Rogue of Gor

Rogue of Gor

John Norman

AN [e-*reads*]BOOK
New York, NY

Copyright © 1981 by John Norman
An E-Reads Edition
www.e-reads.com
ISBN 0-7592-1179-5

The Gor books available from E-Reads:

Table of Contents

Chapter   Page

Chapter   Page

One

I Seek the Whereabouts
of a Slave; I Spend an Evening
in the Belled Collar

I slipped behind the girl and suddenly seized her, holding my hand tightly over her mouth. The trash she carried spilled. I dragged her backwards. She struggled. She made muffled noises. I threw her down, behind the row of trash containers behind the house of Oneander in Ar. My hand was at her throat, thrusting the light steel collar she wore up under her chin. "Make no sound," I warned her. She was blond. She wore the brief, sleeveless white tunic of a house slave. She was barefoot. I recognized her. She was the woman, once free, who had been last on the coffle of Oneander long ago in Ar, the same coffle in which Miss Henderson had been secured. "Rape me swiftly," she said. "I must soon be back."

"Where is Oneander?' I asked, my eyes hard. I had had little fortune with the guards at the gate to his holding. I knew little more than that he was not now in the city.

"Gone," she said. "To the north, business!"

"Where?" I asked. "Where?" My hand tightened on her throat.

"I do not know, Master," she whispered. "I do not know! I am only a slave!"

"Is the slave, Veminia, in the house?" I asked. "The barbarian, the small, dark-haired one, she brought from Vonda, she sold out of the house of Andronicus?"

"It is you!" she said, suddenly, recognizing me. "The slave in the street!"

1

"I am now free," I said. "Where is she?" My grip tightened. "Speak!"

"She was taken north, she with ten others, by Oneander," she whispered.

"Where!" I demanded.

"I do not know," she whispered. "I am only a lowly slave."

"Who would know?' I asked, fiercely.

"Those with him," she said. "Oneander keeps a close counsel."

"Who else?" I demanded. "There must be others."

"Alison," she said, "the dancing slave at the Belled Collar, she might know. Oneander uses her when it pleases him!"

I released her throat. She touched it, frightened, looking up at me. I looked down at her. "I am not now in danger, am I?" she asked.

"No more than any other slave," I said.

She lay back on the cement. Her left hand touched the garbage cans to her left. "You are handsome," she said.

I shrugged.

"You have me at your mercy," she said. "Are you going to press your advantage?"

"Do you beg it?" I asked.

"Yes, Master," she said.

"You are not unattractive," I told her. Then I thrust up the brief house tunic and she put her arms about my neck, lifting her lips to mine.

* * * *

I considered the belly and hips of the dancing girl as she thrust them toward me, undulatingly, as the music pounded in the tavern.

"Have you heard the news?" the man next to me was asking.

"No," I said.

The girl was naked, save that she wore many strings of jewels and armlets. Too she wore bracelets and anklets of gold, which had been locked upon her, and were belled. Her collar, too, was of gold, and belled. She was blond, and it was said she was from Earth. A single pearl, fastened in a setting like a droplet, on a tiny golden chain, was suspended at the center of her forehead.

"There has been a major engagement, one long awaited," said the man next to me, "south of Vonda. More than four thousand men were involved. Fighting was fierce. The mobility of our squares was crucial in the early phases, separating to permit the entrance of charging tharlarion into our lines, then isolating the beasts." Massed men, I knew, could not stand against the charge of tharlarion, not without a defense of ditches or pointed stakes. "But then," said the man, "their phalanx swept down upon us. Then did the day seem lost and retreat was sounded, but the withdrawal was prearranged to creviced ground, to rocky slopes and cragged, outjutting formations. Our generals had chosen their ground well." I knew, too, that no fixed military formation could meet the phalanx on its own terms and survive. Different length spears are held by different ranks, the longer spears by the more rearward ranks. It charges on the run. It is like an avalanche, thundering, screaming, bristling with steel. Its momentum is incredible. It can shatter walls. When two such formations meet in a field the clash can be heard for pasangs. One does not meet the phalanx unless it be with another phalanx. One avoids it, one outmaneuvers it. "Our auxiliaries then drove the tharlarion, maddened and hissing, back into the phalanx. In the skies our tarnsmen turned aside the mercenaries of Artemidorus. They then rained arrows upon the shattered phalanx. While the spearmen lifted their shields to protect themselves from the sky our squares swept down the slopes upon them."

I nodded. I continued to regard the female before me. It was said she was from Earth. I lifted my paga to my lips, from the low table behind which I sat, cross-legged.

She regarded me, as she danced her beauty before me.

"The field was ours!" said the man. "Vonda herself now lies open to our troops!'

I nodded. I did not take my eyes from the dancer. Her eyes, on me, were sensuous and hot, those of a true slave. It was hard for me to believe that she was really from Earth.

"The women of Vonda will soon be emptied into our slave markets," said the man.

"It will lower prices," said another, gloomily.

"I have heard," said another, "that forces from Port Olni are marching to the relief of Vonda."

"Our men will turn northeast to meet them," said another.

"Please, Master," whispered the girl to me. She extended her small hand, still dancing, as though to touch me. On her wrist was a golden bracelet, belled. I saw the small lock, with its key socket, on the bracelet. She could not remove it.

"She likes you," said the man next to me, now paying some attention to the dancer.

Suddenly there was the fierce crack of a slave whip and the girl, terrified, scurried from me. Busebius, proprietor of the tavern, stood at the edge of the sand. "Do you think I have but one customer?" he called to her. "No, Master!" she cried. There was laughter. Then she was dancing, too, before others, and among the tables. I watched her. She was a sensuous dream. It was hard to imagine that she was from Earth.

"There was another dancer here previously," said the man next to me, "one called Helen. She, too, was an Earth blonde. Alison was purchased to replace her."

"What happened to the other girl?" I asked.

"Helen?" he asked.

"Yes," I said.

"She was seen once by Marlenus of Ar, who purchased her. She was chained and sent as a gift somewhere."

"I see," I said.

"Paga, Master?" asked a dark-haired, belled paga slave, in a scrap of diaphanous yellow silk.

I motioned her away. She had short, lovely legs and a sweet, full bosom. The yellow silk was belted tightly about her waist by several turns of yellow binding fiber, more than enough to tie her for your pleasure in an alcove.

I continued to watch the dancer, now some yards away, under the low ceiling.

The girl who had offered me paga had not been truly interested in giving me paga. My cup, clearly, was still almost full. She had been offering me something else, other wares of the tavern.

The dancer now, as the music was mounting in crescendo, was again approaching me. I considered her ankles and thighs, the sweet belly of her, her breasts, and shoulders and throat, the loveliness of her, her face and eyes, the latitudes of her swirling blond hair, the shimmering, restless jewelry on her body, the metal locked on her wrists and ankles, her collar, the pearl at her forehead.

"Master," she said, dancing before me.

I regarded her, through narrowly lidded eyes.

Then she sank to her knees and, on her knees, leaning backwards, danced before me as a kneeling slave.

The music swirled to its climax and, as it ended, she straightened her body and then, from her knees, lowered herself to her right hip and, extending her right arm to me, lay before me, submitted, her head to the floor.

There was Gorean applause in the room, the striking of the right palm on the left shoulder.

I rose to my feet and placed two copper tarsks on the table.

I went to the girl and, with the side of my foot, kicked her.

She looked up, frightened.

I saw in her eyes that she well knew what it was to feel the foot of a master.

Then there was a sudden, different look in her eyes. She put her head down, swiftly, and, holding my foot, pressed her lips to it, fervently.

Then she looked up at me, her eyes shining, her lips softly parted.

"To an alcove," I told her. "Now."

"Yes, Master," she said, and scrambled up, hurrying with a rustle of jewelry and bells to a leather-curtained alcove.

There was more Gorean applause as I followed her and, turning, from the inside, drew shut the curtains of the alcove. When I had them buckled shut from the inside I turned to face the girl.

She knelt in the position of the pleasure slave, back in the alcove, on the scarlet furs, in the light of the small lamp. I looked about. There were some chains in the alcove, and a coil of rope, and a whip.

"If Master desires special equipment," she said, "it will be provided by Busebius."

"There is more than enough here to tame you," I said.

"Yes, Master," she said.

"You are Alison?" I asked.

"In his use of me Master may name me as he pleases," she said.

"You are Alison?" I asked.

"Yes, Master," she said.

"It is an Earth-girl name," I said.

"Please do not be cruel to me on account of it," she said.

"Are you from Earth?" I asked.

"Yes," she said.

"Was Alison your original name?" I asked.

"Yes," she said, "only now Gorean masters have put it on me, by their will, as a mere slave name."

"How did you come to Gor?" I asked.

"I do not know," she said. "I retired one night and awakened later, how much later I do not know, naked, in a dungeon, chained with other girls."

"All slaves?" I asked.

"Yes," she said, "though we did not know it at the time, we were all slaves."

"True slaves?" I asked.

"Yes," she said, "true slaves."

"It is a pretty name," I said.

"Thank you, Master," she said.

"Too," I said, "it is a superb name for a female slave."

"Yes, Master," she said. "Thank you, Master."

I regarded her. "You appear to be a slave," I said.

"I am a slave, Master," she said.

"The men of Gor," I said, "say that the women of Earth are natural slaves. Is it true?"

"Yes, Master," she said. "I, and the other girls on my chain, swiftly learned that we were natural slaves."

"How was this information received by them?" I asked.

"Generally at first with chagrin and shame," she said, "then with helpless resignation, objective recognition and sober acceptance, and then with a liberating and unspeakable joy."

"Are you a natural slave?" I asked her.

"Yes, Master," she said.

I regarded her.

"Try me," she said. "Judge for yourself."

"But you are of Earth," I said.

"Does it dismay you," she asked, "that I, a woman of Earth, should be a natural slave?"

"Get on your back," I said.

"Yes, Master," she said. She unlooped the strings of jewelry from her body, putting them to one side.

"No," I said, "leave the armlets, the pearl drop at your forehead."

of the bells upon her. I saw the barbaric armlets, and the tiny chain that held the small pearl drop at her forehead.

"Yes," I said. My fists were clenched.

"I beg to be fulfilled," she said, "and as the slave I am. I know I have no right to beg this, for a slave is without rights. I do, however, beg it, placing myself vulnerably and fully at your mercy. You may, of course, deny me this fulfillment, for I am a slave. I hope, however, that you will not do so. I hope, rather, that you will see fit to show kindness to a miserable girl in bondage."

I thought I would let her speak.

When one wished, she might be lashed to silence.

She was only a slave.

"It is not just any woman on my world," she said, "who is brought here to serve masters, her betters! Surely we are selected for interest, and beauty. Is it not the fairest and the most fascinating who are harvested for the slave pits of this world, who are found worthy of the collar!"

There was much in what she said, but the professional criteria used in such matters were more complex, more subtle, than she seemed to realize. One of the major criteria utilized by slavers, for example, was the native intelligence of the potential acquisition. Gorean men, as men of Earth seem seldom to do, prize high intelligence in women. Perhaps that is because their own intelligence, on the whole, is high and they might be bored with their properties were the intelligence of the properties not similarly high. Who wants to be served by a stupid slave? Many a girl in a Gorean market, accustomed to, and resigned to, the values of Earth, a world seemingly so enamored of simpler women, is surprised to find herself sooner brought helplessly to the chains of a master, sooner put to her knees, sooner subjected to degradation, sooner given a whip to lick and kiss, than others she esteems far more beautiful, or glamorous. The reason is simple though she may not suspect it for some time. She is thought to be more interesting, and more worth owning, for the Gorean master intends to, and will, own the *whole* slave, *and as a whole slave.* The intelligent woman, of course, now put to her knees, quickly grasps what she now is, and what is expected of her; she now realizes that she is now, presumably for the first time in her life, in the presence of masters, authentic masters of women; she is well aware of the collar on her neck, and its meaning; she wishes to live, but, too, she is strangely stirred and thrilled; intelligent, she trains quickly, and well; emotionally, she is more in touch with her own feelings, and nature, and the secrets of her self, and less the victim of a culture founded on hate and neuterism; female, she relishes her domination, for which she has hungered on Earth; at last she finds herself at the feet of a true man, a strong, virile man, who will master her; at last, accordingly, she can fulfill her womanhood. Too, of course, such women are more sensitive to the master, more attuned to his moods, more alert to his least desires, and they are inventive and appetitious in the furs; most, in time, thankful for the profound, liberating joy of their collars, become hot, devoted and dutiful; most, in time, may be expected to become love slaves. Too, bondage liberates the beauty in a woman, for even a plain girl blossoms in the collar. This has to do, doubtless, with a removal of inhibitions, a fulfillment of her nature, and such. It is hard for a woman to be happy and not beautiful. Another criterion used by slavers which may not be immediately evident to everyone is an initial assessment of the candidate's potential for unusual sexual responsiveness. Thus some women are brought to Gor not because they are unusually beautiful, or intelligent, but because it is recognized, it having come under the judicious, practiced eye of the slaver, that they, doubtless unknown to themselves, will find themselves helpless in the arms of a master, no more than a yielding, dominated, spasmodic love animal. Such are surely worth their coins. To be sure, sooner or later, this doom, or fate, or joy, is the lot of almost every slave girl, for slave fires, as it is said, are lit by cruel men in their bellies, fires which will rage frequently and may be quenched, if at all, by the kindness, and attentions, of the master. Lastly, it might be mentioned that the Gorean's idea of female beauty tends to be far more diversified than that of Earth. Statistically, the Gorean tends to prefer the natural woman, so to speak, who tends to be short, and sweetly bodied. This is not to deny that the "model types," so to speak, are not available in her markets. Surely they are nice, too. Some men prefer one sort; some another; but they are all slave girls, all in their collars. None of this is to deny, of course, that there is anything wrong with a slave candidate who is at one and the same time beautiful, highly intelligent, and sexually needful. Indeed, I think that description fits most of the women who are found in the Gorean markets, whatever may be their world of origin. One thing might be mentioned, in passing, pertaining to Earth-girl slaves. That they have come from a negativistic, antinatural world, that they have been raised, so to speak, in a sexual desert, gives them an interesting piquancy in the markets. Too, of course, one may then easily recognize why it is that such women, now finding themselves in a natural world, with powerful men, often kiss their fingertips and press them gratefully to their collars. Lastly one might note, though one supposes this is of no interest to the slaver, who will have his eye on the market value of the girl, they seem to have a need for, and a capacity for, love.

I said nothing.

"I will strive to be worthy of my fulfillment," she said.

I crouched down behind her, and put my hands on her waist. She shuddered, pressing herself against the wall.

"In what way?" I asked.

"By serving you completely and intimately, and as an abject and total slave," she said.

I did not speak.

"You will not regret it, Master," she said.

I freed her wrists and neck of the rope, leaving it fallen by the ring. I then had her in my arms, she on her knees, by the ring. "Alison will strive to please Master well," she whispered. She then kissed me, softly. Then, softly, she whispered in my ear, "The women of Earth are natural slaves."

"No!" I said.

"Judge by me," she said.

I lowered her to the furs. I began to kiss at her body. "No," I said. Soon she began to gasp and sob in my arms. Then she began to writhe. Then she screamed in the alcove and then, shuddering, shaking, was held in my arms. "Am I not a natural slave?" she asked. "Yes," I said, "you are." There had been no mistaking the nature of her movements, her reflexes. They were clearly those of a natural slave. These things troubled me. She lay back. "And I am a woman of Earth," she said. "You are not typical," I told her. "I am typical," she said. I looked down at her. "What are you thinking?" she asked. "I was thinking," I said, regarding the girl, "that the men of Earth, if they could but see an Earth woman as you are now, would scream with pleasure."

"We are waiting for our masters," she smiled.

13

I listened to the musicians outside of the alcove, the sounds of the tavern. When one brings a girl to an alcove one may keep her there for most practical purposes as long as one wishes. She is yours, for most practical purposes, until one chooses to re-open the curtains. After the tavern is closed an attendant will let you out and, taking charge of the girl, see that she is properly chained at her ring by the girl-wall or kenneled.

"Do you now think it is so terrible a thing to fulfill the needs of a slave?" she asked.

"No," I said.

"And if one is a natural slave," she said, "surely it is acceptable for her to seek, even desperately, the fulfillment of her deepest needs."

"Yes," I said.

"And surely," she said, "it is permissible for the master, though he is under no obligation to do so, for she is only a slave, to deign, in his kindness, if it be his whim or pleasure, to fulfill the needs of the slave."

"It is totally up to him," I said.

"Yes, Master," she said. "She is only a slave."

"That you are a natural slave, Alison," I said, "does not prove that the women of Earth are natural slaves."

"My entire chain, in training," she said, "learned that we were."

"It proves nothing," I said.

"Do you think we were all so rare and different?" she asked.

I shrugged. "I do not know," I said.

"We were not," she said.

"Perhaps, perhaps not," I said.

She smiled.

"How long have you known you were a slave?" I asked.

"Since I was a young girl," she said. "I first discovered it in my thoughts and dreams, and feelings, and fantasies. But I thought I could never be more than a secret slave at the mercy of a secret master. Then I was brought to Gor. Here I wear my collar openly and kneel before my masters, my true masters, for all the world to see."

"It is true," I said.

"Do you object that I have slave needs, Master?" she asked.

"I do not object that you, personally, have slave needs," I said. "Indeed, I rejoice that you have slave needs for they make you a perfection and a dream of pleasure."

"But you would not want all women to be like me?" she asked.

"No," I said.

"But what if they were?" she asked.

I looked at her, angrily.

"Or is it only one woman you would not want to be like me?" she asked.

"No!" I said.

"But what if she is?" asked the girl.

I closed my eyes. The thought of Miss Beverly Henderson as a female slave was almost overpoweringly erotic. With difficulty I controlled myself. I thrust the thought from my mind. I must not even permit myself to think such things.

I opened my eyes.

"Do not deny her nature to her," said the girl.

"Kneel to the whip!" I cried. Terrified the girl scrambled to her knees and knelt down, making herself small, her head to the furs. Her wrists were crossed under her, as though bound. She trembled. I now stood over her, the slave whip in my hand. I drew it back, then I threw it aside, angrily. I crouched down. Then I jerked her head up, by the hair. "Permission to placate," she begged, reaching for me with her lips and mouth. But I held her, by the hair, from me. She whimpered, denied. Then I released her hair and permitted her to touch me.

"Thank you, Master," she whispered.

She was a slave. I would permit her to attempt to placate me, in one of the ancient fashions of the female slave.

* * * *

"I must soon be on my way," I said.

"Master searches for a slave, does he not?" she asked.

"Perhaps," I said.

"Do not ever let her forget that she is a slave," said the girl.

"I must be on my way," I said.

"Have me, but once again," she begged.

I did so, and then, later, I rose to my feet. I unbuckled the leather curtains and threw them back. The tavern was now empty and closed.

15

I turned about and again regarded the girl. She had replaced the loops of her jewelry and knelt before me, in the position of the pleasure slave.

"It is hard for me to think of you as a girl from Earth," I said.

"I am now only a Gorean slave girl," she said.

"You danced well," I said.

An attendant approached from a side door. "I will put her in her kennel," he said. He snapped his fingers at her. "Come, Girl," he said.

"Yes, Master," she said. She rose quickly to her feet and ran softly to him. He took her by the arm.

"She whom you seek is a slave, is she not?" she asked me.

"She is a legal slave," I said. "She is not a true slave."

She was then conducted to the small side door, through which the attendant had emerged. Beyond it, I gathered, would lie such things as the kitchens, the offices, the cellars and pantries, the storage rooms, the dressing rooms, the discipline chamber and the kennels. At the door the attendant let her pause and she turned to me. "Good hunting, Master!" she called to me. "Show her no mercy," she said. Then she brushed a kiss to me with the tips of her fingers in the Gorean fashion. I returned this gesture. She was then conducted through the door. In a short time I heard the sliding downward and locking in place of a kennel gate. Shortly afterward the attendant returned to the floor and let me out, through the main entrance. I heard it being bolted shut behind me. I stood then in the streets of Ar. I looked up at the moons and stars, beyond the cylinders and bridges. I then turned my steps toward the Street of Tarns, that somewhere among its many shops and cots I might arrange transportation northward, toward the Salerian city of Lara.

Two

The Victory Camp

"Greetings, Lady Tima," I said.

"Jason!" she said, struggling in the straps. "Do not hurt me!"

The night sky was red with the glare of the burning city.

"It will be a tarsk bit," said the fellow walking down the long line of pleasure racks.

I placed a tarsk bit in the small leather sack nailed to the frame of the rack.

She pulled back in the straps.

"I will take you no closer to Lara than this," had said the fellow who had flown the tarn which had brought me to this place. "Tarnsmen of Ar," had said he, "patrol the corridor between Vonda and Ar, but are insufficient in numbers to guard the sky beyond the corridor. Too, tomorrow, as the cavalries mass for attack, the guard on the corridor itself will be abandoned." I had nodded and paid him, crawling from the heavy basket. On his return trip he would doubtless take refugees, or perhaps bound girls from Vonda, back to Ar.

"What news of the war is there?" I asked the fellow who was guarding the long line of pleasure racks. "I have just come from Ar."

"We have been successful here," he said, "defeating in battle both the forces of Vonda and those of the tarnsmen of Artemidorus of Cos. Vonda is being sacked. The city burns. This is a victory camp, one for loot and pleasure."

"Surely the Salerian Confederation is now committed to war," I said.

He shrugged. "Forces from Lara march north," said he. "Forces from Port Olni are within a hundred pasangs, marching south. They are delaying now only to match their strike with that of the men of Lara."

I nodded. It would be a pincers move, to take the men of Ar, far from their supply lines, on two fronts.

"We must now retreat," I said.

He laughed. "No," said he. "While those of Port Olni dally in camp we are marching upon them. We will take them separately. Defeating them we will return south to meet the forces of Lara, perhaps even here, in the sight of the ashes of Vonda."

"I see," I said.

"We fear only that the forces of Ti will be committed," he said.

Ti was the largest and most populous city of the Salerian Confederation. It had, to date, refused to involve itself in the machinations of Vonda and Cos.

"Surely it will be only a matter of time," I said.

"I suspect so," said the man. "Even now Ebullius Gaius Cassius, of the Warriors, Administrator of Ti, meets with the high council of Ti."

"Their delay seems inexplicable," I said.

"Those of Cos, enemies to Ar, and merchants of Vonda," said the man, "have precipitated the war, hoping to engage the entire confederation."

"A minority party then," I said, "is maneuvering the situation."

"I think so," said the man. "I doubt frankly that either Ti or Ar wishes a full-scale conflict."

"How much is this one?" called a man, a few racks from us. It was a blonde, strapped on her rack.

"Excuse me," said the man, turning away from me. "A tarsk bit," he said to the fellow.

"Surely," I said.

It was evening. Fires, on high poles, illuminated the area. Many men were about, moving here and there. From where I stood I could see many tents, long tents, and holding areas, where there were temporary stockades or circular embankments. Within these enclosures there were, for the most part, goods and prisoners. Two drunken soldiers staggered past.

"How were you taken?" I asked the Lady Tima.

"By soldiers, in the city," she said, "with others." She looked at me. "Be kind to me, Jason," she begged. "I am absolutely helpless."

"How were you brought here?" I asked.

"On a rope," she said. "I was brought here, stripped, and fastened on the rack."

I looked down the long rows of pleasure racks, aligned under the high torches.

The blonde, a few racks away, in the same line, was crying out for mercy.

"Your market and goods?" I asked.

"The market was burned," she said, "and the goods and slaves taken."

"Did many of those of Vonda escape the city?" I asked.

"Many," she said.

"In flying over this area," I said, "I saw several stockades, mostly filled with women."

"We were hunted more relentlessly," she said, bitterly.

"Yet some women must have escaped the city," I said.

"Yes," she said, "particularly those who fled early. Many have gone as refugees to Lara."

The blonde a few racks away began to squirm and sob in her straps. "No, no," she begged. But she was not being shown the mercy for which she pleaded.

"What of the House of Andronicus?' I asked.

"Gone," she said, "burned, its slaves and personnel fled or taken."

"What of the Lady Gina?" I asked. I remembered her with some fondness.

"Shackled," she said, "in the food tent, where she waits upon men."

"Do you think she enjoys serving them?" I asked.

"They enjoy having her serve them," she said, angrily.

"Doubtless," I said. "Do you recall the slave, Lola, of the House of Andronicus?" I asked.

"Yes," she said. "I do not know her fate." Lola and Tela had been the girls who had first taught me Gorean. They had been the first Gorean slave girls I had ever seen. I had never forgotten my first sight of them. That such women could exist and be slaves had been a stunning and welcome revelation to me of certain of the realities of Gor.

"You had an assistant," I said, "a superb actress, who, pretending to be a mere Earth-girl slave, even to the collar and Ta-Teera, well prepared me for my sale in your market."

"The Lady Tendite," she said. "Don't touch me!"

"Yes, she," I said. "She well made a fool of me."

"Please, don't, Jason!"

"I believed her," I said.

"Jason," she begged. "No!"

"I believed her," I said, "completely."

"I am completely helpless, Jason," she said. "Please have mercy on me!"

"The sale must have been amusing," I said.

"Your hands!" she wept.

"Did you plan it together?" I asked. "Your body seems smaller and more helpless than I remembered it," I observed.

"Yes, yes," she sobbed, "but it was her original plan, her ideas. She thought it would be amusing to do it to you."

"I see," I said.

"Please stop touching me," she begged.

Suddenly, a few racks away, the blonde, throwing her head back, and rearing helplessly in her straps, screamed her submission.

The Lady Tima shuddered, and then, suddenly, lifted herself to me. But my hand did not quite touch her.

"Where is she?" I asked.

"She fled early from Vonda," she said. "She went to Lara. Please do not stop touching me."

"Are you prepared to beg to be touched?" I asked.

"Yes," she said, "I beg it!"

"How do these things work?" I asked, looking at the rack.

"Jason, please!" she whispered.

"I note that you are not yet branded," I said, "nor, I suppose, are these others."

"Jason!" she pleaded.

"Speak," I said.

"We were put on the racks as free women," she said, "that we, the women of the enemy, be properly humiliated. Too, is it not a rich joke for the men of Ar that more than a thousand of the free women of

Vonda adorn their pleasure racks, fastened down like slave girls, their use available for a tarsk bit to the passers-by?"

"Yes," I smiled, "it is a rich joke." The men of Gor are fond of such jokes.

"And only after this, our profound humiliation," she said, "will the men of Ar, if it should please them, see fit to permit us to be divided into lots, and be branded and collared, and sold into slavery throughout the towns and cities of Gor."

"Splendid," I said. "Splendid!"

She looked at me with horror. "Are you a man of Gor?" she asked.

I shrugged. I did not know.

Then again, suddenly, she lifted her body to me. "You have aroused me," she whispered. "You know you have aroused me, and cruelly."

"You lift your body like a female slave, Lady Tima," I said.

She groaned, and lay back. She moaned.

The blonde a few racks down was now sobbing with pleasure. She was alone. "Masters, Masters," she called. "I am only a tarsk bit! Please touch me!"

"What a slut she is," I said.

"Yes, Jason," whispered the Lady Tima.

"These straps seem to hold you quite well," I said.

"I am absolutely helpless," she said. "Touch me, I beg you!"

"The pleasure rack is an interesting device," I said. I examined the wooden wheels, the levers. In virtue of the axes of the device and the various gears and pinions, and the joints, braces, fitted, sliding boards, notches and lock points, it can be adjusted to a variety of positions. To be sure not all the pleasure racks were as sophisticated as that on which was bound my former Mistress, the former female slaver, the Lady Tima of Vonda. This device, like some of the others, had doubtless been brought from the city, perhaps dragged forth by shackled men of Vonda hauling on wagon ropes.

"Jason," begged the Lady Tima.

"I have never seen one this close before," I said.

"Jason!" she cried.

"You look well on your knees before me," I said.

"Jason," she wept.

I then bent her backward, and then, lifting and turning her, examined the left side of her beauty, and then the right. I then put her through a variety of positions, more experimenting with the possibilities of the apparatus than anything else, though the experiments had their aesthetic value, for the Lady Tima was a lovely woman. "Fascinating," I said. "Jason," she protested. I then, as I had grown more proficient with the device, used it for one of its two major purposes, that of exhibiting and displaying its helpless prisoner. Its second major purpose, of course, is to hold the woman in any position one pleases. I rotated her to her back. I then turned away. "Jason!" she cried. "Jason!"

I turned back, again, to face her.

"You have humiliated and abused me," she said. "You have turned me about and examined me on the rack as though I might be a slave girl! You have cruelly aroused me! You cannot leave me now!"

"I can," I told her.

"Please come back," she wept. "Touch me! Touch me!"

"Do you beg it?" I asked.

"Yes," she said.

"As a slave?" I asked.

"Yes, yes," she said. "I beg it as a slave!"

"But that is lower than a mere slut," I said. "Surely you remember the blonde girl," I said, indicating the girl some racks from her.

"I beg it as both a slut and a slave," she said.

I then went slowly to the rack. She looked up at me, frightened. Then I fastened her in position, spreading her legs uncomfortably apart. Then, looking down upon her, I spread her legs by another four inches.

Then I had her.

Three

The Food Tent

"Over here," I told the Lady Gina. "Kneel down." I indicated a place on the straw, at the wall of the food tent, a clear place, between other couples.

She knelt before me, looking up at me. "You are the first man who has ordered me to the straw," she said.

"Do you think you are unattractive?" I asked.

"I know I am unattractive," she said.

"To many men," I said, "you could be very attractive."

"I am a naked and shackled prisoner," she said, "soon perhaps, if it should please the men of Ar, to be branded a slave. I have waited upon your table, and brought you food and drink. Beyond these things, I beg you not to insult and torture me."

"You performed your duties as a naked waitress well," I said, "expertly and deferentially."

"I do not wish to be killed," she said.

"You were a fine trainer," I said. "You taught me much."

"And now," she smiled, "is it your intention to give your trainer a little training?"

"Perhaps," I said.

"I have never had the feelings of a normal woman," she said.

"Lie down," I told her.

"I obey," she said. She looked up at me. "You do not seem angry with me," she said.

I sat beside her. "I am not," I said. "Keeper!" I called. "Give me the key to the shackles of this one."

He came to me and gave me a key, with which I removed the shackle from her right ankle. I returned the key to him. I did not unlock the shackle on her left ankle. She continued to wear it, with its short chain and the opened right shackle.

"He did not seem surprised or startled," I said, "that I should open your shackle."

"No," she said, bewildered. "He did not."

"It is not thus so unthinkable," I said, "that a man might desire to free your legs."

She looked at me, frightened.

"Remember," I said, "you are not now carrying a whip and keys, clad in black leather, in a position of power, men at your mercy."

"No," she whispered.

"And even in that guise," I said, "it is not so improbable but what men might wish to take your whip from you and throw you down, and teach you what it is to be a woman."

"I wanted them to do so," she said. "I wanted them to make me a woman."

"You are a woman," I told her. "Dare to be it."

"No!" she said. "It means surrender to men!"

"Of course," I told her.

"I do not have the feelings of normal women!" she said.

"Perhaps it is only that you are afraid to have them," I said.

"No, no!" she said.

"Then have them," I said.

"No!" she said. "The Lady Gina will never be a submitted slave!"

"You are too proud to be a woman?" I asked.

"Yes," she said.

"Even though you are, in truth, a woman?"

"Yes," she said. "It is wrong to be a woman! It is wrong to be a woman!"

"You could always pretend that to be a woman is to be like a man," I said.

"I am not a fool," she said.

"Do you really think it is wrong for a woman to be a true woman?"

"Yes," she said, "for it is to be a woman, and not a man!"

"But you are not, in fact, a man," I said.

"I know," she said.

"Be a woman, then," I said.

"I dare not," she said.

"Why?" I asked.

"I do not know," she said.

"Is it such a terrible thing to be a woman?" I asked.

"Yes, yes!" she said.

"No," I said, "it is not terrible. It is deeply and profoundly marvelous."

She trembled.

"Take your place in the order of nature," I said.

"At the feet of men!" she said.

"It is where you belong," I said.

She began to shudder at my side. "I begin to feel such emotions, such feelings," she said. "They frighten me. They threaten to overwhelm me."

"It is uncontrollable. It is like a storm," I said.

"Yes," she said.

"Yield to them," I said.

"I do not want to be a woman!" she wept. "I do not want to be a woman!"

"How fared the House of Andronicus?" I asked her.

She looked at me, startled. "The goods and the slaves fled or were taken," she said. "The House itself was destroyed."

"And Andronicus?" I asked.

"He fled," she said, "with others."

"How did Lola fare?" I asked.

"She fled," she said. "I do not know if she was taken by the looters or not."

"Do you think she managed to escape?" I asked.

"The looters, perhaps," she said. "But she wears a collar."

I nodded. Lola was attractive. By now she was doubtless on someone's chain. Lovely female slaves do not remain long at large.

"Did you know she sometimes cried your name aloud in her sleep?" asked the Lady Gina.

"No," I said.

"Yet you failed her as a master," she said.

"That is true," I said.

"It was long ago," she said.

"True," I said.

"You seem much different now," she said.

I shrugged. "Perhaps," I said.

"Jason," she whispered.

"Yes," I said.

"You freed my legs," she said.

"Yes," I said, "but it was a mistake."

"Why?" she asked.

"You do not have the feelings of a normal woman," I said. "It is doubtless nothing that you can help." I then bent to reshackle her. Quickly she drew her legs back. "What is wrong?" I asked her.

"Please do not reshackle me, just yet," she said.

"Why?" I asked.

"I want to be a woman," she whispered.

"Truly?" I asked.

"Yes, truly," she sobbed.

"Then," I said, "you must be prepared, holding nothing back, to yield to your deepest and most profound feelings."

"But then," she said, "I would be only a submitted slave, overwhelmed and mastered."

I took her in my arms. She was tense, and frightened. "You're trembling," I said.

"I am only a woman, and a prisoner," she said.

"Do not forget it," I told her.

"No, Jason," she said.

"You do not seem large and strong," I said.

"I am not large and strong," she said.

"Your body is soft," I said, "and feels good in my hands." I jerked her by the arms to a sitting position, and looked at her.

"Could a man find me desirable?" she asked.

"Yes," I said. "Escape me!"

She struggled, futilely. "I cannot escape you," she said. "You know that!"

I threw her then down to her back in the straw.

"Do not be rough with me, Jason," she said.

"You will now be treated as men please," I told her.

"Yes, Jason," she said.

"Accustom yourself to obedience and submission," I said.

"Yes, Jason," she said.

"Will it be necessary to whip you?" I asked.

"No, Jason," she said.

"Prepare now to yield to your deepest and most profound feelings," I said.

"I will try," she said. "Oh!" she cried, my hands in her hair.

"You will not merely try," I told her. "You will yield to them."

"Yes," she said.

"Yes, what?" I asked.

"Yes—*Master*," she said.

* * * *

"You yielded well, Lady Gina," I said.

"I would never have believed I could have such feelings," she said. "I did not know such feelings could exist."

"Surely you have seen writhing, screaming slave girls?" I asked.

"Yes," she said, "but not until moments ago did I have more than an inkling of what they might be feeling." She smiled. "It is no wonder the luscious little sluts are so fond of their collars."

"There can be progress in such matters," I said. "Perhaps no woman has yet truly sounded the depths of slave joy."

"Yes," she said, "the joy of being owned by a man, of being in his power, completely, of being fully his, and of totally loving and serving him."

"Perhaps," I said.

She kissed me. "You handle a woman well, Jason," she said. "You put me through my paces well."

"Any captor or master," I said, "can put you through your paces."

"It is true," she said, and kissed me. She put her head on my belly. "I have seen women such as myself on the block," she said. "We do not bring high prices."

"Perhaps," I said.

"If I were sent to the kitchens, or the mills or laundries," she said, "I would be under the will of my task master, would I not?"

"Yes," I said.

"Perhaps I might, under his whip, pulling his plow, please a peasant," she said, "or perhaps I might keep the hut of a dock worker, preparing his food and, when he wished, warming his mat."

"Perhaps," I said.

"Did I please you?" she asked.

"Yes," I said.

"Do you think I could please other men?" she asked.

"Yes," I said.

"I know that I am not as desirable as most women," she said.

"You are desirable," I said. "And to some men you will be unutterably desirable."

"How kind you are to a helpless female prisoner," she said, "one soon likely, should it please the men of Ar, to be made a slave."

"I speak the truth," I said.

"You are kind," she said.

I said nothing.

"I will try to please my masters well," she said.

"I would recommend it," I said. She shuddered, against me.

"The men of Ar," she said, "took my freedom from me, when they made me a prisoner. You have taken my freedom from me, when you forced me to yield—as—*as a female slave.*"

"Your yielding," I said, "was not that of a female slave, for you are not yet, truly, a female slave. Yet it was, doubtless, the fullest yielding of which you were at this time capable."

"Can there be more?" she asked.

"You cannot, at this time," I said, "even begin to suspect the depths, the dimensions, the wonders and marvels of slave submission."

"What you have done to me," she said, "is irreversible. I can never go back, now, knowing what I do, to being a proud free woman."

I shrugged. It was nothing to me.

"And yet," she said, sobbing, "I am too plain to be a slave."

"You are a woman," I told her.

"Yes," she said, "I am a woman. I did not know before, truly, what it was to be a woman."

"It is not being a kind of man," I told her.

"No," she said, "it is being a full female, in the order of nature."

"Yes," I said.

"A slave," she said.

"Yes," I said.

She sobbed.

"What is wrong?" I asked.

"I want a master," she said. "I want to be everything, and do everything, for him. I want to give him all of me, holding nothing back. I want to be nothing to him, only his owned slave, totally loving and serving him."

"And so?" I said.

"But I am plain," she said. "No man will want me."

"Are you not done with her yet?" asked a rough voice.

We were startled, and looked up. There, at the edge of the straw, standing, was a large, uncouth fellow, in the garments of the Tarn Keepers. "Yes," I said. I smiled. I sat up and took the Lady Gina's free shackle and jerked her ankles closely together. I prepared to close the open shackle about her right ankle. Her ankles would then be chained together, as before, with about eight inches of chain separating them. The shackles were large, and of heavy iron.

"Do not reshackle her," he said.

"Very well," I said, and got up.

"You look like a tasty pudding," he said to the Lady Gina. She looked up at him, from the straw.

"Are you branded yet, Female?" he asked her.

Her hand went inadvertently to her left thigh. "No," she said, "no."

"Is she any good?" he asked me.

"Yes," I said, "she is pretty good. And there is no telling how good she will be when she is properly enslaved and finds herself in the possession of the right master."

"Of course," he said. He again looked down at her. There was a startled, soft light in the eyes of the Lady Gina as she looked up at the fellow. Suddenly, to me, she seemed very soft, and very vulnerable, in the straw. It was as though a transformation, somehow, had come over her.

"She is beautiful," he said.

"Yes," I said, for, somehow, suddenly, perhaps with the sudden understanding and acceptance of her nature and condition, it had become true.

She gasped, and looked up at him, spoken of as beautiful. She trembled.

He then kicked her, and she cried out with pain. "Split your legs, Vondan slut," he said.

The Lady Gina wasted no time in complying.

"Lie there now before me, thusly," said he, "in the straw."

He let her remain in that position, looking up at him. How far she was now from her whip and keys, her authority, from the House of Andronicus.

"Are you going to be had, Lady of Vonda?" he inquired.

"I do not know, Master," she said.

"What do you think?" he asked.

"It will be as Master wishes," she said.

"Beg," said he, "to be had."

"I so beg," she said.

"I am a man of Ar," said he, "Glorious Ar. Say 'I am a woman of Vonda and I beg to be had by a man of Ar.'"

"It is so said," she said.

"Say," said he, "'The women of Vonda are no more than sluts and slaves to the men of Ar.'"

"It is so said," she said.

"And that you are a woman of Vonda."

"And I am a woman of Vonda," she said.

"You may now beg," he said.

"Did I not beg, Master?"

"Again, slut," said he, "and well understand the words."

"Yes, Master."

"I shall enjoy hearing the words on the lips of a Vondan slut."

"Yes, Master."

"Speak," he snapped.

"I beg!" she said.

"For what?"

"—to be had," she said, "—to be had!"

"And how?" he inquired.

"As a prisoner," she said.

"'As a meaningless slave,'" he corrected her.

"As a meaningless slave!" she said.

"And by whom?" he asked.

"By a man of Glorious Ar!"

"'Though as a slut and meaningless slave I acknowledge myself utterly unworthy of such an honor,'" he said.

"Though as a slut and meaningless slave I acknowledge myself utterly unworthy of such an honor," she said.

He then lowered himself to her side.

"Yes, Master!" she cried out. "Yes, Master!"

I watched for a moment, as she writhed in his arms. "You will look well on the block," he told her.

"Yes, Master," she whispered.

"Perhaps I will buy you," he said.

"Yes, Master," she whispered. "Yes, Master!"

I left the two together, and began to thread my way through the tables, between the soldiers and merchants, and others, and the stripped, shackled women of Vonda, serving as waitresses, toward the opening in the food tent. "Our forces have already moved north," one man was saying. "The troops from Lara will not be here for two days," said another. "By that time they will find here only the ashes of Vonda," laughed another. As I accidentally brushed against a woman of Vonda she trembled, and put down her head, and knelt swiftly. I continued past her. "It is dangerous for merchant caravans," a man was saying. "Many have been attacked," said another. "It is rumored the river pirates are the worst," said another. "They grow bold with the withdrawal of troops from Lara. They have struck even into Lara herself, then withdrawing to their galleys." "Perhaps this will cause the troops of Lara to return," said another, "to protect their own hold-ings." "No," said another, "they are committed." "They are to be sold in the river markets," said someone, as I went past. I did not under-stand the meaning of his remark. It did not, I gathered, pertain to the women of Vonda. It would be difficult to get them to the river markets, which lay beyond Lara, down the Vosk, and higher prices, presum-ably, could be obtained for them in the markets of the south. Most of them, I assumed, women of the enemy, would be sold from the slave blocks of Ar herself.

As I went through the opening of the tent I was jostled by a large man. He wore a mask. "Watch where you are going!" he said, angrily. I stepped back, but did not respond to him. I was angry. It had been he, it seemed to me, who had struck against me. Suddenly, for a moment, he stopped and looked at me, closely. It seemed as though he might have thought he knew me. Too, it seemed to me that I might, in spite of the mask, somehow have found him familiar. Then, saying nothing more, he brushed past me and entered the tent. He was alone. I could not place him. Then I left the food tent and went to the tarn cots. I hoped to be able to arrange for transportation to the vicinity of Lara. I retained five silver tarsks. This is a considerable sum. I felt reasonably certain I could find some tarnsman, perhaps from a neutral city, who might, by a suitably circuitous route, get me into the neighborhood of Lara.

Some tarns had apparently recently arrived from the west. Some of them had apparently been carrying refugees. I saw some wounded men. Here and there small groups of men huddled about, dismally. I saw no women in these groups, even slaves. Some of them wore the white and gold of merchants. Some of them wore masks. They crouched about fires.

"Who are these people?" I asked one of the fellows near the cots.

"Mostly merchants," said he. "These are the victims of the predations of river pirates in Lara."

"Some wear masks," I said.

"Yet most are known to us," said the man. "Even masked. There, not masked, is Splenius, and Zarto. You know Zarto, the iron merchant?"

"No," I said.

"He lost his wagons of ingots," said the man. "Beside him, masked, is Horemius. Eight stone of perfumes were taken from him. There, farther to the left, in the brown mask, is Zadron, the dealer in silver. He lost almost everything. In the red mask is Publius, also of the silver merchants. He retains only the belt of silver on his shoulder."

"I see no women with them, no slaves," I said.

"They were embattled," said the man. "For their lives they bartered their goods and slaves."

"These were all from Lara or her vicinity?" I asked.

"Yes," said he. "They had not realized that the troops of Lara would be moving east, or that the brigands and pirates would move so boldly."

"Are these all of them?" I asked, apprehensively.

"No," said the fellow. "Some of them have gone to the food tent."

"Was one called Oneander, a salt and leather merchant, among them?" I asked.

"Yes," said the fellow.

Four

The City of Lara;
I Renew an Acquaintance

The girl stirred uneasily. Her legs were drawn up. She wore the Ta-Teera, the slave rag, and a collar. She lay in the corner of the main room of the inn. She lay on a slave mat. I had put her there.

I sat, cross-legged, behind one of the low tables in the room. I chewed on a crust of bread. The inn, now, was deserted. It had been evacuated early this morning.

"That is ten copper tarsks," had said the man last night, placing before me a bowl of sul porridge. I had not argued. I had paid him.

"You cannot put me out!" a free woman had been crying to the proprietor of the inn, at his counter to the side.

"You did not pay me for your last night's lodging," he told her. "Pay me now for that, and for tonight, or you may not remain within the inn."

"A silver tarsk for a night's lodging!" she cried. "That is unheard of. It is outrageous. You have no right to charge such prices!"

Others, too, about the counter, uttered such cries. The inn was that of Strobius, in Lara, at the confluence of the Olni and Vosk. It was crowded with refugees from Vonda. Many hundreds had fled from Vonda, and most had taken the river southward, paying highly for their fares on the varieties of river craft, barges, skiffs, river galleys, and even coracles, which had brought them to Lara.

"Those are my prices," said Strobius.

"Sleen!" cried more than one man.

"Whatever the traffic will bear," had grinned a fellow near me at my table.

"I am a free woman of Vonda!" the woman at the counter was crying.

I lifted the sul porridge to my lips. The mask I wore, like those of some others in the room, covered only the upper portions of my face.

There was pounding at the inn door. Guards, sliding back a panel in the door, looked through. Then they admitted another small group of refugees. There would be no rooms for them, as there were none for many of the guests, but they, too, albeit only for a space in a corridor, would be charged a full silver tarsk for their lodging. The inn of Strobius was not thought to be a good inn, but it was a large inn, and a stout one. Too, it was one of the few inns remaining open in Lara. Many of the refugees, destitute, who had come to Lara had not been permitted to land at the quays, but had been driven further downriver. Too, here and there in the city, river pirates, with impunity, sought women and plundered.

Several of the men in the room, other than myself, wore masks. I lowered the sul porridge to the table. It was not good, but it was hot.

"I am a free woman of Vonda!" the woman at the counter was crying. "You cannot put me out!"

Oneander of Ar, the salt and leather merchant, and some others, had worn masks at the loot camp outside the city of Vonda. He had been, perhaps, well advised to do so. He had intended to trade with Lara, a member of the Salerian Confederation. This would not make him popular in Ar, or in the strongholds of Ar. Too, he had been, as I had ascertained, attacked by river pirates on the south bank of the Olni and, embattled, had bargained for his life and those of his men by delivering his goods and slaves to the assailants. It was little wonder that he had chosen to mask his features. He did not wish to encounter the wrath of those of Ar, and he wished, doubtless, to conceal his chagrin and shame over the embarrassing termination of his business venture in the north.

I had waited outside the food tent in the loot camp. The sky to the west was lit with the flames of Vonda.

"Are you Oneander of Ar?" I asked the fellow who emerged from the tent.

"No," he said.

"I think you are Oneander of Ar," I said to him.

"Do not speak so loudly," had said he, looking about, "you fool!"

I had then reached to his tunic and seized him, dragging him toward me.

"Remove your mask," I told him.

"Is there no one to protect me?" he called.

"What is going on here?" inquired a guardsman.

"I think this is Oneander of Ar," I said.

"I had heard he was in the camp," said the guardsman. "Are you he?"

"Yes," said the man, hesitantly, angrily.

"Remove the mask," I said. "Or I shall."

Angrily he drew away the mask.

"It is Oneander," said the guardsman, not pleased.

"Do not leave me here with him!" called Oneander of Ar.

But the guardsman had turned his back and left.

"Who are you?" asked Oneander of Ar, apprehensively.

"I was once a silk slave," I said. "You may recall me, from the streets of Ar, some months ago, in the neighborhood of the shop of Philebus. You set two slaves upon me."

"Do not kill me," he whispered.

"I have heard," said I, "that you were embattled near Lara, and surrendered slaves and goods."

"On the south bank of the Olni," he said, "yes, it is true."

"You did well," I said, "to save the lives of your men, and yourself."

"I have lost much," he said.

"What do you conjecture," I asked, "to be the fate of your goods and slaves?"

"They are no longer mine," he said. "They are now the property of the river pirates, theirs by the rights of sword and power."

"That is true," I said. "But what do you conjecture is to be their fate?"

"It is not likely they could be sold in Lara, or northward," he said. "Usually the river pirates sell their goods and captures somewhere along the river, in one of the numerous river towns."

"What towns?" I asked.

"There are dozens," he said. "Perhaps Ven, Port Cos, Iskander, Tafa, who knows."

"He who attacked you, the pirate chieftain," I said, "who was he."

"There are many bands of river pirates," he said.

"Who was he?" I asked.

"Kliomenes, a lieutenant to Policrates," he said.

"In what town does he sell his wares?" I asked.

"It could be any one of a dozen towns," said Oneander. "I do not know."

I seized him by the tunic, and shook him.

"I do not know!" he said. "I do not know!"

I held him.

"Please do not kill me," he whispered.

"Very well," I had said, and released him. I had then turned about and went toward the tarn cots of the loot camp, that I might arrange with some bold tarnsman to provide me with transportation, by a suitably circuitous route, to the vicinity of Lara.

The girl again stirred in the corner of the room. She rolled to her back. One knee was raised. She was luscious in the slave rag and collar. She turned her head from side to side. She made a small noise. She opened and closed one small hand. I wondered if she were aware, dimly, of the coarse fibers of the slave mat beneath her back. I did not think so, not yet.

"I am a free woman of Vonda!" the woman at the counter had been crying out last night. "You cannot put me out!"

"You will pay or be ejected," Strobius had told her.

"You cannot put me out into the street!" she said.

I had taken another sip of the sul porridge.

The woman at the counter had been veiled, as is common with Gorean women, particularly those of high caste and of the high cities. Many Gorean women, in their haughtiness and pride, do not choose to have their features exposed to the common view. They are too fine and noble to be looked upon by the casual rabble. Similarly the robes of concealment worn by many Gorean women are doubtless dictated by similar sentiments. On the other hand veiling is a not impractical modesty in a culture in which capture, and the chain and the whip are not unknown. One justification for the veiling and for the robes of concealment, which is not regarded as inconsiderable, is that it is supposed to provide something of a protection against abduction and predation. Who would wish to risk his life, it is said, to carry off a woman who might, when roped to a tree and stripped, turn out to be as ugly as a tharlarion? Slave girls, by contrast, are almost never permitted veils. Similarly they are usually clad in such a way that their charms are manifest and obvious to even the casual onlooker. This, aside from having such utilities as reminding the girls that they are total slaves and giving pleasure to the men who look upon them, is supposed to make them, rather than free women, the desiderated objects of capture and rapine. I think there is something to this theory for, statistically, it is almost always the female slave and not her free sister who finds herself abducted and struggling in the lashings of captors or slavers. On the other hand, in spite of the theories pertaining to such matters, free women are certainly not immune to the fates of capture and enslavement. Many men, despite the theories pertaining to such matters, and accepting the risks involved, enjoy taking them. Some slavers specialize in the capture of free women. Indeed, it is thought by some, perhaps largely because of the additional risks involved, and the interest in seeing what one has caught, that there is a special spice and flavor about taking them. Similarly it is said to be pleasant, if one has the time and patience, first to their horror and then to their joy, training them to the collar.

"You cannot put me out into the street!" had cried the free woman.

"I can," he informed her soberly.

"I am a free woman of Vonda," she said, "a member of the Confederation."

"I am an innkeeper," said he. "My politics are those of the ledger and silver."

I had sipped the sul porridge while listening to this conversation.

There are various reasons why Gorean men, upon occasion, resort to masks. Oneander had worn a mask, as had others in the loot camp, because of his fear of the anger of the men of Ar, concerning his trading venture with Lara, and, doubtless, because of his shame at his failure in that venture. Several men in the main room of the inn wore masks now presumably to conceal their identity for various reasons. Times were troubled. It might not well serve their purposes to be recognized, as perhaps men of wealth or position, now in difficult straits. Some might have been seized or held for ransom. Others, perhaps, shamed by the fall of Vonda, or the necessity for their flight from the city, did not wish to be recognized in Lara. Masks, too, are sometimes worn by men in disgrace, or who wish to travel incognito. I recalled the Lady Florence. Doubtless the young men of Vonda, and the estates about Vonda, who would attend her secret auction might wear masks. She might not know who had purchased her until she knelt his slave, before him, at the foot of his couch. I wore a mask because I had not wished to be recognized in Lara. In Lara there were many refugees from Vonda and its vicinity. Some might have watched me in the stable bouts. I did not think my tasks would be either expedited or facilitated by being recognized as a former fighting slave. Now, however, for an independent reason, I was pleased to have worn the mask. Sometimes, incidentally, free young men wear masks and capture a free woman, taking away her clothing and forcing her to perform as a slave for them. She is then commonly released. Afterwards, of course, in meeting young men she does not know for which of them, if any of them, she was forced to perform as a slave. Such a woman commonly begins to take risks inappropriate for a free woman. She is, sooner or later, caught and enslaved. She is then, as she has wished, sold, and will truly wear the collar. Perhaps one of the young men will buy her, and keep her as his own.

"I am a free woman!" the woman at the counter cried.

"That condition," said the innkeeper, "could prove temporary."

"I have nowhere to go," she said. "I am safe here. River pirates may still be within the city. It is not safe for me to be put out."

"You owe me a silver tarsk," said he, "for your last night's lodging. Too, if you would stay here this night, you must pay me another tarsk."

"I do not have them," she wept.

"Then you must be ejected," said he.

"Take my baggage," she said, "my trunks!"

"I do not want them," he said.

It was my plan to arrange transportation downriver in the morning. My business lay not in Lara but further west on the river. Many refugees, incidentally, had not remained in Lara. It was too close, for them, to the war zone. It lay well within the striking distance of a tarn cavalry, such as that which had been employed so devastatingly on the fields and hills south of Vonda. Small ships, coming and going, made their trips between Lara and the nearer downriver towns, such as White Water and Tancred's Landing.

"You cannot put me out into the street!" she cried.

Strobius, the innkeeper, then, in irritation, motioned to one of his assistants. The fellow came up behind the free woman and took her by the upper arms, holding her from behind. She was helpless.

"Eject her," said Strobius.

"You cannot put me out into the street!" she cried.

"Rejoice," said Strobius, "that I do not strip you and sell you into slavery."

"What is going on here?" I had asked, rising to my feet and going to the counter.

"We are putting her out," said Strobius. "She owes me money. She cannot pay."

"But she is a free woman," I said.

"She cannot pay," he said.

"What does she owe?" I asked.

"A silver tarsk for last night," he said, "and, if she would stay here this night, another tarsk, and in advance."

"I believe this is the proper sum," I said. I placed two silver tarsks on the counter.

"Indeed it is," said Strobius. He swept the coins from the counter into his hand, and put them in his apron.

"There is your money, Fellow," said the free woman to Strobius, haughtily, as haughtily as she could manage, still the helpless prisoner of his assistant's grip.

"Yes, Lady," said he, bowing deferentially to her.

"Perhaps, now," she said, squirming in the assistant's grip, "you will have this ruffian unhand me."

He regarded her.

She shuddered. Her Home Stone was not that of Lara, times were troubled, and Strobius was master in his own inn. Too, she had, for a time, owed him money. Would he like to see her stripped, and collared?

"Please, Kind Sir," she said. Gorean men are sometimes slow to release their grip on the bodies of females. They enjoy holding them. They are men.

"Of course, Lady," said Strobius, smiling, again bowing. He then signaled the fellow to release the woman, which he did. She then drew back, angrily, and smoothed down her garments. Then, straightening herself, she came regally to where I stood.

39

"My thanks, Sir," she said, looking up at me.

"It is nothing," I said.

"I am grateful," she said.

"Perhaps you would care to join me at my table," I suggested. "There is little but sul porridge, but I could order you a bowl," I said.

"One must make do in trying circumstances," she said, "with what there is."

"Do you have any wine?" I asked Strobius.

He smiled. "Yes," he said.

"Would you care for some wine?" I asked her.

Her eyes glistened over her veil. It had been some days, I gathered, since she had been able to afford or had had wine. "Yes," she said, "it would give me great pleasure to drink your wine."

"Please go to the table," I said, indicating the table, "and I will make the arrangements."

"Very well," she said, and turned away, going to the table.

"Sul porridge," said Strobius, "is ten copper tarsks. I will charge you forty copper tarsks for the wine, two cups."

"Very well," I said.

In a few moments he had had a fellow bring a tray with the sul porridge and two cups of wine to the counter. I paid him.

"Oh, by the way," I asked, "do you have a packet of Tassa powder?"

He grinned, and reached under the counter. "Yes," he said, handing it to me.

"How much do I owe you for this?" I asked.

"For that one," he said, "it is free. Take it with the compliments of the house."

"Very well," I said.

* * * *

The girl turned uneasily on the mat. She was then again on her side. Her legs were again drawn up. She moaned. I saw the small fingers of her right hand touch the mat. Her finger tips were soft against the rough fibers. On her legs, where she had lain, there were markings from the mat.

I saved a part of the crust of bread I was eating.

She moved uneasily, and made a small noise. She must now sense that it was morning.

I looked about myself. The inn was deserted. It bore the signs of having been hastily evacuated. Tarnsmen of Ar, the rumors had had it, were soon to be aflight toward Lara. The evacuation of the inn had been a portion of the evacuation of the entire city. Outside the streets were empty, and quiet. There were few persons, I conjectured, now left in Lara. There were, of course, the girl and myself.

She rolled onto her belly on the mat. She lay there, the left side of her face against the mat, her small hands at the sides of her head.

I watched her.

I saw her small fingers move slightly, and her finger tips touch the fibers of the mat.

Then, suddenly, I saw her finger tips press down on the mat, and then, suddenly, her fingernails, frightened, dug at it. Her entire body suddenly stiffened.

"You are awake," I observed.

"What is this on which I find myself?" she asked, frightened.

"Is it not obvious?" I asked. "It is a slave mat."

"Where am I?" she asked, lifting her head.

"In the main room of the inn of Strobius," I said, "in the city of Lara."

She rose to her hands and knees. I noticed that her breasts were lovely, inside the rag she wore. "What happened?" she asked.

"You were drugged," I told her.

She shook her head. She looked at me. I did not think she could yet well focus on me.

"You should not have drunk my wine," I told her.

"Where are my clothes?" she asked.

"I discarded, burned or destroyed your luggage and your things," I said, "with the exception of what you now wear, a Ta-Teera and a collar."

"I am collared," she whispered, disbelievingly. She tried the steel.

"It is locked," I assured her.

I saw her hand, subtly, furtively, touch the side of her Ta-Teera.

"The key is no longer there," I informed her. "Too, I have ripped away and discarded the tiny pocket which you had had sewn there.

Girls are not permitted to carry things in their Ta-Teera. Surely you know that."

"Where is the key?" she whispered.

"I threw it away," I told her.

She shook her head. "I remember you," she said. "You paid for my lodging. You gave me wine."

"Yes," I said.

"It was drugged," she said.

"Of course," I said.

"Give me the key to this collar!" she cried, suddenly. She sprang to her feet, her hands pulling at the collar.

"Do not leave the slave mat," I cautioned her. "I threw the key away," I reminded her.

"Threw it away?" she said.

"Yes," I said.

"But it is a real collar," she said. "I cannot remove it."

"No," I said, "it has not been designed to be removed by a girl."

She regarded me with horror.

"Do not leave the mat," I told her.

She stepped back more on the mat.

"Kneel down," I suggested.

She knelt, her knees pressed closely together.

"I found both the Ta-Teera and the collar among your belongings," I told her. "Surely they are unusual objects to be found among the belongings of a free woman."

She said nothing.

"Perhaps you are an escaped slave," I said.

"No!" she cried. "I am not a slave! I am not branded!"

"Reveal your thigh to me," I said, "that I may see whether or not you are branded."

"No!" she said. Then she said, angrily, "It was you, was it not, who put me in the Ta-Teera?"

"Yes," I said.

"Then you know well that I am not branded!"

"That is true," I smiled.

"Beast!"

"You are rather fetching in it," I said.

"It is a rag!" she cried.

42

"I have a reason for permitting you that much," I said. "Otherwise you would have only the steel on your neck."

"I do not understand!"

"Perhaps, later, you will," I said.

"Why are you doing this to me?" she asked. "Who are you? Is this some bizarre joke?"

"No," I said, "it is not a joke."

She turned white.

"Let me go," she said.

"Are you hungry?" I asked.

"Yes, terribly," she said, uncertainly.

I threw her what was left of the crust of bread. It struck the slave mat before her.

"You *throw* me food!" she said.

"Yes," I said.

She reached for it.

"Do not use your hands," I told her.

"I am a free woman," she said.

"Place the palms of your hands down on the mat, and lower your head, and eat," I told her.

"I am a free woman," she said.

"Eat," I told her.

She ate, as I had instructed her, not using her hands. I then placed a pan of water within her reach. "Drink," I told her. She then drank, as she had eaten, not using her hands. I then removed the pan of water from her, threw out the water that had been left and put the pan aside. I then again returned to my place and sat down, cross-legged, behind the small table. She looked at me. I did not think she was displeased to have eaten and drunk.

"What do you want of me?" she asked. "Who are you?"

"Spread your knees," I told her.

Angrily she did so.

"How is it," I asked, "that a free woman should have among her belongings such unusual articles as a Ta-Teera and a collar?"

"I have been associated," she said, "with female slavers, of the house of Tima. I have occasionally used such articles in my work."

"I see," I said.

"Do I know you?" she asked.

43

"Do you?" I asked.

"You are masked," she said. "You have me at a disadvantage."

"It is true that you are well exposed before me," I said.

She reddened.

"Do you know me from somewhere?" she asked.

"Yes," I said.

"From where?" she asked.

"Vonda," I said.

She shrugged, angrily. "You could be any one of a thousand men," she said.

"But I am not," I said.

"No," she said, "I suppose not."

"Come over here," I said, "and lie down on the table, on your back, before me."

She did so.

"What are you going to do with me?" she asked.

"You will learn," I said. The table was low, and sturdy.

"Obviously you intend to treat me as a slave," she said.

"Perhaps," I said.

"I see you have prepared lengths of rope," she said.

"Yes," I said.

Then, slowly, not hurrying, I began to tie her down across the table. I began with her left wrist, fastening it over her head and behind her, to one of the short legs of the table.

"Where are the others?" she asked.

"The city has been evacuated," I said.

"Why?" she asked.

"It was feared there would be an attack of tarnsmen from Ar," I said.

I then jerked tight the rope pulling her right wrist over her head and behind her. I secured it in place.

I thrust up the Ta-Teera, that I might spread her legs.

"Did you truly throw away the key to the collar?" she asked.

"Yes," I said.

"Then you must help me to get out of it soon," she said, "perhaps with tools."

"Why?" I asked. I fastened down her left leg.

"Surely you have read it?" she asked. Such collars usually bear a legend. Usually the legend identifies the master, that the slave, if fled, or lost or strayed, may be promptly returned.

"No," I said. "I cannot read Gorean."

"Does it tell who your master is?" I asked.

"No," she said. "Oh!" she cried, as I pulled her right ankle to the right corner of the table and there, with two loops of the slim, coarse rope, tied it down.

I then jerked apart the Ta-Teera, that she be well revealed to me. She gasped. She squirmed, and trembled. I then stood up and looked down upon her, observing my handiwork.

She pulled at the ropes, and knew herself helpless. She looked up at me. "You have apprehended me boldly," she said.

I said nothing.

She pulled again at the ropes. Then she lay back, helpless. "You have tied me well," she said.

I shrugged.

"I suppose now," she said, "you will wish me to address you as 'Master'."

"As you wish," I said. "It does not matter."

"Tied as I am," she said, "it seems to me not unfitting that I should call you 'Master'."

I said nothing.

"I request your permission to do so," she said.

"It is granted," I said. "What does your collar say?" I asked.

Suddenly she reared in the ropes. "You must help me to remove it!" she said.

"What does it say?" I asked.

"It says, 'I am the slave, Darlene,'" she said.

"It is an Earth-girl name," I said.

"Precisely," she said. "You can well imagine what might be done with me if I were caught in such a collar. Men might think that I was an Earth girl, or one of those girls like an Earth girl, and was thus given such a name!"

I smiled.

"Surely you understand my fears," she said.

"Of course," I said.

"I used to train Earth girls," she said. "I know how men look upon them."

I nodded. Gorean men were not gentle with Earth girls. They regarded them as natural slaves, and treated them accordingly, fully. Some of the most abject slaveries on Gor were assigned to Earth girls.

"So you will help me out of this collar as soon as possible, will you not?" she asked.

"I will if it pleases me," I said.

She lay back. "I am in your ropes," she shrugged.

I crouched then beside her.

"You know me, don't you?" she said.

"Yes," I said.

"You heard my name about the inn," she said.

"Yes," I said, "but even aside from that I would have known you."

"Even veiled?" she asked.

"Yes," I said.

She pulled at the ropes. "You have then," she said, "a shrewd eye for the flesh of women."

"Perhaps," I said.

"Are you a slaver?" she asked, apprehensively.

"No," I said.

"Good," she said. "Good!"

"Why 'good'?" I asked.

"Because then," she said, "I have less to fear."

"Perhaps you are mistaken," I said.

"Oh?" she said.

"Why did you ask?"

"I thought you might be," she said.

"Why?"

"You seemed capable of detecting and assessing my lineaments, even though I was veiled and robed," she said.

"That is something slavers are supposedly good at?" I said.

"Yes," she said.

"Seeing the slave within the robes?"

"If you want it put it that way," she said.

"It seems to me an excellent way of putting it," I said.

"Doubtless," she said, angrily.

46

"I think many men have that ability," I said.

"I trust not!" she said.

I smiled.

"But, too, the authority with which you have handled me and so well bound my limbs."

She looked up at me, and struggled a little, in her bonds.

"I see," I said.

I regarded her.

She was well tied.

This, of course, at least the binding part of it, had nothing to do with the slavers' caste, though they well know their business. It is not at all unusual on Gor for a male, any male, and not simply a warrior, a guardsman, a raider, a slaver, or such, to be familiar with the binding of women. Indeed, boys are commonly trained in these skills once they reach adolescence. It is thought, correctly I suppose, that they will not be likely to need these skills until that time. Indeed, this sort of thing is one of those things that Gorean boys look forward to as it is not only pleasant in itself, but is, in its way, a sign that they are now regarded as having grown up. It is a rite of passage, in its way, one of several toward Gorean manhood. Soon, too, at least in the high cities, they may be able to put away the tunic of boyhood and don their first robe of manhood. Sometimes the manhood robe is associated, as well, with the ceremony of the Home Stone. About this, however, I do not know a great deal, as Goreans tend not to be loquacious in such matters. But, of course, in general, to return to our point, having to do with the binding of women, anyone who owns a slave, or has anything to do with them, would be expected to be familiar with this sort of thing, with a variety of interesting and efficient ties, useful for various purposes, in all of which the woman is utterly helpless, totally at one's mercy. These are, of course, obvious and practical skills, simply called for and to be expected, in a social milieu of the nature of Gorean society. I wondered if it were frightening to be a woman, and to know oneself smaller and weaker than the male, and subduable and leashable by the male, and to recognize, on some level, that one was in nature his rightful property, the smaller, lovelier goods of the larger, stronger beast. This sort of thing, this sort of training, however, is commonly, as much as possible, kept outside the ken of free women, who might find the matter disturbing. On the other hand, some free women doubtless become apprised of such things, one way or another, even if only by rumor. Thus, one supposes, when some free women meet a free male, even under the most innocuous and benign of conditions, at banquets, in the market, at public gatherings, at the song dramas, and so on, they must realize, doubtless uneasily somewhere beneath their cumbersome robes and veils, that they are in the presence of an individual who for all his gentleness and respect could, if he wished, quickly and efficiently, in a matter of moments, render them stark naked and slave helpless, trussed at his feet. Too, obviously the male, at least occasionally, must speculate pertaining to such matters. For example, how would that pretentious, annoying, young lady fare, should she find herself naked, bound hand and foot, at the foot of his couch? Would she not look well there? Might it not be pleasant to look upon the annoying little thing, yours in such straits? Would she then be so irritating, so pretentious and vain? Is she intended for your collar? Is that the destiny you have decided upon for her? Or perhaps you will sell her? As painful and worthless as a free woman she might have been, she would doubtless have some value as a slave. Free women might be good for little or nothing, but one can always see to it that slaves are good for a great deal, for many things. Perhaps this sort of thing gives an interesting undercurrent to some male-female relations on Gor. It is hard to know. But undoubtedly the great majority of Gorean free women do not know of these things. Certainly they are little publicized. And it is doubtless best that they do not know. I myself had received some instruction in these matters from Kenneth, who had been my trainer and friend, when I had been slave in the stables of the Lady Florence of Vonda. We had practiced, of course, on the stable sluts. In these trainings, of course, slaves are used. It would not do at all, obviously, to utilize free women for such purposes.

It might be mentioned in passing that raids to obtain females, "woman raids," or "slave strikes," are not uncommon amongst Gorean cities. The women of one city tend on the whole to be regarded by the men of other cities as attractive candidates for the collar, as potential "slave meat." They are regarded as game, much as tabuk or wild verr might count as game, only in this instance as "slave game," and the men of one city, particularly those of the caste of warriors, often delight in the pleasure of "woman hunt," trying, as it is said, their "chain luck."

Whereas there are bred slaves on Gor, and houses that specialize in such, almost all female slaves have begun their lives as free women. Once enslaved, almost absolutely, they are likely to remain slaves. Who would free them? Indeed, it is said that only a fool frees a slave girl. Those who have owned one find little difficulty in understanding this saying. The woman freed is troublesome and dangerous, the woman enslaved is perfection. The slave girl is delicious and precious. What property can compare with her? She fulfills manhood, and is a joy to own. Too, it might be noted that the slaves on the whole come to love their collars and thrive in bondage. It is the way they want to be, the absolute way they want to live. Indeed, it is regarded as a grievous insult to a girl, and a terrible humiliation, for her to be freed. It is like saying that she is no longer interesting enough, or desirable enough, to be kept in her collar. I suppose this might be difficult for some to understand how this could be, but then, one supposes, their culture is other than the Gorean culture. One merely reports facts. One leaves it to others who are wiser to explain them. One thing seems clear to me, which is that the Gorean culture, for all its perils and occasional cruelties, is much closer to nature than certain other cultures. Those who do not fear nature will perhaps best understand the Gorean culture, and its viability, stability, and fulfilling aspects.

"How is it that you know me?" she asked.

"From Vonda," I said. "You were assistant to the Lady Tima of Vonda, a slaver of that city, of the house of Tima."

"But you do not know me from the house, surely," she said.

"It is from the house, precisely," I said, "that I do know you."

"Who are you?" she asked, frightened.

I drew away the mask.

"Who are you?" she asked.

"Do you not recall me?" I asked. "I was once a silk slave. My name is Jason."

Slowly recognition crept into her eyes. "No," she whispered. "No!" Then, struggling wildly, she tore at the ropes. "No," she screamed. "No!" Then again she lay before me, tied as helplessly and perfectly as before. "No," she whispered. "No, no."

"Yes," I whispered to her. "Yes."

* * * *

The Lady Tendite now lay on the slave mat, where I had put her later in the morning.

"You will help me get this hated collar off, won't you?" she purred, lifting her arms and putting them about my neck, lifting her lips to mine.

"Does Darlene beg it?" I asked.

"Darlene!" she said, lying back, angrily.

"Is that not the name on the collar?" I asked.

"Yes," she said, "it is."

"Does Darlene beg it?" I asked.

"Yes," she purred, again lifting her arms and putting them about my neck. "Yes," she whispered. "Darlene begs it." Then we kissed.

"The request of Darlene is refused," I told her.

Angrily she scrambled to her knees and pulled at the collar. She looked at me in fury. "You sleen!" she said.

I smiled.

"Sleen! Sleen!" she said.

The Ta-Teera had been half torn from her. She had squirmed well.

"Sleen! Sleen!" she wept.

She was soft, and luscious and curved. It was easy to see why men make women slaves.

"Be silent!" I said to her, suddenly.

She looked at me, frightened.

"Do not leave the mat," I told her, getting up. I went to one of the narrow, barred windows in the inn. I saw five armed men running down the street.

"River pirates," I said. "I think they must be."

She moaned, and foolishly tried to cover her beauty. I looked back at her. "Do you think they would permit you modesty in their shackles?" I asked. Then I returned to her side. "They are not coming here," I said. "I think they have decided it is time to leave Lara."

"Why?" she asked.

"Yet I do not smell smoke," I said. "It is interesting."

"What is going on?" she asked.

"Can you not guess?" I asked.

"No," she said. "No!"

I then took her by the arms and threw her to her back on the slave mat beneath me.

"My dear Lady Tendite, or 'Darlene,' as I may choose to call you," I said, "I do not think we have a great deal more time to tarry in this place."

"What do you mean?" she asked.

"And you must leave it somewhat earlier than I," I said.

"I do not understand," she said. "Oh," she said, entered and held. She tried to press me away, but could not do so. Then she clutched at me.

"Excellent, Darlene," I said.

"What are you making me do?" she whispered.

"Can you not guess?" I asked her.

* * * *

"You have won, Jason," she whispered to me, lying on her side beside me, her head on her arm. "You have made me yield to you, irreservedly, helplessly, and as a slave."

"As a free woman," I said, "you cannot yet begin to understand the fullness, the helplessness, of true slave yieldings."

"I sense what they might be," she whispered, "being fully owned, being fully and legally at the mercy of a master."

"Do the thoughts intrigue you?" I asked.

"I must put them from my mind," she said. "I must not even dare to think them."

"Why?" I asked.

"They are too profoundly feminine," she said.

"And thus not fit for a proud free woman?" I asked.

"Yes," she said.

"But suitable perhaps for a collared slave?" I said.

"Yes," she smiled. "Such a woman is permitted to be true to herself."

"I suspect," I said, "she is given no choice but to be true to herself."

"Yes," said the girl. "She is given no choice. She must be true to herself. If she should be reluctant the master and the whip will see to it."

"You seem to speak enviously of the miserable women in bondage."

"Perhaps," she said.

"You yourself wear a collar," I said.

"But I am a free woman," she said.

"For the time, perhaps," I said.

"What do you mean?" she said.

"Get up," I told her. We got up.

She faced me. "You are not going to help me get the collar off, are you?" she asked. She touched me about the shoulder with her finger.

"No," I said.

"You fill me with strange feelings, Jason," she said.

"Oh?" I asked.

"I am accustomed," she said, "to having men do what I wish."

"I suggest, Lady Tendite," I said, "that you begin to accustom yourself to doing what men wish."

"What are you doing?" she asked. I had heard men nearby, the sound of weapons. I dragged her toward the door of the inn. I slid back the panel and looked out. The street, as far as I could tell, was clear. I then shut the panel, and swung up the heavy bars on the door. I opened the door and looked out. The street was clear. I held the Lady Tendite firmly by her left upper arm. She was barefoot, in the torn Ta-Teera and collar. I then flung her down the wide, shallow steps and some fifteen feet into the street beyond. She fell to her hands and knees in the street, and suddenly scrambled up, wildly, looking about herself. I then shut the door, dropping the two heavy beams into place. She ran to the door and began to pound on it. "Let me in!" she cried. "Let me in!"

Within the inn I left the main room and went up to the second floor where, from one of the room's windows, I might command a better view of the street. I could still hear her pounding on the door below. "Let me in, Jason!" she sobbed. "Let me in!" Again and again she struck with her small fists against the door. "I will be your slave, Master!" she cried. "Have mercy on me, Master! Please have mercy on me, Master!"

Then, from the window, I saw her run to the center of the street. She turned from the left to the right, uncertainly. She was sobbing.

"Hold, Slave!" I heard. Men had entered the street. I saw they wore, as I had thought, the uniforms of Ar.

The girl turned wildly in the street and started to run from the men. But she had gone only a step or two when she saw some five other men at the end of the street, also approaching her. She stopped, uncertainly, confused, in the street. The men, not hurrying, then surrounded her.

"I am not what I seem!" she cried. "I am not a slave!"

One of the men seized her by the hair and bent back her head. "Her name is 'Darlene'," he said.

"No!" she said. "I am the Lady Tendite, a free woman of Vonda!"

One of the men then was drawing her hands behind her back. He snapped her wrists in slave bracelets.

"I'm not a slave!" she said.

"'Darlene' is an excellent slave name," said one of the men. "I am hot for her already."

"Wait until we have her in the camp," said their leader.

"A nice catch," said another.

Another man was snapping a leash on her collar.

"Are you an Earth wench?" asked one of the men.

"No," she said, "no!"

"Nonetheless I wager you will whip as well," said another.

"I am not a slave!" "See," she cried, moving her hip to throw back the shreds of the ripped Ta-Teera, "I am not branded!"

"Only a slave would so expose her hip to free men," said one of the men.

"She is not branded," observed another.

"That technicality can be swiftly remedied by a metal worker," said one of the men.

"Why are you not branded, Darlene?" asked a man.

"I am not a slave!" she said. "And my name is not 'Darlene'!"

"You speak much, Darlene," she was told.

"Bring her along," said the leader. "We must finish our patrol."

The Lady Tendite felt the leash grow taut at her collar. She hung back.

"I am not a slave," she said. "My name is not 'Darlene'. I am the Lady Tendite of Vonda!"

"Do all the women of Vonda run about the streets half naked, clad in the rag of a slave, wearing collars?" asked the leader.

"No," she said, "of course not. I was caught and abused, tied even upon a table and forced to give pleasure as a slave. Other things, too, were done to me. I was forced, even, to yield to my captor, as though I might have been a slave and he my master."

"Splendid," laughed one of the men.

She glared angrily at the fellow.

"I bet I, too, can make her yield," said one of the men.

"Later, at the camp," said the leader. Then he again turned his attention to the Lady Tendite. He bowed low before her, in mock courtesy. "I invite you, if you wish, Lady Tendite, to accompany us," he said. "We shall be returning to our loot camp shortly, which is east of Vonda. There you will discover that the women of Vonda are not entirely unknown to us. Many of them have already kindly consented to give us their thighs for branding, their throats for collaring. We trust you will be no less generous."

"She will look well on the slave block," said one of the men.

"True," said another.

"And, Lady Tendite," said the leader, "until you are properly and legally enslaved you will be known by the capture name of 'Darlene'. Say it!" he snapped.

"Darlene!" she cried. "My capture name is Darlene."

"And," said the leader, "in virtue of your collar, and in anticipation of your impending enslavement, you will address us and behave towards us as a slave towards free men."

"Yes," she said.

Then she was struck across the back with the haft of a spear, cruelly.

"Yes, Master!" she cried.

The patrol then continued on its way. I watched the Lady Tendite, her hands braceleted behind her, on her leash, dragged behind the men. She turned once, after about twenty yards, to look back. She saw me. Then she was turned about by the leash and was again dragged, stumbling, down the street.

Five

I Continue My Search for Miss Beverly Henderson

The proprietor of the tavern took the red-haired dancing girl by the arm, she crying out, and thrust her in her costume, ten slender silver chains, five before and five behind, depending from her collar, from the sand. She fell at the side of the sand and, crouching, turned about, looking back.

"This is Jason!" called the proprietor, indicating me. "He wagers ten copper tarsks he can best any man in the house!"

"It is true," I called, stepping to the sand, pulling off the tunic.

"I wager he cannot!" called a large fellow, a peasant, from north of the river.

The proprietor's man, an attendant in the tavern, held the coins.

Bets were taken by the fellows in the tavern.

Men crowded about. Among them, naked, in collars, were paga slaves, with their bronze vessels on leather straps.

The big fellow lunged toward me. I let him strike me. Yet I drew back with his punch in such a way that its impact was largely dissipated. I reacted, however, as though I might have been sorely struck. The men cried out with pleasure. Jabbing, moving, I kept him away from me.

"He fights well," said one of the men.

I then, recovering myself, seized the fellow, that he might not have the free use of his hands. It was not appropriate that I appear too accustomed to this form of sport. I had made that mistake once before, in Tancred's Landing, and there had then been no more eager respondents to my raucous challenge. Rather guardsmen had encouraged me to leave the town with alacrity. I had, as a consequence, picked up only ten copper tarsks at Tancred's Landing.

"Fight!" cried more than one man.

"Clumsy!" cried another.

"Coward!" cried another.

"Coward!" said the peasant.

This irritated me. I relinquished my previous determinations with respect to the manner of handling him. Caught in a swift combination he buckled to the sand. I pretended that I was exhausted, dazed, scarcely able to stand.

"What lucky blows!" cried more than one man.

I looked down at the big fellow who, groggy, was sitting in the sand. I tried to appear as though incredulous that he was down, as though I could not believe that I had somehow struck him from his feet.

"Get up!" cried more than one man.

By the arms he was pulled to the side.

"Ten tarsks," cried another peasant, "that I can best you!"

"Can you fight further, Jason!" anxiously asked the proprietor. Such brawls, supervised, were good for the business of his tavern.

"I will try," I said.

The second fellow, tearing off his tunic, rushed to the sand and then, scarcely hesitating, rushed upon me, fists pummeling. I think he was startled that he managed to strike home so seldom. Soon his arms were sore. I carried him longer than the first fellow. Then, when some interest seemed to lag in the contest, I finished it. He was dragged by his heels from the sand.

"I do not see how one so clumsy, and who fights so poorly, can win so often," said a fellow near the sand.

"He has not yet met Haskoon," said someone confidently.

"I am Haskoon," said a bargeman, stepping to the sand. Haskoon carried his hands too high.

The next fellow, after Haskoon, was more of a wrestler than one who fights with the fists. But I did not break his back.

The fifth fellow was an oarsman on a grain galley. He was strong, but, like the others, was not trained. That his jaw was broken was an accident.

"Jason is surely now exhausted," said the proprietor cheerily. "Who will next step upon the sand?"

But none more, as I had expected, ventured forth to meet me.

I lifted my hands and then drew on my tunic. I was not breathing heavily. I was in a good mood. I bought paga for the five fellows who had helped me earn passage money downriver to the next town. This seemed to assuage their disgruntlement. My financial resources, the ten silver tarsks, obtained from the sale of my former Mistress, the Lady Florence of Vonda, to the slaver, Tenalion of Ar, had been severely depleted. Normally such a sum would last a man months on Gor. In these times, however, given my requirements and the prices, particularly those in Lara, I had been forced to have recourse to alternative sources of income.

"You are no common brawler," said the first fellow to me, the large peasant. "Do not speak it too loudly," I begged of him. "Very well," he said. "I have not felt like this," said one of the other fellows, "since I was trampled by five bosk."

"I am grateful to you all," I assured them.

Slave girls crowded about me, to pour my paga. The collars were lovely on their throats. There were no free women, of course, in the tavern. Gorean taverns can be dangerous places for free women. "Master!" breathed more than one of the lovely slaves, vying to pour me paga. Several knelt about me, breathing quickly, their lips parted, their eyes shining. Several reached out, timidly, to touch me. I had had similar experiences, even with free women, after the stable bouts, though they, of course, had been more discreet, though scarcely more so, than the muchly revealed, ragged, excited, clustering, barefoot, collared slaves. The free woman has her dignity. The slave knows what she is for. The heat in women, when it begins to blaze, speaks to them of being owned, and it is in the collars of the strong, of victors, that they wish to find themselves. It is to such men, the strong, the victors, that they plead to submit.

The free woman, when aroused, thinks collar. The slave, when aroused, rejoices that she is already in one.

The proprietor approached our table and I stood up, holding my goblet of paga, to welcome him. "You fought well, Jason," he said. "Thank you," I said. I looked down. Kneeling at my right knee, her cheek against my knee, was the red-haired dancing girl. She looked up at me timidly, her eyes shining. As she knelt the slender chains at her collar depended to the polished floor. "You fought well, Jason," said

the proprietor. "She is yours for the night. Use her for your pleasure."
"My thanks, Kind Sir," I said. I lifted the paga which I held, saluting
the proprietor and, too, those at the table. "My thanks to you all," I
said. Felicitations were exchanged. I then transferred the paga to my
left hand. I then snapped my fingers and held my right hand, open,
at my hip. Swiftly the girl rose to her feet and, half crouching, put her
head by my hand. I fastened the fingers of my hand deeply and firmly
in her red hair. She winced, and kissed at my thigh. I then, the goblet
of paga in my left hand, her hair in my right, dragged her beside me,
her slender chains rustling, to the nearest empty alcove.

Six

I Hear of the Markets of Victoria;
I Will Travel There

Women are almost always auctioned naked. That way a man can see what he is buying.

I turned away from the block in the barnlike structure in Fina, one of the many towns on the Vosk. I heard the auctioneer's calls fading behind me. I thought he would get a good price for the pretty brunette. She was one of the last items of the evening. Before she had been dragged to the surface of the block, I had examined the remaining girls in the ready cage. She whom I sought was not among them.

Outside the barnlike structure I was stopped by two guardsmen.

"You are Jason, the brawler?" asked one.

"I am Jason," I admitted.

"You will leave Fina by tonight," advised the guardsman.

"Very well," I said.

It had been my intention, anyway, to leave Fina before morning. This had not been the first time, incidentally, that guardsmen had suggested that I leave a town. It had happened once before, at Tancred's Landing.

Several days ago I had departed from Lara. The troops from Ar, tarnsmen, had not burned Lara. Indeed, perhaps surprisingly, they had done little but clear the town of river pirates and, here and there, gather in a bit of loot and some women, mostly female refugees from Vonda who fell into their hands. Their action, however, the strike to Lara, had caused considerable consternation among the forces of Lara, marching toward Vonda. Things, in this sense, had worked out well for the men of Ar, for the troops of Lara had, in consternation, hesitated in their march northward. They were not, thus, involved in the action which took place shortly afterward northeast of Vonda. In this action, however, the forces of Port Olni had been, unexpectedly, abetted by troops from Ti, under the command of Thandar of Ti, one of the sons of Ebullius Gaius Cassius. The battle had been sharp but indecisive. At nightfall of the second day both armies had withdrawn from the field. Ar's committed infantry had been outnumbered but its mobility and its support by their tarn cavalry had compensated to some extent for its lack of weight as a striking force. Thandar of Ti, interestingly, had not challenged Ar in the skies, but had deployed the mercenaries of Artemidorus of Cos in actions against Ar's supply lines. Eventually, after several days of uneasy encampments, the haruspexes of Port Olni, Ti and Ar, meeting on a truce ground, had determined, by taking the auspices, read from the liver and entrails of slaughtered verr, that it was propitious for both armies to withdraw. In this sense, no honor, on either side, was sacrificed. The readings on these auspices had been challenged only by haruspexes of Vonda and Cos. It was generally understood, or felt, that neither the Salerian Confederation nor the city of Ar desired a full-scale conflict. Vonda, it was clearly understood, conspiring with Cos, had initiated hostilities. In burning and sacking Vonda Ar had, for most practical purposes, satisfied its sense of military propriety. Similarly, in stopping the advance of the troops of Ar, the Salerian Confederation could feel that it had maintained its own respect. The tarnsmen of Artemidorus, incidentally, had not molested the slave wagons moving southward. The drivers of these wagons, with their escorts, had only thrown back the canvas to reveal that they carried chained women. The tarnsmen of Artemidorus, then, had flown past, overhead, heedless of the uplifted hands and cries of the women. There is a general Gorean feeling that if a woman has fallen slave she is to remain a slave. The women were then silenced with whips. I think there is little doubt that the cessation of hostilities in the north was in no little part a function of the generosity of the men of Ar, a not impolitic generosity in my opinion, in sparing Lara the fate of Vonda. They had demonstrated that they could have destroyed Lara, but they had not seen fit to do so. This was taken as an expression of disinterest on the part of Ar in all-out warfare with the Salerian Confederation. Also, of course, in the future, this action might tend to divide the confederation in its feelings toward Ar. When it had become clear, incidentally, that Ar had, for most practical purposes, spared Lara, the troops of Lara, not bothering to join with those of Port Olni and Ti, had returned to their city. There would now be sentiment in Lara favoring Ar. This would give Ar political leverage at the confluence of the Olni and Vosk, a strategic point if Cos should ever choose to move in force eastward along the Vosk. Lara was the pivot between the Salerian Confederation and the Vosk towns.

"Hurry!" called the guardsman.

I lifted my hand, acknowledging that I had heard him, and continued my pace toward the wharves of Fina.

For several weeks I had moved from one river town to the next, examining slave markets and attempting to obtain information on the whereabouts of the pirate, Kliomenes. Understandably I encountered few willing informants. Many people, I was sure, knew more of this fellow than they admitted. His name, and that of his captain, Policrates, were apparently feared on the river. These river pirates were not, it must be understood, a few scattered crews of cutthroats. Various bands had their own strongholds and ships. It was not unusual that a single captain had as many as three or four hundred men and eight to ten ships. Similarly there were relationships among these bands, divisions of territory and alliances. They were a power on the river.

I stepped aside to let a free woman, veiled, and a child pass.

I had gone from Lara to White Water, using the barge canal, to circumvent the rapids, and from thence to Tancred's Landing. I had later voyaged downriver to Iskander, Forest Port, and Ar's Station. Ar's Station, incidentally, is near the site where there was a gathering, several years ago, of the horde of Pa-Kur, of the Caste of Assassins, who was leading an alliance of twelve cities, augmented by mercenaries and assassins, against the city of Ar. This war is celebrated, incidentally, in the Gorean fashion, in several songs. Perhaps most famous among them are the songs of Tarl of Bristol. The action is reputed to have taken place in 10,110 C.A., Contasta Ar, from the Founding of Ar. It was now, in that chronology, the year 10,127. Ar's Station, incidentally, did not exist at the time of the massing of the horde of Pa-Kur. It was established four years afterward, as an outpost and trading station, on the south bank of the Vosk. It also commands, in effect, the northern terminus of one of the great roads, the

Viktel Aria, or Ar's Triumph, leading toward Ar. This is also the road popularly known as the Vosk Road, particularly by those viewing it from a riverward direction. West of Ar's Station on the river I had visited Jort's Ferry, Point Alfred, Jasmine, Siba, Sais and Sulport. I had stopped also at Hammerfest and Ragnar's Hamlet, the latter actually, now, a good-sized town. Its growth might be contrasted with that of Tetrapoli, much further west on the river. Ragnar's Hamlet began as a small village and, from this central nucleus, expanded. Tetrapoli, on the other hand, began as four separate towns, Ri, Teibar, Heiban, and Azdak, as legend has it founded by four brothers. These towns grew together along the river and were eventually consolidated as a polity. The four districts of the city, as might be supposed, retain the names of the original towns. The expression 'Tetrapoli' in Gorean, incidentally, means "Four Cities" or "Four Towns."

I made my way now toward the quays of Fina. Here and there men passed me. I was then near the waterfront district. I stepped aside as a string of chained girls, stripped to the waist, was herded past me. They were being taken to one of the stout log warehouses, whose doors were marked with the Kajira sign, to be held for sale. They were sullen in their chains. Some of them looked at me, wondering perhaps if a man such as myself would buy them. The log warehouses for slaves are commonly double-walled and the girls are kept stripped within them, and commonly wear ankle chains, except when the guards wish otherwise. Escape, for all practical purposes, is a statistical impossibility for the Gorean slave girl. Too, the penalties even for attempted escape are often severe. Hamstringing is not uncommon. The hope of the Gorean slave girl is not escape, but to please her master. I inspected the girls as they passed me. She whom I sought was not among them.

"Passage, Master?" inquired a fellow.

"I would deal with others," I told him.

"We are cheap," he called. "Cheap!"

"Thank you," I said to him, and continued on. I had discovered, in various towns, that I was likely to get the best fares at the quays themselves.

On the way down to the river I passed four of the log warehouses whose doors were marked with the Kajira sign. I saw tiny barred windows high in their outer walls. During daylight hours a small amount of light can filter through such a window and then fall through a matching, somewhat lower window, to the interior of the holding area. There are similar apertures, too, sometimes, in the roofs of such structures. In some of the warehouses, incidentally, those which seem to be but one story high, if that, the logged holding areas are substantially underground, as though in a log-walled, sunken room. Windows are commonly small and from eight to ten feet above a girl's head. The light in such structures is, at best, dim. The floor areas are commonly wood except for a central strip of dirt some twenty feet wide. This is primarily for drainage. A network of welded iron bars, set an inch or two beneath the surface, underlies the planking of the floor and the surface of the dirt. Straw is scattered at the edges of the room, on the wood. In the log walls, at various heights, but usually less than a yard from the floor, there occur slave rings. The ground level is commonly reached by ascending a dirt ramp. Such places, as one might suppose, are usually characterized by the smells of held slaves. "Eat!" I heard a man say, from within one of those structures. Then I heard the lash of a whip and a girl's cry of pain. "Yes, Master!" she cried. "Yes, Master!"

I continued toward the quays. Sometimes I almost despaired of finding Miss Beverly Henderson. How could one hope to find one girl among thousands, even tens of thousands, scattered throughout the cities and towns, the fields and villages, of Gor. Too, if she had been transported by caravan or tarn she might, by now, be almost anywhere. Yet I was determined to continue my search. I had two things clearly in my favor. I knew she had been taken recently, and by Kliomenes, the pirate. My search was thus far from hopeless. Indeed, I had little doubt but what I might find Miss Henderson, if I could but find in what market, or markets, Kliomenes would see fit to dispose of his most recent prizes.

"You there, Fellow," said a captain, at the quays. "You seem strong. Look you for work?"

"I am intending to go downriver," I said.

"We are bound for Tafa," he said. "We are short an oarsman."

The next towns west on the river were Victoria and Tafa. West of Tafa was Port Cos, which had been founded by settlers from Cos over a century ago. The major towns west of Port Cos, discounting minor towns, were Tetrapoli, Ven and Turmus, Ven at the junction of the Ta-

Thassa Cartius and the Vosk, and Turmus, at the eastern end of the Vosk's great delta, the last town on the river itself.

"I would go to Victoria," I said. That was the next town west on the river.

"You are an honest fellow, are you not?" asked the captain.

"I think so, reasonably so," I said, warily. "Why?"

"If you are an honest fellow," said the captain, "why would you wish to go to Victoria?"

"Surely there are honest doings in Victoria," I said.

"I suppose so," said the captain.

"Is it a dangerous place?" I asked.

"You must be new on the river," he said.

"Yes," I said.

"Avoid Victoria," he said.

"Why?" I asked.

"Are you a slaver?" he asked.

"No," I said.

"Then avoid Victoria," he said.

"Why?" I asked.

"It is a den of thieves," he said. "It is little more than a market and slave town."

"There is an important slave market there?" I asked.

"You can sometimes get cheap prices on luscious goods there," he said.

"Why are the prices sometimes so cheap?" I asked.

"Girls who cost nothing can be sold cheaply," he said.

"The marketed girls are then primarily captures?" I asked.

"Of course," he said.

"I do not understand," I said.

"It is well known on the river," he said.

"What is well known?" I asked.

"That Victoria is one of the major outlets for the merchandise of river pirates."

"I must go there," I said eagerly.

"I am going to Tafa," he said. "I will not put in at Victoria."

"Let me row for you to the vicinity of Victoria," I said. "Then put me ashore. I will find my way afoot into the town."

"It will be useful to have another oarsman," he said, "even as far as Victoria, and we will have the current with us."

"Yes," I said.

"Perhaps, too," he said, "we could pick up a new oarsman west of Victoria."

"Perhaps," I said.

He looked at me.

"You need pay me nothing," I said. "I will draw the oar for free."

"You are serious?" he asked.

"Yes," I said.

He grinned. "We leave within the Ahn," he said.

Seven

I Arrive in Victoria; I Hear of the Sales Barn of Lysander

"What am I offered for this girl?" called the auctioneer. "What am I offered for this girl?"

It was a blond-haired peasant girl, thick-ankled and sturdy, from south of the Vosk. She was being sold from a rough platform on the wharves of Victoria. She wore a chain collar.

"Two tarsk bits," came a call from the crowd.

I pressed through the throngs on the wharves. The wharves were crowded with goods and men. The masts of river galleys bristled at the quays. There was the smell of the river, and fish.

"I have heard the topaz is being brought east," said a merchant, speaking to another merchant.

"It bodes not well for security on the river," said his fellow.

I thrust past them. Then I drew back, quickly. A brown sleen threw itself to the end of a short, heavy chain. It snarled. It bared its fangs. Such a beast could take a leg from a man at the thigh, with a single motion of those great jaws.

"Down, Taba," said one of the merchants.

Hissing, the beast crouched down, its shoulder blades still prominent under its excited, half-lifted fur, its four hind legs still tensed beneath it. It seemed to me not unlikely that it might, if it had such a will, tear loose the very ring in the boards to which it was chained. I backed away. The merchants, paying me no more attention, continued their conversation. "Victoria has refused the tribute," one of them was saying.

"That is foolish," said a fellow.

"She thinks it is enough to allow them their markets," said a man.

"No," said another, "they will have both, as before, the tribute and the markets."

"They think they can find no other markets," said the second man.

"That is foolish," said the first.

"They could take their business to Tafa," said the second.

"Or return it to Victoria, once she is properly chastened," said the first.

"That is true," said the second.

"Indeed," said the first, "they cannot permit Victoria this insolence. Her example might be followed by every small town on the river."

"They will feel Victoria must be punished," said the second.

"Perhaps that is why the topaz is being brought east," said the first.

"It would be the first time in ten years," said the second.

"Yet, it is interesting," said the first, "for I would not think they would truly need the topaz to subdue Victoria."

"They are strong enough without it," agreed the second.

"Perhaps then it is only a rumor that the topaz is being brought east," said the first.

"Let us hope so," said the second.

"If it is being brought east," said the first, "I think it betokens more than the disciplining of Victoria."

"I would fear so," agreed the second.

I then turned away and left the vicinity of the merchants. I had not understood their conversation.

This morning, before dawn, I had been put ashore some pasangs upriver. I had gone a pasang inland to avoid river tharlarion and proceeded, paralleling the river, toward Victoria. I had come to the town an Ahn ago.

"Candies! Candies!" called a veiled free woman. She carried candies on a tray, held about her neck by a broad strap.

"Hot meat!" called another vendor. "Hot meat!"

"Fresh vegetables here!" called a woman.

"The milk of verr, the eggs of vulos!" I heard call.

Another merchant brushed past me. He was followed by a stately brunette in a brief tunic, collared, carrying a bundle on her head.

I stepped aside as a string of eight peasants, with bundles of Sa-Tarna grain on their shoulders, made their way toward the wharves.

"Now that is what I call really hot meat," a man was saying.

I heard a woman gasping. I looked down. To one side, on her back on the boards, her knees drawn up, her left ankle roped to her left wrist, her right ankle roped to her right wrist, there lay a slave girl. "Please, Masters," whimpered the girl, looking up. "Touch me, Masters." A fat fellow sat on a small stool. He held a light chain, which was attached to her collar. She had been cruelly aroused, but not satisfied. "Please, Masters," she begged. "A tarsk bit for her use," said the fat fellow. I looked down upon her. Then I heard a tarsk bit thrown into the copper bowl beside her. A leather worker pushed past me, crouching beside the slave. Piteously she lifted her body to him.

"Jewelry!" I heard. "Jewelry!"

Nearby there were four girls in a plank collar. This is formed from two boards into which matching semicircles have been cut. The two boards are connected and supported by five flat, sliding U-irons; when the U-irons are slid back, the collar is opened. When they are slid into place, and the two leaves are bolted together, the collar is closed. Two hasps with staples, secured with padlocks, occur, too, at opposite ends of the planks. These lock the collar. The four girls in the plank collar were kneeling, waiting for their master to conduct some business. He was of the peasants. They were nude. Their hands were tied behind their backs.

"When, fleeing from the brigands, I advised seeking refuge in the peasant village," said one, "I did not realize they would take us."

"Peasants are not too fond, generally, of free persons from the high cities," said one of them.

"We were not of their village," said another.

"Doubtless they will use the proceeds from our sale to supplement their income," said one of them.

"If they do not drink it up in the paga taverns first," said the second girl, bitterly.

"We are free women," said the first girl, struggling in the thongs. "They cannot do this to us!"

"Think such thoughts while you may," said the fourth girl. "We are soon to be branded slaves."

"Look at that disgusting girl," said the second girl, indicating with her head the moaning, writhing slave with the leather worker.

"Yes," said the fourth girl.

"Can they make me do that?" asked the second girl, frightened.

"They can make you do anything, my dear," said the fourth girl.

"Jewelry!" I heard. "Jewelry!"

I stepped away to one side and stopped before a blanket spread out on the boards. On the blanket, spread out, were dozens of pins and brooches, clasps and buckles, rings and necklaces, and bracelets and earrings, and bangles and armlets, and body chains. A pleasant-looking fellow in a woolen tunic sat cross-legged behind the blanket.

"Buy jewelry here," said he. "It is cheap and attractive. Bedeck your slaves."

"See, Master?" asked a girl kneeling at his side, collared, nude, lifting her arms. She was almost covered with jewelry. About her throat alone there must have been twenty necklaces. She lifted the necklaces, causing them to rustle and shimmer, holding them forth to me in her small hands. Then she extended her right arm that I might see the armlets, bracelets and rings which scarcely permitted her flesh to be seen.

"Buy some for your slave," said the man. "Here," said he, lifting a necklace from the blanket. "This was taken from a free woman, now scrubbing stones in the plaza of Iphicrates."

"I do not have a slave," I said.

"I will sell you this one," said he, indicating the display slave at his side, "for a silver tarsk."

"Buy me, Master," she laughed. "I am pretty. I work hard. I can well please a man in the furs."

"It is true," smiled the fellow.

"Surely women can be purchased more cheaply in Victoria than a silver tarsk," I smiled.

"True," grinned the fellow. I saw that he had not wished, truly, to sell her.

"You mentioned," I said, "that this necklace had been taken from a free woman."

"By a pirate," he said.

"You speak of this openly," I observed.

"This is Victoria," said he.

69

"May I inquire as to what crew it was of which that pirate was a member?" I asked.

"Of that of Polyclitus," said he. "Their stronghold is near Turmus."

"Doubtless they also harry the trade routes circumventing the delta of the Vosk?" I asked.

"Occasionally," he said. "Indeed, it was there that they picked up this pretty little plum." He indicated the girl at his side. "Would you believe that she was once the daughter of a rich merchant?" he asked.

"It seems incredible," I said.

"He has trained me well to the collar," she purred, kissing at his arm.

"It can be done with any woman," he said.

"Are you familiar with a pirate named Kliomenes?" I asked. I hoped my voice did not betray undue interest.

"He is a bad fellow," said the man. "He is a lieutenant to Policrates."

"Do you know if he is now in Victoria?" I asked.

"Yes," said the man. "He has come to Victoria to sell goods and slaves."

"Where are these to be sold?" I asked.

"The goods have already been sold," said the man, "at the merchant wharves."

"And the slaves?" I asked.

"They are to be sold tonight," said he, "at the sales barn of Lysander."

"I shall take this body chain," I said to the man, indicating one of the body chains on the blanket.

"But I thought you had no slave?" he asked.

"I would still like to thank you, somehow," I said. "You have been very helpful."

"It is a tarsk bit," he said.

The loop of the body chain was some five feet in length. It was made to loop the throat of a woman several times, or, by alternative windings, to bedeck her body in a variety of fashions. The chain was not heavy, but, too, it was not light. It had a solid heft in one's hand. It was closely meshed and strong. It could be used, if a man wished, and perfectly, for purposes of slave security. It was decorated sensuously with colorful wooden beads, semiprecious stones and bits of leather. Detachable, but now attached to the chain at one point were two sets of clips, one of snap clips and one of lock clips. It is by means of these clips that the chain can be transformed from a simple piece of slave jewelry into a sturdy and effective device of slave restraint.

I put down the tarsk bit, and the man took it, and slipped it into his pouch.

"Do not give that to a free woman," he grinned.

"It is pretty," I said. I looped it several times, and put it in my pouch.

"It is a body chain," he said.

"It is still pretty," I said. I wondered why I had bought it. It was pretty, surely. Perhaps that was why I had bought it.

"When I was free," said the girl, "I could not wear such things."

"They are not for free women," said the man.

"No, Master," she said, quickly. "But now," she said, "I may, with my master's permission, make myself as beautiful and exciting as I can."

"It is I who can decide what it is which you can wear," he said.

"Yes, Master," she smiled, "and even if I am permitted to wear anything at all."

"And do not forget it," he said.

"No, Master," she said.

"Tonight," I said, "Kliomenes puts his wares upon the block at the sales barn of Lysander."

"Yes," said the man.

"I thank you," I said, "and I wish you well."

"I, too, wish you well," said he.

I then took my way up a narrow street leading into Victoria.

"Good hunting in the slave market!" called the man after me.

"Thank you," I said. I smiled to myself. Then I continued on my way, wondering why I had purchased so strange an item as a body chain, a form of jewelry obviously designed for the body of a female slave.

Eight

I Have a Close Call in the Tavern of Tasdron; I Hurry to the Sales Barn of Lysander

"Are there any more challengers?" I asked, wiping the sweat and sand from my face with my forearm.

I had tallied my resources, prior to coming to the tavern of Tasdron, off the avenue of Lycurgus, and found them to amount to only seventy copper tarsks, including five tarsks which I had happily, and unexpectedly, received, the captain being a good fellow, for acting as an oarsman from Fina to the vicinity of Victoria. I did not know how much a slave might go for in the market of Lysander, but I wished to have enough to be confident that I could bid realistically and effectively on one item of merchandise, should it be offered to the public.

I spit down into the sand. I rubbed my hands on my thighs.

I had fought seven fellows, and finished them off with a dispatch which, it seemed to me, might have pleased even Kenneth and Barus, my former mentors in such matters. I might have taken more time and enticed more challengers to face me but I wished to be at the market of Lysander when the biddings began. As it was I was not displeased. I had managed to accumulate two silver tarsks and some sixteen copper tarsks. In Victoria I was confident I would encounter no guardsmen who, at the behest of honest folk, might encourage me to take my leave at an early convenience.

"Are there any more challengers?" I inquired.

The room was quiet. I bent down to a small table near the sand to gather in my winnings.

"A silver tarsk," said a voice, not a pleasant one.

I straightened up.

A fellow was now standing, some fifty feet across the room. I had seen the table there earlier. About it had sat some seven or eight fellows, unshaven, dour chaps. Several of them were scarred. Two wore earrings. More than one wore a handkerchief knotted about his head, in the manner of some oarsmen, that their heads be protected from the sun. All were armed.

"Kind Sirs, no!" called out Tasdron, the tavern's proprietor.

There was a sudden sound, that of a short metal blade slipping from a sheath.

"A silver tarsk," said the fellow again, holding the drawn blade. Goreans, I knew, seldom drew steel unless they intended to make use of it. I swallowed hard.

"I am not familiar with steel," I said, as pleasantly as I could manage.

"You should not carry it, then," said the man. Several of his fellows laughed.

"The combat, as has been made clear," said Tasdron, his voice shaking, "is to be unarmed."

"Pick up your blade," said the fellow to me. I saw the point of the short sword move slightly. He gestured to my clothes, and pouch and blade, which lay nearby.

"I cannot fight you with steel," I said. "I am not skilled with it."

"Run," whispered Tasdron.

"Close the exits," said the fellow to some of the men with him. Four of them rose up, one going to the side door, one to the door to the kitchen, and two to the main threshold. They stood there. Their steel, too, was now drawn. At the table, still sitting, were two other men. One of them seemed in his presence as though he might be the group's leader. He observed me, and quaffed paga.

"Pick up your blade," said the fellow.

"No," I said.

"Very well," said he. "The choice is yours." He stepped about his table and then, carefully, watching me, advanced. He stopped about ten feet from me. Then, suddenly, he kicked a table from in front of him to the side, clearing a path to me. Two men scrambled away from the table. A paga slave, cowering in the background, screamed.

"I am unarmed," I said.

He advanced another step. I watched the point of that blade move.

"He is new in Victoria," said Tasdron, desperately. "Take his clothes, his money, his things. Let him live!"

But the fellow did not even glance at Tasdron. He took another step closer.

I backed away, and then felt the tables behind me, against my legs.

"I am unarmed," I said.

The fellow grinned, and advanced another step.

"Permit me to seize up my weapon," I said.

He grinned again, and advanced yet another step. I knew I did not have time to turn and clutch at the weapon in its sheath on the table, with my pouch and clothes, and even had I been able to reach it and remove it from the sheath I did not think it would do me much good. I saw how this man handled steel, and I saw that the blade itself was much marked. It had seen a plenitude of combat. Before him, even with the blade in my grasp, I would have been, I knew, for all practical purposes, defenseless.

"I am unarmed," I said. "Is it your intention to kill me in cold blood?"

"Yes," said the fellow.

"Why?" I asked.

"It will give me pleasure," he said. I saw the blade draw back.

"Hold!" called a voice.

The fellow stepped back, and looked past me. I turned about. There, about twenty feet away, in a dirty woolen himation, stood a tall, unshaven man. Though he seemed disreputable he stood at that moment very straight.

"Do you, Fellow," said he, addressing me, "desire a champion?"

The man was armed. Over his left shoulder there hung a leather sheath. He had not deigned, however, to draw the blade.

"Who are you?" asked the fellow who had been threatening me.

"Do you desire a champion?" asked the man of me.

"Yes," I said.

"Who are you?" demanded the fellow who had been threatening me.

"Do you force me to draw my blade?" asked the tall man. The hair on the back of my neck rose when he had said this.

"Who are you?" demanded the man who had threatened me, taking another step back.

The man did not speak. Rather, with one hand, he threw back the himation, over his shoulders. There was a cry in the tavern.

I saw that the fellow wore the scarlet of the warrior.

"No," said the man who had been threatening me. "I do not force you to draw your blade." He then backed away. When he reached his table he thrust his own blade angrily into his sheath. He then, with the fellows who had guarded the doors, left the tavern.

"Paga, paga for all!" called Tasdron. Paga slaves rushed to pour paga. "Music!" he called. Five musicians, who had been near the kitchen, hurried to their places. Tasdron, too, clapped his hands twice and a dancing slave, portions of her body painted, ran to the sand.

Unsteadily I went to the table of the tall man. He seemed to pay me small attention. When the girl poured him paga his hand shook as he reached for it. He lifted it, suddenly, spilling some to the table, to his lips. He was shaking. "I owe you my life," I said. "Thank you." "Go away," he said. His eyes then seemed glazed. No longer did he seem so proud and strong as he had before, in that brief moment when he had confronted the fellow who had threatened me. His hands shook on the paga goblet. "Go away," he said.

"I see that you still wear the scarlet, Callimachus," said a voice.

"Do not mock me," said the man at the table.

I saw that he who spoke was he whom I had taken to be the leader of the ruffians at the far table, one of whose number had threatened me. He himself had neither supported nor attempted to deter the fellow who had threatened me. He held himself above squabbles in common taverns, I gathered. I took him to be a man of some importance.

"It has been a long time since we met in the vicinity of Port Cos," said the fellow who had come to the table.

The man at the table, sitting, he who had saved me, held the goblet of paga, and said nothing.

"This part of the river," said the standing man, "is mine." Then he looked down at the sitting fellow. "I bear you no hard feelings for Port Cos," he said.

The sitting man drank. His hands were unsteady.

"You always were a courageous fellow, Callimachus," said the standing man. "I always admired that in you. Had you not been concerned to keep the codes, you might have gone far. I might have found a position for you even in my organization."

"Instead," said the man sitting at the table, "we met at Port Cos."

"Your gamble this night was successful," said the standing man. "I would advise against similar boldnesses in the future, however."

The sitting man drank.

"Fortunately for you, my dear Callimachus, my friend Kliomenes, the disagreeable fellow who left the tavern earlier, does not know you. He does not know, as I do, that your eye is no longer as sharp as once it was, that your hand has lost its cunning, that you are now ruined and fallen, that the scarlet is now but meaningless on your body, naught but a remembrance, an empty recollection of a vanished glory."

The sitting man again drank.

"If he knew you as I do," said the standing man, "you would now be dead."

The sitting man looked into the goblet, now empty, on the table. His hands clutched it. His fingers were white. His eyes seemed empty. His cheeks, unshaven, were pale and hollow.

"Paga!" called the standing man. "Paga!" A blond girl, nude, with a string of pearls wound about her steel collar, ran to the table and, from the bronze vessel, on its strap, about her shoulder, poured paga into the goblet before the seated man. The fellow who stood by the table, scarcely noticing the girl, placed a tarsk bit in her mouth, and she fled back to the counter where, under the eye of a paga attendant, she spit the coin into a copper bowl. There seemed to me something familiar about the girl, but I could not place it.

"Drink, Callimachus," said the standing man. "Drink."

The seated man, unsteadily, lifted the paga to his lips.

Then he who had stood by the table turned about and left. I backed away from the table.

"The fellow who threatened me," I said to Tasdron, the proprietor of the tavern, "he called Kliomenes. Who is he?"

"He is Kliomenes, the pirate, lieutenant to Policrates," said Tasdron.

"And the other," I asked, "he who was standing by the table, speaking to the man who saved me?"

"His captain," said Tasdron, "Policrates himself."

I swallowed, hard.

"You are fortunate to be alive," said Tasdron. "I think perhaps you should leave Victoria."

"At what time do the sales begin in the sales barn of Lysander?" I asked.

"They have already begun," said Tasdron.

Hurriedly I ran to the table where I had left my things. I drew on my clothes and hastily slung my sword over my left shoulder. I picked up my winnings from the fighting. I saw the blond girl, she who had the pearls wrapped about her collar, looking at me. It seemed to me that I had seen her somewhere. I placed my winnings in my pouch, and tied it at my belt. I could not recall if, or where, or when, I might have seen her. She was a not unattractive slave. Then I hurried out the door. I made my way rapidly toward the sales barn of Lysander.

Nine

What Occurred at the Sales Barn
of Lysander

"This red-haired beauty," called the auctioneer, "is a catch of Captain Thrasymedes. She can play the lute."

There was raucous laughter. "How good is she in the furs?" called a voice.

The girl went for four copper tarsks.

"Have the girls of Kliomenes been sold?" I asked a fellow.

"Yes," said a fellow. I cried out with anguish. "Most," said another.

"Most?" I pressed him.

"Yes," he said, "I think there are others, taken near Lara."

"What am I offered for this blonde?" called the auctioneer.

"Weren't they sold before?" asked the first fellow.

"Not all, I think," said the second man.

I left their sides and pushed through the crowd, making my way nearer the high, round, sawdust-strewn block.

"Watch where you are going, Fellow," snarled a man.

I stopped by the ready cage. Inside, sitting on a wooden bench, behind stout, closely-set bars, miserable, clutching sheets about themselves, some with glazed eyes, sat some ten girls. I clutched the bars, from the outside, looking within. She whom I sought was not there. One girl rose from the bench, her left ankle pulling against the chain and shackle that held her with the others, and dropped the sheet to her waist. "Buy me," she begged, putting her hand toward me. I stepped back. "This is not an exhibition cage," said an attendant, putting his hand on my arm. "You may not loiter here." "Buy me," begged the girl, reaching toward me. I gathered that she, unlike several of the others, apparently, had had masters. "Are these all the items that remain for sale?" I asked the attendant. "No," he said. "Are there girls of Kliomenes who remain to be sold?" I asked, desperately. "I do not know," he said. "I do not have the manifests."

Miserably I turned about and went back to stand with the others, in the vicinity of the block.

The blonde went for six tarsks.

"And here," said the auctioneer, "we have another blonde. This one, like many of the girls now in the ready cage, was free."

There was laughter. "Make her kiss the whip!" called a man.

"Down, Wench, and kiss the whip!" ordered the auctioneer. The girl knelt and kissed the whip. There was more laughter. He then began to put her through slave paces.

There were some two hundred men at the sale. Such sales occur frequently in the various sales barns of Victoria, sometimes running for several nights in a row. The spring and summer are the busiest seasons, for these are the seasons of heaviest river traffic and, accordingly, the seasons when pirates, after their raids, are most likely to bring in their loot. Many of the men at the sales barn were professional slavers, from other towns and cities, looking for bargains.

"Sold to Targo, of Ar!" announced the auctioneer. Manacles were then clapped on the blonde and she was dragged from the block.

I was angry, for I did not even know if Miss Henderson was to be sold, or if she had already been sold. If she had been sold she might even now, while I stood about, helplessly, be being transported from Victoria, a slave, anywhere. My fists were clenched. My palms were sweating.

The next two girls, brunettes, were sold to Lucilius, of Tyros. The next four slaves were purchased by a fellow named Publius, who was an agent for a Mintar, of Ar.

I waited, as the bidding grew more heated, and as more men entered the building. Five times the ready cage was emptied and filled, and emptied, as girls, freed of their shackles, were ordered to the block's surface for their vending.

"Do none of these women interest you?" asked a man nearby.

"Many are lovely," I said. Indeed, had I not been waiting desperately, miserably, for she whom I sought I might have been tempted to bid hotly on several of them. To own any one of them would have been a joy and a triumph. The man who has owned a woman or women knows of what I speak. Perhaps even those who have never owned a woman can sense, dimly, what it might be like. I know of no pleasure comparable to the pleasure of owning a woman, fully. It is indescribably delicious; it is glorious; it fills one with joy and power; it exalts and fulfills the blood. It teaches a male, in the thunderous currency of intellect and emotion, what is the true meaning of manhood. Compared to it the gratifications of pretense and denial, the insistence on subverting one's blood and virility in the name of a false manhood conditioned by a demented, antibiological society, are pallid indeed. Let those who can climb mountains climb them; let those who cannot climb them console themselves with denying their existence.

"The brunette four sales ago," said the man next to me, "was she not superb?"

"Yes," I said. She had indeed been stunning. In this market, to her indignation, she had gone for only fourteen copper tarsks. She had been sold to an agent of Clark, of Thentis. The next brunette, in my opinion, had been even more stunning. She had gone for a mere fifteen copper tarsks. She had been sold to a Cleanthes of Teletus.

"Sold to Vart, of Port Kar!" called the auctioneer, and a redhead was taken from the platform.

"And here," called the auctioneer, "we have one of the catches of Kliomenes, taken near Lara."

He tore the sheet away from the girl on the block, throwing it to the side.

She wore only her sales collar with her sales disk, on which was written her lot number, wired to the steel.

"A cold, prissy little Earth slut," called the auctioneer, "and yet one not without interest, as you can see." He bent her back, his hand in her hair, exposing the bow of her beauty to the men.

There was a sound of pleasure from the crowd.

"She is already branded," said the auctioneer, "but has served primarily as a display slave, and not a use slave." He then turned her, still keeping his hand in her hair, so that those on his left might better see her. "Accordingly," he said, "she is not yet fully broken to the collar." There was laughter from the crowd. He then turned her so that those on his right might better see her. "In my opinion," said he, "it is now time for this girl to learn the various uses to which a slave can be put." "Yes!" shouted more than one fellow. He then, as she gasped, bent her back a bit more, turning her again toward her left, so that she was presented exquisitely to the men. "Does she not appear ready for taming and heating?" inquired the auctioneer.

"Yes," shouted several men, "yes!" The girl trembled. She knew she might belong to any one of them.

"What am I bid?" called the auctioneer.

"Two copper tarsks," called a man.

"Four!" cried another.

"Six!"

"Seven!"

"Nine!"

"Eleven!"

"This is an exquisite little slut!" called the auctioneer. He then released her hair. "Stand straight," he ordered the girl. She did so. He walked about the platform, with the whip.

"Twelve!"

"Thirteen!"

"She was beautiful enough to be a display slave," said the auctioneer.

"Fourteen!" was called out.

"Now you can have her for your own work and use slave!" pointed out the auctioneer.

"Fifteen!" I heard.

"Consider her, surrendered, squirming in your furs!" he said.

"Sixteen!" I heard.

"Do I hear only sixteen tarsks for this exquisite little bargain?" inquired the auctioneer, incredulously.

"Sixteen," repeated the man.

The auctioneer spun to face the girl. "Kneel, and kiss the whip," he ordered her.

Swiftly the girl, frightened, knelt before him. She took the coils of the whip in her small hands and, lowering her head, kissed them.

"On your feet," barked the auctioneer. "I will have a fit price for you."

The girl, terrified, sprang to her feet.

"Put her through her paces!" called a man. "Let us see what she can do!" called another.

The auctioneer shook out the coils of the whip. He then, rapidly, loudly, clearly, in a series of orders, sometimes cracking the whip, commanded the girl, one by one, swiftly, to assume an intricately patterned series of postures and attitudes. Seldom, I think, in so brief a compass, could a woman be displayed so fully as a female. He then cracked his whip and ordered her to stand straight upon the platform, sucking in her gut. She was breathing heavily; there were tears in her eyes; she was trembling; she was covered with sweat and sawdust. He had permitted her no respite or quarter. The buyers now well understood the nature of the goods on which they were bidding.

"Twenty-two tarsks!" called a man.

"Twenty-three!" called another.

So stunned I was that I had not even entered the bidding. I had never dreamed she could be so beautiful. What fools are the men of Earth, I thought, for the woman on the block was an Earth woman, to let their women off so lightly. What fools they are not to own their women and force them to manifest the true fullness and desirability of their beauty. The woman on the block was an Earth woman. Did she not show, in her own person, how beautiful women of Earth could be. And yet I knew that on Earth such women commonly languished, their beauty denied its meaning and fulfillment, their beauty not summoned forth, not commanded forth, for the pleasure, the sport and service of strong men.

"Twenty-five tarsks!"

"Twenty-six!"

"Twenty-seven!"

"Twenty-eight!"

"Thirty!"

"Buy her," a voice seemed to say to me. "Buy the slave! Make her yours!" "No, no!" I said, half aloud. "I cannot!" "What did you say?" asked the man next to me. "Nothing, nothing!" I said.

"Thirty-five!" I heard.

"Forty!" I heard.

"Forty-two!"

I could not even enter the bidding. I could scarcely breathe. My heart was pounding. I had never dreamed she could be so beautiful. It seemed I could not even speak. I could not take my eyes off the girl under the torches, the collar and sales disk at her throat. I was trembling.

"Forty-four!" I heard.

"Forty-six!"

I trembled. I had seen Miss Beverly Henderson kiss the whip. I had seen her put through slave paces.

Miss Beverly Henderson!

She!

A slave!

Owned!

On this world she was owned, owned as much as would be a pig on Earth!

How could such a thing be?

Quite easily, of course.

And it was the case.

Simply, clearly, and obviously the case.

Legally, and with full perfection, the case.

She was owned.

Literally owned!

Should I have been dismayed?

Rather I was inordinately excited.

I remembered her briefly, wildly, uncontrollably, from the university, from the halls, from the campus, in the severe, pseudomale garments prescribed for her sex by unfeminine women, who arrogated to themselves the setting of ugly, self-serving, hateful, desexualizing fashions, enforcing their decrees by the processes of social pressure, punishing lapses from their requirements by insult, scorn, intimidation, backstabbing, character assassination, diminishment, ostracism and marginalization. I recalled her doing her best to comply with their directives, to fulfill their implacable pathological stereotypes, in dress, in expression and carriage, in attitude and thought. And in this she was surely not other than thousands of other frightened, confused, unhappy women, ordered to deny themselves, to betray their sexuality, women fearing to question propounded absurdities, struggling to be thoughtlessly, uncritically obedient to the dictates of fanatics. But even so her femininity, for all her efforts, had been insufficiently concealed. She was not a surrogate male, a pretend man. She was, willing or no, a beautiful, feminine young woman. How unfortunate for her, I supposed, in such a place and time! And how beautiful she had been in the restaurant, in the off-the-shoulder, white, satin-sheath dress, she somehow then daring to appear so.

I now suspected that that courage had had to do with a change in her, one consequent on her disturbing interlude with a heavy, large-handed, balding, virile man encountered in a Manhattan apartment, an interlude in which she had first found herself put as a female under a man's will, an experience which had shocked her into the understanding that she was quite other than a male, something wondrously and preciously different—and wondrously and preciously beautiful, and wondrously and preciously desirable.

And how dismayed she had been to have been come upon in the restaurant by two of those she so feared, two of her fellow students, gross, mulelike females, politically sanctimonious, smug in dogmatism and power, examples of the ideologically obsessed mediocrities whose intent it was to turn a university into a personal political instrument, one promoting a specialized agenda designed to further particular interests, theirs, an agenda whose fruition would be to replace education with indoctrination, thought with rote reflexes, an indoctrination in which objectivity, logic and reason were to be sacrificed to a specialized, contrived orthodoxy, one alien to evidence, one foreign to nature, one relying on intimidation and falsehood, one predicated upon the utility of harm, pressure, control, censorship, and hatred.

But now that beautiful young woman was no longer in the cold, friendless corridors of a preempted institution, no longer in a desk chair dutifully taking notes on what she was supposed to believe and on the values, like numbing and denying poisons, which she was supposed to imbibe. No longer did she move about a campus in a prescribed garmenture, anxious lest her femininity and her true needs be suspected. And no longer, either, was she in the lovely garmenture of the restaurant, that suggesting her piteous desire to express her forbidden sex, that of her deepest self, that of the true female, the feminine woman, the excruciatingly desirable feminine woman, so preciously, wondrously and gloriously different, in so many ways, from a man.

It seems that some change had come to her life.

She had been found beautiful enough, and desirable enough, obviously, to have been taken by Gorean slavers. Yes, *taken—by Gorean slavers*. They, if none others, had seen the woman in her, the depth, preciousness, and meaning of her beauty. On this world it would not be denied. Indeed, it was why she had been brought here.

The heavy, large-handed, balding, virile fellow of the apartment had doubtless been a Gorean slaver, or perhaps one in league with them.

He had doubtless seen her possibilities.

Perhaps he, even, had passed on her suitability, had marked her for transit to this world.

He doubtless knew she would one day be in a place, and situation, rather as she was now.

Doubtless, gazing upon the scandalized, upset, prideful young lady before him, he had been amused by that thought.

What would she look like, stripped, in a collar, being sold?

I looked upon her, her ankles almost covered in the deep sawdust on the block.

She was terrified, frightened, and confused.

She, the vain, proper, elegant young lady, so prideful, yet so confused and unhappy, so desperately concerned to profess, and adhere to, prescribed views, so conditioned to uncritically accept multiple stupidities, so concerned to be found acceptable by driven, self-seeking, moronic doctrinaires, now found herself in an utterly different reality, in a strange, primitive, wild environment, alien to all she knew—now found herself exposed to the view of numerous, large, strange, powerful, excited, lustful men, men quite unlike those her old world had prepared her to expect or understand—she had not even known such men could exist—now found herself stripped on a slave block on another world, a far world, stark naked, as women are sold, a collar on her neck, with its attached sales disk, bearing her lot number, wired to her collar, in the keeping of a mighty, muscular fellow, an auctioneer, who would not hesitate at the least reluctance, let alone recalcitrance, on her part to instantly use his ready whip upon her, that dreadful instrument of corrective discipline. The university, the restaurant, the city, the world, all she had known were now far away. Others, not she, had decided it. Her life had changed. She had been brought to Gor.

I looked upon her.

She was far from Earth.

She had been enslaved.

She was now a domestic animal.

She was for sale.

She was being sold!

That which was of Earth in me told me I should properly cry out in shame and rage, and shed tears, as doubtless should a true modern male, that she, the innocent creature, should be so exhibited, so exposed, so humiliated.

But something deeper in me, something masculine in me, did not object to seeing her as she now was.

Indeed, I found considerable satisfaction in her predicament.

It all seemed suddenly very appropriate.

An irresistible, overwhelming thought came to me—a thought which I could not banish—that the beautiful Miss Henderson belonged on a slave block.

"Forty-seven!" I heard.

"Forty-eight!"

"Fifty!"

Suddenly the girl cried out, startled. Her reflex had been spasmodic, uncontrollable. Then she put her head in her hands, weeping. Her entire body, under the torches, turned a creamy crimson in color.

"Ninety tarsks!" called a man.

The auctioneer stepped back from the girl, the whip in his hand.

"I have ninety tarsks," he called.

"She is not so cold," said the man next to me.

"No," I said, "no."

"Ninety-two tarsks!" called a man.

"Ninety-four!" called another.

"I have ninety-four tarsks," called the auctioneer. "Do I have more? Do I have more?"

There was silence.

"I prepare to close my hand," called the auctioneer.

"Ninety-eight!" I cried out, suddenly. I was startled to hear my own voice.

The girl lifted her head, dully.

"Ninety-eight, I have ninety-eight," called the auctioneer. "Do I hear more? Do I hear more?"

There was silence.

"I prepare to close my hand," said the auctioneer. "I close my hand!"

I owned Miss Henderson.

Ten

We Leave the Sales Barn of Lysander; Miss Henderson Will Share My Lodgings

Miss Henderson was thrust from the block. I made my way toward the foot of the block. My head seemed to swim. I was scarcely conscious of my movements. I moved as though in a dream.

"Jason?" she asked, from within the bars of the holding cage at the right of the sales block. Already her left ankle had been shackled. "Jason?"

I handed the receipt to the cage attendant. At the table I had paid ninety-eight tarsks.

I saw the sales disk removed from her collar and put in a small, wooden box. I saw the shackle removed from her ankle. I saw the door to the cage open and saw her pushed forth, before me.

"Do you not know enough to kneel before your master?" asked the attendant.

Swiftly she knelt.

I lifted her to her feet and held her in my arms. "Is it you, Jason?" she whispered. "Is it truly you?"

"Yes," I said. "It is I."

She began to weep, and I held her close to me. She shuddered in my arms. She sobbed. I felt her tears through my tunic. "Jason," she sobbed, "Jason, Jason."

I held her to me, and caressed her head. "I am so happy," she said. "I am so happy!"

"Yes," I said, "yes." I continued to caress her head, and hold her to me.

"You purchased me. You own me, Jason," she said. "I am your slave." I scarcely understood what she was saying. "I know that you will be strong with me, but I will try to serve you well," she said.

"What are you saying?" I asked.

"I will try to be pleasing to you," she said. "I do not want to be whipped."

"What are you saying?" I asked.

She drew back a bit in my arms and lifted her head. There were tears in her eyes. Her lips trembled. She seemed incredibly happy. "I remember the girl at the shop of Philebus, in Ar," she said, "she who, wrists bound, was neck-leashed to the ring. Doubtless I now, too, as the mood seizes you, now that you own me, will be subjected to such ruthless and peremptory considerations. Doubtless you will respect my will no more than hers and rape me, too, when it pleases you."

I looked at her, puzzled.

She again put her head against me, pressing her cheek against my shoulder. "All the things that you may have wanted to do with me," she said, "you may now do. Everything that you may have wanted from a woman I must now give. You may do with me as you please. I must obey you in all things." She lifted her head again. There were tears in her eyes. "Show me no mercy," she said. "See that I serve you well."

"Key!" I cried. "Key!"

"What will you name me?" she asked.

"Key!" I cried.

"Key?" she asked. "Master?"

The key to the sales collar was placed into my hand by one of the cage attendants. I saw the snug fit of the steel on her throat. It was incredibly exciting. She could not remove it. Then, sweating, getting a grip on myself, hurriedly, fumbling, I thrust the tiny key into the lock.

"Master?" she asked, frightened.

"Do not call me 'Master'!" I said, almost shouting. My voice choked.

Men looked at us.

I turned the key and opened the tiny, heavy, single-action, seven-bolt lock on the collar. Each of the bolts is said to stand for one of the letters in the spelling of 'Kajira', the most common Gorean expression for a slave girl.

"Where is your collar for me?" she asked.

"I have no collar for you," I said.

"Master?" she asked.

"Do not call me 'Master'!" I said.

"Yes, Master," she said. "I mean 'Yes, Jason!'"

I put my hands on the collar, to tear it from her throat. But she clutched at the collar, holding it on her throat.

"Master?" she asked. "Jason?"

"You are a woman of Earth," I said. "You know how to behave and act."

"I do not understand," she said.

"Do not speak to me of pleasing me," I said. "Do not speak to me of obeying me or serving me."

"But I am a slave," she said, "and you own me!"

"No," I said.

"I am branded," she said.

"It is nothing," I said.

"Be a girl, and wear a brand," she said, "and you will see if it is nothing!"

"It is not your fault that you are branded," I said.

"But it is the fault of men," she said, "and I am nonetheless branded!"

I went to pull the collar from her throat and, again, her small hands tightened on it.

"You own me," she said. "What are you going to do with me?"

"Free you," I said. "I will give you what your heart most desires, your total liberation and freedom!"

She looked at me, aghast.

I pulled away the collar and flung it, the key in the lock, to the side.

"You do not want me," she whispered.

"Have no fear," I said. "I will not take advantage of you, nor abuse you, nor exploit you. You will be accorded all dignity and respect. In all things you will be my full and lovely equal." Then I realized I had made an error. "Excuse me," I said, "I did not mean to demean you.

I did not mean to say 'lovely'. You will be in all things, simply, and straightforwardly, my equal."

"How can a slave be the equal of her master?" she asked.

"You are free," I told her.

"I might have been bought by a Gorean man," she said, "one who might have treasured me, and cherished me, and made me serve him well, and used me richly."

"I have freed you," I said. "Are you not happy?" I asked, puzzled.

"I am naked," she said.

"Forgive me," I cried. Quickly I hurried to one of the cage attendants. For a tarsk bit I purchased one of the discarded sheets torn from the slave beauties who were still being sold from the block.

I hurried back to the girl and stood before her, the sheet in my hand. For the briefest instant I felt sick. She was so beautiful. Should I not have marched her through the streets of Victoria naked, an exhibited slave, for my own joy, that of her master, and that men might rejoice in her beauty and call out to me their congratulations, commending me on the splendid fortune that was mine, that of having such a woman in my total power?

"Please," she said.

I stepped more closely to her and, standing before her, held the sheet behind her, preparing to draw it about her.

"Do not look at me, you lustful beast," she said. "Cover me, quickly!"

Swiftly I drew the sheet about her and she, from within it, clutched it even more closely about herself. I could see, as she had gathered the sheet, the outline of her small fists beneath it.

"Do not look at my calves and ankles," she said, "please."

"Forgive me," I said. "Let us hurry from this place."

"Yes," she said, "it is offensive. I smell here the stinking of slaves."

Quickly we left the sales barn of Lysander.

"Where do you live?" she asked.

"I have taken a small room, near the wharves," I said.

"I, too, will need a room," she said.

"I cannot afford much," I said.

"Then we shall manage to divide the room," she said, "somehow, with a screen, or partition, of some sort."

"Of course," I said.

"You must, too, go out and purchase me clothing," she said. "I cannot wear a sheet."

"What about a slave tunic?" I asked.

"Do not jest, Jason," she said.

"It is in this direction," I said, indicating a street leading toward the river front.

"I have no money," she said. "And I have no Home Stone. What is that?" she asked.

We heard the sound of a bell, and then, a moment later, that of coins in a metal box. A girl in a brown rag, slave, emerged from the shadows. About her neck, chained, there was a bronze bell, hollow, flattish, with sloping sides, with a flat top and ring, and a slotted, metal coin box, locked. Swiftly she knelt before me. She bit at my tunic, and licked at the side of my leg. She lifted her head. "Have me for a tarsk bit, Master," she begged. Her hands were braceleted behind her back.

"No," I told her.

"Get away, you filthy thing," said Miss Henderson.

"If I do not return with the equivalent of a copper tarsk," said the girl kneeling before me, "I will be whipped."

"Get away!" said Miss Henderson.

"Your slave requires discipline," said the girl kneeling before me.

"She is not my slave," I said.

"Whose slave is she?" asked the girl. "I know various masters."

"She is not a slave," I said.

"She is obviously a slave," said the girl, "thus someone's slave. Who has her?"

"No one *has* her," I said. "She is free."

The thought passed my mind that it might be nice to *have* Miss Henderson, not in some simple sense, merely, say, that of a transitory physical conjunction, but in a full proprietary sense, that of an uncompromised and absolute ownership, thus one in which not only all physicalities, and possessings, of whatever nature, and however frequent or lengthy, might be enjoined upon her at one's least whim, that would go without saying, but one in which would be involved as well many other things, for example, strippings, kneelings, bellyings, lickings and kissings, posings and writhings, crawlings and dancings, and such, at as little as the snapping of one's fingers, and surely, too, having at one's disposal, deliciously, all her conceivable labors and services. Does one truly own a slave until she is at your feet diligently polishing your leather, looking up occasionally, hoping you will be satisfied; she does not wish to be beaten; until she is in your kitchen, preparing your food; until she is serving it, humbly, perhaps nude, as you might wish her then, and then kneeling to one side, waiting to see if she will be fed; until she, hair bound in a scarf, perhaps nude otherwise, attends to your quarters, perhaps while you watch, she sedulously tidying up for you, dusting and cleaning, mopping and scrubbing; and be sure she will clean, too, beneath the sparse furniture; that is important, too; and should she not air out the furs of love, adjust the wick on the rape lamp, and buff and kiss the slave ring at the foot of your couch, to which at night she is chained; until she, at the public troughs, with other girls, laughing and chatting, launders for you, until she, the coin bag tied to her collar, shrewdly markets for you, such things. That is to truly have a woman, to have her wholly yours, to have her totally at your beck and call. That is, of course, as one has a slave. Indeed, a good slave, like many domestic animals, should anticipate the interests and desires of the master.

The thought of Miss Henderson as a domestic animal, and mine, was not unpleasant.

"She should be a slave," said the girl.

Miss Henderson cried out in anger.

"She is free," I averred.

"It seems she would make a good slave," said the girl.

"She is free," I repeated.

"She needs the lash," said the girl.

Miss Henderson drew back, not looking at me. She drew the sheet more closely about her ill-concealed nakedness.

I wondered if, indeed, the rather haughty, troublesome Miss Henderson might not profit from a bout with the lash. I thought it might improve her, considerably.

The lash is useful in removing objectionable faults, both major and minor, in a woman.

Once a woman has felt the whip, one often requires no more than a casual glance in its direction.

Her behavior is likely to be ameliorated instantly.

But I suppose it is not surprising that a woman who realizes that she will be punished if she is not fully pleasing, and in all particulars, should then be seriously concerned to be pleasing, fully pleasing—*and in all particulars.*

As a little Gorean saying has it—whip in hand, girl at feet.

I drew out a copper tarsk, and prepared to place it in the girl's coin box.

Swiftly the girl, before I could put the coin in the box, lay on her back, on the stones of the street, before me. "You must use me first," she said, "and then put the coin in only if I please you."

"No!" said Miss Henderson.

"No?" I asked.

"She is a terrible person!" said Miss Henderson.

"She is a lovely slave," I said.

"That is it," she said. "She is a slave, a slave!"

"But a lovely slave," I said.

"She is nothing, a slave!" scolded Miss Henderson.

"She is not nothing," I said. "She is a lovely slave, and, indeed, pretty enough to be put out as a coin girl."

"A coin girl?"

"That is the expression," I said.

"How despicable!" said Miss Henderson. "How shameful! How I hold such a one in contempt! What a pathetic creature, with a bell on her neck, and a coin box! It is clear that coin girls, as you call them, are amongst the most degraded, the lowest and most worthless of slaves!"

"Perhaps you, lofty lady," said the coin girl, "are insufficiently desirable to be put out as a coin girl."

"I am beautiful!" said Miss Henderson.

I was pleased that she had said this. It was true, of course, but I would scarcely have expected Miss Henderson to have said so. Gor, it seems, had improved her sense of self-awareness or, at least, had freed her to be somewhat less circumspect about such matters.

Too, she had been a display slave, and that spoke well for her appeal to the eye, and ear, and hand.

All women are vain.

This is one of the endearing features of the sex. Certainly it is one which appeals greatly to me. But this vanity has a peculiar charm in the case of the slave girl. It is, you see, not merely free women who have this delicious fault, if fault it be, but, too, radically, the half-naked, ragged, collared slave, competing for a cosmetic or a comb. It is interesting how a girl in a simple rag with steel on her neck will clean and brush herself, and pose and display herself, with the same zest and pleasure with which a free woman arranges ornate robes and a multitude of colorful veils. To be sure, the slave knows she is desirable. She has been put in a collar.

"Perhaps then, one day, you, too, will wear a bell and coin box," said the girl.

"Never!" snapped Miss Henderson, in rage.

To be sure, I thought, if she were a slave, and put in such devices, and sent forth, she had best return with a jingling coin box. She and her desirability would be all that would stand between her and a displeased master, and his whip.

I looked down at the kneeling slave. She was indeed lovely.

It was of interest to me that she did not show Miss Henderson the respect that a female slave commonly accords a free woman. In general, the Gorean female slave lives in mortal fear of the Gorean free woman and usually endeavors, as much as possible, to avoid them. Obviously the slave did not see Miss Henderson in any way as a free woman. To be sure, the Gorean free woman is not accustomed to frequent the streets barefoot and unveiled, and clad in no more than a tiny sheet. Clearly the slave saw Miss Henderson as no more than another slave, rather as herself, except, perhaps, for being a bit more or less beautiful. I was not interested in taking action in the matter. If Miss Henderson had been suitably robed and veiled I might have felt more as though I should require the slave to exhibit a proper deference in her presence. But then, had she been suitably robed and veiled, one supposes the whole matter would not have arisen, and the slave would have been on her knees, not daring to speak, eyes cast down, if not on her belly, trembling, utterly silent, hoping not to be beaten, before Miss Henderson.

"Do not give away our money," said Miss Henderson.

"It is my money," I said.

"Do not squander our meager resources," she said.

"They are my resources, not yours," I pointed out. "I will do what I please with them."

"Of course, Jason," she said, irritatedly.

"I will not use you," I told the girl, "but I will give you the coin." I made as though to place the coin in the box, which now, as she lay, back on her elbows, hung beside her left breast, swelling against the thin slave cloth.

Quickly she scrambled back, and rose to her feet. "I am worth the tarsk bit," she said. "And my master is a proud man. He does not send us into the streets to beg."

"But you may be whipped," I said.

"I will get the money elsewhere," she said. "And if I were you I would whip the slave beside you."

"Get out of here!" cried Miss Henderson.

The girl then fled with a sound of her bell and the jangling of the coins in the box.

"Disgusting! Disgusting!" said Miss Henderson. "Terrible! Disgusting!"

"Some men," I said, "buy such girls and send them out into the streets. They keep them in kennels and send them out in the afternoon. It is how they earn their living."

"Terrible! Disgusting!" said Miss Henderson.

"You were saying?" I asked.

"I was saying," she said, "that I have no money, and that I have no Home Stone. Too, there is no practical trade of which I am the Mistress."

"There is one trade, which is available to all women," I said.

"Do not jest, Jason," she said. "It is not amusing."

"That of cook," I said.

"Very funny," she said.

"How do you expect to earn your keep?" I asked.

"I do not expect to earn my keep," she said. "I expect you to earn my keep."

"And what do you expect to do in return?" I asked.

"Nothing, absolutely nothing," she said. "I did not ask to be purchased."

"I see that you are scarcely likely to prove to be an economic asset," I said.

"You could always, I suppose, put a bell and coin box about my neck and send me into the streets," she said.

"It is a thought," I admitted.

She made an angry noise, and we continued on, toward the river front.

"Have you a job?" she asked.

"No," I said.

"You must get one," she said.

"I expect that would be advisable," I said. I supposed I might work as an oarsman or a dock worker. I was strong. It no longer seemed a good way to make money by challenging fellows in the taverns. One might respond with a knife or sword. Tonight my life had been saved by a dissolute fellow, a man called Callimachus, perhaps from Port Cos, farther west on the river, a derelict. Had it not been for him I would doubtless have been slain by the pirate, Kliomenes.

"We will need the money," she said.

I said nothing.

"You may call me 'Beverly'," she said.

"What about 'Veminia'?" I asked. The veminium is a small, lovely Gorean flower, softly petaled and blue.

"That is a slave name," she said. "That is what I was called in the house of Oneander of Ar."

"Most Goreans," I said, "would regard 'Beverly' as a slave name."

"What of 'Jason'?" she asked, angrily.

"I am sorry to disappoint you," I said, "but that is a not uncommon name on Gor, particularly, as I understand it, west on the river, and on the islands of Cos and Tyros."

"Oh," she said.

"Too," I said, "it is commonly regarded as the name of a free man."

"Oh," she said.

"Unlike 'Beverly'," I said.

"I see," she said, acidly.

"Beverly," I added.

"The name 'Beverly' may be worn as a free name, as well as a slave name," she said. "I shall wear it as a free name."

"Very well," I said.

"We shall have to make careful arrangements to govern our sharing common lodgings," she said.

"Of course," I said.

"I shall bathe first," she said.

"There is a small copper tub," I said.

"And each of us shall do his own share of the cooking, the cleaning, and the housework," she said. "Each will have full responsibility for his own portions of these labors."

"I am to work the day," I said, "and then, do half the work of the room or lodgings?"

"Do not expect me to perform menial labors for you," she said. "I am a free woman. I shall take care of my things. And you shall take care of yours."

"I see," I said.

"I trust your room is not in this dismal structure," she said, looking up at a swinging lantern hanging over an inn's threshold.

"Yes," I said.

"We shall have to do better than this," she said. I looked down at her. I considered tearing the sheet from her. I wondered what she would look like with a bell and coin box on her neck. Then I reminded myself that she was a free woman, and that she was from the planet Earth, my old planet. She was not a Gorean girl, but something nobler and finer, an Earth woman.

"You did not even pay a full silver tarsk for me," she said, looking up at me, angrily. "There were girls who were sold for as much as two or three silver tarsks."

"They were very beautiful women," I said, "and some were of high caste, two were exquisitely trained pleasure slaves."

"Surely I was worth more than any of them," she said, petulantly.

"Are you angry?" I asked.

"Yes," she said. "I am worth much more than ninety-eight copper tarsks."

"I am not sure you are worth ninety-eight copper tarsks," I said. She cried out with anger.

"If you had been worth a silver tarsk in a Gorean market," I told her, "you would have brought a silver tarsk in a Gorean market."

"You are hateful!" she said.

"You are not a silver-tarsk girl," I told her.

"Hateful!" she said.

"I do not think you are worth two copper tarsks," I said.

"Beast!" she said. "Beast!"

"Remember," I told her, "you have no Home Stone."

"What are you telling me," she asked, "that I keep a civil tongue in my head?"

"It would not hurt," I told her.

"Oh, yes!" she said. "I know! I have no Home Stone! You might just tear the sheet from me. You might just throw me down in the threshold, on the stones, under the lantern, and rape me, and re-enslave me!"

"I could!" I said, angrily.

"You would not dare," she said.

"Do not tempt me," I said, in fury.

"You are too weak to treat me as a woman, and a slave!" she said.

I seized her by the upper arms, under the sheet, and shook her, violently. "Oh," she cried, "please, Master, be gentle!" Then she looked at me, frightened.

"The word 'Master' came easily from your lips," I said.

Quickly she pulled the sheet back about her. She looked down.

"Forgive me," I said. "I'm sorry. I behaved like a cad."

"Am I in danger, Jason?" she asked.

"No," I said, "of course not."

She looked up. "I am a woman of Earth," she said, "not a Gorean girl."

"I am well aware of that," I said. "I am really very sorry."

"I know that you will not treat me with power, and strength," she said.

"Forgive me," I said. "I had become angry."

"You are a man of Earth," she said, "and are decent and kind. You are tender and gentle. You are accommodating and wish to be pleasing. Remember that women have nothing to fear from men such as you. Keep that clearly in mind."

"Forgive me," I said. "I am very sorry."

"In the future," she said, "keep your hands off me."

"I'm sorry," I said.

"I am a person," she said.

"Of course," I said. "I'm sorry."

"I am not a pleasure toy," she said.

"I'm sorry," I said. "I'm sorry." How grievously I had insulted Miss Henderson!

"Tonight," she said, "when I was being displayed before Gorean buyers, did you see me move in certain ways, and cry out in certain ways?"

"Yes," I admitted.

"Put such things from your mind," she said. "The auctioneer, the beast, caught me off guard. His action took me by surprise. He did not permit me to be myself. I am stronger than that, as you will learn. It was like another girl, a slave girl, who moved like that, and cried out like that. Have no fear. The delicious pleasures which may have been suggested by her movements or cries will not be yours."

"I see," I said.

"I am not a licking and kissing pleasure girl, one who can scarcely control herself and fears the whip."

"I see," I said.

"I shall endeavor to see that I am fully worthy of your respect, and of my own respect, as a free woman."

"I understand," I said.

"Let us go inside now," she said. "The room must be properly partitioned."

"Are you not grateful that I rescued you from bondage?" I asked.

"I am extremely grateful," she said. "You have no idea how wonderful it is to be free. It is just what every woman wants."

"You have not much expressed your gratitude," I said.

"And how do you, a man, suggest that I express it?" she asked, acidly.

I looked down, reddening.

"I am not a slave, Jason," she said. "I am a free woman."

"I understand," I said.

"Is that why you bought me," she asked, "that I, a weak, silly woman, overwhelmed with gratitude, would grant you my favors?"

I did not raise my head.

"Favors which you were too weak to obtain in any other way?" she asked.

"I'm sorry," I said.

"But do not think I am not grateful," she said. "I shall teach you how to be a true man, solicitous and tender, and that sort of thing."

"I see," I said.

"Do not touch me!" she said.

I drew back. "Permit me to kiss you," I said. She was so beautiful.

"No," she said. "I am not a pleasure object."

"I'm sorry," I said. Again I had insulted Miss Henderson. It seemed I could do nothing right with her.

"But I am grateful," she said. "You may give me a small kiss, a quick kiss."

I touched her cheek with my lips, kissing her.

"It is enough!" she said. My hands had tightened on her arms, under the sheet. "You are very strong, Jason," she said. I had lifted her to her toes and, holding her, pressed her back against the door to the inn. She looked at me, frightened. I saw her lovely cherry lips, the small, fine white teeth behind them. I considered administering to her the kiss of the master to the female slave. "No!" she said.

I held her, my own hands trembling, power in my body.

"I am a woman of Earth," she said. "You are a man of Earth!"

I held her.

"Do not rape me, Jason," she said.

"I'm sorry," I said. I put her down.

"Beg my forgiveness!" she said.

"I'm sorry," I said. "I'm sorry!"

"Never look at me again like that, with such lust and power," she said. "I am a woman of Earth!"

"Forgive me," I said.

"I see it will not be easy to teach you to be a true man," she said.

I shrugged, angrily.

"But I think you will learn, Jason," she said. "You are a man of Earth."

"Perhaps," I said.

"We must now go inside," she said. "The room must be properly partitioned."

"Please let me kiss you," I said.

"It has been a trying day for me," she said. "I am weary. Surely you must understand."

"Please," I said.

"After what happened a moment ago," she said, "I do not think I will permit you to kiss me again for a very long time, if ever."

"Perhaps you will permit me to kiss you from time to time," I suggested, "just to keep me performing properly."

"Perhaps," she said, angrily. "We shall see."

"Please, Beverly," I said.

"No," she said.

"Please," I said.

"I am weary," she said. "And I have a headache."

"Let us remain here but a moment longer," I said.

"It is growing chilly here," she said. "And I do not feel well."

"Please," I said.

"Do not be insensitive, Jason," she said. "I have told you that I have a headache."

"I did not mean to be insensitive," I said. "Forgive me." I wondered what she would look like naked, tied at a slave ring, being lashed.

"We must go in now," she said. "In the morning you must rise early. You must buy me clothing and go to the market. You must then find work."

"Yes, Beverly," I said.

I held the door open for her and she preceded me inside. The inn-keeper looked up from behind his counter, puzzled that a woman such as she was not heeling me.

I indicated the stairs, and she preceded me up the stairs.

"We shall certainly have to find better lodgings than these, and soon," she said.

"Yes, Beverly," I said.

The stairs were dark, save for small, trembling yellow pools of light, cast from flickering tharlarion-oil lamps.

I considered her ankle as she ascended the stairs before me. It had not looked bad in the shackle at the market. Too, I recalled the moment in the taxi cab, long ago, before I had lost consciousness. She had been lying on the back seat of the cab, her legs drawn up. I had seen her ankle then, too. I recalled thinking then, too, that it would have looked well in slave steel.

Eleven

"I will use the one in that alcove," I said to Tasdron, flinging down a tarsk bit on the stained counter.

"She is yours," said Tasdron, wiping a paga goblet with a large, soft cloth.

I strode across the floor of the tavern of Tasdron and entered the alcove. The blond girl knelt there, nude, against the back wall of smooth, rounded red tiles.

I turned about and buckled shut the heavy curtains of the alcove, and then again faced her.

Her wrists, by several narrow loops of red leather, on each wrist, were tied to iron rings on each side of her body, a little below the level of her shoulders. The former customer had left her tied in this fashion, not bothering to release her. I was just as well pleased. I wished to interrogate her. She knelt on red furs. The light was from a tiny thar-larion-oil lamp in the alcove. Tasdron's collar was on her throat.

"Master?" she asked, pressing back against the rounded, red tiles.

"Do you recall me?" I asked. "Do you recall I was the fellow who challenged in this tavern, and who was threatened by Kliomenes, the pirate, the fellow who was saved, happily, by one called Callimachus."

"Yes, Master," she said. "I was here. I remember. He is Callimachus, of Port Cos."

"He was once of the warriors?" I asked.

"It is thought so," she said. "So it is said among the girls."

"Have you seen me before?" I asked.

"It does not seem possible, Master," she said. "I am only a slave."

"It seemed to me, before," I said, "that you reacted to me as though you might once have seen me, as though I might be somehow familiar to you."

"It is true," she said. "It seemed to me that, somehow, I had seen you before. Yet I do not see how, actually, that could be. I am only a miserable slave."

"Were you always a slave?" I asked.

"No, Master," she said. "I was once free."

"On Gor?" I asked.

"No, Master," she said. She smiled. "I am afraid that women such as I are slaves on Gor."

"Where were you free?" I asked.

"On a far world," she said.

"Where slaves are not enslaved?" I asked.

"Yes, Master," she smiled.

"What is your name?" I asked.

"Peggy," she said, "if it pleases Master."

"That is an Earth-girl name," I said. "Are you from the planet Earth?"

"Yes, Master," she said, "but please do not whip me. It is not my fault that Earth is my planet of origin. I will try to be pleasing to you."

"Earth girls make excellent slaves," I said.

"Thank you, Master," she said.

"Do you speak the Earth language, English?" I asked.

"Yes, Master," she said.

"I, too, speak English," I said. "Let us converse in that tongue."

"Yes, Master," she said, in English.

"What was your Earth name?" I asked.

"Peggy," she said. "Peggy Baxter."

"Where did you work?" I asked.

"In a city called New York," she said, "as a hat-check girl, at a restaurant."

"Yes!" I said. "That is it!"

"Master?" she asked, frightened.

"I had thought I had seen you," I said. "It was there."

"There?" she asked.

"You wore black, low-cut shoes, with high heels, without strap or ties," I said.

"Pumps," she said.

"You wore black-net stockings or panty hose," I said. "You wore a black miniskirt, and a long-sleeved, smooth, white silk blouse, open at the throat. You had a black ribbon for your hair."

"Panty hose," she said. "But they were taken from me."

I nodded. Gorean men seldom permit a slave shielding for her warm intimacies.

"Apparently I was not the only one who saw you there," I said. "Some other, or others," I said, "must have seen you as well, and adjudged you worthy to be brought to Gor as a slave girl."

"Yes, Master," she said.

"I commend their judgment, and taste," I said.

"Thank you, Master," she said.

"How is it that you were originally captured on Earth?" I asked.

"After work, late," she said, "I left the restaurant. A cab was nearby. I thought myself fortunate. I entered the cab. It was a specially designed capture vehicle. I found myself helplessly sealed within it. Gas entered my mobile prison. I lost consciousness. I did not recover consciousness until I found myself chained in a girl-dungeon on Gor. I awakened to the whip and the hands of a brute upon me. I swiftly learned I was a slave."

"I think that I myself, and a friend," I said, "were captured by the same cab, the same devices." I recalled that the cab driver, in the garage, had said that he had another pickup to make that night. His next pickup, doubtless, had been the lovely, long-legged Miss Baxter.

"Did you get off work at two A.M.?" I asked.

"Yes," she said. "How did you know?"

"I heard the pickup of someone referred to who got off work at two A.M.," I said.

"Doubtless it was I," she said, shuddering.

"I think so," I said.

"Master speaks English fluently," she said, apprehensively. Her hands twisted in the straps.

"Were you brought to the House of Andronicus, in Vonda?" I asked.

"Yes," she said, "where I was given rudimentary slave training and learned a smattering of Gorean. I was sold in Vonda to a taverner in Tancred's Landing. Tasdron saw me there and fancied me. He bought me and brought me here, where I now wear his collar." She looked at me. "Is Master a slaver?" she asked.

"No," I said.

"How is it that Master speaks English?" she asked.

"It is my native tongue," I said. "I was brought to Gor, rather accidentally, as a slave. I became free."

"Master is cruel to tease a miserable slave," said the girl.

"How am I teasing you?" I asked, puzzled.

She laughed. "Do not expect me to believe that Master is a man of Earth," she said. "I am not a fool."

"I am from the planet Earth," I said.

"You are cruel to a miserable slave," she said.

"Why do you not believe I am from Earth?" I asked, puzzled.

"You are not pathetic and weak," she said. "And your eyes, they look at me, and see me as a female slave."

I smiled. Indeed, she was beautiful.

"The men of Gor," she said, "are strong. They are not weak and divided against themselves. They are not tortured. They are integrated and coherent, and proud. They see themselves in the order of nature. They see females as females, as slaves, and themselves as men, as masters. If we do not please them they punish us, or slay us. We quickly learn our place in the order of things. Only where there are true men can there be true women."

"But you are a naked and collared slave," I said, "bound in a paga tavern."

"I am a woman," she smiled, "something that I never was, truly, on Earth."

"I see," I said.

"We are small, and weak, and soft and beautiful," she said, "and we have dispositions to yield, and to love and serve, selflessly. We long for masters. We cannot be fulfilled until we find them." She smiled. "And then, on Gor," she said, "we look up and, startled, find them standing over us. The whip is in their hand. They will take no nonsense from us. Is it any wonder we love them so?"

"I was once from Earth," I said.

"I find that hard to believe," she said.

I shrugged.

"Look at me," she said.

I grinned, and she reddened.

"What do you see," she asked, "an abused woman to be hastily freed, or a slave tethered for a man's pleasure?"

"A slave," I said, "tethered for a man's pleasure."

"You see," she smiled, "you are Gorean."

"And as what do you see yourself," I asked, "as an abused woman, hoping to be hastily freed, or as a slave, tied to rings, who hopes her master will see fit to linger over her?"

"A slave," she smiled, "one fastened helplessly, tied to rings, who hopes that she will be found sufficiently pleasing that a master will see fit to linger over her, driving her to a madness of embonded joy."

"Do you wish to be freed?" I asked.

"A woman such as I, on Gor," she laughed, "has no hope of freedom."

I smiled. I did not doubt that. She had even been named 'Peggy'. That name, an Earth-girl name, made it perfectly clear that her master regarded her categorically, and totally, as a slave. It had been her name on Earth. Now, of course, she wore it as a slave name, by the decision of her master. Slaves in their own right have no names. They are animals.

"But do you wish to be freed?" I asked.

"No, Master," she said.

"But you are a woman of Earth," I said.

"So, Master?" she asked, puzzled.

"Surely, then, you wish to be free?" I asked.

"Why?" she asked.

"You are a woman of Earth," I said.

"Do you think that in the bellies of the females of Earth there does not lurk a true woman?" she asked.

"I do not know," I said.

"We are not men, really," she said.

"You would be well advised not to say things like that on Earth," I said.

"I know," she said. "On Earth, I did not speak the depths of my feelings. I did not dare. I did not wish to be criticized by men, or by unhappy, frustrated women."

I nodded. The cultural penalties inflicted on those who speak the truth can be severe.

"I kept silent," she said, "and longed for a master."

"Is not freedom precious?" I asked.

"I have been free," she said. "I know what it is like."

"Is it not precious?" I asked.

"Yes," she said, "it is precious, very precious. And sometimes I miss it very much. Sometimes I wish I were again free. Sometimes, when I am chained at night, or whipped, or commanded, and must do things I do not wish to do, I wish I were again free. And sometimes I am terribly afraid when I think of the power my masters have over me."

"I see," I said.

"But then, too," she said, "I find myself exquisitely thrilled, and responsive to, the very power, the force and discipline, to which I am subject. To know that I am a slave and must obey fulfills something very deep in me."

"I see," I said.

"Sometimes, at night," she said, "I find myself, almost without thinking about it, licking the bars of my cage, kissing the steel on my wrists."

"Do you fear your masters?" I asked.

"Of course," she said, "they hold over me the power of life and death."

"But yet," I asked, "you find them exciting?"

"I find them terribly exciting," she said, "both emotionally and physically. I can scarcely be near them without catching my breath, without feeling slightly afraid and trembling."

"They own you," I said.

"Yes," she said.

"When they look upon you, do you feel sexual heat?" I asked.

"Often," she said.

"And if they should snap their fingers and point to the floor?" I asked.

"Then I would swiftly lie before them, and as a slave," she said.

"You are eager to please them?" I asked.

"Yes," she said. "I am eager to please them, fully and totally."

"Because they are your masters?" I asked.

"Yes," she said, "and I am their slave."

She smiled at me. "Do these responses," she asked, "startle you, coming as they do from a woman once of Earth?"

"There seems little in you now of Earth," I said.

"True," she smiled. She pulled at the thongs. "I am now only a Gorean slave girl," she said.

I said nothing.

"The women of Earth are also women," she said. "Do not despise them for it. Accept them for what they are. There is nothing wrong with being a woman. It is the complementary sex to that of the male. It is not our fault if, when placed in a proper context, a biological context, in a biologically congenial civilization, we behave as we desire, and must. Is your anger or dismay actually an envy of the Gorean brutes who throw us to their feet and put collars on our necks? Consider that. It may be true. Would you not like some delicious Earth woman as your total slave? If so, how are you so different from the brutes of Gor, who do with us as they wish? It is not our fault if, for whatever reasons, the men of Earth seem determined to turn us into men, and deny to us our precious and ancient natures. It is hard to be a woman on Earth." She then pulled again at the thongs. "But it is not hard, Master, on Gor," she smiled. "Gorean men see to it."

"You are a slave," I said. "Are you happy?"

"Yes," she said, "radiantly happy."

"Why?" I asked.

"I am now in the power of uncompromising and dominant males. I must serve them and please them, and as a woman, fully. I am owned by them. They bring the fullness of my womanhood out of me, and are content with nothing less. On Gor, for the first time in my life, I am a total woman. I am completely fulfilled. I am incredibly happy."

"You are fond of your slavery?" I asked.

"I love my slavery, Master," she said.

"Would you like to go back to Earth?" I asked.

"No, Master," she said.

I regarded her.

"See my brand," she said.

I did so. It was the common Kajira mark. It was the same brand worn by Miss Henderson. Both girls were left-thigh branded.

"My collar," she said.

I regarded it. It was simple, narrow, close-fitting, of gleaming steel.

"The thongs on my wrists," she said.

I looked at her bound wrists.

"And my naked body," she said, "tied for a master's pleasure."

"Yes," I said.

"Am I not an exquisite slave girl?" she asked.

"Yes," I said.

"And yet," she said, "I am from the planet Earth. Can you doubt, truly, then, that the women of Earth can be slaves?"

"No," I said. "I do not doubt it."

"Perhaps you do doubt it," she said.

"No," I said. "No."

"Untie me," she said.

"Why?" I asked.

"I will prove to you that I am a slave," she said.

I looked at her, not speaking.

"Have you held slaves in your arms?" she asked.

"Yes," I said, "many times."

"See, then," she said, "if I am different."

I regarded her.

"Touch me," she begged.

I smiled, ignoring her plea.

She leaned back, her wrists, bound, at the rings. "You are clearly Gorean," she said. "I see that I must wait upon your will."

I sat, cross-legged, for some time, watching her. Then her eyes looked pleadingly at me. I could smell the heat of her.

"Do you beg to be had, and as a slave?" I asked.

"Yes, Master," she whispered. "I beg to be had, and as a slave."

I then slowly untied her.

* * * *

"So," she asked later, smiling, lying on her stomach beside me, "am I so different?"

"No," I said.

"You put me well to the test," she laughed.

I touched the collar, lightly, at her throat.

"Do you doubt that I am a slave?" she asked.

"No," I said.

"You see," she said, "that I am a superb slave."

"It is true," I said.

"Have I not been appropriately and fittingly embonded?" she asked.

"You have been," I said.

"Do I not belong in a slave collar?" she asked.

"There is no doubt about it," I said. "You do."

"Tasdron had me for a silver tarsk," she said.

"A cheap price," I said. "You are worth more."

"I am better now," she said, "than when Tasdron bought me. I have learned much."

"I would say you are worth now at least two silver tarsks."

"Thank you, Master," she said, warmly, kissing me.

"It is hard to believe that you are from Earth," I said.

She laughed. "But I am, Master," she said. "You saw me there yourself, in the restaurant."

"Yes," I said.

"When you saw me there," she asked, "did you want to have me?"

"Yes," I said.

"And now," she laughed, "you have done so, and may again, and again, as it should please you."

"Yes," I said.

"Master," she said.

"Yes," I said.

"When I saw you, too, at the restaurant," she said, "I wondered what it would be like to lie in your arms."

"A bold admission," I said.

"For an Earth girl, who thinks she is free, perhaps," she laughed, "but not for a slave. Slaves may speak such truths."

"That is true," I said.

"But never for a moment did I dream," she said, "that I would lie naked in your arms as an obedient, collared slave on an alien world."

I then took her by the arm and threw her again beneath me. She looked up, happily. "Is Master going to have me again?" she asked.

"Yes," I said.

"Peggy is pleased to have been found worthy of the attentions of Master," she said. "Oh," she said, "Master is strong." Then she said, "You are Gorean. I know you are Gorean!" Then she said, "I yield me to my Gorean Master!"

It is pleasant to have a woman yield to you as a slave. I know of nothing which so exalts the power and manhood of the human male. Too there is apparently nothing which so deeply releases the emotions and yielding sensuality of the human female. In these matters something is touched which obviously bears deeply on the fundamental nature of the sexes. Here, in human relations, is yet another exemplification of one of the major and incessantly recurrent themes of nature, that of dominance and submission. The realities of nature must be denied, I suspect, only at one's own peril. And certainly human beings cannot be fulfilled, nor can they know themselves, until they have become themselves. The nature of human beings precedes the fleeting parades of mottoes and slogans. It lies latent and obdurate, in ambush, if you like, in the genetic codes.

"Permit me to kiss you," she said.

"You may do so," I told her.

Is there a human animal beneath the conditioned ideologies? It seems not improbable. We may torture and mutilate the human animal; we may deny that it exists; but it lies within us, in the chemistry of every living cell in our bodies. In denying it we, truly, deny only ourselves. In hating it, we hate our own hearts, and our own blood. We are not so terrible, really. It is only that we are men and women, and not something else. Perhaps it is wrong to be men and women. Perhaps we should be something else. Perhaps we should consider ourselves images and inventions. Perhaps we should participate in the mythologies convenient to the manipulative purposes of self-serving, self-proclaimed elites. Doubtless the question is difficult. It is always hard to know the truth and pretend not to believe it. Perhaps we should not be men and women. Perhaps we should not be true to ourselves. But even if we should deny ourselves, and starve, and torture and frustrate ourselves, we would still, in the end, be ourselves. We would remain men and women, only then, perhaps, mutilated and sickened men and women, useful tools in the schemes of others, of cunning and pathological frustrates, themselves often as confused and miserable as the uncritical creatures they would systematically delude.

We are what we are, and will remain so, regardless of what we may be taught to believe. Fearing ourselves does not make us not ourselves. Can the human reality, in the fullness of its truth, be truly so fearful a thing. I do not think so. Human nature may be despised; it may be thwarted; it may be distorted and denied. This may be accomplished by conditioning programs, obedient to their own antecedents and developing in accord with their own histories and social dynamics. It is clearly possible to educate the young to distrust and fear themselves, and to injure and torture themselves. And, in turn, as a function of their own conditioning programs, they may dutifully bequeath their own tortures to their own young in turn. Yet how much pain must be endured, how much crime and madness, how much unhappiness and misery, before human rationality, that pathetic reed, that frail staff, that small weapon, that fragile tool, must revolt and cry, "No!" How obvious must it be before human beings are willing to realize that a grotesque and biologically inimical inversion of values has taken place? What would be accepted as evidence, if not disease, madness, misery, irrationality, frustration, criminality and sickness, that a tragic disparateness now exists between the needs of human beings and the imperatives of society. Must it be human beings who must be wrong? Perhaps it is, rather, those sociological imperatives which have, gradually, over the centuries, diverged from their original instrumentalities to follow their own disconnected and remote trajectories.

In ancient Attica it is said there was a giant, Procrustes. He would seize upon travelers and tie them upon an iron bed. If the traveler was too short for the bed, he would disjoint and break their bodies until they fitted it; if they were too long for the bed, he would cut their feet from them, until they, again, fitted the bed. Perhaps the bed of Procrustes is the truth and men must be broken or cut to pieces that they may fit it. On the other hand, clearly there is an alternative, although Procrustes seemed not to have heard of it. The bed could be made to fit the guest. Is the bed to conform to the guest, or is the guest to conform to the bed. From my own point of view, I would prefer a bed which considered the nature of human beings. I would make the human being the measure by which I judged the value of beds. I see little of profit in making the bed the measure of the human being, and requiring that we remake, if by torture and mutilation, the human being until it fits the bed. Besides, we cannot remake the human being to fit the bed, truly. We do not make new human beings or better human beings by this method. All we make by that method is broken or mutilated human beings.

"Have me again, Master," she begged.

"Very well," I said.

And as she moaned and gasped in my arms, and cried out, and I held her so closely she could not escape, I pondered the nature of human beings. And then I, too, cried out and with force owned her as a woman. In those obliterating moments I knew who I was, and who she was. "Be had, Slave," I told her. "You give me pleasure." "Yes, Master," she wept.

Later we lay quietly together, side by side.

Perhaps it is wrong to be men and women. But, on the other hand, perhaps it is not wrong to be men and women. It is what we are. Perhaps it is not wrong to be what we are. That is a genuine possibility. Perhaps it is not wrong to be what we are. If that is so, then it may quite possibly be right, or at least morally permissible, to be what we are. And if that is true, we may be entitled to our own natures, and the happinesses attendant upon the fulfillment of those natures. How then I envied the Gorean brutes, to whom such questions could scarcely arise. The Goreans, for example, have not been conditioned to exalt thirst, or to wonder if it is morally permissible to drink water, and, if so, under what conditions and subject to what restrictions. In dehydration they find nothing morally commendable. Indeed, naive folk, it does not even occur to them to debate such questions. They are, however, in virtue of this attitude, at the least, spared certain eccentric neuroses.

"On Gor," whispered the girl next to me, "I have learned that men and women are not identical."

"Yes," I said. I smiled to myself. I knew at least one culture in which this obvious, biological truism would count as political heresy, to be punished by ostracism, slander and, when possible, by economic penalties. What a tragic world and culture that was. How I pitied those who, in order not to jeopardize their careers in an antibiological environment, were forced to subscribe publicly to such doctrines. How rare is courage.

"And men," she said, "or Gorean men, or men of a Gorean type, are the masters."

"Yes," I said.

"And women such as I are their slaves," she said.

"Yes," I said. "Lick and kiss me."

"Lick and kiss you?" she said.

"Yes," I said.

"You command me like a Gorean slave girl," she said.

"That is what you are," I told her.

"Yes, Master," she said.

"You do it well," I told her.

She trembled. "Tasdron taught me," she said.

I smiled. I could well imagine Tasdron teaching her and she, knowing him her legal master, desperately striving to learn. If she did not do well she would know that she might be whipped to within an inch of her life or fed, alive, to hungry sleen. Under such circumstances, girls learn quickly and well.

"Ah," I said.

"Is Master pleased?" she asked.

"Yes," I said.

"Then Peggy, too, is pleased," she said.

"Complete your work," I said.

"Yes, Master," she said.

Later she lay beside me, her head at my thigh. My hand wandered to her hair, and then to her neck, enclosed in the narrow, steel collar. I fingered the lock at the back. She put her mouth to my thigh. I felt the warmth of her breath on my thigh. I felt her lips, the pressing of her teeth. Then she kissed me, and lay again, quietly, beside me.

"You treated me like a Gorean slave girl," she said.

"That is what you are," I told her.

"Yes, Master," she laughed. "It is true." She kissed me again. "I knew that I had convinced you," she said.

"How did you know?" I asked.

"In the past Ahn," she said, "you commanded me as casually and thoughtlessly as you might have any Gorean slut in a collar. Thus, in joy, I recognized that you had come to regard me, quite properly, as one of them."

"I see," I said.

"You see," she said, "I am the same. I am no different. I am only another girl in the collar, another woman who must obey you and serve your pleasure."

"Are you content?" I asked.

"Yes, Master," she said, "as would be any woman in the arms of a man such as you."

"Are you happy?" I asked.

"I am joyful, in the fulfillment of my nature," she said. "I am a slave. At last I have come to a world where there are men who wish for me to please them, and will see that I do so, and want me, and will have me, a world where there are masters."

"I must be going," I told her.

She looked up, frightened. "Do not go yet," she said. "Let me please you again."

"Appetitious slave," I said.

"On Gor," she said, "my appetites have been ignited. It has pleased men to ignite them."

"Are you dismayed?" I asked.

"No, Master," she said. "On this world I need not be ashamed of my appetites. On this world it is appropriate that I am hot, and belong to men."

"In your belly there is slave fire?" I asked.

"Yes, Master," she said. "In my belly there burns slave fire. I do not pretend that it does not."

"Shameless slave," I said.

"Yes, Master," she said.

"For whom, in this moment," I asked, "do your slave fires burn?"

"You, Master," she whispered.

I hesitated.

"Be merciful, Master," she begged. "Satisfy me."

I put her beneath me, in the capture position, and subjected her to swift slave rape.

She cried out with pleasure, yet used so harshly and brutally.

I struck her away from me and drew on my tunic. I must to work early at the wharves. At dawn I wished to be in the hiring yard. I looked down at her.

"Are all women such slaves as you?" I asked.

She smiled up at me, curled on the furs. "Yes, Master," she said.

I turned to go.

"Master," she said.

I turned again, to face her.

"You have made much of the fact that I am an Earth girl and a slave," she said.

"Yes," I said.

"There is another girl in whom you are interested, isn't there," she asked, "an Earth girl?"

"Perhaps," I said.

"Is she a slave?" she asked.

"No," I said. I had freed her.

"That is unfortunate," she said.

I shrugged.

"Does she have a Home Stone?" she asked.

"No," I said.

"Then enslave her!" she said.

"She is different from you," I said.

"Is she pretty?" she asked.

"Yes," I said.

"Then she is not so different," she said. "Have I seen her?"

"Long ago, once," I said, "at the restaurant. She was with me."

"She!" laughed the girl.

"Yes," I said.

"She was very pretty, Master," she said.

"Yes," I said.

"Is she on Gor?" she asked.

"Yes," I said.

"And free?" she asked.

"Yes," I said.

"I do not like that," said the girl. "Why should I be a slave, and she be free?"

"If she were here," I said, "you would have to kneel before her, and obey her."

The collared girl shuddered. Slave girls fear free women, greatly. There is little to wonder about in this. Free women, perhaps envying them their collars, are often extremely cruel to them.

"Do you think she would make a good slave?" I asked.

The girl smiled. "I think she would make an excellent slave, Master."

"I shall have to keep that in mind," I said.

Swiftly the girl knelt before me. "I assure you that she is a slave," she said. "I remember her. She is a slave. It is wrong for her not to be put in a collar. She is a slave, truly. Thus she should be made a slave, and be used, and treated and handled accordingly."

"You do not know her," I said.

"Perhaps it is you who do not know her," she said.

I smiled.

"I am an enslaved woman," said the girl. "Do you not think that one slave knows another?"

I laughed.

'Take her in hand," she said. "Take away her clothes. Put her in a collar. Throw her to your feet. Use her. You will see!"

I smote my thigh, laughing, in the Gorean fashion, so preposterous were the urgent words of the lovely, kneeling slave. How preposterous it was even to think of the lovely Miss Henderson as a slave.

The girl knelt back, on her heels. "I assure you, Master," she said, "she is as much, or more, a slave than I."

"Watch your tongue, Girl," I said, angrily, "lest it be slit."

She shuddered, and put down her head. "Forgive me, Master," she whispered.

"She is different from you," I said. "You are only a shameful and degraded slave."

"Do you wish her to be herself," she asked, "or to conform to some alien image which your culture has devised for her?"

I did not speak.

"She is not a man," she said. "She is a woman."

"They are the same," I said.

"That is stupid," she said.

"I know," I said. Then I said, angrily, "I know that she is not a man. I know that she is a woman."

"And if that is so," she said, "how do you consider her differently, how do you treat her differently?"

"I don't know!" I said.

"Perhaps Master is indeed from Earth," she said.

"I was once from Earth," I said. "I must respect her."

"Do not respect her," she said. "Fulfill her."

"How?" I asked.

"Make her your full and total slave," she said.

"I cannot," I said.

"Surely Master knows he is of the dominant sex," she said, "and that it is those of our sex who must submit."

"I know that it is true," I said, "but it is my duty not to believe it."

"Can it truly be one's duty not to believe the truth?" she asked.

"Yes," I said. "It is important to hold the correct opinions, whether they conform to reality or not."

"Perhaps such opinions subserve the purposes of ambitious and eccentric minorities," she said, "and that is doubtless an important point in their favor, but they do not seem to advance the cause of a civilization congenial to the nature of the human species as it is in actuality constituted."

"It is important to cater to the few," I said, "though it may, in time, spell doom and pain to the many."

"That is madness," she said.

"It is the principle on which my world is based," I said.

"That is no longer your world," she said.

"How do you know?" I asked.

"I could tell, a few Ehn ago," she said, "by how you held me."

I shrugged.

"Abandon disease and madness," she said. "Return to the order of nature."

"To look upon truth, openly," I said, "could be a fearful thing."

"Yes, Master," she whispered, and put her head down, the collar on her throat.

I reached to her hair and, twisting her head, she crying out, threw her to the furs. "But it might not be unpleasant to do so," I said, and then took her.

Almost instantly she had writhed in my arms, surrendering as a female slave to her master.

Then, trembling, held, she looked up at me. "You took me well, Master," she said.

I laughed, pleased with my conquest and triumph over her. I then knew what was the order of nature.

And she, too, knew it well.

"The other girl," she whispered, "is she unpleasant or difficult to get on with?"

"Perhaps," I said.

"Do you find her at times a bother, or troublesome?"

"Yes," I said.

"May I make a suggestion?" she asked.

"Yes," I said.

"Buy a whip," she said.

Twelve

I Become Irritated with My Kept Woman; I Kennel Her

"Do not forget you are a kept woman," I told her.

"Kept woman!" she cried.

"Precisely," I said.

"I do not care to think of myself as a kept woman," she said.

"Unfortunate," I said, "for it is exactly what you are."

"Where were you last night, and today?" she demanded.

"I owe you no accountings," I told her. "Is my supper ready?"

"I have already eaten," she said.

"Is my supper ready?" I asked.

"You may prepare it yourself," she said.

"The house is dirty," I said.

"Such work is not mine to do," she said. "If you wish such work done buy yourself a slave."

I had rented a small house a few blocks from the wharves. It had an upstairs and a downstairs. It was small, but stout, as are most Gorean dwellings. On the small earnings I made at the wharves it was somewhat expensive for me, but it was not altogether impractical. There were two bedrooms upstairs, and there was a hall, living room and kitchen downstairs. Miss Henderson's bedroom had a porch, which overlooked a small garden, surrounded by a high wall.

"Would you be pleased," I asked her, "to return to an inn?"

"The house is not unpleasant," she said, "but it has certain distressing features."

"And what are those?" I asked. I thought the house was rather nice, considering the modesty of the budget which must needs sustain its rental.

"My couch," she said, "in the master bedroom, has a heavy iron ring set in its base."

"That is a slave ring," I said. "Surely you know its purpose."

"Yes," she said, acidly.

Such rings are commonly used for chaining slave girls, generally by the neck, or left ankle, to the foot of their master's couch.

"And, too," she said, "I do not like the slave kennels in the hall."

I shrugged. "It is a Gorean house," I said.

"Did you bring the suls from the market?" she asked.

"No," I said. "I did not."

"How much money did you earn today?" she asked.

The amount of money earned varied from day to day, depending on the galleys in port and the need for men from the hiring yard.

"It is none of your business," I told her.

Her shoulders stiffened under the robes of concealment and her eyes flashed angrily over the silk of the house veil. I could see her lips and mouth, vaguely, beneath the veil.

"You brought nothing from the market," she said. "Accordingly there is very little for you here to eat."

"Were you not to shop?" I asked. "I gave you money."

"I did not feel like it," she said.

"I will eat out," I said.

"That is expensive," she said. "There is some bread and dried meat left."

"I will eat out," I said.

"The girls are pretty at the paga taverns, aren't they?" she asked, pointedly.

"They had better be," I said, "or they would bring in little money for their masters."

"I have heard such girls are 'hot,'" she said.

"It is one of the features for which they are purchased," I said.

"I see," she said, in cold fury. "And what if they are not 'in the mood'?" she asked.

"They know enough to be in the mood," I assured her.

"And what if the customer is not pleased?" she asked.

"The girl, then, would be well whipped," I said.

"Would you," she asked, "if not pleased, have such a girl whipped?"

"Yes," I said.

"And if I were such a girl," she said, "and you were not pleased, would you have me whipped?"

"Yes," I said.

"I see," she said, in cold fury. She then rose to her feet. She drew her robes haughtily about her. "I am weary," she said. "I shall now retire."

"Do not throw the bolt on your door," I said. She had been doing this, and it irritated me.

"It is my bedroom," she said.

"Of these lodgings," I said, "I am the rental master. It is your bedroom only upon my sufferance."

"Of course," she said, coldly. "I am your kept woman."

"You may leave when you wish," I said.

"Of course," she said. "I need only walk out upon the Gorean streets and see what will happen to me."

"You could sell yourself to an impotent master," I said.

Her eyes flashed angrily over the white silk of the house veil.

"I invite you to leave," I said.

"I do not want to leave," she said.

"You prefer to be kept," I said.

"Yes," she said, coldly, "I prefer to be kept."

She then turned about and left the kitchen, where we had been talking. She went through the living room and, going through the hall, passing the kennels, began to ascend the stairs.

"Do not bolt the door," I called after her.

"Why not?" she asked, angrily.

"There will be no iron between a keeper and his kept woman," I said, "unless it be by his will, such as a collar for her, or shackles or the bars of a cell."

"I will do as I please," she said.

"A keeper must always have access to his kept woman," I said.

"I will do as I please!" she said.

I listened to her door shut. I listened, carefully. Then I heard the iron bolt slid shut.

I sat, cross-legged, behind the small table in the kitchen. Then I rose up and went to the storage box and took out some bread and dried meat. I chewed on it for a time. Then, finishing it, I wiped my mouth. I then walked through the house to the stairs, and climbed them.

She screamed, suddenly, clutching clothing about her.

I stood in the threshold, the door awry, hanging off its hinges. The bolt with its brackets was splintered from the heavy wood.

She backed away, holding the clothing about her. "Don't hurt me," she said. "I would have opened the door!"

I strode to her, and stood before her.

"I would have opened the door," she said.

"A slave might be slain for such a lie," I said.

She did not meet my eyes. "You should knock," she said, "before entering a lady's bedroom."

I tore away the clothing she held before her, casting it aside. She wore then only a light Gorean slip, white, which came high on her thighs.

"I am not fully dressed!" she said.

I took her and threw her on her belly on the couch. "What are you going to do to me?" she asked.

"Strip you," I told her.

From the back I ripped apart the white slip until she lay upon it.

"Get out of my bedroom!" she sobbed.

"Be pleased that I do not this night make you earn your keep," I said.

"Get out of my bedroom!" she cried.

"For the night," I told her, "this is not your bedroom." I seized her by the hair and pulled her, naked beside me, down the stairs. Before the first slave kennel, that farthest to the left, as you face them, I stopped. With my left hand I flung up the sturdy, barred gate. I put the startled Miss Henderson on her hands and knees before the small opening. Then, my left hand in her hair, and my right hand on her left thigh, I thrust her bodily into the kennel. "This is your bedroom for the night," I told her. I then threw down the iron gate. She turned about, clutching the bars. I turned the key in the lock, fastening her within. "There will be no iron between a keeper and his kept woman," I said, "unless it be by his will, such as a collar, or shackles for her, or the bars of a cell." I then walked over to the wall. I held the key up, where she could see it. "A keeper must always have access to his kept woman," I said. I then hung the key on a peg, where she might, from time to time, look upon it, as it might please her.

"Jason," she said.

"I am going out," I told her.

"Let me out," she begged. "I am uncomfortable. The kennel is of cement, the bars of steel."

"Have a pleasant night," I said.

"I am uncomfortable," she said. "I am cold!"

"I wager," I said, "you will be far more uncomfortable and cold in the morning."

"Jason!" she cried. "Jason!"

But I had gone out.

"You beast!" I heard her cry. "I hate you! I hate you!"

I locked the door from the outside, and left.

Thirteen

The Topaz

I returned to the house near the fifth Ahn. I had slept some at the tavern of Cleanthes. I frequented various taverns in Victoria. There were several in the city. There were attractions, so to speak, in each. My favorite, on the whole, I believe, remained the tavern of Tasdron. It was in that tavern that the former Peggy Baxter, now a branded, encollared Gorean slave girl, served her master's customers.

I had lit a small tharlarion-oil lamp in the hall. I had fetched down from the bedroom near the top of the stairs a robe. I looked down on the girl who knelt in the small kennel, holding the bars. Her flesh looked lovely behind the bars. "Take your hands from the bars," I said. She knelt back in the kennel, and I unlocked the gate and thrust it up. I put the key to the side. She crawled out, on her hands and knees, and I threw her the robe. She stood up, belting it about her. "It is my short robe," she said, "not my long robe."

"Yes," I said. It came high on her thighs.

"It is suitable, doubtless," she said, "for a kept woman."

"Yes," I said.

"I am cold, and hungry," she said.

"There is some food in the kitchen," I said. "I left some of the bread and dried meat. There is some money there, too. You could go to the market. Did you sleep?"

"No," she said.

"I must go to the hiring yard," I said.

"You stink of the paga taverns," she said.

I turned away from her and put my pouch to the side. I did not, normally, carry it to the wharves.

"Were the girls pretty?" she asked.

"Yes," I said.

"As pretty as I?" she asked.

"I suppose so," I said. "Some of them."

"Did you have a good time?" she asked.

"Yes," I said. I went to a bucket of water in the corner of the room and, uncovering it, and using a bowl, dipped out water which I then used for washing my hands and face.

"Did anything unusual happen at the tavern?" she asked.

"There are some guardsmen from Ar's Station in Victoria," I said.

"What are they doing here?" she asked.

"Have you heard of the topaz?" I asked.

"Yes," she said. "I heard people in the market speaking of it."

"It is a pledge symbol," I said, "apparently used among pirates on the river, when combining for massive assaults."

"The men of Ar's Station are searching for the topaz?" she asked.

"Yes," I said.

"They fear that their post will be subjected to attack."

"Yes," I said, drying my face with a towel. "And if Ar's Station should be destroyed, the eastern river, between Tafa and Lara, would lie much at the mercy of the raiders."

"Then Port Cos would be next?" she asked.

"That is the speculation," I said, putting aside the towel.

"Did the guardsmen of Ar's Station find the topaz?" she asked.

"Not to my knowledge," I said. "They stopped me, and others, outside the tavern of Cleanthes. Later they searched all in the tavern, save those whom they remembered from outside, as having been previously examined."

"You were not searched a second time then?" she asked.

"No," I said. "It was the same men who were conducting the search."

"If the topaz should reach the stronghold of Policrates," she said, "the way would be clear for the uniting of the raider forces of both the east and west."

"It has perhaps already reached the stronghold of Policrates," I said.

"Surely routes to such a citadel have been invested," she said.

"They cannot be adequately invested," I said, "without consider-able forces. I do not think a careful courier would have difficulty reaching the citadel."

"What hope, then, have those who would wish to keep the topaz from reaching Policrates?"

"The hope is to apprehend the courier before he can reach the cita-del," I said.

"A slim hope," she said.

"I agree," I said.

"I would not wish to be who carries the topaz," she said.

"Nor I," I said, smiling.

"You kenneled me last night," she said.

"That is not unknown to me," I said.

"I will no longer try to keep a door locked between us," she said.

"That is advisable," I said.

She came then and stood near me. I restrained myself from seizing her in my arms and throwing her to the floor of the hall.

"Jason," she said.

"Yes," I said.

She drew her robe down, slightly, from her shoulders.

"Yes?" I said.

"I am ready to earn my keep," she said.

"You speak like a slave girl," I scorned her.

"Slave girls do not earn their keep," she said. "They do what they are told."

"If you were a slave girl, would you do what you were told?" I asked.

"Of course," she said. "I would have to."

"That is true," I said. She looked into my eyes and saw that it was indeed true, absolutely.

"I wonder if you would make a good slave," I said.

"Enslave me," she said, "and see."

"You are a woman of Earth," I said.

"On this world," she said, "many women of Earth are kept as the total slaves of their masters."

I looked at her.

Suddenly she knelt before me. "Enslave me," she begged. "I will make you a good slave."

"Get on your feet," I said, confused. "You are a woman of Earth. Must I teach you, of all people, a little feminist, how to be a true person?"

"This is Gor," she said, "not Earth. Such things are behind me now. I have learned too much."

"Get up," I said.

"On Gor," she said, "I do not need to pretend any longer. Here I do not need to be a political puppet. Here I am free at last to be a woman."

"Get up!" I cried.

"Fulfill my needs, please!" she begged.

"No!" I cried. Then I said, again, "Get up, quickly. You shame me."

She rose to her feet, tears in her eyes. She drew her robe tightly about her. "It is I who have been shamed," she said.

"You have shamed yourself," I said, angrily.

"No," she said, "that is not true, Jason. I have been honest to myself. It is you who have shamed me, punishing me for permitting myself this careless honesty. It is my fault, in a sense. You are a man of Earth, still. I should have known better."

"You should not have such needs," I told her.

"I have them," she said.

"Change them," I said.

"I cannot," she said.

"Surely you desire to do so," I said.

"No," she said, "no longer, I love them. They are the deepest part of me."

"You must then, at the least," I said, "pretend that you do not have them."

"Why?" she asked.

"I do not know," I said, "perhaps because they do not conform to the values of the glandularly deficient and sexually inert."

"This is not Earth," she said. "Why should I conform to such values?"

"I do not know," I said. "I do not know!"

"Such men and women," she said, "must make virtues of their deficiencies. Otherwise, to their humiliation, they would confess themselves less than others."

"Perhaps," I said. "I do not know."

"Why do you let others, the petty and resentful, the fearful and inadequate, legislate for you in this sphere?"

"I do not know," I said.

"What are their credentials?" she asked. "Where are their proofs?"

"I do not know," I said.

"Heeding their advice produces misery and frustration, impairments, physical and mental, anxiety, pain, sickness and self-torture. It can even shorten lives. Do these sorts of things seem to you the manifestations of a correct moral position?"

"I do not know," I said.

"Is it only the stupid, and the mutilated and crippled, who are to be accounted healthy?"

"I do not know," I said. "I do not know!"

"I am sorry if I have embarrassed you," she said.

"Go to your room," I said.

"You have refused me as a woman," she said.

"Go to your room, Miss Henderson," I said.

"Of course, Keeper," she said. She turned away from me. She went toward the stairs. At the foot of the stairs, she turned, again, to face me. "I am still prepared to earn my keep," she said.

"You are a woman of Earth," I said. "It is not necessary for a woman of Earth to earn her keep."

"Take me to the market, and sell me," she said.

"Why?" I asked.

"Perhaps a man will buy me," she said.

"I do not deny you your freedom," I said.

"You are refusing me my slavery," she said.

"You are displeasing me," I said.

"Then beat me and rape me," she said, "and put me under discipline."

"Go to your room, Miss Henderson," I warned her.

"And shall I strip and await your pleasure?" she asked.

"No," I told her.

"Clearly," she said, "a girl is safe with you."

I said nothing.

"Do you behave in this fashion with the sluts in the paga taverns?" she asked.

"They are different," I said. "They are slaves." And I added, not pleasantly, "And only slaves."

"I see," she said. "I envy the miserable creatures."

"Do not," I said. "You do not know what it is to be a slave."

"I have been a slave," she said.

"You were only a display slave," I said. "You were not a full slave. You do not have the least idea of what it would be to be a full slave."

"Collar me, and teach me," she said.

"You are a woman of Earth," I said. "I have no intention of abusing you."

"I am grateful, Keeper," she said, acidly.

I bent, angrily, to my pouch. I would find some money which I would insert in the lining of my tunic, a common thing among manual laborers on Gor.

"What is wrong?" she asked, from the stairs.

"This was not here before," I said. I drew the object from the pouch.

"What is it?" she asked.

I turned the object slowly in my hand. It was a fragment of polished stone, a fragment of what appeared to have once been a beveled, rectangular solid. It was about the size of a fist. It was a yellowish stone, with an intricate and unusual brownish discoloration at the point where it had apparently been broken from a larger stone.

"What is it?" she asked.

"I am not sure," I said. "I think it is a topaz."

Fourteen

Lola

I went back outside and brought in the other materials which I had purchased here and there in Victoria. I then closed, and bolted, the door.

"Who is there?" called down Miss Henderson, from upstairs.

"It is Jason," I said. The slave did not count.

"Who is she?" asked Miss Henderson, from the head of the stairs.

"Is it not obvious?" I asked. "It is a female slave. I am calling her Lola." This seemed to me appropriate, as it was the name which she had worn in the House of Andronicus.

"Who is she?" asked Lola. I smiled to myself. She would not have dared to speak so peremptorily before another male on Gor.

Miss Henderson stood aghast at the top of the stairs, that a slave should have so spoken.

"She is pretty, and in your house," said Lola to me, "and yet she is not in a collar. I see that you have not changed since the House of Andronicus, Jason."

"Insolent slave!" cried Miss Henderson. She had not worn a house veil since the night I had kenneled her.

I noted that Lola had used my name. That would cost her, I decided, an additional five strokes.

"There is shopping to be done," I told Miss Henderson. "Attend to it."

"I do not wish to," she said.

"Attend to it," I told her.

"Yes, Jason," she said, angrily. She descended the stairs, took some coins from the kitchen, unbolted the door, and left. I rebolted the door, after her.

Lola looked at me. "At least I shall have an easy slavery," she said.

I had found her this morning, near noon, when I had been on my luncheon break. At such times, for my amusement and interest, I occasionally frequented some of the dock markets, where, though cheap girls tend to be sold there, one may occasionally see a real beauty being vended. It is pleasant, of course, to see women being sold, particularly if they are beautiful.

She was kneeling, back on her heels, naked, on the hot boards of a slaver's platform. The boards were rough and splintery, and there were tiny droplets of tar on them. She was shackled by the wrists, on a short chain, to an iron ring, heavy, whose plate was bolted into the boards.

"Lola," I had said, my mouth full, chewing on the meat I had bought on the wharves.

She had jerked back, seeing me. The sales had not yet begun.

"What do you want for her?" I asked the slaver on the platform, carrying his keys and whip.

"Ten copper tarsks," he said.

"Done!" I said.

"No!" she cried.

"Be silent, Wench," he ordered her.

I removed a ten-tarsk piece from the lining of my tunic. Workers do not commonly carry pouches at their work.

"Do not sell me to him," begged the girl, "please!"

But he kicked her brutally to silence.

I paid him and he unshackled her. He also removed his collar from her throat.

"Come along," I told her. She descended from the platform and, naked and miserable, heeled me as I threaded my way slowly from the place. She did not try to escape. She knew there was no escape for her. She was a Gorean slave girl.

I stopped at the warehouse where I had been working and collected a half day's wages. My employer did not object, for he could see that I had purchased something of interest. Doubtless I was eager to get her home. "Continue working, Jason," called one of the fellows. "Leave her here in the warehouse. We will see that no harm comes to her!" There was much laughter. I waved to them as I left the warehouse. "Have her once for me!" called one of my fellow workers after me.

"Little do they know you," she said, bitterly.

On the way home I stopped in the market to buy a few things, some articles for which I thought I might find a use.

"Why are you buying a slave whip?" she asked me.

"Be patient," I told her. "Perhaps you will learn."

I also bought some chains, and binding fiber, and other things. Interestingly, for no reason I clearly understood, I bought two sets of certain articles.

Also on the way home I purchased her a slave tunic and stopped at the shop of a metal worker, where I had her measured and purchased a collar for her. I had the collar inscribed according to my specifications. I put it in my sack, with its two keys, tied to it with a string.

* * * *

I snapped my fingers, and the girl, to the side, rose from her knees and lightly hurried to the table, beside which she again knelt, head down.

"You may clear, Lola," I told her.

"Yes, Master," she said, and began to remove the dishes from the table.

"A deferential slut," said Miss Henderson, who knelt across the table from me.

Lola kept her head down.

"Rather different than when you brought her into the house this afternoon," she said. "What did you do to her?"

"Reminded her she was a slave," I said.

"I see," said Miss Henderson.

Lola rose to her feet and padded softly, barefoot, carrying the dishes, to the kitchen.

"Her tunic is sleeveless, and too short," said Miss Henderson.

"It pleases me," I said.

"Of course," said Miss Henderson. "She is yours."

* * * *

"Why have you tied me like this?" had asked Lola.

I had tied her wrists together before her body, before the opened door of the house, leaving a dangling, loose strap of about a foot in length.

I then swept her from her feet and carried her across the threshold and put her down, on her feet, near the side wall to the left.

"Why have you carried me into the house as a capture, and a slave?" she asked.

I had rebolted the door, after Miss Henderson, sent on her shopping errands by myself, had exited.

I had then turned again to face Lola. We were alone in the house.

She looked at me. "At least I shall have an easy slavery," she said.

"Stand here," I told her, positioning her about five feet from the wall, facing it, to the left of the door as you enter, beneath a stout beam.

"I shall make you a poor slave," she said.

I went to the side of the room and, loosening the chain, lowered the chain. Attached to the end of the chain, on the other side of the beam ring, now descending, was a wide circle of steel, a steel ring, some six inches in diameter. I stopped the chain when the steel ring dangled at her belly.

"You know what that is?" I asked her.

"I am a slave girl," she said.

"Speak it," I said.

"It is a whipping ring," she said.

I tied her tethered wrists, by the free end of the strap, to the ring.

"Why have you tied me to the whipping ring?" she asked.

"Why do you think?" I asked.

"You're bluffing," she said.

I went back to the wall and pulled the chain again through the beam ring. Then her hands were held well over her head.

"I will make you a poor slave," she said. "Oh!" she said.

"Perhaps, not," I said.

"Release me," she said, tensely. She stood now, painfully, on the tips of her toes.

I hooked a link of the chain on the holding hook, lifting her a quarter of an inch higher, securing her in place.

"Let me go," she said.

I walked about her, and then faced her, looking upon her.

"You are luscious," I told her. "I think you may make an excellent slave."

"Let me go!" she said, squirming in the leather.

"Yes, an excellent slave," I said. Then I went behind her.

"What are you going to do?" she asked.

"What do you think?" I asked her.

"You cannot frighten me," she said. "I know you cannot strike me. You are too weak to whip me, and make me obey you. You are a man of Earth!"

"Long ago you had me beaten in the House of Andronicus," I said. "In your role as a free woman in the slave training you deliberately spilled wine and blamed me, and ordered me whipped. The whipping was very painful. Do you recall?"

She said nothing.

"You have never adequately paid for that," I said.

"Paid?" she asked.

"Yes," I said.

"Do not forget you are a man of Earth," she said.

"Oh, yes," I said, "the men of Earth never make a woman pay for anything. She may even humiliate them and destroy them as men and with total impunity. Is that right?"

"Yes, yes!" said the girl.

"Not always," I said.

"Master?" she asked.

"And this is not Earth," I said.

"Master?" she asked.

And then, suddenly, she screamed, caught fully, helplessly, in the blurred, whistling slash of the five-stranded Gorean slave whip.

Ten strokes did I give her.

Then she hung weeping, shuddering, at the ring. "How can you whip me?" she asked. "You are a man of Earth."

I went to her and, by the hair, jerked back her head, and she cried out with pain. "Is this the touch of a man of Earth?" I asked.

"No," she said, frightened.

"Too," I said, whispering in her ear, "you are a new slave who has been brought recently to my house."

"No," she begged. "No!"

Sometimes a girl is whipped when she is first brought into a new house. It is regarded, in some cities, including Victoria, as a way of making clear to her that the house in which she now finds herself is a house in which she is a slave.

Ten strokes more then did I administer to the fair beauty.

"Too," I said, "earlier you dared to speak my name."

"Forgive me, Master," she sobbed.

"That has earned you five extra strokes," I informed her.

She moaned, and then was shaken five times, encircled in the burning lashes, being repaid for her insolence.

When I lowered the whip she sagged in the leather, fastened at the ring, and slipped from consciousness. I went before her and slapped her awake. She looked at me, startled, awakened, in pain, terrified. "And one more stroke," I told her, "to remind you that you are a slave."

"Yes, Master," she whispered.

I delivered the blow, letting it be the fiercest of her beating.

I then put aside the whip and lowered the chain. She collapsed to the floor. I unbound her hands from the ring, freeing her, too, of the tether which had confined her wrists.

She lay on her stomach on the tiles of the hall. She lifted her head, slowly. She shook her head to clear her vision. She looked at me, disbelievingly.

I removed my sandals and threw them to the tiles, near where she lay.

Obediently, on her hands and knees, one by one, putting her head down, she brought them to me in her teeth, and put them before me. She then looked up.

"Kiss the whip," I told her.

"Yes, Master," she said.

She took the whip, held before her, in her small hands and, pressing her lips fervently to it, kissed it. She then looked up at me, and I saw in her eyes, moist and awe-stricken, that I was her master.

I then collared her.

"Your duties in this house, Lola," I told her, "will be numerous and complex. In particular, you will be a house slave. You will dust and clean the house, and keep it neat. You will mend and sew. You will wash and iron clothing. You will shop, and cook and serve. All manners of domestic tasks, trivial and servile, unfit for free women, will be yours."

"Yes, Master," she said.

"Too, you will take orders in this house from Lady Beverly, Miss Henderson, who is a free woman in the house, as you would from me, but you are to remember always that it is I who own you, and not she."

"Yes, Master," she said. "But for such a handsome Master am I to be only a house slave?"

"Foremost among your duties," I said, "for you are beautiful, will be to attend to the pleasures of your Master."

"Yes, Master," she said. "Please forgive me, Master, for not having been pleasing to you before."

"Do you wish to be whipped again?" I asked.

"No, Master," she said. "No!"

The whipping had convinced her that she was under discipline. This understanding, of course, goes far beyond the mere pain of a particular episode. The whipping in itself, though of considerable moment, is insignificant when compared to the lesson it teaches. It teaches the girl that she is under the total domination of a man. It teaches her that she is at his mercy, and is owned, truly. This fulfills something very deep in the female. This is the lesson of the leather. This is not to deny, of course, that a woman who is fully conscious of her embonded condition, does not fear the whip. She does, for she knows what it can, and will, do to her if she is not pleasing. The only woman who does not fear the whip is she who has not felt it.

"Then, perhaps you should begin to be pleasing to me now," I said.

"Yes, Master!" she said, and began to kiss at my body.

"But on the other hand," I said, "perhaps you should merely tie my sandals."

"Let me tie them later," she said. "Let me please you now."

"Do you beg it?" I asked.

"Yes, Master," she said.

"Very well," I said.

* * * *

Lola, kneeling behind the bars of the slave kennel, looked up at me. "You are so different now from before," she said.

I shrugged.

She put her arm timidly through the bars, to touch me. "Will you not again, sometime, subject me to slave rape?" she asked.

"Perhaps," I said.

"I am pleased that you bought me," she whispered. "I will try to serve you well."

"Do not think things will be easy here for you," I said, "for there is a free woman in the house."

"I will obey her," said Lola, "and with perfection."

"But do not forget," I said, "that it is I who own you, and not she."

"I shall not forget, Master," she smiled. Then she kissed her finger tips and, putting her hand through the bars, put her hand to my waist. "I know well who owns me," she said.

"Rest now," I said. "The Mistress will be home soon, and then, doubtless, you will be soon set to chores."

"Yes, Master," said Lola.

* * * *

Lola now returned to the small table and, kneeling, head down, served us our dessert, slices of tospit, sprinkled with four Gorean sugars.

"I see there may be some advantages to having a slave in the house," said Miss Henderson.

"I have never doubted it," I said.

"You may serve the black wine now, in small cups, Lola," said Miss Henderson.

"Yes, Mistress," whispered Lola.

This was a delicacy. I had purchased some, some days ago, but we had not yet served it. In a few Ehn Lola returned with the tray, with the vessel of steaming liquid, the creams and sugars, the tiny cups, and the small spoons for mixing and measuring.

"Delicious," said Miss Henderson.

"Thank you, Mistress," said Lola. She then drew back a bit, and knelt, to be unobtrusive, and yet available, instantly, to serve, should free folk wish aught.

"You are a very pretty girl, Lola," said Miss Henderson, regarding her.

"Thank you, Mistress," said Lola, her head down.

"Men must find you attractive," said Miss Henderson.

"Perhaps, Mistress," said Lola, "some men." I smiled to myself. The man who did not find Lola attractive must indeed be an inert dolt.

"How long have you been a slave?" asked Miss Henderson.

"Four years, Mistress," said Lola.

"Have you had several Masters?" asked Miss Henderson.

"Yes, Mistress," said Lola.

"Have you served them as a slave?" she asked.

"Yes, Mistress," said Lola.

"As a full slave?" asked Miss Henderson.

Lola lowered her head further. "Yes, Mistress," she whispered.

"Do you enjoy their hands on your body?" asked Miss Henderson.

"Yes, Mistress," whispered Lola.

"I see that you are a true slave," said Miss Henderson.

"Yes, Mistress," whispered Lola.

"Incidentally," I said to Miss Henderson, "move your things out of the master bedroom."

"It is my bedroom!" she said.

"No," I said. "I am taking it. It is larger. And it has a porch, and a view of the garden and sky. I am renting the house. I am making it mine."

"No!" she said.

"Too," I said, "it has the great couch, the one with the slave ring at its foot."

"I see," said Miss Henderson, looking angrily at Lola. Lola did not raise her head, but knelt there, her knees close together, in the brief slave tunic. "I see," said Miss Henderson, and rose to her feet, hurrying angrily upstairs.

I finished my black wine, enjoying it. When I had finished I permitted Lola to clear the table and address herself to the work in the kitchen.

After a time I went upstairs. Miss Henderson had cleared the room. I looked at the heavy iron slave ring, about eight inches in diameter, set in the stone of the great couch. I then went into Miss Henderson's room. She was sitting on the couch. "You did not knock," she said. "I need not knock to enter the room of my kept woman," I said. I then took my things from the room and put them into the master bedroom. I looked over the balustrade to the sky beyond. It was lovely. As I again started downstairs I met Miss Henderson on the landing. She, too, was going downstairs.

"You seem angry," I said.

"Not I," she said.

"Why are you going downstairs?" I asked.

"To supervise the slave," she said. "Such girls are lazy and will do no work if they are not closely watched."

I stepped aside and let her precede me down the stairs. She was a free woman, and a woman of Earth. She was not a slave, who must heel her master.

* * * *

"Come here, Lola," I said.

It was now in the early evening. Miss Henderson and I, with small cups of a Turian liqueur before us, lounged in the living room. A tharlarion-oil lamp lit the room.

"Stand here," I told Lola.

"Yes, Master," she said.

"Surely you are not angry," I said to Miss Henderson, "that I bought her." I faced Lola away from me. I put my hands on her ankle. "Look at this ankle," I said. Lola trembled. "And these calves and thighs," I said, "and the luscious, central curves of her, and these breasts and shoulders." I was now standing beside the slave. I put my hand under her chin, lifting it up. "And this neck, in my collar," I said, "and this head and face, and this hair. Surely you can see that she is an excellent buy."

"Yes," said Miss Henderson, angrily, "she was an excellent buy!"

"When you have finished your work tonight, Lola," I said, "go upstairs to the master bedroom. Take your clothes off, and kneel there, by the slave ring, and await my pleasure."

"Yes, Master," she said, and went then, hurriedly, to the kitchen.

"Just like that?" asked Miss Henderson.

"Of course," I said. "She is a slave."

"It must be pleasant to have such absolute power over a woman," she said.

"Yes," I said.

In time Miss Henderson and I had finished our liqueur. Lola cleaned the glasses and put them away. Then, head down, quietly, when she had finished, she slipped past us and made her way upstairs to the master bedroom.

"Do you find her more beautiful than I?" asked Miss Henderson.

"She is quite beautiful," I said. "But I do not think that she is more beautiful than you. You are quite beautiful, you know."

"Yet it is she whom you kneel at your slave ring, not I," said Miss Henderson.

I gritted my teeth, forcing the thought of Miss Henderson kneeling naked at my slave ring, awaiting my pleasure, from my mind. It was all I could do to control myself. She was the most incredibly attractive female I had ever known.

"You are a free woman," I said.

"Perhaps I would make a good slave," she said.

"I doubt it," I said. "You are a woman of Earth."

"Gorean men say that we make excellent slaves," she said. "It is only necessary that we understand clearly that we are slaves, and are put under discipline. We then blossom in our slavery, beautifully, as much or perhaps even more so than Gorean girls."

"I have given you respect," I said. "I have given you freedom. I have given you money. I have relieved you of work. I have denied you nothing. Yet you remain dissatisfied."

"You have denied me one thing," she said.

"What is that?" I asked.

"A collar," she said.

"Go to your room," I said.

"Of course," she said. "Let me not keep you from your slut."

She rose from the table and, lifting the hem of her robes, went to the stairs.

"She is doubtless already naked, and at your ring," she said.

"She had better be," I said, "unless she wishes to be whipped."

Angrily Miss Henderson ascended the stairs.

"Miss Henderson," I called.

"Yes, Mister Marshall," she said.

"Remember that your door is to be left unbolted," I said.

"I know," she said. "That my door be bolted is not permitted. A keeper must always have access to his kept woman."

She then entered her room, the smaller room which, previously, had been mine. She closed the door firmly, decisively, angrily.

I listened carefully.

She did not bolt it.

I then, not hurrying, went upstairs. I entered my room and closed the door behind me, bolting it.

I looked down at Lola. She knelt naked, at the ring. She looked up at me, and smiled. "I await your pleasure, Master," she said.

"Spread the furs," I said, "and light the ravishment lamp."

I removed my tunic, throwing it aside.

In a few moments Lola lay on the furs, at the foot of the couch, on her belly, her hands at her sides, the backs of her hands to the furs, the palms of her hands vulnerably up, exposed.

I crouched beside her and took the nearby chain and collar. I fastened the chain to the slave ring and then closed the heavy collar about her neck, over the other collar. She was then chained by the neck to my slave ring.

I took her body in my hands and turned her to her back. Her weight was light for my strength.

She looked up at me, breathlessly. She lifted her arms and put them about my neck. "I am yours, Master," she whispered.

"That is known to me," I said.

"Yes, yes, Master," she whispered, lifting her lips to mine.

Fifteen

The House Has been Ransacked; Miss Henderson Has been Bound as a Slave; I Do Not Abuse Her

The door was ajar.

I had returned early from the wharves. There had been little work.

I was apprehensive that the door was ajar.

"Lola!" I called, stepping within the threshold. "Lola!"

I heard a tiny sound, a pathetic, tiny whimper, muffled, almost inaudible, from a few feet away.

I ran to the slave kennel on the left. Lola was within, naked, sitting, bound hand and foot. She was tightly gagged. Only the tiniest, muffled sounds could escape her.

The key was nearby. I opened the kennel. I pulled and lifted her out. I fumbled with the knots on the gag. I loosened them and pulled the binding down about her neck. I pulled the deep, heavy wadding from her mouth.

"The Mistress," she said. "She is upstairs."

I looked about. The house was a shambles. Goods were cast about. My pouch, left home, had been emptied out upon the floor.

"Who did this?" I asked.

"A man," she said. "A large man. He wore a mask, purple."

"Is he in the house?" I asked.

"No," she gasped.

I untied her hands. I glanced at the knots on her ankles. I did not think that she, with her woman's strength, could well undo them. I loosened them.

"What did he want?" I asked her.

"I do not know, Master," she said.

I hurried upstairs. Miss Henderson was in the master bedroom. She was on the great couch. She looked at me, pathetically. There were bruises on her body. She was tied as a slave. She tried to speak, but she had been well gagged.

My things in the bedroom had been gone through, and thrown about.

I looked at Miss Henderson. Her small legs, by the ankles, had been tied cruelly apart. Her wrists, too, were tied widely apart. Small rings, on either side of the couch, at the head and foot, anchoring the binding fiber, permitted this tie. It is not an uncommon tie for slaves. There were tears in her eyes. She made tiny, muffled noises. I could scarcely hear them, though I stood at the foot of the couch.

Lola, her slave tunic now drawn on, stood in the threshold of the master bedroom. "The Mistress was not circumspect," she said. "She opened the door. The man thrust in. He turned her about and held her, a knife at her throat. 'Do not run or cry out,' he said, 'or your Mistress dies. Bring cloths and binding fiber.' I obeyed. 'Strip,' he ordered me. I obeyed. 'Lie on your stomachs, side by side,' he told us. We obeyed. Then, while he knelt across the body of the Mistress, that she might not flee, he bound me, hand and foot, and gagged me. Then, at his leisure, garment by garment, with his knife, seeming to enjoy having her progressively revealed to him, he stripped the Mistress. He then, though she was free, trussed and gagged her identically as he had me. He then stood up and regarded us. We lay before him, though I was a slave and she free, side by side, identically helpless. I was put in the slave kennel, and the kennel was locked. She he carried upstairs."

I looked at Miss Henderson with irritation. What a fool she was to have so thoughtlessly opened the door.

She struggled in the binding fiber. Her eyes begged me to release her. She made tiny noises, helpless, pathetic, almost inaudible.

"Shall I free her, Master?" asked Lola.

"No," I said, angrily.

I then went to Miss Henderson's bedroom. It, too, was a shambles.

"The kitchen, I assume, was searched," I said to Lola, returning to the master bedroom.

"Yes," she said.

"What did he take?" I asked.

"As far as I know," she said, "he took nothing."

"Go to the kitchen, Lola," I said. "Set things in order."

"Yes, Master," she said.

I shut the door behind her. I had little doubt for what it was that the visitor had sought.

Miss Henderson whimpered.

"What a fool you are to have opened the door, not knowing the nature or identity of your guest," I said.

Anger, as well as tears, welled up in her eyes.

"Yet," I said, regarding her, "you are a pretty little fool."

She twisted, angrily, in the binding fiber.

I knelt upon the couch and, turning her head to the side, untied the knots at the back of her neck. Then, turning her head to face me, I pulled the wet, heavy packing of the gag from her mouth.

"Your gag was quite effective," I told her, "as was Lola's. He who gagged you is apparently no stranger to the control of prisoners."

"After he had brought me upstairs and tied me, as you find me," she said, "he removed my gag, temporarily."

"Yes?" I said.

"He struck me until I begged to be raped," she said. "He made me beg to be raped!"

"And what happened," I asked, smiling, "after you had begged to be raped?"

"He laughed, and then raped me," she said, in fury.

"Of course," I said. "Had you not asked him to do so?"

"He looked upon me as though I might be a slave," she said, "and he treated me, thoughtlessly and casually, as though I might be a slave. He even called me 'Slave'!"

"Gorean men are expert in such matters," I said. "Perhaps he knows something about you that I do not know."

"Look!" she said. "He tied me as a slave!"

"You look well," I told her, "tied as a slave."

She squirmed in the binding fiber angrily, helplessly. "Please, unbind me," she said.

I looked at her.

"The topaz is gone," she said.

"Speak softly," I said. "Lola is a slave. She need know nothing of the topaz."

"It is gone," she said, softly.

"Oh?" I said.

"I was terrified," she said, "and so I told him, immediately, where it was." She looked at me, angrily. "And then, in spite of my cooperation, he called me 'Slave' and, in amusement, subjected me to his will."

"Where did you tell him it was?" I asked.

"In your pouch, downstairs," she said, "where you keep it."

"It has not been in the pouch for days," I said.

"Where is it?" she asked.

"Elsewhere," I said.

She looked up at me.

"It is fortunate," I said, "that he, rightly or wrongly, took you as a slave. Else he might have returned to cut your throat. Thinking you a slave he would presume you ignorant of the location of an item of such value." I smiled. "You could then be left alive, perhaps to please him again as an interesting and compliant pleasure object, should you fall again into his clutches."

"He then, finishing with me, regagged me," she said.

"And effectively," I said.

"Yes," she said, angrily.

"If he had found the topaz immediately," I said, "why did you think he would continue to search the house?"

"For valuables," she said. "But I did not understand his anger, his frustration."

"He had not, actually, found the topaz," I said.

"I did not understand," she said. "It had not occurred to me that you would have removed it from your pouch without telling me."

I shrugged.

"In that," she said, "not taking me into your confidence, you treated me as a slave, did you not, Jason?"

"I may have saved your life," I said. "Slave girls have value—as articles of property."

"I see," she said, angrily.

"Besides," I said, "obviously you were willing to reveal the location of the topaz with alacrity, as I had feared. It is important that it not reach Policrates. If it does, the major forces of the pirates of the eastern Vosk would achieve unification, at least for a time, with those of the western Vosk. This is to be prevented, if at all possible. If you did not know the location of the topaz it seemed obvious to me that you could not reveal its location, unless by some chance inadvertence. Doubtless the fewer that know of its location, the better."

"Do you think I am a slave, Jason?" she asked.

"I assumed that any who might search for the topaz would be likely to regard you in such terms," I said. "You are the type of woman, sexually stimulating and curvaceous, desirable, whom Gorean men, rightly or wrongly, look upon in terms of the parameters of bondage, in terms of such things as their potential for yielding incredible gratification and service. Too, do not forget that your left thigh bears a certain lovely brand, that of many Gorean Kajirae."

"Do you think I am a slave, Jason?" she asked.

"Why do you ask?" I asked.

"You have not untied me," she said. "You have left me bound as a slave."

I did not speak.

"I lie before you, bound as a slave," she said. "Use me, if you wish. I am tied, helplessly. I cannot resist you. Take me, and as a slave, if you wish!"

I did not speak.

"Untie me," she begged.

"No," I said.

"Why not?" she asked.

"You look well, tied as a slave," I told her.

"Perhaps that is because I am a slave," she said.

"Perhaps," I said.

"You are punishing me, aren't you?" she said.

"Yes," I said.

"And as a slave," she said.

"Yes," I said.

"You do regard me as a slave," she said.

"You are a woman of Earth," I said. "How can you be a slave?"

"I am a woman of Earth," she said. "How can I not be a slave?"

I rose from the couch and went to the door.

"Where is the topaz, Jason?" she inquired.

"I choose not to inform you of its location," I said.

"Excellent," she said. "You keep your slaves in ignorance."

"Do not confuse yourself with a slave, Miss Henderson," I said. "If you were my slave, you would be in no doubt about the fact."

"I wonder," she said.

I considered her throat. I did not think it would look bad in a close-fitting steel collar, properly inscribed, identifying her as mine. Then I forced such thoughts from my mind. She was Miss Beverly Henderson, of Earth.

"May I inquire as to the duration of my punishment?" she asked.

"An Ahn or two, I expect," I said. "I will have Lola restore the house to order. When she is finished you will be freed and sent to your room. You may emerge in the morning."

"And little Lola will come in here to lick your feet," she said, bitterly.

"She will do what she is commanded," I said. "I may have her do that. I may not. It will depend totally upon my will."

"What manner of man are you?" she asked, horrified.

"One who does not mind having a beautiful woman, naked, collared, a slave at his total mercy, licking his feet," I said.

"How pathetic to be a slave!" she cried.

"Rejoice in your freedom," I told her. I then opened the door and prepared to exit.

"Jason," she said.

"Yes," I said.

"I yielded to my rapist," she said.

"As a slave?" I asked.

"Yes," she said. "Am I not then a slave?"

"Perhaps," I said.

"I will never yield to you," she said. "You cannot make me yield to you!"

I smiled to myself, for was she not female? Then I put such thoughts from my mind. She was Miss Beverly Henderson, of Earth.

I exited and closed the door, quietly. "I hate you!" she cried out, from within.

Sixteen

Lola Has Not Greeted Me as I Return Home; I Hurry to the Wharves

"Lola!" I called. "Lola!"

The day's work had been long on the docks, I was looking forward to receiving the attentions of the lovely little slut.

"Lola!" I called.

Where was she? By now she should have run to me and knelt before me, happily, waiting to be commanded.

"Lola!" I called. "Lola!" I began to grow slightly irritated. Was the girl lax? Perhaps it would be necessary to put her under some unpleasant discipline.

"She is not here," said Miss Henderson, lightly.

"You have sent her shopping?" I asked.

"No," she said.

"Where is she?" I asked. "You know I like her at my feet when I come home."

"She is not here," said Miss Henderson, somewhat evasively I thought.

"Where is she?" I asked.

"She was a poor slave," said Miss Henderson. "She was lazy. Her work was not adequate."

"Where is she?" I asked.

"I grew displeased with her," said Miss Henderson.

"Where is she?" I asked.

"I sold her," said Miss Henderson.

I looked at her, disbelievingly.

"Her work was not satisfactory," she said. "I ordered her to submit to binding, as a slave must. I then, with a switch, conducted her to the wharves, where I sold her."

"To what merchant?" I said, angrily.

"I did not inquire his name," she said.

"The market was on what wharf?" I asked.

"I received two copper tarsks for her," she said.

"The market was on what wharf?" I asked.

"I will give you the two copper tarsks, if you wish," she said.

"The market was on what wharf?" I asked.

"I did not pay any attention," she said. "Doubtless, by now, she has been sold off anyway. Jason! Take your hands off me!"

I held her rudely by the arms, almost lifting her from the floor.

"She was not yours to sell!" I said.

"Her work was not satisfactory," she said. "I share this household."

"She was not yours to sell," I said.

"I will give you the two copper tarsks, if you wish," she said. "We can buy another work slave, if you wish, a better worker, one mutually agreeable to us."

"Lola was a splendid worker," I said.

"I did not care for her," said Miss Henderson. "Jason!"

I had flung her halfway across the room, in fury. "Beware!" she said. "I am free!"

"You had no right to sell her," I said.

"I am free," she said. "I do what I please!"

I glared at her, in fury. Then I turned about.

"Where are you going?" she asked.

"To the wharves," I said.

"She will have been sold by now!" she cried. "You will never find her!"

"When did you take her to the market?" I asked.

"Early this morning," she said, "as soon as you had left."

"You planned well," I said.

"You will never find her!" she cried.

I left the house, in fury, slamming the door.
"You will never find her!" she cried, from within.
I began to run toward the wharves.

Seventeen

I Ponder the Contentment
of a Slave

"You take me with bitterness, Master," she said. "Has Peggy displeased you?"

"No," I said. "I am angry."

"Ah," she said, "then ventilate your emotions upon me, for I am only a slave." She kissed me. "I must submit to whatever men choose to do to me. Do you wish to whip me?"

"No," I said. "It is not you whom I should make suffer."

"Some free woman has displeased you?" she asked.

"Yes," I said.

"Then take your vengeance upon her," she said. "Collar her. Make her your slave."

"She is from Earth," I said.

"We are not different from other women," she said, "unless it might be, perhaps, that we make better slaves." She leaned back on the furs of the alcove. "Is this the same female concerning whom we once spoke, she who was with you in the restaurant?"

"Yes," I said.

"The pretty little beast," she said.

"Yes," I said.

"And you have not yet enslaved her? Master is dilatory."

"Do you think so?" I asked.

"A Gorean man would soon have her lovely little throat locked in his steel collar," she said.

"But she is from Earth," I said.

"Master is quaint," she laughed. "Forgive me, Master," she smiled.

"Very well," I said.

"What did she do?" asked Peggy.

I then grew again bitter. "She sold a slave of mine," I said, "unknown to me, and without right."

"For a man," said Peggy, "such an offense is punishable by exile. For a woman, remanded to a praetor, the penalty is commonly that she herself will then wear the collar."

"Oh?" I asked.

"Yes," she said. "Enslave her."

"I cannot," I said. "She is from Earth."

"The women of Earth," she smiled, "are never to be punished, no matter what they do?"

"No," I said.

"Gorean men," she laughed, "are not so tolerant of our flaws. We may be severely punished even for displeasing them in the slightest."

"You may be severely punished even at their whim," I said.

"Yes," she said.

"But you are slaves," I reminded her.

"That is true," she said. "We were brought to Gor to be collared, and made slaves."

"She is free," I reminded her.

"Enslave her," said Peggy.

"But then she would be only another Gorean slave girl," I said, "no different from others."

"True," said Peggy.

"And she would be mine, to do with exactly as I pleased," I said, "totally."

"Precisely," said Peggy. "Oh," she said, suddenly, "you are so strong."

"I must put such thoughts from my head," I said.

"Why?" she asked, clutching me, pressing closely against me.

"Men must not think such thoughts," I said.

"Why?" she asked. "Because they so considerably increase their virility?" She held to me, tightly. "I would rather they put thoughts from their heads," she said, "which made them miserable and weak. How can thoughts be good which make men miserable and weak? How can thoughts be wrong which make men great and strong? I am a slave in your arms. Does your blood not call you to your destiny, my Master? My blood, racing in my weakened body, opened like a flower to you, yielding, calls me to mine. I submit to you, my Master. I beg you to be strong with me, to own me. Peggy begs Master to take her!"

I then took her, and she screamed with pleasure, a taken slave.

Later I held her closely. "Are you a contented slave?" I asked her.

"I am a slave," she whispered, "whether I am contented or not."

"Speak," I said.

"Yes, Master," she whispered, softly, "I am a contented slave."

Eighteen

I Make the Acquaintance of
Guardsmen from Port Cos; I Do
Not Take Action Against Miss
Henderson; She is a Free Woman

I hung in the ropes. My back was still sore from the whipping.

"As far as we can determine," said the guardsman from Port Cos, "he is ignorant as to the whereabouts of the topaz."

"I vouch for him," said Tasdron. "He is an honest worker, well known on the wharves. He has been in Victoria for weeks."

When I had emerged from the tavern of Tasdron I had been suddenly surrounded by guardsmen in the livery of Port Cos. Several crossbows were trained on me.

"Do not draw your weapon," I had been told. "Do not resist."

"Is this he?" had asked the leader of the guardsmen.

"It is he," had said Miss Henderson.

"You are under arrest," had said the leader of the guardsmen.

"On what charge?" I asked.

"Vagrancy," said the leader of the guardsmen.

"That is absurd," I said.

"Your innocence, if you are innocent, may always be established later," said the man.

"This is Victoria," I said.

"The power of Port Cos marches with the men of Port Cos," said the man. "Bind him."

My hands had been tied behind my back.

"I am finished with you, Jason," said Miss Henderson, facing me. Then she had turned to the leader of the guardsmen of Port Cos. "Pay me," she said.

"Bind her, as well," he had said. To her consternation her small wrists were tied behind her back. "Bring them both to our headquarters," had said the leader of the guardsmen.

* * * *

"I vouch for him," said Tasdron. "He is an honest worker, well known on the wharves. He has been in Victoria for weeks."

"Did he come from east on the river, or west?" asked the guardsman.

"From the east, from Lara, as I understand it," said Tasdron.

"That is much what he, too, claims," said the guardsman.

"In my own tavern," said Tasdron, "he had difficulty with Kliomenes, the pirate. He could have been killed. That scarcely seems what one would expect from the courier of Ragnar Voskjard. Too, he does not seem skilled with the sword."

"It is not claimed he is the courier," said the guardsman. "It is claimed only that he knows the whereabouts of the topaz."

"Is there any reason to suppose that that is true?" inquired Tasdron.

"Only the word and story of a free woman, whom he keeps," said the guardsman.

"I see," said Tasdron. "And have you had similar situations before?"

"Four times," said the guardsman, disgustedly.

"Doubtless you have searched his compartments," said Tasdron.

"He has a small house," said the guardsman. "We have searched the house and the garden."

"What did you find?" asked Tasdron.

"Nothing," said the guardsman.

"Does the woman seem well disposed towards him?" asked Tasdron.

"She hates him," said the guardsman.

"And does she seem interested in the reward for information leading to the acquisition of the topaz?" asked Tasdron.

"Yes," said the guardsman. "The money seems quite important to her."

"Ten silver tarsks is a considerable sum," said Tasdron. "The guardsmen from Ar's Station, also in Victoria searching for the topaz, are offering only six silver tarsks."

"Cut him down," said the leader of the guardsmen to one of his men.

When the ropes were cut from my wrists I fell to the floor but did not lose my footing.

"He is strong," said the leader of the guardsmen.

My tunic was torn down about my waist. "My thanks, Tasdron," I said to him, "for your helpful words."

"It is nothing," he said, and left.

"You may go," said the leader of the guardsmen to me. "You may pick up your things at the door."

"Had you found the topaz," I asked, "what would have been done with me?"

"You might have looked forward," said he, "if fortunate, to a lifetime chained at the bench of a state galley."

"I see," I said.

"Do not forget your things at the door," he said.

"Very well," I said.

At the door, I drew the shreds of my tunic about me. I picked up my pouch and the sword belt, with its scabbard and sheathed steel. Among these things, in the robes of the free woman, her hands tied behind her, and her ankles tied, knelt Miss Henderson.

"Do not leave her behind," said the leader of the guardsmen. "She is yours."

I looked down at her. She did not meet my eyes.

"Those in your situation before," said the leader of the guardsmen, "stripped such women and took them, bound, to the market, where they sold them."

I crouched beside Miss Henderson and freed her ankles. I then helped her to her feet, and untied her wrists. I then left the small headquarters of the guardsmen of Port Cos, in Victoria. She followed me outside. Once outside, and a few yards from the headquarters, I turned about, and faced her.

"If you needed money, or wanted it," I said, "I would have given you money."

"Stay with me tonight," she said.

"I am going to the paga tavern," I told her.

"Why?" she asked.

"There are more interesting women there," I said.

"Slaves!" she said.

"Yes," I said.

"I am a free woman," she said. "Do you find slaves more interesting than I?"

"Of course," I said.

"Why?" she asked.

"For one thing," I said, "they are owned."

"That makes them fascinating, doesn't it?" she said, bitterly.

"Yes," I said.

"And doubtless," she said, angrily, "they do not have the inhibitions and frigidities of their free sisters!"

"They are not permitted them," I admitted.

"I hate female slaves," she said.

I shrugged.

"Why are they preferred over free women?" she asked.

"Because they are slaves," I said.

"What are the differences?" she asked.

"There are thousands," I said. "Perhaps, most simply, the female slave is submitted to men. This makes her the most total of women."

"Disgusting," she said.

"Perhaps," I said.

"No man could ever break my will," she said.

"That is the sort of thing which is usually said by a woman who is yearning for her will to be broken, by a strong man," I said.

"I hate female slaves," she said.

I did not speak.

"Do you think I would make a good female slave?" she asked.

"I think you would make an excellent little slave," I said.

"Stay with me tonight," she said.

"Why?" I asked.

"Break my will," she said. "Make me a slave."

"You are a woman of Earth," I told her.

159

"I see," she said. "I am too fine, and different."

"Of course," I told her. "Do you need to be told that?"

"No!" she said. "I know it!"

"Very well," I said, angrily.

"Stay with me tonight," she begged. "Make me your slave!"

I looked at her.

"My will, broken, will lie before you as yielding, as supine and vanquished, as my body," she said. "I beg of you, Jason, make me your slave!"

"I am going to the paga tavern," I said.

"I hate you!" she cried.

I turned away from her then and began to make my way toward the house. She, after a moment, running in her sandals, followed me.

"Jason," she said, "wait! Wait for me!"

But I did not wait.

* * * *

I opened the door and looked within. Then I stepped back, and indicated that she should precede me into the house.

"I expected to heel you into the house," she said.

"You are a free woman," I said. "You will enter first."

She looked at me, warily. "What is to be done with me inside?" she asked.

"You are a woman of Earth," I reminded her. "Nothing."

"Where is the topaz?" she asked.

"What topaz?" I asked.

She cried out in anger, and then entered the house. She would enter first, for she was a free woman.

Nineteen

Glyco, of Port Cos; I Obtain a Silver Tarsk; He Seeks Callimachus

"Stop, Thief!" cried the portly fellow, his robes swirling.

Darting away from him was a small, quick fellow, clutching in his hand a bulging purse, its strap slashed. In the small fellow's right hand there was clutched a dagger. Men stood aside to let the thief run by them.

"Stop him!" cried the portly fellow, stumbling, puffing, trying to pursue the running man.

I watched, a bale of rep fiber on my shoulder, near the rep wharf.

As the running man approached me I lowered the bale of rep fiber and, as he came within feet of me, suddenly slid it before him. He struck the bale and stumbled over it, rolling on the boards. Instantly I was upon him. He slashed at me, on his back, with the knife and I seized his wrist with both hands and yanked him to his feet. He dropped the purse. I spun him about twice by the wrist and then, with this momentum, hurled him into a tower of nail barrels on the side. They cascaded down. I jerked him back, groggy. He was bloody. There were splinters in his tunic and face. I then, with two hands, broke his wrist and kicked the fallen knife to the side. I then turned him about to face me. He looked at me wildly, clutching his wrist. A bone fragment was jutting through it. I then kicked him squarely and he threw back his head, screaming with pain. I then turned him about again and, holding him by the back of the neck, ran him to the edge of the wharf where, seizing his ankle, and holding his neck, I upended him into the water below. He struck out toward the shore, then clambered toward it, getting his feet under him. He screamed twice more. When he stood in about a foot of water, among pilings, near the next wharf, he struck down madly at his legs with his left hand, striking two dock eels from his calf. Then, painfully, he moved himself up the sand, staggering, holding his legs widely apart.

"Where are the guardsmen, to apprehend him?" puffed the portly fellow, who wore the caste colors of the merchants, white and gold.

"There are no guardsmen in Victoria," I said.

"Two copper tarsks, one to each of you," said the merchant to two dock workers who stood nearby, "to apprehend and bind that fellow!"

Swiftly the two dock workers set out after the thief.

Though men stood about none had attempted to steal the purse of the merchant, which lay nearby. Most of those of Victoria are honest fellows.

One of them handed the purse back to the merchant, who thanked him.

"What is your name, Fellow?" asked the merchant of me.

"Jason," I said.

"Of Victoria?" asked the merchant.

"It is here that I am now," I said.

He smiled. Drifters among the river towns are not uncommon. They come from all over Gor. "You have had difficulties with guardsmen?" he asked.

"I had some difficulties with guardsmen in Tancred's Landing and Fina," I admitted.

"I am Glyco," said he, "of the Merchants, of Port Cos. You are a bold fellow. I am grateful for your aid."

"It is nothing," I said.

Whining, the thief was dragged before us by the two dock workers. He was still in great pain. He could scarcely stand. The dock workers had torn off his clothes and, ripping his tunic, had made a rope of twisted cloth, with which they had bound his hands behind his back. They also had him on a short neck leash, also fashioned of twisted cloth, from his tunic. His right hand was bleeding, and his left leg, in two places. The leg seemed gouged. The dock eels, black, about four feet long, are tenacious creatures. They had not relinquished their hold on the flesh in their jaws when they had been forcibly struck away from the leg, back into the water. The thief shrank back from me. The dock workers threw him to his knees before the merchant.

The merchant turned to me. He handed me a silver tarsk from the purse.

"You need give me nothing," I said. "It was not important."

"Take, if you will," said he, "as a token of my gratitude, this silver tarsk."

I took it. "Thank you," I said. Several of the men about, striking their shoulders in the Gorean fashion, applauded the merchant. He had been very generous. A silver tarsk is, to most Goreans, a coin of considerable value. In most exchanges it is valued at a hundred copper tarsks, each of which is valued, commonly, at some ten to twenty tarsk bits. Ten silver tarsks, usually, is regarded as the equivalent of one gold piece, of one of the high cities. To be sure, there is little standardization in these matters, for much depends on the actual weights of the coins and the quantities of precious metals, certified by the municipal stamps, contained in the coins. Sometimes, too, coins are split or shaved. Further, the debasing of coinage is not unknown. Scales, and rumors, it seems, are often used by coin merchants. One of the central coins on Gor is the golden tarn disk of Ar, against which many cities standardize their own gold piece. Other generally respected coins tend to be the silver tarsk of Tharna, the golden tarn disk of Ko-ro-ba, and the golden tarn of Port Kar, the latter particularly on the western Vosk, in the Tamber Gulf region, and a few hundred pasangs north and south of the Vosk's delta.

The merchant then looked at the thief. "I will have him taken to Port Cos," he said, "where there are praetors."

"Please, Master," said the thief, "do not deliver me to praetors!"

"Are you so fond of your hands?" asked the merchant. I noted that the thief's left ear had already been notched. That had doubtless been done elsewhere than in Victoria.

"Please, Master, have mercy on me," begged the thief.

"He has had a rather hard day already," I said, putting in a word on the thief's behalf.

"Let us then just slit his throat now," said a fellow standing nearby.

The thief squirmed. "No," he begged. "No!"

"What do you suggest?" asked the merchant of me.

"Give him to me," I said.

"No, please, Master!" whined the thief to the merchant.

"He is yours," said the merchant.

I yanked the fellow by the neck leash of twisted cloth to his feet. I thrust the silver tarsk into his mouth, so that he could not speak. "Seek a physician," I told him. "Have your wrist attended to. It appears to be broken. Do not be in Victoria by morning." I then turned him about and, hurrying him with a well-placed kick, sent him running, awkwardly, painfully, whimpering and stumbling, from the dock.

"Surely you are a guardsman," said the merchant.

"No," I said.

The men gathered about watched the thief hurrying, bound, away. There was laughter.

"You are magnanimous," said the merchant.

"He was not a woman," I said. "Too, it was not my purse he stole."

The merchant laughed.

I looked after the fleeing fellow, now disappearing between warehouses. I did not think honest folk in Victoria would again find him troublesome.

"One thing more, Fellow," said the merchant. "I am in Victoria on business. I seek one once of Port Cos, a warrior, one whose name is Callimachus."

I was startled to hear this name, for it was the name of he who had saved me, some weeks ago, from the steel of Kliomenes, the pirate.

"At night," said I, "he often drinks at the tavern of Tasdron. You might find him there, I think."

"My thanks, Fellow," said the merchant, and, smiling, turned about and made his way back among the boxes and bales on the crowded wharf.

"Have you no work to do this day," asked the man in whose fee I was that afternoon.

"That I have, Sir," I grinned, and turned again to my labors.

Twenty

The Tavern of Hibron; I Return Home Alone

"Stand back," said the pirate.

Two blades, his, and that of a companion, were leveled at my breast.

"Beverly!" I said. My hand, palm sweating, was poised over the hilt of my sword.

"Make no unfortunate move," said the pirate, he who had spoken to me before.

"Who is that fellow?" asked Beverly, airily. She knelt, in the position of the free woman behind the small table.

"Come home with me now," I said. "I have sought for you long." Returning from the wharves to the house I had not found her on the premises. There had been no sign of forced entry or struggle. Anxious, I had begun to search the public places of Victoria. Then, after two Ahn of searching, I had found her here, near the wharves, unattended, in the tavern of Hibron, a miserable tavern, a low place, called the Pirate's Chain.

"I do not wish to come home with you now," she said, lightly, a bit of Ka-la-na spilling from the silver goblet she held. At a gesture from Kliomenes, who sat, cross-legged, beside her, a half-naked paga slave, whose left ankle was belled, refilled Miss Henderson's cup.

"Come home with me," I said, "you little fool." I felt the points of the two swords, through my tunic, against my flesh.

"If you may pleasure yourself in taverns," she said, "surely so, too, may I."

"Free women," I said, "do not come here. It is too close to the wharves. It is dangerous. This is Gor."

"I am not afraid," she laughed.

"You do not know the danger in which you stand," I said to her.

"May I introduce my new friend," she said, "Kliomenes, a river captain."

"Surely you remember him well," I said. "It was he, and his men, who captured you from Oneander when you were a slave, and sold you."

"Perhaps that was a mistake," said Kliomenes. He grinned at her. She had thrust back the hood of her robes and unpinned her veil. Her face was bared; her hair, darkly brown and silken, cascaded down about her shoulders. These things were not unnoted by the men in the tavern. There was probably not a man there but was wondering how she would look stripped and in a collar.

"That you captured me?" she asked, puzzled.

"No," said he, "that I sold you."

She laughed merrily, and shoved at him, playfully. "Do not insult a free woman, Sleen," she laughed.

There was much laughter, but there was an undercurrent of menace in the laughter which, I think, the girl did not recognize.

"But that sort of thing is behind me now," she said to me, throwing back her head and quaffing deeply of the ruby-red Ka-la-na in her cup. She again looked at me. "Kliomenes is a merchant," she told me. "I am now a free woman. We are met now on different terms. We meet now as equals. He is really a nice man, and my friend."

"Come with me now," I said to her. "Come home with me, now."

"I do not wish to do so," she said.

Kliomenes again gestured to the half-naked slave, with the belled ankle, that she refill the girl's cup. The slave did so, deferentially, smiling. Her hair had been cut short. There was a steel collar on her neck.

"Come home with me, now," I said to the girl.

"Kliomenes is buying me a drink," she said. "He is a gentleman, and a true man."

"I did not know she was yours," said Kliomenes, amused. "That is delightful."

"I am not his!" said the girl. "I am a free woman!"

"Are you his companion?" asked Kliomenes.

"No!" she said.

"Is she your wench slave?" asked Kliomenes.

"No," I said, angrily.

"I share his quarters," she said, angrily. "We are not even friends."

"Are you concerned for her?" asked Kliomenes, amused.

"I wish her to return home with me now," I said.

"But she does not wish to do so," he smiled. "Do you wish to go with him now?" he asked.

"No," she said, snuggling against him.

"You see?" asked Kliomenes.

"I am a free woman, in all respects," she said, "and may, and will, do precisely as I please."

"You have heard the lady," said Kliomenes, putting his arm about her shoulders.

"Kliomenes, meet Jason," she said. "Jason, meet Kliomenes."

Kliomenes inclined his head, amused.

"We have met," I said. I remembered the tavern of Tasdron. I would presumably have been slain there had it not been for the intervention of the derelict, Callimachus, once a warrior of Port Cos.

"Begone, Buffoon," said Kliomenes, not pleasantly. I felt again the points of the swords of the two pirates at my chest.

"Begone, Buffoon," laughed the girl.

"Have no fear," grinned Kliomenes. "I will see that she is taken care of properly." There was laughter in the tavern.

"Begone, Buffoon!" laughed the girl.

"Unless," said Kliomenes, rising to his feet, "you care to meet me with steel."

My hand, wet with sweat, fingers moving against one another, opened and shut at the hilt of the sword I wore.

Kliomenes looked at me, grinning.

"Please, Master," said Hibron, the proprietor of that low tavern, "I do not wish trouble. Please, Master!"

I turned about, angrily, and strode from the tavern. There were tears of fury, of helpless rage, in my eyes. I knew myself no match for Kliomenes, or the others. I did not even know the first uses of the steel which I wore at my hip. As I left the tavern I heard the laughter of Kliomenes and his men behind me, and the laughter, too, of the girl.

Outside the tavern I paused, fists clenched. I heard Kliomenes, within, call out. "More wine for the Lady Beverly, the free woman!" There was laughter. "Yes, Master," I heard the slave with the wine vessel say, and heard the sensuous ring of the bells locked on her ankle as she hastened to comply.

I then returned home. I waited late for the return of Beverly. In the morning I went as usual to the hiring yard. When I returned home that night she had still not arrived, nor, again, by the next morning.

Twenty One

I Hear the Ringing of an Alarm Bar; I am Not Accompanied to the Wharves

"Forget her, Master," whispered Peggy. She lifted her head from the furs, and kissed me. There was a tiny rustle of chain and collar. She was fastened by the neck to a ring at the back of the alcove. It had pleased me to so secure her this evening.

"I have," I said.

Peggy laughed. "I am a slave," she said, "but do not think we are stupid."

"I have never thought that," I smiled.

I supposed there were stupid slaves, but I did not think them abundant. Most female slaves I had encountered on Gor, whether natively Gorean or of Earth origin, had impressed me as being sensitive and intelligent, as well as feminine and beautiful. And, too, in time, as the slave fires began to burn in their bellies, they became helplessly, needfully, passionate. I think that I have already, earlier, given some general indications as to the sort of criteria apparently used by Gorean slavers in, as it is sometimes said, harvesting from the slave fields of Earth. Another saying pertinent in these matters, which is occasionally heard, is "picking fruit from the slave orchards of Earth." Certainly many women of Earth, fallen to the slave noose or net, seem to have been taken as easily as one might consider, select and pick excellent fruit, luscious fruit, simply waiting to be picked, from the sweet, fragrant branches of an unguarded orchard. One might mention in passing that some Goreans find it difficult to believe that the Earth girls brought to Gor were not already collared on Earth. How could such a woman, so feminine and beautiful, not have been a slave? Surely the men of Earth are not such fools as to allow such desirability out of their collars? Do they not wish to own them? And if they do wish to own them, why do they not do so? A second reason has to do with the readiness of the Earth girl for bondage, and her gratitude for the collar. At last she is provided for, and protected, and comforted, and loved. At last she can be in the arms of a true man. She loves what she is, and her master. Choiceless, she obeys and strives to please. She is sexually and psychologically fulfilled in ways unthinkable on her more artificial world. She is owned, and dominated, and treasured. She is subject to the whip and chains, and loves it. She knows that she has value, and is admired by men, and even lusted for, and that she is envied, and even hated, by free women. She thrives in the culture. She can now be a true woman as she now has, at last, a true master. The third reason is a more Gorean reason; it is that many, perhaps most, slave raids, as opposed to major attacks on cities, have as their principal object not the acquisition of free women, who are commonly well protected, but rather of slaves. Thus, some Goreans, denied what is called "the second knowledge," who do not realize that Earth is a different planet, but think of it rather as simply some remote district, suppose that "girls from Earth" are simply slave booty similar to that obtained in other far places, all on their own world. Gorean, for example, is not spoken on all parts of Gor. On the other hand, as Earth women in Gorean markets have become more familiar and numerous, most Goreans have come to accept that their origin is a different world. Certainly Earth women are seldom whipped today for lying about their antecedents, which, I fear, may have been too frequently the case in the past. How they have come to Gor, of course, remains largely mysterious to most Goreans, and often, at least in detail, to the girls themselves. Some Goreans, interestingly, but understandably enough, unaware of the absence of an adequate atmosphere between worlds, as were most intellectuals of Earth for centuries, as well, suppose simply, and naturally enough, that these new crops of slave beasts have been brought in lashed in tarn baskets, or chained to saddle rings, or perhaps strapped naked, supine and arched, across saddles, before the bold raiders who have taken them. That is often the way slaves are transported between camps and cities. Between geographical points, of course, long coffles, sometimes pasangs in length, are not uncommon. In these the girls are usually marched naked, in single file, chained together by the neck, under the surveillance of armed guards. Dalliance is discouraged by means of long-bladed whips and the prodding and striking of reversed lances. After such a journey, a destination of slave pens and auction blocks is joyously welcomed. Will each woman, sooner or later, in one sale or another, passing through various hands, sometimes many, find the master of her dreams? It is not known.

"You have not forgotten her," said Peggy.

"No," I said.

"But you should," she said.

"Perhaps," I said.

"Then do so," she said.

"It is hard to forget the little slut," I said.

"It is well known in Victoria, how she betrayed you," said Peggy.

"Where did you hear that?" I asked. "And am I, only a dock worker, known in Victoria?" I looked at her.

"Tasdron spoke of it in the tavern to free men," she said, "and I, and other slaves, overheard him speak."

I supposed there was little in Victoria that was not known to its nude or half-clad tavern slaves. Such girls, in spite of their collars, often know more of what transpires in a town or city than many free folk.

"Doubtless I am a laughing stock in Victoria," I said, bitterly.

"No, Master," she said. "But it is true that many are puzzled as to why you did not, at that time, make her your total slave."

I said nothing.

"You are known and respected in Victoria," she said. "You are known for your ability with your fists, a thing which Gorean men can understand, and for your work on the docks, and for your strength."

"Is it also known how I withdrew from the tavern of Hibron, the Pirate's Chain, when I sought there the Lady Beverly?" I asked.

"You call the little slut a lady?" she asked.

I looked at her, sternly.

"Forgive me, Master," she smiled, "but I saw her in the restaurant, on Earth. I assure you that she is as much, or more, a slut than I, and as fully worthy as I, or perhaps even more worthy than I, for the degrading circlet of bondage."

I looked up, lying on my back, at the low ceiling of the alcove.

"Yes," she smiled, "it is well known in Victoria what occurred in the tavern of Hibron, but none blame you. You are not the master of the sword and even had you been, you were grievously outnumbered. None blame you, I assure you. Indeed, many feel you were courageous to have even entered the tavern under the circumstances, to attempt to extract the unwitting little fool from the situation in which she had placed herself."

"I did not fight," I said.

"You had no choice," she said.

"I withdrew," I said.

"You had no choice," she said.

"I am a coward," I said.

"That is not true," she said. "In such a situation only a master swordsman, or a fool or a madman, would have fought."

"I see," I said.

"A wise man would have withdrawn, as you did," she said.

"Or a coward," I said.

"You are not a coward," she said. "Glyco, the merchant of Port Cos, has spoken freely of your bravery on the wharves, in your recovery of his purse."

"Oh," I said.

"And the thief, Grat, the Swift, who has long been a nuisance in Victoria, has fled the town, obedient to your command."

"That is interesting," I said. I had not even known his name.

"There are even those who say there should be guardsmen in Victoria, and that you should be chief among them," she said.

I laughed. The thought of a guardsman who did not even know the sword was an amusing one.

We were silent for a time.

"The stronghold of Policrates is impregnable," she said.

"You are an intelligent woman," I said.

"Do not attempt it," she said.

I was silent. I had, I knew, the means whereby I might, if I wished, gain admission to that dark, rearing fortress, the walled river cove at its base.

"Forget her, Master," advised Peggy.

"I have seen Glyco, of Port Cos, in the tavern," I said. "He had wished to see Callimachus, once of Port Cos. I have seen them more than once, on various nights, engaged in converse, Glyco earnest, and Callimachus sullen and noncommittal."

"It is true," said Peggy.

"Of what do they speak?" I asked.

"I do not know, Master," said Peggy. "We girls are warned away from their table, save when we are called forth to serve, and then they remain silent, except to give us our commands."

"How long is Glyco to remain in Victoria?" I asked.

"I do not know, Master," she said. "Perhaps he is gone now, for he has not been tonight, to my knowledge, in the tavern." Peggy fingered the chain dangling from her collar. "Master seems curious," she said.

"I would like to know the business of Glyco with Callimachus," I said.

"I will tell you one thing I know," she said. "Glyco stays with the guardsmen of Port Cos, near the wharves."

"Not in an inn?" I asked.

"No," she said.

"Interesting," I said.

"And it is said, too," she whispered, coming close to me, the chain on her neck touching my chest, as she put her head over me, "that Glyco is not only a merchant but stands high in the merchant council of Port Cos."

"I wonder what such a man is doing in Victoria, speaking with Callimachus," I said.

"I do not know, Master," she said. Then, suddenly, she pressed her softness against me, in a slave girl's piteous need. "I am only a slave, permitted to live on the sufferance of men, that she may please them," she said.

I then took her in my arms.

* * * *

Later we lay quietly, softly, together. Her head was at my waist.

I again looked at the ceiling of the alcove, at the roughened texture, and the tiny cracks, of its plaster and wood, reddish in the flickering light of the tiny lamp.

"Is Master distracted?" she asked.

"Perhaps," I said.

"You still remember her, do you not?" she asked.

"Perhaps," I said. I put my hand, with rough gentleness, in her hair, holding it.

"You have well ravished me, Master," she whispered.

"You are a responsive wench," I said.

"I cannot help but be responsive in your arms," she said.

"You merely fear the whip," I smiled.

"I do fear the whip," she said, "and I know that it will be well laid upon me at the merest suspicion on the part of Tasdron, my Master, that a customer may not have been fully pleased, but even if it were not for the whip, I know I could not help but respond to you as a vulnerable and spasmodic slave."

I released her hair and took her again in my arms, throwing the chain back over her shoulder.

"What woman would not be a slave in your arms?" she asked. "I beg to be had again."

"Very well," I said, and then, lengthily, contented her.

It is pleasing to have a female slave.

* * * *

"The stronghold of Policrates is impregnable," she said. "Forget her."

"How is it that you know what I am thinking?" I asked, smiling.

"Slave girls must pay close attention to men," she smiled, "for they are her masters."

I smiled. It was true. Slave girls are extremely sensitive to the moods, the feelings and thoughts of men. They must be, for they are their masters.

"By now she doubtless wears the steel loops of a pirate's pleasure girl," she said.

I thought this not unlikely.

"You have money," said Peggy. "Buy another girl, one to lick your feet and content you."

Slave girls tend to speak openly and honestly. They are under few delusions as to the desires of men. Hypocrisies are not encouraged in them, as they often are in their free sisters. Similarly Gorean men tend on the whole, unabashedly, to be perfectly frank about such matters. What true man, in his vitality, does not want a beautiful woman as a slave? Two major differences between the men of Earth and the men of Gor are, first, that the men of Gor are perfectly straightforward and open about this and, secondly, that such women may normally be purchased at a modest price in a convenient market. On Gor the order of nature, as old as the switch, the rope, the cave and the raid, has never been denied.

She put her lips close to my ear. I heard the tiny, heavy sound of the links of the chain, moving against one another, depending from her collar. "Buy Peggy, if you wish," she whispered.

"Do you wish me to buy you?" I asked.

"I would rather be purchased by only one other man on all Gor," she said, "and he has never even had me. He scarcely notices me and seems not even to know I exist. Yet I almost faint with joy at the very thought of serving him."

I looked at her. She was very beautiful.

"I am unworthy even to think of him," she said. "I am only an Earth woman, and a branded slave."

"Who is he?" I asked.

"Please do not make me speak his name, Master," she said.

"Very well," I said.

We lay together quietly, for a time, not speaking. We could hear conversation outside, from the floor of the tavern.

"Have you heard more of the topaz?" I asked.

"No, Master," she said. "But it is thought to be in Victoria."

"The men of Victoria," I said, "seem adamant in refusing to pay the tribute to Policrates."

"Yes, Master," she smiled.

I thought this was courageous on their part, but I did not know if it were wise. It had been the first time in five years that this had happened. The last time the pirates of the dark stronghold had carried fire and sword to a dozen wharfed ships. The tribute, then, had been rapidly forthcoming. To be sure, in the past years the pirates had become more and more dependent on the markets of Victoria to dispose of their loot and captures. In the light of this many in Victoria regarded themselves as having at last attained a position in which they might succeed in evading the humiliating burdens of tribute.

"Master is kind to spare my feelings," said Peggy.

I smiled. I had not pressed her on the matter of he whose collar she longed to wear.

"Put her from your mind," whispered Peggy. "There are many lovely women in the markets. Buy one. Put her in your collar. Teach her with the whip who it is to whom she belongs. Make her yours."

I looked up at the low ceiling.

"Is she so special to you because she is from Earth, or because you knew her from Earth?" she asked.

"I do not know," I said.

"Is that why you cannot forget her?" she asked. "Is that why you are so concerned about her?"

"I do not know," I said.

"There must be hundreds of girls from Earth, perhaps some thousands, who wear their collars on Gor," she said.

"Yes," I said. "That is doubtless true."

"What, then, is so special about her?" she asked.

"I do not know," I said.

"Imagine a wall," she said, "of eight feet in height, of heavy stone, a hundred yards in length. Imagine, too, a hundred women, beautiful, and stripped, chained helplessly to this wall. It is, of course, a market wall. In the company of a slaver, their owner, you examine these women. Each, in her chains, kneels before you, and begs you to buy her. One of these women is the girl we shall call Beverly. But you have never seen her before. Which of all of these women would you buy?"

I looked at her.

"Which, of all these women," she asked, "would you have released from the wall? On the throat of which, of all of them, would you lock your inflexible collar. On the wrists of which, of all of them, would you lock your unyielding slave bracelets. Which, of all of them, would you lead home, as your slave?"

"She," I said, "the one whom we might call Beverly."

"Ah," said Peggy, drawing back, "I fear she is your love slave."

"She is too fine to be a slave," I said, "let alone the most complete of slaves, the total and utterly abject love slave."

"Even if it should be what she wants most deeply, in her deepest heart?" asked Peggy.

"Of course," I said, angrily.

"But what if she is a slave," asked Peggy, "in reality a true slave?"

"It does not matter," I said.

"Surely you have recognized Gorean women can be slaves, and have treated them accordingly," said Peggy.

"Yes," I said.

"And surely you have recognized some Earth women can be slaves, and have treated them accordingly," she said.

"Yes," I said. I looked at Peggy. She blushed deeply, and smiled. I had often treated her, thoroughly and completely, as the mere slave she was.

"How then," asked Peggy, softly, smiling, "is this other woman different?"

"She is different," I said, angrily.

"Can you admit the possibility that she might not be different?" asked Peggy.

"No," I said. "No!"

"Why not?" asked Peggy.

"Then she would be only a slave," I said, angrily.

"But if this is what she is, and what fulfills her, and makes her joyful?" she asked.

"It does not matter," I said, angrily.

"The nature of the woman, and her fulfillment and joy, does not matter to you?" she asked.

I was silent. I was furious.

"Do you not, honestly, want her in your chains?" asked Peggy.

"The first instant I saw her," I said, "I wanted her in my chains." Peggy kissed me.

"But I must put such thoughts from my head," I said, bitterly.

"Why?" she asked.

"I do not know," I said.

"Nature is harsh, but it is not so terrible, truly," she said.

"I must go," I said.

"It is not yet even the Twentieth Ahn, Master," she said. Swiftly she knelt beside me, head down. "Have I displeased Master?" she asked.

"No," I said, smiling, looking up at her.

"Dare to become Gorean, Master," she said, "please."

"Perhaps," I said.

Swiftly she nestled down beside me, holding me. She did not want me to leave the alcove.

"Thank you for talking with a mere slave," she whispered.

"Why do you not simply place yourself on your belly before he whose collar you wish to wear," I asked, "and with tears, kissing his feet, implore him to buy you."

"I dare not," she said. "I am only a low slave, and an Earth woman."

"I see," I said.

"He might be offended, and slay me, or Tasdron, my master, discovering my crime, might slay me, for my insolence."

"I see," I said.

"And so I must see him daily," she said, "and cannot reveal in the least my feelings for him, beyond those of the silken slave who must serve any man who can afford the price of a cup of her master's paga."

I put my arm about the girl.

"You see, Master," she said, "we are not so different. You have lost your slave, and I cannot even permit myself to be found by my master."

I kissed her, softly.

She began to sob in my arms, and I held her gently, closely. She looked up at me, with tears in her eyes.

"It is hard being a slave girl," I told her.

"Yes, Master," she said. "Master," she said.

"Yes," I said.

"Please have me, with gentleness, Master," she begged, "though I am a slave."

"Very well, Slave," I said.

"Thank you, Master," she said, softly.

* * * *

She lay beside me. She fingered the chain depending from her collar. "I love being chained," she said.

"Chains are useful in impressing her slavery on a woman," I said.

"They leave little doubt in her mind so as to who is master," she smiled.

I did not respond. What she said, however, was doubtless true. The effect of a chain, or a rope, on a woman's sexuality is sometimes incredible. This is particularly true with the new slave girl. With the older slave girl, one who has already learned something of the meaning of her collar, a mere snapping of the fingers or a small, imperious gesture can have a similarly devastating, triggering effect on her sexuality. The readiness and excitability, indeed, the almost helpless sexual vulnerability of the slave girl, is something for which the men of Earth, whose experience has been limited to the free females of Earth, are totally unprepared. It commonly takes fifteen to twenty minutes to bring a free Earth female to orgasm. A slave girl, on the other hand, whether Gorean or an embonded Earth girl, finding herself on Gor, once trained and understanding, fully, her condition, will often find herself on the brink of orgasm, simply finding her master's eyes casually upon her. The differences, of course, are almost entirely psychological. Sexuality, as is well known, is almost entirely a function of the imagination and brain. The slave girl knows that she is a slave, truly, and that passion is not only permitted to her but required of her. Indeed, she may be whipped or slain if she is insufficiently passionate. Her sexual needs are thus liberated. Frightened, she often begins by acting, and this is known to the master, but soon, perhaps to her horror, she discovers that she, obedient to the master's touch, and no longer acting, and this, too, is known to the master, has become, truly, suddenly, a yielding, spasmodic slave. Too, of course, her slavery and her sexuality is impressed upon her in a thousand, subtle ways. Certain modes of speech are expected of her and certain gestures and postures. She must, for example, address free persons deferentially and, commonly, will kneel in their presence. Her garb, too, is commonly distinctive; it is usually inexpensive and brief; sometimes it is only a rag; it is designed to remind her of lowliness; it is designed, too, of course, generally, to leave little doubt as to her charms. Needless to say, too, her throat is encircled by a collar, which will identify her master; sometimes, too, the collar will bear the name by which he has decided to call her; and her thigh, or some other part of her body, will be branded. She is an animal, sensuous and beautiful, marked as property, and has a name only on the sufferance of her master; he need not even give her a name, if he does not wish to do so. Beyond this, of course, she finds herself in the Gorean civilization. It is a complex, vital, bright, colorful, deeply sensuous civilization; it is a harsh, gorgeous world in which the slave girl has a special role and place; her condition is unquestioned and categorical; it is supported by history, by custom and law; there is absolutely no escape for her; she is slave. Accordingly, an animal and property, without even a name in her own right, she kneels before her master; she waits to be commanded.

"I love it when you are strong with me," said Peggy. She lay beside me, on her elbow, the chain dangling from her collar.

"You are a woman," I said.

"I despise weak men," she said. "I respect only men who will treat me as a woman, and do with me what they please. I know I am a woman. I want to be treated as one. How can I take my place in the order of nature if men will not treat me as they wish? That is what I want, to be treated, even with insolence, as men wish. Only then can I know them as my master, and yield to them in my fullness."

"Before," I said, "you wished to be taken with gentleness."

"And you did so," she said. "That was then my mood, and I am grateful that you deigned to respect it."

"Sometimes I might not," I said.

"I know, Master," she said. "And then later," she said, "when your appetites grew again upon you, you took me as a mere slave, with brutality."

"You yielded well," I said.

"I could not help myself, Master," she said.

She then lay beside me, and began to kiss at my arm. She took my arm in her two hands, kissing it. "You are strong," she whispered.

I did not respond.

"Master," she whispered.

"Yes," I said.

"Have Peggy again. Peggy begs it."

"Perhaps," I said. "Perhaps not."

She whimpered, and put her head against my arm.

I supposed that it was not surprising that women reduced to bondage, collared and branded, denied by the strictures of their condition the mockeries of male imitation, and finding the impediments to the manifestation of their deepest and most secret nature removed, should gradually find themselves more and more at the mercy of their needs.

I found this amusing, perhaps because I had come from Earth. How humiliating for an Earth girl, in particular, I thought, to discover that she now had, ignited within her, deep, feminine needs, for the satisfaction of which she found herself dependent on masters. This aspect of the sexuality of the female slave, her need as well as her responsiveness, would also be found astonishing by the men of Earth, accustomed only to the suppressed dispositions and conditioned inertnesses of the women with which he is familiar. It is not unusual for a slave girl to kneel, head down, before even a hated master, and beg his touch. Slavers, not unoften, deprive a female slave of a man's touch for two or three days before her sale. She then, almost invariably, brings a higher price. Her need, manifested in her piteous display of herself, in her physical attitudes, her gestures and expressions, is evident and often arousing, to the buyers. How many women of Earth, I wondered, strip themselves slowly before a man and then kneel before him, and kiss his feet, and then, looking up, beg him for his touch. Perhaps only those who are slave girls.

"You are chained," I said.

"Yes, Master," she said.

I took Peggy's chain in my hand and jerked it, lightly but firmly. She felt the chain, then, pull at the snug collar and jerk it against the back of her neck.

"You are truly chained," I said.

"Yes, Master," she said.

"Why are you chained?" I asked.

"It pleased Master to chain me," she said. She kissed me. "Please, Master," she said, "have your chained slave."

"Perhaps," I said. "Perhaps not."

She sobbed in frustration, and continued to kiss me.

Even with girls used to slavery, who have well learned their collars, of course, the chain never loses its meaning. Masters commonly use it, even with experienced girls. It never loses its effect.

"Please, Master," she sobbed.

"Be silent," I said.

"Yes, Master," she said, sobbing.

Sometimes a slave girl must be struck away from one's feet. Sometimes she must be chained to one side, to a wall or in a corner.

I laughed.

"Master?" she asked.

I then took her in my arms and threw her, roughly, beneath me.

She cried out with pleasure.

* * * *

"What is that sound?" I asked.

"You make a slave very happy, Master," she said, snuggled beside me.

"Do you not hear it?" I asked.

"I hear conversation, the clink of goblets from the floor of the tavern," she said.

"Sandals!" I suddenly snapped.

A Gorean command need not be repeated. Peggy, startled, wild-eyed, rose to her knees and seized my sandals. I stood up, bending over in the low alcove. I pulled on my tunic. She thrust the sandals to her lips, kissing them. "Master?" she asked. She placed the sandals on my feet, thonging them tightly. I buckled my belt, with its dependent pouch. I slung the sword belt, with its attached scabbard, with its sheathed steel, over my left shoulder. "Master?" asked Peggy.

"Can you not hear it?" I asked.

She finished tying the sandals. As she knotted each she kissed the knot, and then, when finished with both, put her head to my feet in a graceful gesture of submission. Tying his sandals, and often thusly, is a small, homely service often performed by the slave girl for her master. Then she looked up at me, puzzled.

"Now," I said, "cannot you hear it?"

"The conversation has stopped on the floor of the tavern," she said, frightened. "It is quiet there."

"Listen," I said.

"I hear it!" she said. "What is it?"

"It is an alarm bar," I said. "It is coming from the wharves."

"What does it mean?" she asked.

I began to unbuckle the leather curtains of the alcove, swiftly. "I do not know," I said.

"Where are you going?" she asked.

"To the wharves," I said.

"Do not go!" she said.

I threw back the curtains. I looked back at her. She knelt frightened, on the furs, the chain on her neck. "Do not go!" she begged.

I turned about and made my way rapidly through the tables. I heard her sob and jerk at the chain in frustration but it, of course, held her, perfectly. The men among whom I strode had not risen to their feet. None met my eyes. None volunteered to accompany me.

"Do not go," advised Tasdron.

I did not answer him, but left the tavern and then, running, made my way toward the wharves.

Twenty Two

What Occurred at the Wharves; What Occurred in the Vicinity of the Tavern of Tasdron

"Stand back, lest you be hurt!" cried a man.

I was seized by two men, citizens, and dragged back into the encircling crowd. I was bleeding. My tunic was cut. The sword of the pirate, in a drunken swing, had grazed my chest. Other citizens, with ship poles, of the sort used on Gorean galleys in casting off and thrusting from the wharves, pressed back the crowd. I felt the side of the pole against my belly. I was jostled by the crowd. The pirate turned away, laughing.

"Where are the guardsmen of Port Cos?" I asked. "Where are the guardsmen of Ar's Station?" There were several guardsmen, from each of these towns, in Victoria.

There was smoke in the air. Five warehouses, and some ancillary buildings were afire.

"They maintain their posts," said a man, grimly. "They protect their own headquarters."

"Victoria is not their concern," said another, bitterly.

I watched the pirates, perhaps some fifty or sixty of them, unchallenged, moving between warehouses and the wharves, where two pirate galleys were moored. Some townsfolk, at swordpoint, were loading goods onto the galleys. Some of the pirates bore torches.

"The tribute will be paid by morning," said one of the men near me.

I saw several of the pirates with bottles of paga, swilling from them, as they strutted about, sometimes pausing to cut into a bale of goods or overturn a barrel, kicking it open, permitting its contents to run out, over the boards.

The alarm bar continued to ring futilely. The pirates made no effort to stop the desperate fellow who, meaninglessly, continued to strike it.

"We outnumber them fifty to one," I said. "Let me rush upon them. Let us stop them!"

"They are the masters in Victoria," said a man. "Do nothing rash."

I heard a woman scream and saw her, thrown over the shoulder of a laughing pirate, a brawny fellow, being carried to one of the galleys.

"What will be done with her?" whispered a woman, near me, terrified.

"If she is beautiful," said a man near us, "perhaps she will be kept to serve in the stronghold of Policrates. If she is not, perhaps her throat will be cut."

The woman gasped, her hand at her veil.

The pirate threw the woman to his feet near the nearest galley and there stripped her and handed her to a comrade who stood on board the galley. He put her on the outside of the railing, facing outwards, with the small of her back tightly against it, her arms hooked over it, and behind it, as with the others. He then, with a length of binding fiber, running tight across her belly, fastened her wrists together, as he had similarly those of the others. All were well displayed. Too, the exposition of captures in this way tends to discourage retaliatory missile fire from the scene of the pillaging.

The woman was comely. I did not think she would have her throat cut. Lusty men have better uses to which to put such women. I did think, however, that they would soon, all the captures, be marked and put in collars.

"If I were you," said the man near the woman in the crowd, "I would draw back in the crowd and hide. Then I would flee."

"But I am free," she said.

"So, too, were they," said the man, angrily, gesturing to the bound woman at the railing of the pirate galley.

She shrank back, suddenly frightened.

I saw Kliomenes, some seventy yards away, directing his men and the enforced laborers, citizens of Victoria, loading the galleys.

"You there, Female," called a pirate, his eye roaming the crowd, "step forth!"

The men holding the ship's pole, frightened, lowered it.

"Step forth!" said the pirate.

The woman shook her head, pressing back against the men.

"Unhood her, face-strip her," ordered the pirate.

"Protect me, save me, please," she begged.

Her hood was thrust back. Her veil was torn away. She was lovely. The price she would bring would be good. I wondered why such a woman would come to the wharves in a time of such danger. Surely she must have understood the peril to which she would be exposing herself.

"Step forth, Beauty," said the pirate.

Numbly, she approached him. I made to move, but two men restrained me.

Swiftly, before us all, in the light of the flames, was the woman stripped by the pirate's blade.

"Lie down," said he.

She hesitated, and looked at him in anguish. "Or do you wish to be slit like a larma?" he asked. His sword jabbed into the sweet roundedness of her belly.

Swiftly, then, she lay at his feet, her back on the harsh, tarred boards.

The pirate then looked at us, and laughed. "Here, at my feet, supine, stripped, is a free woman of Victoria. Do any of you dispute her with me?" Two men restrained me. No others moved.

"Kneel," he ordered the woman. She did so.

He then placed the point of his blade against her fair throat.

Numbly, slowly, lifting her arms, the blade between her arms, her fingers trembling, she tied the bondage knot in her own hair. She looked at him. "Please, spare me, Master," she said.

For a long moment or two the point of the blade remained at her throat, as the pirate considered the girl's plea. I saw his eye roam her now-embonded curves.

He laughed. He thrust his blade back in its sheath. She almost fainted with relief.

"On your feet!" he said. "Run to the nearest galley! Beg to be displayed there, as the loot you are!"

"Yes, Master!" she cried and, leaping up, fled toward the galley, a commanded slave.

"We do what we wish with Victoria," said the pirate. "Do any of you gainsay me?" None spoke. He then laughed again, and, turning about, went back toward the galleys.

I watched the new slave being bound at the railing, with the others.

"I say she wanted the collar," said a man.

"They all do," said another.

They did not know, of course, a woman such as Miss Beverly Henderson.

She could not be a slave.

But what, I asked myself, if she were, in her secret heart, as Alison, in Ar, and Peggy, in Victoria, both themselves surely slaves, had claimed, a true slave? If she were she had made a great fool of me, in pretending to be free, in being often displeasing, in daring to sell Lola, in attempting to betray me to the guardsmen of Port Cos, in disparaging me in the tavern of Hibron. What if she were a slave? Could she be truly a slave? The very thought almost made me wish to cry out with fury and pleasure. If she were a slave I would find this out. And then, somehow, against all obstacles, I would make her mine, mine own. I would own her, nor would I be gentle with the slave. She owed me much. Yes, I vowed, if she were a slave, I would have her in my collar! And she would soon then well know herself a slave! I would treat her, the desirable little slut, and slave, with a ruthlessness and a power that would become legendary in Victoria!

I then could no longer deny it. I wanted Miss Beverly Henderson— and in the fullest and most perfect way a man could want a woman— as a slave! I wanted her to be mine, to be owned by me, to be my actual property, socially, culturally, legally, to be mine completely, mine to command, mine to do with as I pleased, mine to buy and sell, to give away, if I chose. This was not Earth, with its negativities, confusions, refusals, entanglements and hypocrisies! This was not Earth. This world was no stranger to the glories and honesties of human nature. This was not Earth. This was a different world, a brighter, fresher world, a healthier, more vigorous, more virile, more natural world. This was Gor, Gor! Here the equations of dominance and submission were not denied. Here ancient winds blew uncurtailed. Here lambs did not legislate for lions. On a world such as this, a natural world, a woman such as Miss Beverly Henderson might well be found on her knees in a man's collar. I recalled her from Earth, from the university, from the restaurant. How unnatural she then seemed in such purlieus.

Perhaps she belonged on Gor, stripped and collared.

I thought of her.

Could it be, I wondered, that she might be a slave, truly?

And, if so, what ought, in the claimant justice of biology and truth, to be her disposition?

But, of course, she, of Earth, could not be a slave!

Not she!

I recalled her.

How unhappy she had been on Earth!

How absurd and piteous had been her attempts to conform to imposed stereotypes so heinously alien to her nature. How zealously earnest she had been to dress in certain ways and behave in certain ways, to deny her beauty and its meaning, how desperately she had tried to live up to ideological strictures foreign to her needs; how pathetically she had dutifully repeated slogans; how sincerely she had tried to believe lies; how blindly she had tried to convince herself that axiological toxins were salubrious nourishment, how dutifully she had attempted to subscribe to the views of others, with self-serving agendas, not herself. How she had feared to listen to her blood, and her heart. How powerful are the forces of socialization! How rare the individual who has the intelligence and strength to examine inflicted orthodoxies! How few can detect the subtle encompassing walls, let alone break or scale them. The shaping of heads and the bindings of feet, such gross interferences with nature, are common knowledge; but the shapings and bindings of minds, even more hideous, seems seldom detected.

I recalled her.

She had gone about her business, and studies, and such, on Earth, trying so seriously to conform to political and social pressures, fearing not to, being anxious to dress as required, to think as required, to feel as required, trying fearfully to please others who regarded her softness and femininity as a reproach, or threat, others who despised her.

But even those garments, and those attitudes, however desperately presented, or brandished, could not conceal the woman of her.

I had not seen her, despite her best efforts, as a neuterized embodiment of a prescribed ideology. Who could have done so? Perhaps that was why she had been so looked down upon, and scorned, by gross, dogmatic peers. I had seen her as I wanted to see her, as she was, not as she wished to be seen, not as she pretended she was. I had seen her, despite all, as a young, attractive woman, a beautiful, desirable young female, the sort to be enfolded naked, lovingly, helplessly, in a man's arms.

That was, of course, politically inappropriate. But then that is one of the inconveniences of nature, that it can upon occasion prove a political embarrassment. On Earth politics and nature do not live in the same house, and, indeed, nature does not live in a house at all. It is outside the house, like the land, and space, and stars. Those who prefer to stay indoors need not ask what lies outside the house. Let them stay indoors, if they wish; but, too, let them not interfere with those whose destiny calls them to the greater, beckoning, healthful, sunlit world outside.

I recalled the lovely, preoccupied, fearful, inhibited, conforming Miss Henderson.

I doubt that she knew how she was looked at.

Could she have even understood it?

Did she know how she was looked at, could she have suspected it, that she was looked at, despite her prescribed garmenture, despite her ideology and views, her smugness, her vaunted pride, as a woman is looked at by a man?

Had I not a thousand times, in my mind, seeing her in the corridors, on the campus, on the streets, unbeknownst to her, conjectured her luscious lineaments; had I not a thousand times, noting her in a thousand places, in my mind, had her revealed to me, and collared? And now the lovely, vain, pretentious, troublesome Miss Henderson was no longer on Earth. She, as I, was on Gor. And she, such as she was, was accordingly subject to the risks, and appropriatenesses, of that world.

It is very different from Earth.

I considered her.

Much pain had she caused me.

But there are remedies, and compensations, for such things, the remedy of the mastery, for example, and the compensations of plenteous labors and services, and inordinate pleasures derived from the erstwhile pain object. A free woman can be a source of inconvenience and annoyance, even of intolerable agony; a slave, on the other hand, is an object of utility and gratification.

I thought Miss Henderson, taken well in hand, would make an excellent slave.

Too, from a thousand indications, even on Earth, I suspected, despite myself, that she might be a natural slave, a woman who belonged in the collar.

So why then should she not be in mine?

But something in my heart cried out that she, the lovely Miss Henderson, could not be a slave, not she!

I must deny it!

Was she not from Earth, from Earth?

But I could no longer deny one thing—that I wanted Miss Beverly Henderson, that I wanted to own her. To own her, literally. I wanted her—as my slave.

But perhaps she was not a slave?

It was important to determine that.

She was, after all, from Earth.

But if she were a slave, it was in the collar of no one other than myself that I wanted her.

On Earth slaves are free; on Gor they are not.

So it was important to learn what she was.

Was she a slave?

That must be determined.

If she should be a slave, it was right that she should be in the collar. And if she was a slave, I wanted her for my own.

I could no longer deny it. I wanted Miss Beverly Henderson as my slave.

But, alas, could she, from Earth, be a slave?

But what if all women were slaves?

If all women were slaves, so, too, then, would be the lovely Miss Henderson.

Do all women belong in collars?

The Goreans have a saying that all women are slaves, only that some are not yet in collars.

If Miss Henderson were truly a slave, if she truly belonged in the collar, I wanted her.

She had caused me much grief. I had many scores to settle with the beauty.

In my collar she would be in no doubt as to her bondage. I would see that she gave me everything, and more.

It would be pleasant to have her at my feet, as I wanted her, as my helpless, abject slave.

If I thought it in the least helpful, or if it pleased me on even an idle whim, she would instantly learn the bite of the whip.

I would teach her to crawl, and beg, and please.

I would have all from her, and more!

She would learn what bondage was, and being in the keeping of a master.

It would be pleasant, after Earth, and all this time, to own her.

I did not think I would soon sell one such as she.

"We will pay the tribute in the morning," said another man.

"We have no choice," said another.

"We should never have entered into difficulties over the matter," said another man.

"True," said another man.

The smoke stung my eyes. The man had, by now, stopped ringing the alarm bar. The crowd was mostly silent. One could hear the flames.

"We have been taught our lesson," said one of the men.

"Policrates owns Victoria," said another.

"It is true," said another.

I turned about and left the crowd. I made my way slowly away from the wharves. I began to walk slowly back toward the tavern of Tasdron.

Many were the thoughts in my head.

I had seen a free woman of Victoria stripped with no more mercy than would have been shown to a slave. I had seen her kneel naked before a pirate and, his blade at her throat, with her own hands, tie the knot of bondage in her hair, in full view of hundreds of her fellow citizens.

I had seen the disorganization, the fear, the demoralization of the men of Victoria. I had seen the insolence of the pirates, the burning of buildings.

And the men of Victoria, though greatly outnumbering the pirates, had not fought.

The tribute would be paid.

And, too, I had learned, and I mused on this, that I wanted to own Miss Beverly Henderson, yes, literally own her, as a man on Earth might own a pair of boots, or a pig or a dog, or as a man on Gor might own, say, a tarsk or a pet sleen, or, lower than either, as he might own a slave.

* * * *

"Do not!" I cried. I seized the figure, his body poised, hunched over the sword, its point to his belly, its hilt in his hands, braced against the stones of the dark street. "No!" I cried. I struggled, briefly, with him. Then with the bottom of my foot I kicked the sword to one side and it slid upward, tearing through the tunic. He dropped to his hands and knees, vomiting, and scrambled for the sword, seizing it. He cried out in fury, and frustration, the blade now in his hands. He rose to his feet, reeling. "Who are you to interfere in this matter?" he howled. He lifted the blade and approached me. I saw it waver. He steadied it, placing one hand upon the other, on the hilt. It again lifted. I stood my ground. I did not think he would strike me. Then the blade lowered and the man sobbed, and backed against the wall, and lowered himself, sitting to its base, the sword on the stones beside him. He bent over, his head in his hands. "Who are you to interfere?" he wept.

"Surely there are others better than yourself against whom you might turn your sword," I said, angrily.

"Give me a drink," he said.

"Has it come to this," I asked him, "the glory, the codes, the steel?"

"I want a drink," he said, sullenly.

"I have but returned from the wharves," I told him. "Surely you, and the others, from the tavern of Tasdron, did not fail to hear the alarm?"

"There is no business of mine at the wharves," he said.

"Yet," said I, "you had left the tavern. Will you tell me you were not bound for the wharves?"

"I can do nothing," he said. "I could do nothing."

"Yet sick, your senses swirling, you left the tavern," I said. "This street leads to the wharves."

"I fell," he said. "I could not even walk."

"Do you wish to hear what occurred at the wharves," I asked, angrily.

"I am useless," he said. "I could do nothing. I am no good."

"At the wharves," I said, "there were pirates, few more than half a hundred of such men, under the command of Kliomenes, lieutenant to Policrates."

"I do not wish to hear of these matters," he said.

"In the view of hundreds of those of Victoria these men, so few of them, burned and looted, laughing and with impunity, as it pleased them. And in the view of hundreds of those of Victoria, angry, but inactive and cowering, not daring to protest, were lofty free women of this town publicly stripped and bound, thence to be carried into shameful slavery, to wear their collars at the feet of buccaneers."

"Women belong in collars," he said, angrily.

"And would you then," I asked, "willingly deliver them, prizes more fittingly yours, into the hands of such men as Kliomenes and Policrates. Are they more men than you, that such beauties should kneel at their feet rather than, fearfully, at yours?"

He lowered his head again, putting it in his hands.

"I would have thought," I said, "that it would be men such as you who might strike terror into the hearts of men such as they, that it would be men such as you whom groveling slave girls, wary of the whip, might fear even more to displease than they."

"Give me a drink," he said.

"You are, then, so fond of Kliomenes and Policrates that you are willing, graciously, to surrender to them the women and other treasures of this town."

"I am not of Victoria," he said.

"Few in Victoria," I said, "are of Victoria, it seems. Yet many reside here. If not men such as we, who, then, is of Victoria?"

"I am sick," he said.

"There was no leadership at the wharves," I said. "Insult was done upon this town with impunity. I saw hundreds of men, fearful, milling about, with no one to lead them. I saw them intimidated by a handful of organized, ruthless fellows, strutting and vain as vulos. I saw free men impressed into the service of loading the goods of the town onto the galleys of the thieves. Men, unprotesting, fearful, saw their properties purloined and burned. Flames linger yet on the wharves. Smoke hangs in the air."

He was silent.

"We missed you on the wharves," I said.

"Why did you interfere in my affairs?" he asked.

"Once," said I, "in the tavern of Tasdron you saved my life. Is it not my right, then, to save yours?"

"We are, then, even," said he, bitterly. "We now owe one another nothing. Go now, leave me."

"I have seen Glyco, a merchant, a high merchant, of Port Cos, these several days in earnest converse with you. I think, surely, that he, fearing the union of the pirates of the east and west, was entreating you to lend support to some scheme of resistance."

"You are shrewd," said the man.

"Yet his entreaties, I gather, have proven fruitless."

"I cannot help him," said the man.

"Yet that he came to you suggests that your courage, your brilliance in such matters, have never been forgotten."

"I am no longer who I once was," he said.

"I gather you once stood high among the guardsmen of Port Cos," I said.

"Once I was captain in Port Cos," he said. "Indeed it was I who once drove the band of Policrates from the vicinity of Port Cos." He looked up at me. "But that was long ago," he said. "I no longer remember that captain. I think he is gone now."

"What occurred?" I asked.

"He grew more fond of paga than of his codes," he said. "Disgraced, he was dismissed. He came west upon the river, to Victoria."

"What was his name?" I asked.

"I have forgotten," he said, sullenly.

"Had you been upon the wharves," I said, "things might have gone differently."

"Why did you not lead them?" he asked, angrily.

"I am only a weakling and a fool," I said, "and I am untrained."

He said nothing.

"One such as you might have made a difference."

He extended his right hand. It was large, but unsteady. It shook.

"At one time," he said, "I could strike a thousand blows, to the accuracy of a hair, I could thrust a thousand times, within the circle of half a hort, but now—now, see what has become of me." His hand, shaking, then fell. He closed his fist and pressed it against the stones of the dark street. He wept. "Policrates could have killed me in the tavern," he said. "He knew my weakness. But he did not do so. For the sake of old memories, I deem, vestiges of vanished realities, he spared me." He looked up at me. "We were youths together on the wharves of Port Cos," he said. "Each of us turned to the trades of steel, I to that of the guardsman, he to that of the marauder."

"What did Glyco wish of you?" I asked.

"A plan, a rallying point, a flag of memory, a leader, an assault upon the stronghold of Policrates."

"And what did you tell him?" I asked.

"It would take a hundred siege ships, and ten thousand men to take the stronghold of Policrates," he said.

I nodded. I did not think his estimates in error. For all practical purposes, considering the forces that could realistically be marshaled upon the river the stronghold of Policrates was impregnable. I had heard similar asseverations from others. Miss Beverly Henderson, and her beauty, the thought crossed my mind, were now locked behind those lofty, dark walls.

"The situation, then, is hopeless?" I asked.

"Yes, hopeless," he said.

"Tomorrow," I said, "the tribute is to be paid to Policrates."

The man shrugged.

"It is said," I said, "that the pirates own Victoria."

"It is true," he said. "It is true."

"And are there none to gainsay them?" I asked.

"None," said he.

"What can I do for you?" I asked, sadly.

"Give me a drink," he said.

I turned away from him and walked up the street, to the tavern of Tasdron, which was still open, though much subdued. I entered the tavern. I did not speak to anyone, nor did any meet my eyes. I purchased a bottle of paga which I then took from the tavern, retracing my steps to the slumped, dark figure sitting against the wall. I stopped before him, and he lifted his head from his knees, and looked at me, blearily. I handed the bottle to him, which, fumbling, quickly, he reached for. He bit and pulled the cork from the bottle. He clutched the bottle with both hands. He looked up at me, sitting by the wall.

"I am sorry," I said, "to have spoken cruelly to you. It was not my right. It was in anger, in rage, in frustration, that I spoke. I am truly sorry."

"Do you pity me?" he asked.

"Yes," I said. "I pity you."

Slowly, by an act of will, in cold fury, movement by movement, the man struggled unsteadily to his feet. There was a terrible fury in his eyes. "Pity?" he asked. "Me?"

"Yes," I said. "You have fallen. You cannot rise. You cannot help yourself. It is not your fault. I do not blame you."

"Pity?" he asked. "Me?"

"I know that you have been disgraced," I said. "I know that the scarlet has been taken from you."

"No one," said he, "can take the scarlet from me, once it is granted, unless it be by the sword."

He tore open the tunic he wore, revealing beneath it, dark, blackish in appearance, in the moonlight, the scarlet.

"This," said he, "can be taken from me only by the sword. Let him dare to do so who will."

"You are finished," I said. "Drink."

He looked dismally, angrily, at the bottle clutched in his right hand.

"You have forgotten the name of the warrior," I said, "who was once of Port Cos. He is no more. Drink."

The man then held the bottle near the neck, with both hands. For a long moment he looked at it. His shoulders then hunched forward, and he moaned in pain. Then, slowly, painfully, he straightened his body. He lifted his head to the Gorean moons and, in the dark street, in anguish uttered a wild cry. It began as a cry of anguish, and pain, and ended as a howl of rage. He turned about and, with two hands, broke the bottle suddenly into a thousand fragments against the stone. In the darkness he was cut with glass and soiled with scattered paga.

"I remember him," he said.

"What was his name?" I asked.

"Callimachus," he said. "His name is Callimachus, of Port Cos."

"Is he gone?" I asked.

Then the man, with two fists, struck against the wall. "No," he said, with a terrible ferocity. There was blood on his hands, dark, running between the fingers.

"Where is he?" I asked.

Slowly the man turned to face me. "He is here," he said. "I am he."

"I am pleased to hear it," I said. I reached down and picked up the fallen blade. I handed it to him. "This," I said, "is yours."

He sheathed the blade. He looked at me, for a long time. "You have done me service," he said. "How can I repay you?"

"I have a plan," I said. "Teach me the sword."

Twenty Three

I am Made Welcome in the Holding of Policrates; Kliomenes Makes Test of Me; I Select a Girl for My Night's Pleasure

The naked slave girl, in her bells and jewels, writhed on the scarlet tiles of the floor before us.

Policrates, sitting beside me, behind the broad, low table, musingly fitted together the two pieces of yellowish, brown stone, the two halves of the once-shattered topaz. Again I found it startling, and impressive, how the figure of a river galley emerged from the brownish discolorations in the two pieces of stone, once they were fitted together. There was no mistaking that they were the two halves of what was once an unusual, divided stone.

"Fascinating," said Policrates. "And how is my friend, Ragnar Voskjard?"

"Well," said I, "and he, of course, inquires after your health."

"I am well," said Policrates, "and you may, upon your return, assure him that I am eager to participate in our common venture."

"In twenty days," I said, "allowing for my return and the fitting of our ships, we shall be at your sea gate."

"Excellent," said Policrates.

"We shall then," I said, "proceed to Ar's Station, to sack the stores and burn her vessels. Following that we shall wreak similar havoc upon Port Cos. These two major ports crippled the river, then, for all practical purposes, will be ours."

"It is amusing," said Policrates, "that the tension between Cos and Ar prevents the linkage of their powers upon the river."

"Their foolishness in this respect," I said, "should redound considerably to our advantage."

"True," laughed Policrates. "And let us drink to that!"

He lifted his goblet and we clinked our goblets together, and I reached across, before Policrates, extending my goblet, too, to Kliomenes, who, surlily, sat on the right of Policrates. We three, then, touched goblets, and then we drank. Kliomenes eyed me narrowly.

I turned away and gave my attention to the slave writhing on the tiles before us.

She was performing a need dance, of a type not uncommon among Gorean female slaves. Such a dance usually proceeds in clearly defined phrases, evident not merely in the expressions and movements of the girl but in the nature of the accompanying music. There are usually five phases to such a dance. In the first phase the girl, dancing, feigns indifference to the presence of men, before whom, as a slave, she must perform. In the second phase, for she has not yet been raped, her distress and uneasiness, her restlessness, her disturbance by her sexual urges, must become subtly more manifest. Here it must be evident that she is beginning to feel her sexuality, and drives, profoundly, and yet is struggling against them. Toward the end of this phase it must become clear not only that she has sexual needs, and deep ones, but that she is beginning to fear that she may not be, simply as she is, of sufficient interest to men to obtain their satisfaction. Here, need, coupled with anxiety and self-doubt, for she has not yet been seized by strong men, must become clear. In the third phase of the dance she, in an almost ladylike fashion, acknowledges herself defeated in her attempt to conceal her sexuality; she then, again in an almost ladylike fashion, delicately but clearly, with restraint but unmistakably, acknowledges, and publicly, before masters, that she has sexual needs. Then, with smiles, and gestures, displaying herself, she makes manifest her readiness for the service of men, her willingness, and her receptivity. She invites them, so to speak to have her. But she has not yet been seized by an arm or an ankle, or by her collar, a thumb hooked rudely under it, or hair, and pulled from the floor. What if she is not sufficiently pleasing? What if she is not to be fulfilled? What if she must continue to dance, alone, unnoticed. At this point it becomes clear to her that it is by no means a foregone conclusion that men will find her of interest, or that they will see fit to satisfy her. She must strive to be pleasing. If she is not good enough she may be chained, unfulfilled, another night alone in the kennel. There are always other girls. She must earn her rape. Too, if she should be insufficiently pleasing consistently it is likely that she will be slain. Goreans place few impediments in the way of the liberation of a slave female's sexuality. In this phase of the dance, then, shamelessly the woman dances her need and, shamelessly, begs for her sexual satisfaction. This phase of the dance is sometimes known as the Heat of the Collared She-Sleen. The fifth, and final phase, of the dance, is far more dramatic and exciting. In this phase the girl, overcome by sexual desire and terrified that she may not be found sufficiently pleasing, clearly manifests, and utterly, that she is a slave female. In this portion of the dance the girl is seldom on her feet. Rather, sitting, rolling, and changing position, on her side, her back, her belly, half kneeling, half sitting, kneeling, crawling, reaching out, bending backwards, lying down, twisting with passion, gesturing to her body, presenting it to masters for their inspection and interest, whimpering, moaning, crying out, brazenly presenting herself as a slave, pleading for her rape, she writhes, a piteous, begging, vulnerable, ready slave, a woman fit for and begging for the touch of a master, a woman begging to become, at the least touch of her master, a totally submitted slave. The fourth phase of the dance, as I have mentioned, is sometimes known as the Heat of the Collared She-Sleen. This portion of the dance, the fifth portion, is sometimes known as the Heat of the Slave Girl.

"I had expected the topaz to be delivered earlier," said Policrates. "I had sent word to Ragnar Voskjard more than fifty days ago."

"There were many deliberations in the holding of Ragnar," I said. "Junctions of this kind are not to be entered upon lightly. Too, I was detained in Victoria. There are many guardsmen in Victoria, both of Port Cos and Ar's Station, who search for the bearer of the topaz."

"I would feel better," said Kliomenes, "if I could see your face."

"The mask I wear," I said, "must be to conceal my identity."

"It is common, Kliomenes," said Policrates, "for the courier, he carrying the topaz, to cover his features in foreign holdings. The concealment of his identity is essential to his work."

"For all you know," I said to Kliomenes, "I might be Ragnar Voskjard himself."

Kliomenes shrank back.

"But you are not," said Policrates, "for Ragnar, a shrewd fellow, would not venture upon such dangerous work as the personal transport of the topaz."

"I think that is true," I grinned. "At any rate it is certainly true, at least, that I am not Ragnar Voskjard."

"There is something about you which seems familiar," said Kliomenes. "Have I ever seen you before?"

"Perhaps," I said.

"You see, Kliomenes," said Policrates, "our friend may be well known upon the river. If so, it is scarcely in Ragnar Voskjard's interest, or in ours, or in the interest of our friend here, to be recognized as the courier of the topaz. If he is highly placed in some town on the river then his utility to Voskjard and to us would be considerably diminished if it were understood such a highly placed person was secretly in league with men such as ourselves and Voskjard."

"True," said Kliomenes.

"And I think we may be certain," said Policrates, "that our friend is indeed well known in at least one town on the river."

"That is true," I admitted. Indeed, I was reasonably well known in Victoria.

The music ended with a swirl of sound and the girl, with a jangle of bells, lay before the table of Policrates, whimpering, her hand extended. She lifted her head. I read the unmistakable need in her eyes. She was indeed a slave female.

"Master!" she whimpered. "Please, Master."

Policrates glanced at her. He had scarcely paid her attention in the dance.

"Have me thrown to your men, please, Master," she begged.

Policrates gestured to a brawny fellow who, coming up behind the girl, bent down and, by her upper arms, lifted her from the floor. She was helpless in his arms. Only her toes, with painted, scarlet nails, touched the floor. Policrates gestured again, to a table to the side, and the fellow, carrying the girl, went to the table. He then threw her, with a jangle of bells, and a clatter of plates and goblets, to the surface of the table. Instantly the girl was held down on the table, on her back, her arms and legs held apart, and several men crowded about her. I heard her cry out with pleasure.

"I know who you remind me of," said Kliomenes.

"Who?" I asked.

"A brawler and dock worker of Victoria," he said, "one called Jason."

I smiled.

"There is a resemblance," said Policrates.

"Jason, of Victoria," said Kliomenes, "did not know the sword."

"Then how could I be he?" I asked.

"Draw!" cried Kliomenes, leaping across the table, and whipping out his blade.

I looked, unconcernedly, at Policrates. "My identity is surely established sufficiently by my former possession of the topaz," I said. "Surely, too, none who were not of the party of Ragnar Voskjard, should they come into the possession of the topaz, would dare to bring it here. What could be the point?"

"These things seem to me true," said Policrates, "but, as Kliomenes has said, there seems a resemblance."

"Surely I am not to be blamed for that," I smiled.

"Will it hurt to make test of the matter?" inquired Policrates.

I grinned. "No," I said. "But, on the other hand, it is well known upon the river that Kliomenes is an excellent swordsman. Surely I should be forgiven if I do not find myself eager to be spitted upon his blade."

"Draw," smiled Policrates.

I threw the cloak behind me and drew forth the blade which was slung at my hip. With one foot I moved aside the low table, watching Kliomenes, that he not attack me as I step upon the table, maintaining an uneven balance.

Kliomenes, I saw, noted this.

There was then silence in the hall. The pirates, feasting at the low tables, stopped eating, and watched. The girls, too, with their vessels and trays, serving, many of them nude, save for their collars and bangles, stood or knelt quietly, not moving, watching. The torches could then be heard, crackling at the walls.

Kliomenes thrust suddenly at me and I parried the blow, smartly. I did not attempt to strike him.

He thrust then thrice again and, each time, I turned aside the steel.

Men murmured at the tables. He had been too easily thwarted. Suddenly, angrily, Kliomenes attacked. For three or four Ehn he struck and slashed at me. Then, sweating, he lowered his blade, angrily. I had, of intent, particularly in the last two Ehn, parried heavily. Strength, as well as skill, is significant in swordplay, something which is insufficiently understood by many unfamiliar with weaponry. It is particularly telling if the action is prolonged. Whereas one may turn aside steel deftly one may also, if one chooses, turn it aside with power, which necessitates an additional exertion on the part of the antagonist to return his steel to the ready position. He must, in order to protect himself, under such conditions, bring his blade back through a greater arc, and with additional speed and pressure. Similarly, as may be understood in terms of a simple simile, if one is holding an implement and it is struck with greater force it will be more difficult and tiring to return it to its original position than if it has not been struck heavily and has not been moved significantly. Sometimes, though I had tried not to make this obvious, I had, in effect, beaten his blade to the side, rather than merely turned it away.

"Obviously this man cannot be Jason of Victoria," smiled Policrates.

Kliomenes angrily thrust his steel into its sheath. I dropped my blade, too, into my sheath. I had not attempted to respond to him, truly, but had only defended myself. Since I had limited myself only to defense, and had not risked the exposures of attack, I had been in little danger, at least for a time. It is difficult, of course, to strike a swordsman who is both competent and careful. It is dangerous, of course, over a period of time, to rely solely on defense. For one thing the antagonist, emboldened, may press more and more dangerous attacks, far more difficult to avert than if he were subject to the necessity of protecting himself. Secondly, of course, one's defense might falter or become imperfect, particularly over time. Obviously the consequences of even a moment's inadvertence in the dialogue of blades could be irremediable. One who limits oneself solely to defense, and is unwilling to attack, obviously can never win. Too, sooner or later, it seems, he must be doomed to lose. There is no wall so strong that it will not one day crumble.

Kliomenes returned to his place, and I, replacing the table to its original position, returned, too, to my place.

"Kliomenes," observed Policrates, "you seem weary."

"I only wished to make test of him," said Kliomenes, "to determine whether or not he knew the sword."

"And what is your opinion?" asked Policrates.

"His skills seem adequate," said Kliomenes.

"I thought so, too," said Policrates, smiling.

I was grateful to Callimachus, he of Port Cos, my teacher. In long hours, from dawn to dusk, and even in the light of lamps, over the past several days, in my house in Victoria, he had labored with me, instilling in me techniques, and anticipations and reflexes, subjecting me, too, to a tutelage of apprehensions and tactics. I had proved, I think, a not inapt pupil. Yet I remained clearly aware of my limitations. A high order of skill with steel is not easily purchased. This is particularly true with the subtle differences, and dimensions and increments, which tend to divide masters.

"I only wished to make test of him," said Kliomenes, "to see whether or not he knew the sword. I did not wish to kill the courier of Ragnar Voskjard."

"That is clearly understood," smiled Policrates. "Music," then he called, "and a new dancer, and wenches to serve! Let the feast continue!"

The musicians then again began to play, the sensuous, melodious, exciting, wild music of Gor.

I picked up a leg of vulo and bit into it. I was relieved, though I gave little sign of it. Kliomenes, angrily, continued to swill wine. A new dancer came forth upon the floor and began, a tall brute near her with the leather, to perform a whip dance. Girls, some nude, some scantily clad, hurried about the tables, serving food and drink. I looked about, considering the wenches. I did not see Miss Beverly Henderson among them. I did see several, however, whom I would have been delighted to own.

"Wine, Master?" asked a red-headed girl with two leather straps wound about her body.

I took wine from her, and gave my attention then to the dancer, a luscious, dark-haired girl. In the whip dance, though there are various versions of it, depending on the locality, the girl is almost never struck with the whip, unless, of course, she does not perform well. When the whip is cracked, however, the girl will commonly react as though she has been struck. This, conjoined with the music, and her beauty, and the obvious symbolism of her beauty beneath total male discipline, can be extremely, powerfully erotic. In an elegant, civilized context, one of beauty and music, it makes clear and bespeaks the raw and essential primitives of the ancient, genetic, biological sexual relationship of men and women, the theme of dominance and submission, that man is master by blood and woman is slave by birth. Neither, too, as say the Goreans, will know their fulfillment until they become true to themselves. We can be conquered, but nature cannot. In attempting to conquer nature, we defeat only ourselves. True freedom and happiness, perhaps, lies not in denying and repudiating our nature but in fulfilling it.

"Bread, Master?" asked a blond-haired beauty, kneeling down beside me. She offered me a silver tray on which, hot and steaming, were wedges of Gorean bread, made from Sa-Tarna grain. I took one of them and, from the tureen, with the small silver dipper, both on the tray, poured hot butter on the bread. I then dismissed her with a gesture of my head and she rose lightly to her feet and left, to serve another. She was unclothed.

"I would prefer," said Kliomenes, "that he did not wear a mask."

"Surely you must understand," said Policrates, "that his identity must remain concealed." Policrates gestured about himself, to the tables. "What if one here should turn traitor, and later identify and betray our guest, say, for gold? Or, what if his features might be seen by a slave, say, a mere serving wench, who might later, herself being sold or given away, inadvertently, by her reaction, give suspicion as to his identity?"

Kliomenes nodded glumly, and turned again to his wine.

"Do even the slaves here know that I am the courier of Ragnar Voskjard?" I asked.

"Of course," said Policrates. "To celebrate your arrival, and the bringing of the pledge of the topaz, this very feast has been commanded. Indeed, even if it were not so, it is difficult to keep rumors of such matters from the kitchens and kennels. The little sluts, even in their chains, are prone to gossip and are eager for the least tidbit of news."

I smiled.

"Meat, Master?" asked a girl, nude, who knelt now beside me. She offered a tray on which small cubes of roasted bosk, on tiny sticks, steamed. I took several, dipping them by the sticks, in a sauce, carried on the same tray. I returned the tiny sticks to the tray and looked at the girl. She put down her head. Her hair had been cut quite short, probably as a punishment. She must now, nude, offer meat to men. It is understood, of course, in such a situation, that in asking such a question that the girl is offering herself to the male, as much, or more, than the steaming, nourishing delights on her plate. This sort of thing, incidentally, is quite common in Gorean serving. This sort of question, generally, is understood more broadly than merely being an inquiry into the male's culinary preferences of the moment. The classical question in this respect, almost universal on Gor, is "Wine, Master?"

"Do you think, truly," asked Policrates, "that the fleet of Ragnar Voskjard, fully rigged and fitted, can be here in twenty days?"

"I see no difficulty in the matter," I assured him.

"Good," he said.

I looked about, at the girls among the tables. Some, but not all, wore five steel loops on their body, a rounded, narrow collar loop, and, rounded and narrow, loops on their wrists and ankles. Such loops, in a variety of ways, can provide a variety of ties. Only a bit of binding fiber, slipped behind the loops, is required. Gorean men are sometimes ingenious in the ties to which they subject slave girls. Different ties, of course, have different purposes. One may generally distinguish among such things as control ties, discipline ties and pleasure ties. These ties are not mutually exclusive, of course.

"Grapes, Master?" said a soft, feminine voice near to me. I looked about, but I did not react. It was the free woman, or the woman who had been free, who had been ordered from the crowd on the wharves of Victoria. I recalled her having been stripped by the pirate, and his blade at her throat. She had tied the knot of bondage in her own hair. She had been ordered to run to the galley. There I had seen her bound helplessly at its railing, her back to it, exposing her beauty, with others. "Master?" she asked. Her voice, and mien, were deferential, and totally submissive. An incredible transformation had come over her. She was now soft, and lovely, and beautiful, a woman who was, and knew herself, owned. I wanted to take her in my arms. She lifted the tray of grapes to me, proffering it. They were Ta grapes. I smiled. Each, I noted, had been carefully peeled. Doubtless that had been the task to which she had set that afternoon. Such trivial, painstaking tasks are often useful in teaching a woman that she is a slave. "Master?" she asked. I wanted to take her in my arms. I permitted her to feed me a grape. Then she withdrew. I watched her withdraw. She was beautiful. She wore a snatch of yellow silk.

"I see that she pleases you," said Policrates. "You may have her this evening, in your chambers, if you wish."

"Perhaps," I said. I shrugged.

The whip dance continued before us.

"Fruit, Master?" asked a girl, softly, timidly, kneeling down lightly beside me. Her head was down. She was frightened. I turned, sitting, to face her. She trembled. She did not raise her head.

"She fears you," said Policrates, "for she knows you are the courier of Ragnar Voskjard. Too, she is perhaps intimidated by my presence, and that of Kliomenes, for we are highest in this holding."

I smiled. Such men, of course, held over her the total power of life or death.

I regarded the girl.

There were five, narrow, rounded loops of steel locked upon her fair body, one serving as collar, and the others for her wrists and ankles. In her hands she carried, held, ripe, rounded fruit. She wore, like the girl before her, tantalizing to the eye, what might constitute a master's conception of a garment suitable for a lovely female slave, a fragment of silk which made unmistakably clear that the beauty to which it clung, and which it made little pretense to conceal, lay fully at the disposition and mercy of lusty men. Yet it was, in its way, more demure than that which had been worn by the girl before her. In particular, as it was tied snugly, it gathered her breasts, holding them together and lifting them.

"She is a new slave," said Policrates, "and is not yet fully broken to her collar."

Her dark hair was coiffured loosely and high upon her head. It was bound with a braided yellow cord, strong enough to hold her wrists, should she be bound with it. If the cord were jerked loose the hair would fall, unbound, to the small of her back.

"She is exquisite, isn't she?" asked Policrates.

I put my thumb under her chin and lifted up her head. Her soft brown eyes, frightened, met mine. There was a look in them which I had seen before, I thought, in other girls, in the eyes of a slave girl as she looks into the eyes of a master. That interested me. Then she turned aside her head, though it was still held much in place by the obdurate pressure of my thumb. She did not recognize me. Her delicate lips wore lipstick, red. There was a subtle shading of blue on her upper eyelids.

"She fears that you will find her pleasing," said Policrates, "but yet, I think, desires that you will."

The girl trembled.

I removed my thumb from beneath her chin, and she put her head down.

Policrates regarded her.

"Little fool," he said, "for what purpose have you come to this table?"

The girl lifted her head then and, timidly, lifted the ripe, rounded fruit which she held in her hands, Gorean peaches and plums, to me. Her eyes met mine, and then she looked down, blushing. I then understood the purpose of the gathering of her brief yellow garment at her breasts, lifting them, sweet, rounded and swelling, for the inspection and delectation of masters. In her gesture, her offering of the fruit, it was clearly understood that she was offering to me as well the lovely fruits of her service and beauty.

I took one of the peaches and bit into it, watching her. She shuddered.

"You are dismissed," said Policrates.

"Yes, Master," she said, frightened, and rising quickly, lightly, hurried away, barefoot on the tiles, to serve others.

I thought Miss Beverly Henderson made a lovely slave girl.

The whip dance was now approaching its climax.

"She is a pretty little thing," I said, looking after Miss Henderson. "What do you call her?"

"Beverly," said Policrates.

"You are cruel," I said, smiling, "to give her an Earth-girl name."

"She is an Earth girl," he said, grinning.

"Oh," I said.

"Do you like Earth girls?" he asked.

"Yes," I said.

"That one is raw," he said, "but, in time, like the others, I think she will make an excellent slave."

"Do you think she is a natural slave?" I asked.

"Undoubtedly," he said. "I meant that she was not yet fully trained, not yet broken fully to the collar."

"I see," I said.

"Kliomenes fell in with her at the tavern of Hibron, the Pirate's Chain, in Victoria," he said. "He immediately sized her up as slave meat. Thinking herself in delightful converse with him she informed him that her name on Earth had been Beverly. Accordingly it seemed fitting that we should put that name again upon her, though now only as a slave name, by our whim."

"Of course," I said.

"She herself," said Policrates, "repudiated the assistance of a fellow desiring to extricate her from her peril, mocking and dismissing him, one called Jason, of Victoria, he to whom you bear some physical resemblance."

"I see," I said.

"Kliomenes did not even use Tassa powder on her," he said. "He simply bound her and carried her, struggling, to his ship." He indicated the girl, among the tables, moving about, kneeling and serving fruit. I thought her thighs and ankles, and her back, which was much exposed, were beautiful. "She now serves us well," he said.

I turned my attention to the dancer on the floor. She lay now on her back, one knee lifted, her arms at her sides, palms down, before the brute with his whip, who towered over her. Her head, too, was turned to the side. Then she turned her head to face the brute who tyrannized her. She looked deeply into his eyes. Then, delicately, in a graceful gesture, she turned her hands, putting their backs to the floor, exposing her palms, and the soft flesh of her palms, to him, indicating her surrender, her submission, her vulnerability and her readiness.

There was applause, the striking of the left shoulder, from the tables.

The brute then crouched beside her and encircled her neck with the coils of his whip. He drew her to her knees then before him. She looked up at him, her neck in the whip coils, his.

There was more applause. Then the brute looked to Policrates, who indicated a table. He then pulled the girl to her feet and, running her over the tiles, and then releasing the coils from her neck, threw her stumbling into the arms of waiting pirates who, with a cry of pleasure, seized her and began to work their lusty wills upon her. There was more applause, and laughter.

I rose to my feet.

"The feast has but begun," laughed Policrates.

"I am weary," I said. "I think I shall retire to my chambers."

"Certainly!" he laughed. "Your journey has been long. I shall, of course, send a girl to wash your body, and content you."

"Policrates is generous," I said.

"It is nothing," he said.

This form of hospitality, of course, is common on Gor. It is common to provide a guest with a girl for the night, to see to his comfort. My compliment, nonetheless, was appropriate, as was his reply. Ritualistic amenities, and pleasantries, on such occasions are invariably observed.

He rose to stand beside me. Together we looked about the tables, at the various girls, slaves, nude and partially clothed, who served there.

"Take your pick of the wenches," he said.

I looked about, at the girls, attending dutifully to their serving, many of them not even conscious of my attention. One of them could discover later that she had been selected to be sent to my chambers for the evening.

"Tais is interesting," said Policrates. A dark-haired girl quickly averted her eyes from ours, putting down her head and hurrying to pour wine nearby. Two silver chains ran from a large loop on her collar to her wrists. The snug metal bracelets there were jeweled. "There is Relia there," he said. "Consider her." He indicated another dark-haired girl. She wore a long, lovely red gown, but it had been pulled down about her waist. She carried a tray of tiny cups, filled with liqueurs. She was willowy and sweetly-breasted. A silver collar graced her throat. "Tela, when captured," he said, indicating a blonde, "begged to be permitted to be kept in white silk." He laughed. "After throwing her to a crew, for their pleasure, we put her, as she had asked, in white silk." "Amusing," I said. "She now often begs for red silk," he said. "Perhaps we will one day permit it to her." "I see," I said. "She is now quick to lick a man's feet," he added. "Excellent," I said. "Bikkie," said he, indicating a short, dark-haired girl, "is good. Too, there are Mira and Tala, the matched blondes. They are sisters from Cos." He indicated two girls, one older than the other, one perhaps nineteen, the other seventeen. They were fastened together, by the neck, by a knotted red strap some four feet in length. They were slender, and nude. "You may have both," he said.

I continued to look about.

"I saw that you were interested in Lita," he said, referring to a girl in a diaphanous bit of swirling yellow silk. She was the woman who had been free, whom I had seen enslaved on the wharves of Victoria, only a few nights past. In her own hair she had tied the knot of bondage. "She is trying hard to improve her skills," he said. "I think she will be ready for sale in another month. Perhaps you could assist in her training."

"Perhaps some other time," I said.

"There are others, of course," said he, "below, in cages."

"I think I see one in which I might be interested," I said.

"Which?" asked he.

"That one," I said.

"Beverly," said he, "the Earth girl?"

"Yes," I said.

"Choose another," he said.

"Why?" I asked.

"She is raw, and untrained," he said. "She is a poor slave."

"I find her, nonetheless, not to be without interest," I said.

"Very well," he said. "I will have her sent to your chambers within the Ahn."

"My thanks, Policrates," I said. "Oh," I said. "I may wish, in the privacy of my chambers, to remove this mask."

"I understand," said he. "I will send her to you blindfolded."

"My thanks, Policrates," I said.

"It is nothing," he said.

I then bowed graciously to my host, Policrates, and to Kliomenes, his lieutenant and confederate, and then turned about, and made my way to my chambers.

Twenty Four

What Occurred in My Chambers, When Miss Henderson Thought Me to be the Courier of Ragnar Voskjard

"Master?" she asked.

She stood within the door to my chambers. The door had been shut behind her. A guard had conducted her to my chambers. He had opened the door. Timidly, blindfolded, conducted by his hand on her arm, she had entered. The door had then shut behind her. She stood now within my chambers. We were absolutely alone.

"Master?" she asked. "I have come to serve you," she said.

I did not respond to her, but observed her. She stood timidly, blindfolded, near the door. She wore a tiny, diaphanous bit of brown silk about her body. It was high on her thighs. It was off her right shoulder and held loosely on her by a casually knotted, narrow disrobing loop, fastened over her left shoulder. A single tug would open the garment, dropping it to her ankles. She carried, folded, several large, colored, soft towels, with two sponges, and oils, for the bath. On the towels, too, were certain other articles. Among them was, opened, the rounded steel loop she had worn about her neck, earlier. It, with its key, lay on the top towel. It had been removed from her for she was to assist me in the bath. It accompanied her, that it might be again, when she had bathed me, replaced on her. Similarly the steel loops from her wrists and ankles had been removed. They, however, had been kept elsewhere. They did not accompany her. On the towels, however, coiled, there was a whip, and slave cuffs, and anklets, of leather, with snaps. Too, it might be mentioned, there were, as is usual, chains at the foot of the great couch, which might be lengthened or shortened. One chain terminated in a collar, which might be locked about a girl's neck. The other chain terminated in a smaller loop of steel, an ankle ring, suitable for a girl's ankle.

I regarded her.

Her hair was still coiffured high upon her head, and held, as before, with the braided yellow cord, stout enough to bind her with. She was barefoot, as is common with slaves.

"Master?" she asked. "Are you in the room?"

I moved, that she might know my presence.

"Forgive me, Master," she said, "if I have awakened you, or disturbed you."

I pulled away the mask I wore and discarded it, to one side on the great couch.

I snapped my fingers.

"Yes, Master," she said. She approached the sound, and knelt before me.

"I am Beverly," she said. "I have been sent to serve you."

I did not speak.

"It is a great honor for me, Master," she said, "that one such as you should select Beverly to serve you."

I did not respond to her.

"The water will have been readied," she said. Near the couch was a large, round, sunken tub, with some six inches of water in it. Too, to one side, there were rinsing jars.

She put the objects she carried on the floor, to her right.

"Here, Master," she said, feeling for it, "is a slave collar. You may place it on me when you wish." She put it, with its key, at my feet. "Here, too," she said, putting the objects near the collar, "are slave cuffs, and anklets." I regarded the objects, with their tiny belts and buckles, with their attached, sewn in, metal snap rings. "And here, Master," she said, "is your whip." She kissed it and put it, too, at my feet.

"Beverly is now ready to serve her Master," she said.

I again snapped my fingers, and the girl stood.

She stood lovely, and straight, her hands now empty, the towels and oils, and other articles on the floor near us.

"Am I to bathe you now, Master?" she asked.

I regarded her blindfold. It was efficient, and Gorean. Most blindfolds, of a sort used on Earth, are inefficient, for one may see under them. This is not the case with the common Gorean blindfold. It consists, commonly, of three pieces, usually two rounded pieces of soft felt, three to four inches in diameter, and the binding, which usually consists of two or more turns of a dark, thick, folded cloth, or scarf, knotted behind the head. The pieces of rounded, face-hugging felt, the eye coverings, in the girl's blindfold were about three and a half inches in diameter. They were yellow. The binding, some three turns of folded, opaque, thick black cloth, knotted tightly behind her head, held the eye coverings securely in place. The blindfold, of course, is seldom used in the transportation of a slave. Slave hoods are much more common in such a role. Some of these are fitted with gags. Also, they may be, or some of them, locked upon the girl. The blindfold, of course, as will be recalled by those who have seen a girl in one, has its own advantages. It permits, for example, something of the beauty of her face, such as her trembling lips, to be seen. Also it permits you to place your teeth upon hers, to test her tongue for responsiveness with yours and, if one wishes, to run the tip of one's finger lightly inside her mouth, between her teeth and the interior of her cheek.

"May I bathe Master now?" she asked.

I jerked loose the disrobing loop at her left shoulder. Beverly Henderson was stripped before me.

I walked around, behind her. She lifted up her chin. She trembled, slightly. She was extremely aware of my presence. I bent forward, slightly. She had been subtly perfumed. She shuddered. She had felt my breath at the left side of her neck, and on her left shoulder.

I then walked about her and stood before her.

"Yes, Master," she said. She reached out and, gently, first touching my chest, her hands lingering there for a moment, found the knot in the belt of soft cloth with which I had closed the casual tunic I had donned. She undid the knot and parted the tunic, kissing me at the belly. She then went behind me and, gently, removed the tunic, kissing me beneath the left shoulder blade. She then stood again before me. She folded the tunic and belt, kissing them, and then knelt down, placing them to one side. She then stood again, before me, her head down.

I smiled. The girl had been taught how to disrobe a master for the bath.

I then placed the articles for the bath in her hands, and conducted her to the side of the tub. She placed the articles where she might find them. She then took a vial of oil and one of the sponges in her hands. I then helped her step within the tub.

I looked at her.

She stood in the water, blindfolded, waiting for me. Miss Beverly Henderson, once a proud girl of Earth, now only a Gorean slave girl, waited to bathe a free male, one whom she must address as master and serve as he pleased.

I stepped down within the tub.

Then, kneeling or standing, as was fit, humbly, Miss Beverly Henderson, with the oils and sponges, and rinsing waters, bathed me.

Then, after a few Ehn, she toweled my body dry and then knelt before me, head down.

I snapped my fingers, and she stood.

I then looked at her, carefully. I assessed the nature of her breathing. I touched my fingers to her side, and noted her sudden, involuntary movement. I smiled. The Gorean bath, of such a sort, has many purposes. The cleansing of the body, of course, is only one such purpose. It has two major purposes with respect to its effect on the girl. The first is that she is performing a lowly and humble task for a man. This helps to remind her that she is a slave. Also, of course, serving a man, particularly in small and humble ways, probably for biological reasons, tends to be sexually arousing for a woman. Many men, I think, fail to understand that. When a girl brings a man his sandals and ties them on his feet she is having a sexual experience. Many men, I think, fail to understand the pervasiveness and radiance, the depth, and contextual richness, of female sexuality. It is such a wondrous, deep and marvelous thing. He who denies a woman her right to serve man, and particularly in such small ways, denies to her a portion of herself; that man is not only a fool, for he is the natural recipient of such attentions, but he is cruel; such a denial, too, can make a woman ashamed to seek sexual gratification for such small services, usually unbeknownst to the boorish male, are intimately connected with such gratification; this is one reason, incidentally, that those who secretly fear sexuality, and would repudiate it, will be among the first to denounce such homely services of love. In the case of the slave girl, of course, such services are commanded of her. She must perform them. This tells her then, on some deep level, that it is all right, truly, to be a woman. Indeed, she is given no choice but to be a woman. Thusly is her love unqualifiedly liberated. This type of thing, I think, accounts for something of the joy which is experienced by many slave girls, a joy which, otherwise, would seem inexplicable. The second major purpose with respect to the effect on the girl, of course, is that she is touching and, in effect, in the bathing, caressing a man's body. She is intimately close to the male, even to the extent of sensual tactuality. Being alive and hormonally active, of course, this is arousing to her. And it is, of course, particularly arousing to a slave female, for she knows she is fit meat for the lust of men. Does her very condition not tell her that? Too, of course, she herself, though touching, is not touched. This is frustrating to her, naturally, and intensifies her desire, usually near the surface in a slave, to be taken in the arms of the master. From the point of the man, too, of course, there are several purposes of the bath. Some of these are related to those pertinent to the girl. First, he is served, as the master. He is master. Second, it is not unpleasant to be washed humbly by a beautiful woman. Third, such service tends to arouse the girl. It is not uncommon, when such a bath has been finished, and he has been toweled by the beauty, that she kneels before him and begs to be raped.

"The bath is finished, Master," said the girl, standing before me.

I jerked loose the yellow cord from her hair. I then, with the cord, tied her wrists behind her back. I thought it well that she should feel herself tied.

I then threw thick love furs at the foot of the couch. She heard them. I lifted the chains there and put them on top of the furs.

I then conducted her to a place at the foot of the couch. She stood there on the furs. Often slave girls are not permitted on the couch. They are used at its foot. I took the steel collar, the rounded, narrow metal loop, with its lock, which she had brought with her into the room. I snapped it about her throat. It fitted closely.

"I am now a collared female," she said. I walked away from her, and placed the key among my things.

I returned to her, then, and looked at her. Gorean men truly look at women, and they know themselves looked at, truly.

"My brand," she said, "is the common Kajira mark. I hope it pleases Master." I regarded it, the staff and fronds, delicate and incisive, beauty subject to discipline.

Quickly I snapped my fingers, sharply. She knelt immediately on the furs, among the chains. She knew well where she knelt. She knelt back on her heels, spreading her knees.

I then sat on the edge of the couch, at its bottom, the palms of my hands resting on its furs, and looked upon her.

I wanted to howl with pleasure.

Beverly Henderson, naked and bound, knelt before me, in the position of the pleasure slave.

"Master?" she asked.

I noted that she had assumed the position spontaneously. That interested me.

"Master?" she inquired.

I knew that come what may I must have her, and have her well. If she were not sent forth in the morning, perhaps bruised and sobbing, as a well-ravished slave, the men of the holding of Policrates, and its master himself, would grow thoughtful. My failure to subject her uncompromisingly to the predations of my mastery would be certain to generate suspicion. The true courier of Ragnar Voskjard, I knew, would be expected to handle women well.

She pulled at the loops of braided yellow cord which held her well.

"Master has not deigned to speak to me," she said. "Am I to be whipped? Am I not pleasing?"

I did not, of course, as was my intent, respond to her.

"Is Master not going to rape me?" she asked. "Did Master not select me out from the other girls for his pleasure?"

She squirmed, miserably, before me.

"Perhaps I am not pretty enough now for Master," she said, "now that he has seen me closely. I know that I am not as beautiful as many of the girls. I know that they say that I am not a good slave, and that I am not well broken as yet to my collar, but I will try to please you well."

It interested me to hear her speak. She spoke as might have a slave. Did she not know she was from Earth?

"I cannot dance," she said. "And I do not know the love songs of slaves."

I said nothing.

"They have not taught me to dance," she whimpered, "nor have I been permitted to learn the desire songs of heated slaves."

I said nothing.

"What does Master want of me?" she asked, piteously.

I did not respond to her.

"I acknowledge you as the courier of Ragnar Voskjard," she said. "I acknowledge you as a great and important man. And I acknowledge myself as only a miserable slave. It is a great honor for me that you have selected me out, from the others, to be sent to your chambers this night, to serve you." She looked toward me, piteously, though she could see nothing in the dark confines of the blindfold. "I will try to be worthy of your choice," she said. "I will try to please you."

Again I did not respond to her.

"I am frightened!" she said. "Obviously I must not be pleasing to you. Then whip me, and call for another girl!"

I did not move.

"But you are not at this moment whipping me," she said, "nor calling for another girl. Now I am truly frightened, for I know that, somehow, now, you must find me pleasing, or of interest. But I am terrified that a man such as you might find me pleasing, or of interest. What will he do to me? Oh, please, Master, speak to me! Let me tell, if only by the tone of your voice, what are your intentions with respect to me! Oh, I am so helpless! I am so helpless!"

I regarded her, and the steel collar on her throat, placed there by my own hand.

"I am so helpless," she wept.

Then she tossed her head, and smiled. "You have me at something of a disadvantage, Master," she laughed, "for whereas you may see, I am blindfolded, and whereas you are free, I am kneeling collared, nude and bound." Her lower lip suddenly trembled. "Please, speak to me, Master," she begged.

She was very beautiful.

She squirmed in the loops of yellow cord holding her wrists behind her back.

"I understand," she said, "why I must be blindfolded, that you have doubtless here, in the privacy of your own chambers, removed your mask. I am not to be permitted to see the face of the courier of Ragnar Voskjard, no more than others, even though I am only a lowly slave. Who knows through what sales or changings of hands a girl who is mere property such as I might pass? You cannot risk that I might, someday, somewhere, if only by inadvertence, perhaps by a startled cry or gesture, or a too-eager licking at your feet, compromise your secret."

I was interested that she had spoken, and naturally, of the licking of feet. That sort of thing is common in a slave girl. Did she not know she was from Earth?

"But you cannot even speak to me, Master?" she begged. "Ah!" she said. "That you do not speak to me must also be intended to conceal your identity! You would not wish me to be able to recognize even your voice!" She trembled. "Or is it, rather," she asked, "that I am so low a slave that you do not concern yourself even to speak to me?"

I smiled. Whereas the frightened, deferential slave had not recognized me sitting regally with Policrates and Kliomenes in the feasting hall, in the robes and mask of the courier of Ragnar Voskjard, I did not doubt but what she might quickly recognize my voice.

"I have it, Master," she said, happily. "If you do not speak to help protect your identity, touch me once upon the left shoulder. If you do not speak because you regard me as only a contemptible slave, unworthy to be spoken to, touch me once upon the left arm."

She lifted her body, tensing to see where she might be touched.

"Please, Master!" she begged.

But I did not move.

She then knelt back, on her heels. "I see, Master," she said, miserably. "Not even that is to be made known to me." She shuddered. "Do you not know how terrifying it is to be in a room, blindfolded, with one who does not speak to you? Ah, perhaps you do!" She smiled. "You well know how to treat a slave, Master," she said.

I was interested to note that she spoke of herself, naturally, as a slave.

"But yet," she said, "you are permitting me to speak. You have not struck me to silence, nor put a block of wood in my mouth, or gagged me. I may gather, then, that at least until I feel your blow, or the lash of your whip, that you wish to hear me speak. But why would this be? What could I, a mere slave, have to say that might interest you?"

She pulled at the cord loops. She seemed genuinely puzzled.

"How am I different from the other girls?" she asked herself, aloud, thinking.

"Of course!" she said, suddenly, delightedly. "Now I have it! I am the only Earth girl in the holding! They told you I was from Earth, didn't they! You are not familiar with Earth girls. That intrigued you! They must have told you. You did not take me in your hands and force open my mouth, to look for bits of metal in my teeth. I do not think my accent betrayed me, for there are many barbarian accents on Gor, and I speak Gorean excellently."

I smiled, the vain little thing, but it was true that she did speak a liquid, fluent Gorean. Her linguistic skills in this respect, and I have unusual aptitude in such matters, approached my own.

"That my masters call me 'Beverly'," she said, "would not in itself tell you that I was from Earth. Not unoften Gorean girls, particularly if they are to be consigned to a low slavery, are given such names. Perhaps, then, you might have seen the tiny scarring high on my left arm. It is called a 'vaccination mark.'"

I smiled. Such marks, and fillings in the teeth, are used by slavers as almost infallible signs of Earth origin. And woe to the girl who has them, for she is almost certainly then to be marked out for heavier chains and more ruthless treatment.

"But, on the whole," she said, "I think it most likely that you were merely told that I was from Earth. This, then, you found of interest. You decided, then, that it was to be I who would come to your chambers this evening. Did you wish merely to see if we, being lower, were juicier puddings than our Gorean sisters, or, beyond this, as a matter of curiosity, did you wish to learn something of our nature?"

It amused me that Miss Henderson had used the graphic Gorean expression that she had, an expression almost always applied to a slave, a hot and helpless lay. From my own experience I did not think Earth girls were juicier puddings, so to speak, than Gorean girls, nor, really, that Gorean girls tended to be juicier puddings than Earth girls. It is true, of course, that the slave tends to be a far juicier pudding, so to speak, than the free woman of either world. Some Earth girls are marvelous in the furs, and some Gorean girls are. Much depends on the individual girl. This is to be expected, of course, for all Gorean girls, as far as I know, have ultimately an Earth origin. I think it is true, however, that an Earth girl may sometimes have an extra dimension of lovely, yielding slavishness in her, which is perhaps natural, considering the sexual desert from which she has been rescued. She can remember her loneliness and frustration, how she, a slave, languished in a world where she could find no masters. Such women, in time, find themselves overwhelmed in gratitude for the collar. For the first time, in spite of the world from which they come, they are forced to become true women. Thus they find fulfillment, and joy. To the Gorean free woman the joys of the slave girl, though they may be despised and disparaged, are at least culturally not unknown, and are the envy of such free women. To the Earth woman, on the other hand, who finds herself in the collar of a Gorean master, such joys come as a revelation. Only in her wildest and most secret dreams had she dared even to suspect their existence. Then she finds herself a slave girl.

"I think," said Miss Henderson, "that it is your intention to try me, to try me out, to sample an Earth girl, to see if we might be of interest, but as of yet, in spite of my helplessness before you, you have not done so. Further, you have permitted me to speak. I gather, thus, that you will use me when it pleases you and, in the meantime, that I, though only a slave, am to speak before you." She smiled. "I shall do so, Master."

It was natural for her to think that I, whom she believed to be Gorean, would be interested to hear of her world, and of the nature of the female slaves taken from it. Earth slave girls are controversial on Gor, though I think they are now more accepted than formerly. Some men have a taste for Earth females. Other men will not even own them. A not uncommon task for an Earth female on Gor is to attempt to secure the affections of a Gorean master who regards her as nothing and despises her. For months, through assiduous application, through attentiveness and study, through a selfless love and service, such a woman may labor to convince the brute who owns her that she is worthy to wear his collar. Then perhaps one day he looks down upon her kneeling before him. His hand touches the side of her head. Was it a gentle gesture? She takes his hand and presses her lips, sobbing, fervently to it. He takes her by the arms and presses her back, gently, to the tiles, a love slave. When he is finished with her he takes his whip and orders her to her knees. Perhaps he strikes her, perhaps he puts the whip to her mouth, and she kisses it. Well then does she know she is still a slave. He turns away. She, kneeling, her head down, smiles shyly, happily.

"My name was Beverly Henderson," she said, "and I am from a world called Earth. Doubtless you have heard something of it. I assure you that it exists. I was captured there by slavers and brought to Gor, that I might wear a collar and learn to serve true men—such as you, Master, who are so strong that you have stripped me, and bound me and put me at your feet, your slave." She smiled. "No man of Earth," she said, "is strong enough to do that."

I smiled.

"The women of Earth," she said, "are starved for strong men. I cannot tell you the restlessness, the misery and frustration they feel. The men of Earth are not true men. Perhaps once they were, long ago, but that is now history. Now they are weak and ineffectual. Manhood among them is measured by its lack. No longer are they capable of true manhood."

I doubted what she said, but, surely, I had no intention of explicitly gainsaying her. I thought it best to let her speak.

"Females," she said, "are the natural property of men such as Goreans, not of men such as those of Earth. It is men such as Goreans, and not men such as those of Earth, who recognize the meaning of our beauty and simply take us, and make us serve them. But I have bathed Master and now kneel naked and bound before him. I tell him nothing."

She squirmed in the close confines of the loops of braided yellow cord. They held her well.

"I was taken to the House of Andronicus, in Vonda," she said. "There, with other girls from Earth, more than fifty of us, I was branded. I remember one of the girls, pulled sobbing and in pain from the rack, crying out, joyfully, "I am a slave girl!" How startling, and strange, seemed her cry. Yet I, too, later, after I had screamed and sobbed, and had been pulled, my thigh stinging from the iron, from the rack, and found myself alone, chained on the straw by the damp wall, was filled with strange emotions. Though I could scarcely admit it to myself I knew, with wild, strange feelings, that I was glad that I, too, had been branded. "You were born for the brand," I whispered to myself, "and now, incomprehensibly, wonderfully, on this strange world, it has at last been put upon you. In your pain, rejoice, Slave Girl. You are now publicly marked, clearly and incontrovertibly, as what in your secret heart you have always been. Serve your masters well, Slave Girl."

I sat on the couch. My fists were clenched. Did she not know she was from Earth!

"Most of us, of course, including myself, dared not yet admit we were pleased with our brands. We lamented together, pretending to bemoan the misery of our plights. Our masters, of course, did not give us a great deal of time to indulge our self-pity. We must be prepared for markets. We were then separated and sent to different training rooms. There I was forced to kneel, and was put in a house collar. I was then chained at a ring and given my first whipping. Thus did I learn what the lash might feel like upon me, and that I was under discipline. My slave reflexes were tested and found, as is the case with most Earth females, initially inert. Held on my knees, my head held back, my nose pinched shut, my mouth forced open, slave wine was poured down my throat. I must needs swallow. I was then hooded and men were called in, who abused me, as it pleased them. Then, a day later, still hooded, I was returned to the central dungeon."

She paused. "I have not been struck," she said. "Therefore I gather that I have Master's permission to continue."

"How beautiful you are," breathed a girl in the dungeon to me, when I had been unhooded. "How beautiful you are," I whispered, seeing her. "Were you whipped?" she asked. "Yes," I said. "I, too," she said, head down. I looked about the dungeon, at the girls there. How soft, and beautiful they were, in their collars. The collar, as Master well knows, considerably enhances the beauty of a woman. "Were you raped?" asked the girl, a lovely blonde. "Yes," I said. "They used me well." "I, too," she said. "I enjoyed my rape," said a redhead, collared, in an ankle ring, and chain, lying near us in the straw. "Slave!" hissed another girl to her. "Yes, slave," smiled the redhead. My intimacies sprang aflame when I heard her words. How bold she was! I myself would not have dared to admit such a thing to another woman! What might she think of me? I had not even, scarcely, dared to admit to myself, or recall, that in the arms of the fifth man my body had clasped his, and my arms, and I had, in the darkness of the hood, a moaning slave, subdued, cried out with pleasure. Then, too soon, they had been finished with me. That night I had lain in the darkness of the hood, hungry, recollecting the sensations they had induced in me. Now, though I could scarcely admit this to myself, I feared, and feared correctly, that the first fires of a slave's passion had been ignited within me. I had known that I was a slave, and a true slave, before they had touched me, but I had not known, until they took me in their arms, how helpless and low a slave I could be."

I could scarcely believe my ears. It seemed that Miss Henderson, without thought, before me, was confessing herself a slave. She was from Earth!

"What is to be done with us?" asked one of the girls. "I think we are to be readied for markets," said another girl. There was then a beating on the bars of the dungeon and we knelt. A man entered, with a whip. Our training began."

She smiled at me. "We were taught to kneel, and to crawl, and to move and walk. We were taught the use of our hands, and of our total body, and our hair, and of our mouth and tongue. We were taught many things. The first words of Gorean I learned were 'I am a slave girl.' But our masters did not waste much time on us. Our new masters, those who would buy us, could teach us more. The night before we were to be sold, we were permitted to speak to one another. We kissed one another, and cried, for we knew that we might soon never see one another again, and we did not know what lay before us, outside the confines of the House of Andronicus, in the harsh world of Gor. None of us, of course, had been sold before. Interestingly, however, we were looking forward to our sales. It was not just that we wished to be out of the House of Andronicus. It was rather, I think, that we were now eager to belong to masters. You see, Master, in the past few days, a startling transformation had come over us. Few of us mentioned this, but I think there was not one amongst us who did not clearly recognize it. We had become, honestly, female slaves. Here we may distinguish between two concepts of slavery, that which can be imposed and constitutes an absolute and legal condition, and that which is instinctual and innate, which, under certain conditions, can be manifested and released. The fullest slave, of course, is she who is a natural slave, and then, beyond this, truly wears the collar, that slave who is a slave by nature and whose slavery, released, is then confirmed and fixed upon her openly, publicly, by all the sanctions of custom and law, for all the world to see. What we discovered, Master, all of us, in the dungeons and training rooms of the House of Andronicus, was that we were natural slaves. There our slavery had been, by such devices as brands and collars, and whips and hoods, fully, for the first time, released in us and made manifest. Many of us were timid and thrilled to discover that we were natural slaves. At last there could be an end to the lies and pretenses. At last we could stop fighting ourselves and pretending to be what we were not. We now, though women of Earth, could admit to ourselves what we were. This gave us great joy. Beyond this, of course, we knew we were, categorically and absolutely, legal slaves, lovely properties which might be bartered and sold, and who might figure in transactions which would be upheld in any court of law. This we found frightening, but absolutely thrilling. It so confirmed our slavery upon us! There was no escape for us! Even if we should pull at our chains, or cry or rebel, we would still be only troublesome slaves, who might then be disciplined and brought swiftly into line. Any person on the street, seeing us, would know what we were. Even children would know us as mere slaves, for, categorically, and legally, that is what we would be. Owned animals, that is what we would be! You are a man, Master, so perhaps you cannot understand, or fully understand, how exciting it is for a woman to be owned, to find herself a slave. But I am a slave, and a natural slave, and a legal slave. I am fearful. But I am joyful!"

Angrily I rose from the couch. I seized up the whip. I thrust it to her mouth. "I kiss your whip, joyfully, Master," she whispered.

I looked down at her, enraged. Beverly Henderson had kissed the whip.

"Master?" she asked, frightened. She was very beautiful, bound before me, on her knees.

I returned to the couch, angry, and sat down upon it. I again regarded her.

She smiled, uncertainly. "I have kissed Master's whip," she said. "Does he not now wish to use me? Does he not now wish to try out an Earth girl?"

I did not respond.

"Surely I have told Master enough, now, about girls of Earth," she said. "Is his curiosity not now satisfied? Does he not understand us now to be natural slaves, the rightful properties of men such as he?"

I did not respond.

"After that night," she said, "we were divided into smaller lots and distributed throughout various markets. I think they did not wish, for some reason, to sell too many Earth girls in a given market. I found my own sale indescribably thrilling. I was exhibited naked. I was forced to perform lasciviously on the block, as a female slave. Even my slave reflexes were exhibited to the crowd. I was auctioned. I was sold to the highest bidder." She smiled. "I have had various Masters, and various names. Eventually I came into the possession of the holding of Policrates, wherein you find me. There is little more to tell."

I did not respond.

"Here I am called 'Beverly'," she smiled. "It was my name originally, on Earth, as you may recall I mentioned earlier. Now of course I wear it only as a slave name, by the whim of Masters. Still it pleases me. I think it is an excellent slave name."

I, too, thought so, looking upon her.

"You understand, of course, Master," she said, "that I would not have spoken to a man of Earth, those pathetic and ineffectual fools, with the intimacy, the frankness and honesty with which I have addressed you, a man of Gor."

I said nothing.

"What miserable weaklings they are," she said.

I said nothing.

Suddenly she leaned forward. She strained against the loops of yellow cord which confined her wrists behind her body. Her knees moved on the furs, among the chains. I saw the steel at her throat. "The slut in me desires to serve a Master," she whispered, suddenly, intensely. "Please, Master!"

I rose to my feet, and looked down at her.

"I am the slave of a man such as you!" she said.

I then, suddenly, savagely, seized her by the upper arms. I dragged her to the center of the room. I lifted her high above me, bound, her dark hair, unbound, loose and wild about her. I then, slowly, lowered her, to where her toes could just touch the floor. Then, suddenly, angrily, I shook her. "Master!" she cried out, miserably. I then dragged her back before the couch, where I stood her on her feet, before me. She felt the furs beneath her feet, the chains. I regarded her, in fury. I snapped my fingers. Immediately she knelt before me, bound, among the chains. She looked up, though she could see nothing in the confines of the blindfold.

I looked down at her.

Beverly Henderson, a self-confessed slave, and the most desirable woman I had ever seen, was at my feet. She was naked and bound, mine!

I was filled then with emotions so powerful, so primitive and exultant, so ancient, so overwhelming, so mighty and glorious, that I knew then I had caught the scent of the meaning of man, and of woman. Could I again deny my blood? Could I again repudiate the heritage of my manhood? How could it be? The meat of the mammoth roasted then again upon the greenwood spit. Once again, after an interim of ten thousand years, sparks were struck from blue flint, as heavy, hairy hands shaped the head of a spear. Once more were heard the love whimpers of the thonged female, who had been displeasing, begging to be released that she might lick the thighs of her master.

I looked down at her. I knew then that I had always wanted Beverly Henderson as my slave. From the first instant I had seen her I had wanted her as my slave!

"Master," she whimpered. "Master!"

Then I stood before her with my fists clenched and threw back my head and wanted to howl with misery. Surely she must be a free woman! She must be free! She was from Earth! But could everything that my blood, my instincts and impulses told me be wrong? But it must be, else a civilization structured upon, and predicated upon, pathologies must disintegrate and perish. But could there not be a civilization congenial to the truths of the blood, to the nature of human beings. Is man so foolish, so naive and habit-bound, so fundamentally irrational, so ready to believe anything that he might be taught, no matter how absurd, that he cannot understand that torture cannot be truth. The test for truth, surely, must not be pain, misery and frustration, but happiness and joy.

"Master," she whimpered.

But surely she must be free!

But what if she were a true slave, as she had indicated?

But she could not be a true slave. She was from Earth!

But what if, even though she were from Earth, she were a true slave, as in accord with her own avowals? Could such a thing, she from Earth, be possible, even thinkable?

I scarcely dared even consider this possibility, for then she, a slave, could be mine!

I determined, cruelly, to make test of the matter.

I untied her hands. I waited then for her to shrink back in terror, to, feeling her way, try to retreat to the far wall, perhaps cowering there, at my mercy.

But her head was at my feet. I felt her lips kissing my feet. Beverly Henderson was at my feet! "Forgive me, Master," she said, "if I have displeased you." She was then holding my legs, putting her cheek against them, and kissing them. "Forgive your slave," she said, "and let your slave please you."

I then seized her by the arms and jerked her to her feet. She was startled. Savagely I jerked her small hands behind her back and, with the yellow cord, tied them there, tightly. "Master?" she asked, frightened. I snapped my fingers. She knelt. I snapped my fingers again. She stood. I then threw her, bodily, onto the deep furs on the surface of the couch. She lay there, on her side. I picked up the whip and shook out its coils. She heard the sound, and moaned. I approached her. She was tense, frightened. She, in the darkness of the blindfold, could see nothing. She shuddered in fear as I touched the whip lightly to her body, moving it upon her right calf. She gasped. Then I moved the whip about on her body, slowly, curiously, observing her responses. She was tense, and frightened. "Please do not whip me, Master," she said. I put the flat, leather coils of the whip then to her mouth. She, lying on her side, fervently, frightened, kissed them, again and again. "Please do not whip me, Master," she begged.

I put the whip on the couch, to one side, where I might have it at hand, to lash her if she were not totally pleasing.

I then had her, and as the bound slave she was.

She cried out, startled, taken with such force. I looked down at her, gripped in my arms. I dragged her from the couch and threw her then on the chains and furs at its foot. In my desire, and in my eagerness, and in my fury and joy, I had had the wench on the surface of the great couch itself. But she now lay bound at the foot of the couch, in the shadow of the slave ring, trembling, in a more fit place for a slave such as she. I then again took her. She was gasping, and shuddering. It is sometimes months before a girl is permitted, commanded, to ascend her master's couch. Even then she commonly enters it not as a free person, directly, but as a slave, from the lower left, or bottom, after first kneeling and kissing its furs. She cried out, shuddering in my arms, suddenly had again. "Oh, Master," she sobbed, "Master!" My hands were again hard on her arms. I, kneeling then, pulled her, too, to her knees. Then I shook her and threw her to her side, on the furs and chains, against the bottom of the couch. She was sobbing, and gasping. She pulled against the cord loops on her wrists. There were marks, from my hands, on her arms. "Please, Master," she sobbed. She rose, terrified, to her knees, and then to her feet, trying to escape. She stumbled, in the blindfold, against the edge of the couch, crying out, bruising herself. She then stumbled from the couch, frightened, lost her footing and, crying out, turning, fell into the tub. She tried to scramble, weeping, to her feet, but I was on her in an instant. I forced her to her knees in the water and then, holding her by the hair, not permitting her to leave her knees, I forced her head back until her dark hair, beneath where I had it knotted in my hand, was loose, floating in the water, and the bow of her exquisite slave beauty was well exposed to me. I regarded her for a time, so held. "Please, Master," she wept, "be gentle with me." Angrily then, my hand still in her hair, I jerked her head forward and, still keeping her on her knees, crouching over her, I thrust her face beneath the water. I held it there for a time, and then pulled it up. Sputtering, half blinded by the water, gasping, she wept, "Please, Master, forgive me! I did not mean to displease you!"

I then flung her on her back in the water and, she struggling, gasping, trying to keep her head above water, again had her. Then I thrust her up, half sitting, half lying, against the edge of the tub. She turned her head toward me, gasping. The blindfold was sopped, but secure. Her hair and body were soaked and wet. The cord loops, soaked, were still tight on her small wrists. Her body, wet, was interesting to touch. Then I again had her.

"Master," she sobbed.

I rose to my feet and stepped from the tub. I walked slowly, shuddering, about the room. Then I was calm. I looked back at her. She was half lying, half kneeling, against the side of the tub. I went to her and took her by the collar and pulled her to her feet, and from the tub, and to the foot of the couch, where I put her to her knees. Crouching near her I toweled dry the steel loop on her throat. It, like her, belonged to Policrates. I then, gently, dried her hair, and wrapped a towel about it. Also, because I intended to put her in the ankle ring, I dried her left ankle. I did not dry her beyond those things, however, what was necessary to protect the collar and steel of Policrates. I then locked her left ankle in the ankle ring, thus fastening her, by a length of chain, to the foot of my couch. Had she been my own girl I probably would have dried her completely. It is pleasant, as one may well imagine, to towel one's slave.

"Master," she wept. "Master."

I made her lie down there, at the foot of the great couch. I then, satisfied, and fulfilled as I would not have believed possible, entered upon the great couch and lay wearily upon its furs.

"Master," she sobbed.

I was soon asleep.

* * * *

I dreamed that Beverly Henderson was chained naked at my slave ring.

Then I awakened. I left the couch and walked about it, to its foot.

Beverly Henderson was chained there, naked, at my slave ring.

I kicked her, softly, with the side of my foot.

She was not asleep.

She rose to her knees, and put her head down, humbly.

It was near dawn. Gray light entered the room. Her wrists were still tied behind her. I had not released them. "It must be near morning, Master," she said. She could not be certain. She wore the blindfold.

I took her by the upper arms and lifted her to her feet. The towel, in the night, had come loose from her hair. I touched her hair. It was still damp.

I lifted her in my arms, gently, and placed her on the furs of the couch.

"Thank you, Master," she said, "for permitting me the honor of your couch."

I said nothing.

"I gather that it must now be near morning," she said, "though I cannot know that. I gather, too, that Master is now refreshed. I have been lifted and placed upon his couch. Doubtless I am now to please him, his slave."

I said nothing.

"Master well brutalized me last night," she said. "He taught me well that I am a slave. I shall endeavor to please him well."

I said nothing.

"But how can I please him?" she asked. "I am bound!"

I did not, of course, respond to her.

"Ah, yes!" she said. "I am an Earth girl! Master is still curious about Earth girls! He wants to know if we know how to give pleasures to masters."

So saying, attentively and lasciviously, as a bound slave she addressed herself to my pleasures.

She did well.

When she had finished, and I had rested, I threw her to her stomach and unbound her hands. Swiftly then, and eagerly, feeling for me, she knelt beside me. "I will show you now, Master," she said, "what truly an Earth girl can do!"

I lay there then and wondered if ever other men of Earth had experienced such pleasures, if ever they had had such pleasures from their females. Perhaps only, I thought, if their females, like Miss Henderson, were their slaves.

"It is thus," whispered Miss Henderson to me, "that we serve our Gorean masters!"

I said nothing.

"Do you now wonder," she laughed softly, holding me, quietly snuggling against me, "why it is that we are sought in the slave markets, why it is that we bring high prices?"

Though I did not respond to her her services had come as a revelation to me. I had not even suspected that Earth women were capable of such marvels. Collared, and under discipline, what incredible treasures they were! They were joys, and priceless! Men, I knew, would kill to possess such women. Petty, arrogant, smug, cold, proud, inert, frustrated, the women of Earth trod the sands of their native world; the men of Earth, I thought, did not begin to suspect the gold into which such pain and dross could be transmuted; how long, I wondered, before such creatures were brought naked to their knees before masters.

"How I despise the men of Earth," said the girl to me. "How I love my Gorean master!"

I then began, for the first time, to truly, attentively caress her.

"You are going to make me yield, aren't you?" she gasped. I then continued, patiently, carefully, to touch her. She then began to tremble, and sometimes tried to pull away from me, and at other times to press against me. I controlled her, sometimes letting her do as she wished, and at other times not permitting it. She lay on her back, her lips parted. She began to moan, the whimpers of a collared slave girl. I felt her. She was hot and open, gaping, saturated with the lubricating oils of her readiness. I smiled to myself. The slut was a hot slave. I was pleased with Miss Henderson. "I'm yours, Master," she whispered. "Please have me." I then took her, and she cried out with the unmistakable, rapturous submission of the surrendered slave girl. She then grasped me tightly, fearing that I would leave her. When she understood that I was content to hold her, she lay warmly in my arms, sometimes kissing me. "You have conquered me, Master," she said, "as you have doubtless conquered many other girls before me."

I said nothing.

"I am owned," she said. "That pleases me."

I began to kiss her about the neck and throat. She put her head back, laughing. "I am an Earth girl," she said. "Do you like us?"

I continued to kiss her.

"Are we not juicy puddings?" she laughed. "Is it not clear now why men will buy us?"

She clutched me to her, and kissed me. "Would you not like to buy one of us?" she said.

I held her from me.

"Buy me, Master," she said, suddenly. "Buy me!"

I did not let her touch me, though she strained toward me, the pretty slut, the clever slut, to press her beauty, piteously, entreatingly, against me.

"I have never been in the arms of a man such as you," she said. "I love you! I want to be your slave!"

I did not speak.

"Put me beneath your whip," she said. "Put me in your chains. Lock your collar upon my throat! Own me!"

I regarded her.

"Please buy me," she begged. "Please own me! I will try to be a good slave to you!"

I did not permit her to touch me.

Then she laughed, a tear running from beneath the blindfold. "How brazen we Earth girls are," she laughed, "how shameless, that we would beg to be purchased! How you must despise us, such lowly, desperate slaves!"

I then entered Miss Henderson and she gasped, clutching me.

I smiled. It was not unusual for a slave girl, fervently, to desire to be purchased by a given man, one before whom she knows she could kneel as a superb slave. In such a case it is natural for her to present herself as piteously and excitingly before him as possible, in order that his interest might be aroused. She, obviously, has nothing to say about her purchase. The choice is his, fully. It is he who is the buyer. This sort of thing is not unusual in slave markets, particularly on open platforms. I have seen, many times, a girl attempting to interest a given man, singled out, in the crowd, in buying her. And, not unoften, such a fellow will bid upon her, knowing well the wonders which she, purchased from her owner, is offering him. Still, in the end, it is his which is the choice. She can do no more than present herself, displaying her owner's merchandise as attractively as she can. It is he who will buy or not. He is the master.

"I love my Gorean master," breathed the girl. "Buy Beverly, please!"

I have also seen girls attempt to influence their sales in public auctions, while being exhibited naked on the block, trying to present themselves particularly to a given man, but this disposition is usually curbed by the auctioneer's whip. She is not there to be sold to the man of her choice but to the highest bidder. Indeed, in most public auctions, such actions on the part of the girl are for most practical purposes impossible. Such auctions are usually held at night, when men are off work, and can come to the biddings, under torches. The block tends to be illuminated and the house is much in darkness. The girl, naked, in the light, exhibited, can be well seen, but she herself can see few of the buyers. She is intensely aware, of course, of their presence, in the crowds, in the tiers. Their sounds, their cries, their breathing, their movements, the sweat, the smells, their interest, are clearly evident to her, almost engulfing her on the block, almost like possessive hands upon her body. She can then influence her sale, guided by the auctioneer's whip, only in such a way as to present herself as the most luscious slave meat she can, hoping thereby to improve her price, that she may be purchased by a more well-to-do master. Yet most girls are sold for prices in similar ranges and there are few men who cannot, by spending an extra coin or two, secure the slave of their choice. Often when the hand of the auctioneer has been closed a girl will not know to whom she has been sold. She may not have seen the bidder, or she may have been purchased through an agent. Sometimes it is a day or more before she learns to what chain she has been sold. In this time she does not know if she has been purchased by the man of her dreams, who will control her well, or by some harsh, cruel brute, before whom she must kneel in terror. To be sure, she will soon learn.

"Buy me, Master," begged Beverly.

I then made her respond to me, and she began to moan. "I want to be bought," she moaned.

To beg to be purchased is a slave's act. That is a saying of Goreans. I think it is true. In this, then, Miss Henderson provided further confirmation of the rightness of the collar upon her throat, that she was a natural and true slave.

"If I yield well to you, Master," wheedled Miss Henderson, "will you buy me?"

I then, savagely, struck her face, back and forth, with the palm of my hand, and then its back.

"Forgive me, Master," she cried, "I did not mean to bargain! I will yield to you fully, and perfectly, at your least command! Do not kill me, Master, please!"

There was blood on my hand, and at her mouth. Her lip was swollen.

I kissed her upon the swollen lip, and she whimpered. I tasted her blood.

"Please do not kill me, Master," she begged.

I then took her.

When I finished with her I rose up from the couch. She lay there, frightened.

"I did not mean to displease my Gorean master," she said. "I did not think. Take pity on me. I am only a slave."

I pulled her from the couch, to her knees at the slave ring.

"Permit me to placate you, Master," she begged.

I permitted her to perform intimate services for me. I then buckled the thick leather slave cuffs on her wrists. "Master?" she asked. I then thrust her right wrist through the slave ring and, with the heavy metal snaps, sewn into the cuffs, secured her there.

She heard the strands of the whip shaken out. "Please do not whip me, Master," she begged. Then she put down her head. Then I lashed her, for she had been displeasing.

I cast aside the whip and drew on my tunic, and gathered together my things.

At the door I turned, to look back at the sobbing girl. She turned her head toward me, it still secured in the blindfold. She knelt naked at the ring, fastened to it by the cuffs, and, too, by the ankle ring, still locked upon her left ankle. She wore her collar.

"I love you, Master," she said. "It is to such a man as you that I wish to belong."

I put down my things at the door. I went back to her. I pulled her out from the ring, half on her back, her hands above and behind her, twisted and helpless in the slave cuffs, held at the ring.

"Forgive me, if I was displeasing to you, Master," she begged.

I looked at her.

"I love you, my Gorean master," she said.

I then, again, took her. Spasmodically she shook and yielded, as I would not have thought it possible for a woman to do. She sobbed and shuddered in ecstasy, a had slave.

"I submit to you, Master," she wept, "totally and completely. You are my Master. I am your slave."

I withdrew from her, and stood, and looked down upon her.

"Do not leave me, Master," she begged. 'Take me with you. You have made me yours, my Gorean master. I am yours. Take me with you. Policrates, my master, would give me to you, if you should but ask!"

I picked up my things at the door. I slung them about me. I donned my mask. There was a knock on the door, and I opened it. A pirate stood there, he who had brought Beverly to me last night, who had now come to fetch me to breakfast. I must soon leave the holding of Policrates, theoretically to journey downriver to the holding of Ragnar Voskjard, that his fleet might be soon launched, that the two fleets, in fierce force, might overwhelm the garrisons of Ar's Station, and then of Port Cos, that the river, for hundreds of pasangs, would then become theirs, subject to their predations or levied tributes as they saw fit.

I nodded to the pirate, indicating my readiness to accompany him.

He looked beyond me, to the slave ring. The girl now knelt there, cuffed to the ring. He seemed startled. "Is it Beverly?" he asked. The girl, suddenly, shrank back against the stone of the couch, a slave's movement. Curious, the pirate brushed past me, going to the girl. He crouched down beside her. "It is Beverly," he said. She trembled. He put forth his hand, touching her at the shoulder. She shuddered beneath his touch, putting down her head. "What have you done to her?" he asked, grinning. "Last night she was an enslaved female. This morning she is a female slave." He put forth his hand and held her, with one hand, his fingers about her chin and throat. She shuddered. "I would say," he grinned, "that she is now more truly aware of her condition, that you have much improved her." He did not remove his hand from her throat and chin. "Were you much improved last night, Beverly?" he asked.

"Yes, Master," she said.

"Policrates," he said, "told me that if you were troublesome you were to be fed to sleen."

She shuddered.

"But I see that you were not troublesome," he said.

"No, Master," she said.

He removed his hand from her throat and chin, and continued to regard her. She knelt, soft and helpless, trembling, held in the leather cuffs at the slave ring.

"I see that you are much different this morning, from last night," he said.

"Yes, Master," she said.

He then, with his hand, touched her left calf, running his fingers lightly over it. She whimpered, and drew back. "Interesting," he said.

Her response had been that of a helpless, superb slave.

"What was done to you last night?" he asked.

"I was mastered," she said.

"It is obvious," he said, and rose to his feet. He turned to face me, and grinned. He jerked his thumb back toward the kneeling slave. "Policrates will be pleased," he said.

I shrugged.

When a girl has been mastered, of course, she is more fit for any man.

Miss Henderson, in the blindfold, on her knees at the ring, turned to face us, as she could.

We looked back upon her. It was a superb slave who knelt there. Miss Henderson, in the night, I saw, now clearly, remembering her from the evening before, had been brought to a new dimension in her slavery.

The pirate laughed.

The girl shrank back against the stone of the couch. The snaps on the cuffs rubbed against the slave ring.

The pirate then walked slowly towards her. She cowered back, fearing to be struck.

He stopped, standing before her.

She lifted her head to him but was, of course, unable to see him, prevented with perfection from doing so by the efficiency of the Gorean blindfold. She squirmed in the cuffs, unable to see, in a slave's fear.

The pirate stood looking at her, his hands on his hips.

Every inch of her was beautiful, and enslaved. She would now be a dream of pleasure for any man.

"Who owns you?" he asked.

"Policrates," she said.

"And more generally," he said, "who owns you?"

"Men," she said.

The pirate then turned about and rejoined me, by the door. He then went through the door, and I was to follow him. I did turn about, once, to look again upon the girl. "Master!" she cried out to me, piteously, in the darkness of the blindfold, stretching her small cuffed hands, as she could, entreatingly, toward me. "Master! Master!"

Then I went through the door and closed it behind me. "Master!" I heard her cry. "Master!"

Then I had left her behind me, merely a girl fastened at the foot of a couch, only a slave who had served one of her master's guests.

Twenty Five

In the Tavern of Tasdron Men Meet in Secret

"Withdraw, Slave," said Tasdron, proprietor of the tavern of Tasdron, in Victoria, off the avenue of Lycurgus.

"Yes, Master," said Peggy, bowing her head, deferentially, and backing gracefully from the table, as a slave. She was barefoot, and wore a brief snatch of diaphanous, yellow pleasure silk. Her long blond hair was tied back with a yellow ribbon. The close-fitting steel collar was lovely on her throat. The rustle of the slave bells locked on her left ankle was subtle and sensual. She withdrew to the far side of the room and knelt there, back on her heels, knees wide, as befitted the sort of slave she was, a mere pleasure slave.

Callimachus, sitting across from me, regarded her. She put her head down, unable to meet the eyes of such a man. I saw that she trembled under his gaze. I smiled to myself. I had seen how she had looked upon him, in her serving, and when she had knelt near the table. Her eyes had been soft and moist, and tender, and vulnerable and helpless. I had sensed how she had restrained herself from lowering herself softly to her belly on the floor before him and extending her hand to him, begging his touch, and that he would make her his. But she did not wish to be slain for such insolence, she only a lowly Earth-girl slave. I had seen the look in her eyes. In her eyes had been the light of a helpless slave girl's love. I recalled that once she had told me that there was only one man on all Gor to whom she would rather belong than myself, and that he did not even know, or scarcely knew, of her existence. I had not pressed her to reveal his name. But now I had no doubt I had penetrated her secret. In her heart the embonded

Earth girl was the secret love slave of Callimachus, a warrior once of
Port Cos. But she dared not make her feelings known to him. She did
not wish to be slain. Accordingly she could be to him little more than
any other slave, only another girl, self-effacing, deferential, scarcely
noticed, who served him in the establishment of her master, Tasdron
of Victoria. In spite of her beauty and his frequent use of the tavern of
Tasdron he had never ordered her, whip in hand, to strip and hurry to
an alcove for his pleasure. In the misery of his dereliction and afflicted
by the devitalizing consequences attendant upon it he had preferred
the indulgences of self-pity and the delusory solaces of paga to the
exultant and proud imposition of his will, as a dominant male, on
the hearts and bodies of writhing female slaves. Then when he had
recalled himself to the codes of his caste he had resolved to forgo the
victories and the rights, and the joys and triumphs, of the mastership
until certain serious, projected works had been accomplished. It was
in connection with such works that we had met this night in the tavern
of Tasdron.

"You understand," said Tasdron, "that it is dangerous for me even
to be a party to these matters."

Callimachus looked away from the girl, kneeling, head down, by
the far wall. She was only a slave.

"If men such as Kliomenes or Policrates should understand that we
are met on such subjects, my tavern, at the least, would be speedily
reduced to ashes."

"That is understood, Tasdron," said Callimachus. "We are sensitive
to the danger that there is in this for you."

"But there is surely," said Tasdron, "much greater danger for you."

"We will accept the risks," said Callimachus.

"I, too, then," said Tasdron, "will do no less."

"Good," said Callimachus.

We spoke softly. We sat about a small table in a back room in
Tasdron's tavern. Callimachus had kept the repudiation of his dereliction a secret from those in Victoria. When he went about in public it
seemed his shoulders were bent, his eyes bleared, his step uncertain,
his hand unsure. It was only at times like now, when with trusted
men, that he sat, and carried himself, and spoke, as a warrior. Victoria
knew him still as only a fallen man, one defeated, one lax in his caste
codes, one inert and whining in traps of his own weaving. They knew

him still, as we had decided fit for our plans, as only a self-forsaken ruin and drunkard. They needed not know that he who had fallen had now risen; that once more the codes were kept with pride; that the cords with which he had once, with such pain and skill, bound himself, he had now sundered and torn from him, like an enraged larl emerging fiercely from a net now too frail to hold him. He had recalled that he was Callimachus, of the Warriors, one entrusted with steel, one entitled to wear the scarlet of the proud caste. I did not think it likely that he would forget these things again.

"I have spoken to Glyco, Merchant of Port Cos," said Callimachus. "He will fetch Callisthenes, who is captain of the forces of Port Cos in Victoria, he in search of the topaz. He will come to this place at the twentieth Ahn."

"He must come in disguise," said Tasdron. "Spies are everywhere."

"That will be made clear to him by Glyco," said Callimachus.

I observed Peggy, the long-haired, long-legged, blond Earth-girl slave, kneeling, head down, by the far wall. Her shoulders shook with a sob. She was so near to him whom she so vulnerably and desperately loved and yet, as a slave, must remain helplessly silent.

"Have you made inquiries among those of Victoria?" asked Callimachus of Tasdron. "Is there support for our work in the town?"

"I have with circumspection made these inquiries," said Tasdron, dourly, "but I fear there is little support in this place for such dangerous labors."

"We can expect no aid, then, from Victoria?" said Callimachus.

"None," said Tasdron.

I continued to watch the girl, her head down, at the far wall. She, a female and a slave, had been banished to that place, that she might not be privy to the discourse of men and masters. Yet she was close enough to be promptly summoned, to serve instantly if aught might be required of her. Her shoulders shook with sobs. I looked away from her. She was only a slave, and slaves are nothing.

"We must arrange that Aemilianus, Captain of the forces of Ar's Station in Victoria, also attend this meeting tonight," said Callimachus.

"Surely it has not escaped your attention," smiled Tasdron, "that Cos and Ar are currently at war."

"No," said Callimachus. "Yet I think the common interest on the river of Ar's Station and Port Cos, and, indeed, of Cos and Ar themselves, should persuade them to regard our plan with care."

"Those of Port Cos and Ar's Station would sooner cut one another's throats than share wine in Victoria," said Tasdron.

"The problems of Port Cos are not identical to those of Cos," said Callimachus, "nor are those of Ar's Station identical with those of Ar."

"Ar's Station is, in effect, an outpost of Ar," said Tasdron. "It is unlike Port Cos, which is a colony, and whose ties with Cos are largely historical and cultural."

"Yet guardsmen of these two places have been for weeks in Victoria and have made no effort to seek one another out."

"Indeed," said Tasdron, thoughtfully, "they have studiously avoided one another."

"The location of their diverse headquarters are surely known, the one to the other," said Callimachus.

"That is true," said Tasdron.

"And yet neither has stormed the headquarters of the other."

"True," said Tasdron.

"Does it not then seem that they may have things on their mind more important than the indisputable differences which separate them."

"Perhaps," said Tasdron.

"I suggest," said Callimachus, "that the security of the river is of greater concern to them both than the distant wars of their allies."

"This may be true," said Tasdron, "but surely it is nothing they could admit openly."

"What could admit it more openly than their common presence in Victoria, without strife?" asked Callimachus.

"Aemilianus will never confer with us should he learn that Callisthenes is to be party to our proceedings, nor will Callisthenes permit himself to attend a meeting at which he knows that one of Ar's Station is to be present."

"Each need not know in advance of the projected attendance of the other," said Callimachus.

"And what will you do when they learn of this matter?" asked Tasdron.

"Attempt to prevent bloodshed," said Callimachus.

"I trust that you will be successful," said Tasdron, glumly. "If either Aemilianus or Callisthenes should be felled in my tavern, I think the incident would be unlikely to escape the attention of their allied guardsmen."

"To be sure," smiled Callimachus, "their vengeance would doubtless be merciless and prompt."

Tasdron shuddered. Gorean men, in certain matters, tend not to be patient.

"Glyco, to whom I have spoken, being a merchant of Port Cos, can meet openly with Callisthenes without arousing suspicion. There will be no difficulty, thus, in bringing Callisthenes to our meeting. The matter, however, will be otherwise with Aemilianus. It is unlikely that he can be subtly contacted. Here there is danger. He, like Callisthenes, is doubtless under surveillance by spies of pirates."

"I am hungry," I said.

"Peggy," said Tasdron, raising his voice.

Swiftly the girl leaped to her feet and, with a sound of slave bells, hurried to the table, beside which she knelt. "Yes, Master," she said.

"Bring me bread and meat," I said to her.

"To me, too," said Callimachus, seeming to look through her, without really seeing her. She was only a girl who was owned, and must obey.

"Yes, Master," she said. Her lip trembled.

"And to mc, too," said Tasdron, "and, too, bring forth some cheese and dates."

"Yes, Master," she said. "Do Masters desire drink?"

Tasdron looked at Callimachus.

"Water," said Callimachus.

"Black wine," I said. I thought it best to keep my head clear until the conclusion of our evening's business.

"Black wine," said Tasdron.

"Yes, Master," said the girl, and hurried away.

"It is just as well not to have paga this night," said Tasdron.

"I think so," smiled Callimachus.

"Do you fear it?" asked Tasdron.

"Of course," said Callimachus. "I am not a fool."

"I would have thought you feared nothing," said Tasdron.

"Only a fool fears nothing," said Callimachus.

"What do you know of Callisthenes?" I asked Callimachus.

"He is a captain, a guardsman of Port Cos," said Callimachus. "He is skilled with the sword. He is shrewd, I regard him as a good officer."

"It was he, was it not," I asked, "who acceded to your command in Port Cos, following your being relieved of your duties?"

"It was," smiled Callimachus, "but I assure you I shall not hold that against him, nor will it interfere with my capacity to work closely with him."

"If he chooses to work with you," I said.

"Of course," shrugged Callimachus.

"Do you think he will remember you?" I asked.

"I would think so," said Callimachus, ruefully.

"It was evidence brought against Callisthenes in Port Cos five years ago by Callimachus," said Tasdron, "which cost him an early promotion, a matter of minor peculation."

"Such things are not unknown," said Callimachus, "but I chose not to accept them in my command."

"I understand," I said. I had a respect for caste honor. Honor was honor, in small things as well as great. Indeed, how can one practice honor in great things, if not in small things?

"And later," said Tasdron, "it was the testimonies of Callisthenes which resulted in Callimachus' loss of command."

"He did his duty, as I had done mine, earlier," said Callimachus. "I cannot, as a soldier, hold that against him. My only regret is that I had not resigned my command. In that way I might have precluded the disgrace of the hearing, the admonishment of my fellow officers, the embarrassment of being publicly relieved of my duties."

"Be these things as they may," said Tasdron, "they surely do not bode well for the future of our plans."

"It cannot be helped," said Callimachus. "If you wish I shall withdraw from participation in these matters."

"Nonsense," said Tasdron. "You are well remembered, and with affection, in Port Cos. I know this from Glyco. Why else do you think he sought you in Victoria?"

"I pledge you that I will work well with Callisthenes," said Callimachus.

"What do you know of Aemilianus of Ar's Station?" I asked Callimachus and Tasdron.

"Victoria is closer to Port Cos than Ar's Station," said Tasdron. "Indeed, Ar is substantially a land power. We know little of men such as Aemilianus. I have heard that he is a good officer."

"I know nothing of him," said Callimachus, his voice slightly hardening, "save that he is from Ar."

"Your Cosian sympathies are showing," I cautioned him. "Nothing will be much advanced if you and this fellow find it necessary to slice one another into pieces."

"Particularly in my tavern," grumbled Tasdron.

"The immediate problem remains," said Callimachus. "How can we contact this Aemilianus, and bring him to this meeting, without attracting the attention of the spies of Policrates?"

"We have no choice, I think," said Tasdron, "but to contact him directly and take what risks are unavoidable."

"Even so," said Callimachus, "do you think that he, a warrior of Ar, a captain, will simply disguise himself and hurry off to a rendezvous in Victoria? He is surely aware that many in Victoria bear those of Ar little love. He will be suspicious."

"He will doubtless demand that the meeting be held in his headquarters," said Tasdron.

"Then all we have to do," said Callimachus, bitterly, "is to convince Callisthenes to put himself in the power of the men of Ar's Station."

"He may be bolder than we think," I said.

"I do not understand," said Tasdron.

"For what purpose has he come to Victoria?" I asked.

"To find the topaz," said Tasdron.

"I have a plan," I said.

"What?" said Tasdron.

"Do you have the common keys to the collars and bells of your girls on the premises?" I asked.

"Surely," said Tasdron.

I then drew from my pouch a piece of silk. It was heavy, from what it was wrapped about. I placed it carefully on the table. "I think the matter will not be as difficult as you might suspect," I said.

"I understand," said Tasdron. He eyed the silk-wrapped object which I had placed upon the table. He had detected the telltale sound.

"Masters," said Peggy, approaching the table, kneeling beside it, bearing a tray. She placed the tray on the table, and removed three plates of bread and meat from it, a dish of assorted cheeses, a bowl of dates, a pitcher of water, a pot of black wine, steaming, and tiny vessels of sugars and creams, and three goblets. On the table, too, she placed small spoons, of silver, from Tharna, for use with the black wine, and, at each place, a kailiauk-horn-handled eating prong, from distant Turia. Finger towels, then, and a silver finger bowl, too, she placed upon the table. The bowl was also of Tharnan silver. When she had placed these things on the table, she looked about, still kneeling, and saw me close the door to the room, locking her within, with us. She suddenly trembled. She knew that she was a slave, and that absolutely anything could be done with her.

"Leave the tray where it is," said Tasdron. "Remove your silk, and remain kneeling."

"Yes, Master," she said, swiftly slipping the silk back from her shoulders.

She reddened, kneeling as a naked slave before the man she loved. Yet he looked upon her as though she might be any girl casually stripped by the command of a master.

I smiled to myself. Peggy had obeyed immediately and unhesitantly. Gorean slave girls do not dally in their compliance.

I unwrapped then the object from the silk on the table. There was the sound of the metal clapper in the narrow, flattish, triangular-shaped bell, the rustle of the chain and lock, the sound of the small, metal, sturdy, rectangular, locked coin box. I dangled the chain, the girl bell and the coin box before her eyes.

"Do you know what this is?" I asked her.

"Yes, Master," she whispered, frightened.

"Excellent," said Tasdron, "excellent," and he rose from the table, letting himself out of the room with a key, by means of a side door, one which led up a flight of stairs, presumably to private compartments.

He locked the door behind him. He would return shortly with the keys to her bells and collar.

* * * *

"Stand, Slave," I said.

Peggy stood, beautifully.

Tasdron crouched beside her left ankle and, with his key, removed the slave bells from her left ankle. Such bells are seldom put on by the slave or removed by the slave. Almost always they are put on or removed by one who is in authority over the slave. The girl seldom puts them on or removes them; rather it is hers to wear them, and as a slave, for as long or briefly as masters see fit.

I then, not hurrying, lifted the heavy chain, with its bell and box, about the girl's neck. I stood behind her. I then, not yet dropping the chain about her neck, but holding it about her neck, closed the lock. She shuddered. It was on her, though she could not yet feel its weight as I had not yet released it, that it might fall against the back of her neck. Tasdron then, with a key, removed his collar from her throat. I then dropped the chain about her neck. The heavy black links were obdurate against the small, soft hairs on the back of her slender, lovely neck. I then threw her hair back again, in place. I then walked about her, and before her. She who had once been Peggy Baxter, of Earth, then stood before me in the apparatus of a Gorean coin girl.

"An excellent idea," said Tasdron. "Now she will attract only the attention natural to a coin girl in the streets."

"Some may recognize her, of course," I said.

"I do not think many will," said Tasdron, "and if some do, they will simply assume that she has been put into the streets for discipline."

"That, too, was my conjecture," I said. Though the Gorean coin girl is commonly one of several girls, one of a stable thereof, so to speak, sent daily into the streets to earn money as the chattels they are for their master, under the penalty of whippings or tortures, or death, if their day's work does not prove sufficiently lucrative, it is not unknown for this sensual charge to be also placed upon a private girl, usually as a punishment for having failed in some way, often trivial or negligible, to be fully pleasing. After having been sent into the humiliations and dangers of the streets it is a rare girl who does not hurry back, eager and chastened, to the intimate joys of a private slavery.

"Do you know what you are to do?" I asked the girl.

"Yes, Master," she said. "You have explained the matter fully to me."

"Do not fail, Slave Girl," I said to her, menacingly.

"I shall do my best, Master," she whispered.

"It may work," said Tasdron, regarding the slave. He looked to Callimachus. "What do you think?"

"It may quite possibly work," said Callimachus. "We shall hope so."

"She is pretty, isn't she?" said Tasdron. "What do you think of her?"

Peggy straightened her body, scarcely daring to breathe. She was beautiful.

"She is not totally displeasing," said Callimachus.

Tasdron then took the girl by an arm and thrust her toward a rear door, before which he stopped, the girl then standing beside him, to unlock it.

The girl turned to face us. "But am I not to be given even a Ta-Teera to wear?" she asked.

"You will be more alluring, more fetching, without it," I told her.

"Yes, Master," she said, half choking.

Tasdron then had the door open, and he took her again by the arm.

"But in the streets," she said, "seen as I am, what if others should wish to use me?"

"You are in the guise of a Coin Girl," I told her.

"But what should I do?" she asked.

"See that you serve them well," I said.

"Yes, Master," she whispered, and then Tasdron, by her arm, half dragging her, pulled her through the door and down the corridor toward the alley door. The sound of the bell on her neck was exciting. Then, the door unbolted and opened, she was thrust into the darkness of the alley. She looked at us, once, and then turned about and sped away, the bell on her neck, on our business. Tasdron closed the door and resecured it.

"Do you think she will be successful?" asked Callimachus of Tasdron, when he had returned to the room.

"She is a slave," said Tasdron. "It will be in her best interest to be so."

"Let us eat," I said. "I am hungry."

"I, too," said Callimachus.

"I, too," said Tasdron.

Twenty Six

Florence; Miles of Vonda

"Florence!" I said.

"Master!" she said, pleased.

"Is it you!" I laughed.

"Yes," she said.

"How wonderful to see you," I said.

"Doubtless it is wonderful for a man to see me, as I am now," she laughed.

It was the eighteenth Ahn, two Ahn before the twentieth Ahn, the Gorean midnight, when we would hold our secret meeting in the back room of Tasdron's tavern. I had finished my supper in the room and had, leaving Callimachus and Tasdron in conversation, emerged through the now-opened door into the main room of the tavern. I intended to walk until the twentieth Ahn.

"I see that you are well secured," I said.

"My master has seen to it," she said, proudly.

In Tasdron's paga tavern, as in many, along one wall, there is a set of slave rings, to which one may chain or tie one's slaves while drinking or dining in the tavern. This is a convenience for the customers.

"How beautiful you are," I said. I crouched down beside her.

"Thank you, Master," she said.

"I see that slavery agrees with you," I said.

"Yes, Master," she said, softly.

I turned her face toward me, gently, with my hand.

"What an incredible transformation has come over you," I said.

"It is only that you are not used to seeing me in the tunic and collar of a slave," she said.

"No," I said, "it is far beyond such things." I lowered my hand.

"Yes, Master," she smiled.

I examined her, with attention, as a man does an enslaved woman, as she put her head down, shyly. She wore a brief slave tunic, of gray rep-cloth. It was demure, as such garments go, but it left little doubt as to her charms. I saw that her master was proud of his slave's beauty. She knelt with her back to the wall and slave ring, her knees wide. Her hands were braceleted above and behind her head, the linking chain on the bracelets passing behind the slave ring. She also wore an ankle ring with a chain which looped up to the same slave ring, and was locked about it. The soft, rounded flesh of her forearms, below the steel, and the sweet, swelling flesh of her palms, above the steel, were lovely. I examined the lineaments of her body, the beauty of her breasts held high, as she was braceleted, the latitudes of her belly, the flare of her hips, the sweetness of her knees and thighs, the lovely curve of her calves, her ankles, the left clasped in steel, and her small feet. She was barefoot, of course, as slaves are commonly kept.

"You are astonishingly beautiful, Florence," I said.

"Thank you, Master," she said.

"You are doubly chained," I said.

"Yes, Master," she said.

This type of chaining, a double chaining, is usually done only by a man who is in a strange city, and does not know, fully, what to expect. If one is familiar with the city a single chaining is usually regarded as sufficient. Indeed, sometimes the girl is merely told to grasp the ring and to remain there until the master returns. She may not release the ring until given permission by a free person. Some girls have been raped at such rings, as helplessly as though they might have been chained to them, so great is the fear of their master, and so strict is the Gorean discipline to which they know themselves subject.

"Are you always, in a tavern, chained in this fashion?" I asked.

"Yes, Master," she said.

"It would be hard to steal you," I smiled.

"Yes, Master," she smiled.

"Your master must find you very precious," I said.

"I am only a slave," she said, putting her head down, smiling.

"I wonder as what sort of slave your master keeps you," I said.

She looked up, puzzled.

I glanced down then, rather obviously, meaningfully, at the spread of her sweet knees.

"Master is cruel," she smiled. "He teases a poor, helpless, chained slave."

"Perhaps," I said.

Then she laughed, delightedly. "Yes, I must so kneel. Of course! Certainly! He will have it so. My despicable status by his will is thus proclaimed to all. Of course he keeps me as that sort of slave—his pleasure slave!"

"You are that beautiful?" I asked.

"I hope so, Master," she said.

"That is the lowest of all slaves," I said.

"Yes, Master," she said, happily.

"So the proud Lady Florence of Vonda is now a mere pleasure slave."

"Yes, Master!"

"Is it what you want to be?" I asked.

"Yes, Master," she said.

I regarded her.

"Forgive me, Master, if that distresses you," she said, "but I am no longer a free woman. I am now a slave, and a slave must speak the truth. She may be terribly punished, or even slain, for lying. So do not punish me for speaking the truth, I beg of you! I am a slave! I have no alternative, Master!"

"Is it then, truly," I asked, "what you want to be?"

"Oh, yes, Master! Yes, Master! That is what I want to be, and what somehow I have always wanted to be, a master's pleasure slave!"

"Why is that?" I asked.

"Because I am a woman, Master," she said, "because I am a woman"

"You have become very beautiful," I said.

"Thank you, Master," she said.

"Who is your master?" I asked.

"Miles of Vonda," she said.

"I thought he might be," I said.

"He purchased me at a secret auction," she said, "held in the camp of Tenalion, the Slaver."

"What did he bid?" I asked.

"A hundred pieces of gold," she said, smiling, not lifting her head.

"Vain little she-sleen," I laughed.

"It is true," she smiled.

"Marvelous," I said. "I myself received only ten silver tarsks for you when I sold you to Tenalion."

"The gold was doubtless much more than I was worth," she said.

"Not to Miles of Vonda," I smiled.

"No," she said, smiling.

"Are you happy?" I asked.

She lifted her head, happily. "Oh, yes," she said, "yes, yes! I am so happy! I am so happy, Master!"

"Wonderful," I said.

"He stripped me, and put me under his whip, and taught me instantly that I was his slave, his total slave."

"I am very happy for you," I said.

"I had never dreamed, when I was free, that he could be such a man. Had I even suspected it I would have torn away my clothes and thrown myself to his feet, begging his collar."

"Had you been free," I said, "he could not have been such a man."

"That is true," she said. "Had I been free he could not have handled me and treated me as he wished, and as I wished, as his lovely beast, to be ravished, and trained and taught her duties."

I nodded. Enmeshed in legalities, negativities and socialized expectations it was difficult to relate as biological human beings. But the slave girl, standing outside the protections of such devices, stands before her master as an exposed, raw human female, without rights, his to do with as he pleases. Similarly the master, owing the slave nothing, and knowing that she is completely his, his very property, may relate to her freely in the order of nature. In his treatment of her he is untrammeled by either conscience or law, and this she knows, and loves, and, accordingly, hastens to obey and be pleasing. She knows that she is owned, and that he is her unqualified master. The order of nature, and the obdurate and thematic equations of dominance and submission, denied though they might be, and even if hysterically repudiated, will continue to lurk in the microstructures of every cell in the human body. The master/slave relationship is the institutionalization of dominance and submission. It is, under the enhancements of civilization, the institutionalization of the primitive biological relationship of the human male and female, he the master, she the slave. How lonely is the man who has not yet found his slave; how forlorn is the woman who has not yet found her master.

"I am pleased that you are so happy," I said.

"But he is strict with me," she said. "I must obey him in all things."

"Of course," I said.

"I fear only that he will tire of me, or sell me," she said. "I try so hard to please him."

"You do not wish to be whipped," I said.

"I love him," she said. "I love Miles of Vonda!"

"With the love of a free companion?" I asked.

"Certainly not," she said, "rather with the helpless and total love of the slave girl for her master."

"He is a fortunate man," I said.

"I am his, fully," she said. She smiled, shyly. The auburn-haired beauty was radiant. I looked at her. How marvelous is the transformation which slavery works in a woman.

"What are you called now?" I asked.

"'Florence'," she said.

"He put your old name on you, as a slave name," I said.

"Was it not appropriate?" she asked.

"Yes," I said.

"Yes," she laughed, delightedly, "it was fully appropriate. I was a slave before, when I was free. I knew it in my heart, even then, that I was a slave. It is thus fully appropriate that I now wear my old name openly, and with full explicitness, as a slave name."

"That pleases you, doesn't it?" I asked.

"Yes, Master," she said, happily. "It pleases me very much."

"Florence, the slave," I said.

"Yes, Florence, the slave," she said.

"How is Miles of Vonda?" I asked.

Her eyes clouded. "He has fallen on hard times," she said. "Warriors of Ar made hostel in his holdings, in their withdrawal to the south. He, in anger, spoke ill of Ar in their presence. Accordingly they burned his holdings and scattered his hurt and tharlarion."

"What is he doing in Victoria?" I asked.

"He is on his way west on the river," she said, "to Turmus, where he has friends, that he may negotiate a loan to rebuild and replenish his holdings."

"It is now dangerous to travel on the river," I said. "River pirates are now bold and active."

"We must take our chances," she said.

"How large is his retinue?" I asked. This could make a difference with respect to the security of his venture.

"Only myself," she said, "and Krondar, a fighting slave."

"Only two?" I asked.

"Yes," she said. "He sold his other slaves, to obtain moneys for the journey."

"But he did not sell you," I said.

"He kept me," she smiled, moving in the chains.

"And Krondar," I said.

"Yes," she said. "He is fond of Krondar, and a fighting slave may be useful upon the river."

"That is true," I said.

I remembered Krondar. Indeed, I had once fought him in the pit of leather and blood, when I, too, had been a fighting slave. Krondar was a veteran of the fighting pits of Ar. He had fought even with the spiked cestae and the knife gauntlets. He was a short, stout, thick-bodied, powerful man. His face and upper body were disfigured with masses of scar tissue, lingering records of a bloody history in the pits.

"You should not leave Victoria," I said, "until several ships, in convoy, are prepared to move westward."

"My master is impatient," she said.

"It has been wonderful to see you," I said, adding, "Female Slave." I stood up.

"It has been wonderful for me to see you, too, Master," she said.

I turned away.

"Master," she said.

I turned back to regard her.

"Thank you," she said, "for, long ago, having captured and sold me. It was you who first taught me my womanhood. It was you who first taught me, incontrovertibly, that I belonged to men."

I shrugged.

"If it were not for you," she said, "I might never have come into the possession of my master, Miles of Vonda."

"I wish you well, Slave Girl," I smiled.

"And I, too, wish you well, Master," she said.

I then left the tavern. Outside, looking about, I saw a burly, crouched figure, one crouching near some bundles by the tavern wall. I grinned. I approached the figure, and it lifted its head. It growled, and opened its hands, warning me not to approach more closely.

"Krondar!" I said.

The heavy head, scarred, whitishly streaked in the moonlight by the wall, looked at me, puzzled. On its throat was a heavy metal collar. "Master?" it asked.

"Do not call me 'Master'," I said. "I am Jason, now free. Once near Vonda we fought."

"Free?" asked the brute. Then it knelt.

I drew him to his feet. "I am Jason," I said. "Can you remember Jason?" I asked.

It looked at me, in the moonlight. Then there was a heavy chuckle in its throat. "It was a good fight," he said.

In the moonlight, then, we embraced. We had shared the fellowship of the pit of leather and blood.

"It is good to see you, Krondar," I said.

"It is good to see you—Jason," said he.

I turned suddenly for I heard steel slipping from a sheath behind me.

Miles of Vonda, angry, stood there, his sword drawn. Behind him, frightened, in her brief gray slave tunic, stood his lovely slave, Florence.

I stepped away from Krondar, and backed up a step. Miles of Vonda, sword ready, advanced a step.

"In the tavern," said Miles of Vonda, "was it not you who accosted my slave?"

"I spoke with her," I said.

"Draw your weapon," said he.

"Do you not know me?" I asked.

"You are Jason," said he, "who was once a fighting slave."

"Yes," I said.

"Draw your weapon," said he.

"Please, Master," begged the slave. "He meant no harm! Please!"

"Be silent, Slave," he snapped.

"Yes, Master," she said, miserably.

Two or three other men had now gathered about.

"Will it be necessary to slay you with your sword in your sheath?" inquired Miles of Vonda.

"Please, no, Master!" wept Florence, falling to her knees beside him, clutching at him. He spurned her to the side with his foot. She lay there, then, on the stones, weeping. She had spoken without permission. She had sought to interfere in the affairs of men. Tonight she would doubtless be whipped.

"Draw your weapon," said Miles of Vonda.

More men had now gathered about. One of them had muttered something angrily, when Miles of Vonda had spoken as he had. I saw the hands of several on their swords. I suddenly realized, with a certain amount of gratification, that these fellows were not pleased with what was ensuing. I had learned from Peggy that I was not unknown in Victoria. Men, I now gathered, knew me from the docks. Too, perhaps they had learned of my dismissal of Grat, the Swift, the thief, from Victoria, and how I had entered the tavern of Hibron to extract Miss Henderson from her danger there, though in this I had been unsuccessful. Perhaps they knew, too, of my outspoken displeasure at the wharves when the pirates had looted and burned there, punishing Victoria for having at that time refused their demands for tribute. With some of these fellows I had drunk, and worked.

"Draw," said Miles of Vonda.

I do not think Miles of Vonda knew the danger he was in. My major concern now was to save his life.

"I had thought you a man of honor," I said.

"It is my hope that I am so," said Miles of Vonda.

"I work on the docks," I said. Out of the corner of my eye I noted Krondar squaring about, to face several of the men tensed about us. He, at least, knew the danger in which his master stood. I had little doubt Krondar would charge against several of these men, though he might take five swords in his chest doing so. "How then, as I am a worker on the docks, could I have had the leisure to develop skills with the blade which might be the match of yours?"

Angrily Miles of Vonda thrust his sword back in its sheath. He need not know that I had taken the leisure, and much of it, as it pleased me, to develop blade skills, nor need he know I was, for my times of training, reasonably adept with the blade. Callimachus was a master and he had lavished intelligence and time on my development. Too, I had discovered, as did not displease me, perhaps as a result of my reflexes and aggressions, that I possessed something of an aptitude for the manipulation of that wicked Gorean blade. Indeed, I suspected that I might find myself at no disadvantage in bladed contest with the proud Vondan. Indeed, I was curious to know if I might kill him. On the other hand, I had no wish to do him injury. And beyond these things, I did not wish for those of Victoria to know of my skills with the blade. Jason, the worker on the docks, and a fellow of some popularity in Victoria, was not thought to be skilled with the blade. As Callimachus pretended still to dereliction to further our projects so, too, I must pretend to ineptness with the blade.

"I shall not kill you," said Miles of Vonda, irritably.

"That is welcome news," I said.

I saw the men about relax. Miles of Vonda, although he did not know it, had just saved his own life, and that of Krondar, and possibly that of the slave. Before he could have reached me a dozen blades might have cut him down.

I felt a fondness then for the men of Victoria.

"Krondar," said Miles of Vonda, indicating me, "beat him."

"I shall attack him if you wish, Master," said Krondar, "but I cannot beat him."

"How then," asked Miles of Vonda, looking at me, "is my honor in this matter to be satisfied?"

"I do not know," I said.

He walked up to me and, with the flat of his right hand, gave me a stinging slap. He then drew back and spit upon me. Men cried out angrily. Krondar gasped. Florence cried out with misery. I tensed, but did not respond.

Miles of Vonda then turned about and, gesturing to Krondar to shoulder the burdens he had been guarding, left, walking down the avenue of Lycurgus, followed by Florence, and then later, a few feet behind, by Krondar, bearing his gear.

I wiped my tunic, and then wiped my hand on my thigh.

"Why didn't you break his neck?" asked one of the men about.

"He is really a good fellow," I said. "Besides," I added, "look at the slave girl." We looked after her, the scantily clad, auburn-haired beauty heeling her master. "Who would not be jealous of such a slave?" I asked.

"Perhaps you are right," grinned the man beside me.

Twenty Seven

What Occurred on the Wharves, Shortly Before Midnight

It was now the nineteenth Ahn, an Ahn before the twentieth Ahn, the Gorean midnight.

I was more careless than I should have been. I had been thinking of Miles of Vonda and the slave he owned, who had once been the Lady Florence of Vonda. I was pleased with her happiness, and regarded him as a fortunate fellow.

"Hold!" said a voice, menacingly.

I spun about, near a pile of lumber on the wharves. It was lonely there now.

I had no opportunity to draw my sword. The point of the other's blade was entered into my gut. I backed against the lumber.

"So you have followed me, Miles of Vonda," I said. He did not respond.

"The mask is not necessary," I said. "It is dark here, and we are alone."

The blade drew back a few inches. "Hold your hands at your sides, and kneel, very slowly," said the man.

I did so.

"Now, slowly, very slowly, place your sword belt and scabbard on the boards," said the voice.

I slowly slipped the belt and scabbard, with the sheathed blade, from my shoulder, and placed them on the boards.

"You are not Miles of Vonda," I said. I could now tell that it was not his voice. "Who are you," I asked, "a brigand?"

He said nothing. I watched the sword.

"I have some money with me," I said. "I will give it to you. You do not need to slay me."

"Do not be a fool," he said. "Where is it?" he said.

"What?" I asked.

"The topaz," he said.

"You are the courier of Ragnar Voskjard," I said. It would have been he who would have, to protect himself during the search of the tavern of Cleanthes, by the guardsmen of Ar's Station, placed the topaz in my pouch. I had not been searched within the tavern because I, like certain others, had been searched outside the tavern, but moments before. He would presumably be an important man, and the security of his identity a closely guarded secret.

"Where is the topaz?" he pressed.

"It was you, was it not," I asked, "who raided my house, who ransacked it, and put the Lady Beverly under interrogation in the matter of the topaz?"

"I did not find it there," he said, menacingly.

"But you received something for your trouble," I reminded him. "You tied the Lady Beverly as a slave and made her beg for her rape, after which you courteously acceded to her request."

"She was not displeasing," he said.

"The rape of a free woman is a serious offense," I said.

"I know women," he said. "She was a natural slave."

"I cannot gainsay it," I said. I had learned in the stronghold of Policrates, the pirate, that the beautiful Miss Henderson was, in her heart, a slave among slaves. It was not inappropriate, thus, but quite appropriate, that she had been subjected to merciless slave rape.

The most complete, overwhelming and shattering orgasm of which a woman is capable is the slave orgasm. Once it has been experienced a woman remains the captive of its memory and will do anything to know again its ecstatic torments. She lives in the desperate hope that her master will deign again to subject her to the those merciless storms of degrading, possessing, obliterating sensations available only to a slave in her collar. It is little wonder that she may often beg on her knees or belly for her master's touch. The sexual needs of the female, as is well known, are amongst the strongest chains in a woman's bondage. The only stronger chains are those of love, that of the slave for her master. Besides such things the roughness of hemp, the weight of iron, the cruel, tight clasp of the closely encircling leather straps, are bonds as of gossamer.

One makes love in many ways, in many moods, to a slave, gently, brutally, cruelly, lovingly, with abrupt disdain, with lengthy, patient, irresistible ministrations.

And one of the attentions to which a slave may occasionally look forward is slave rape. For example, a master may simply seize her, tear her bit of cloth away and fling her to the floor or carpet, putting her to peremptory slave use. That, of course, is a swift use. Some slave rapes are leisurely affairs, which may last two or three days. It depends on what the master pleases.

It might be mentioned, in passing, that the slave is to be readily available to the master at all times. Indeed, most Gorean slave garments have no nether closure. One of the rare exceptions is the Turian camisk. Indeed, it is often the case that a slave tunic will have a disrobing loop at the left shoulder, convenient to the hand of right-handed master. A tug drops the garment to the girl's ankles.

"Remove your garments. I want you now," are words familiar to a slave girl, and words she hopes to hear.

"Strip," she might hear.

She hastens to comply.

Dalliance is not acceptable in a slave.

"The guardsmen of Port Cos, who, too, searched your house, and the gardens, upon the informings of the Lady Beverly, who turned against you, were no more successful."

"You are well informed," I said.

"Where then is the topaz?" he asked.

"Safe," I said. He surely need not know I had delivered it, in accord with a plan, to Policrates myself.

"Do you wish to be slain now?" he asked.

"If you slay me," I said, "how, then, will you find the topaz?"

He drew back the sword a little. "I have watched you," said he. "I have been patient. But you have not led me to the topaz. You must understand I cannot wait indefinitely. There are those to whom I must answer."

"I am sensitive to such matters," I said.

"Where is the topaz?" he said, angrily.

"If I give it to you," I said, "of what value, then, would be my life to you?"

"None," he said.

"Under such circumstances," I said, "I think you can easily understand that I might not be eager to surrender it to you."

"I, myself," he said, menacingly, "if I do not deliver the topaz, may be slain."

"Your identity is known, of course, to Ragnar Voskjard," I said.

"Of course," he said.

"Your situation is not an enviable one either," I admitted.

"In such a situation," he pointed out, "I have little to lose by slaying you."

"That point has not eluded me," I admitted.

"But there is a simple solution to our mutual difficulty," he said, "one which is in our common interest."

"That you will spare me, if I give you the topaz," I said.

"Of course," said he.

"But what guarantee have I," I asked, "that you will abide by the terms of such a bargain?"

"I give you my word," said he, "in it pledging my honor."

"With all due respect," I said, "pirates, and those in league with them, are not noted for their honor."

"Do you have a choice?" he asked. The sword drew back.

"I will show you where I put the topaz," I said.

"Rise slowly," he said. "And walk slowly. Do not pick up your sword."

I got to my feet, not hurrying, leaving the sword, with the belt and scabbard, on the boards. I began to walk, slowly, among the materials on the wharves. He was behind me, sword drawn. If I were to turn on him I was sure he could cut me down before I could get my hands on him. Similarly, before I could dodge or run, it seemed to me not unlikely that he could strike at the back of my neck.

"Slowly," he said. "Slowly."

"Very well," I said.

"It is here," I said, "that I put the topaz." It was true that I had put it there. I had also, of course, removed it later from that place when I had carried it to the holding of Policrates. Carefully, I removed one of the heavy granite blocks of stone, building stone, rectangular, some six inches by six inches, by eighteen inches, from the tiered pile of stones. It was building stone brought in by a quarry galley several weeks ago. The intended purchaser had defaulted on his contract and the stone was to be stored over the winter, beside the quarry warehouse, until the following spring, when it was to be auctioned. In the spring prices tend to be highest on such materials. In virtue of the temporary commercial inertness of the stone, and its weight and cheapness, it had seemed to me to provide an ideal hiding place for the topaz. Also it lay no more than four hundred yards from the hiring yard on the wharves, to which I often went in seeking work.

"None would expect that the topaz would be hidden in such a place," I speculated.

"Do you have it yet?" asked the fellow behind me, masked, with the sword. He was a tall, spare man. Originally I had taken him to be Miles of Vonda.

I realized I had little time. Carefully I moved another stone. Then I took another stone in my hands, seeming to struggle with it.

"I am to be spared, if I give you the topaz," I reminded him.

"Yes, yes," he said.

"It is here," I said.

He struck down with the sword and I, turning, thrust up the block of granite to block the blow. Sparks showered off the stone, and particles of rock. I kicked him back from the stone, which I still held in my hands. He staggered back. I waited until he was upright, in the moment he had caught his balance. Then, underhanded, with two hands, I slung the block of granite at him. It caught him in the left shoulder. He gasped, and spun about, turned by the stone. I lunged toward him, but, he turning swiftly, stopped. The thrust of the sword was short by a foot. I stepped back a foot. He did not advance. He breathed heavily. His left arm and hand hung beside him. I suspected that his left shoulder and side must be ringing with numbness.

"It was not there after all," I said. "It seems I was mistaken."

Gasping, he staggered toward me, and I turned and, swiftly, fled from the place, making my way swiftly back to the piled lumber. It was there that I, in a moment, bending down, seized up the sword which I had left there. I turned, then, to see him, painfully, following. When he saw that I now held my blade ready, he stopped. That action convinced me that whoever he was, he was not of Victoria. In Victoria it was thought I did not know the blade. Thus, had he been of Victoria I think that he, even in pain, might have advanced. As it was, not knowing my capacity with the sword, I not being known to him, and knowing himself better than I how his injury might have impeded his swordplay, he hesitated. I saw he did not know what to do.

"Treacherous sleen!" he said.

"It was not I who struck down at you," I pointed out.

"Sleen!" he said.

"Ho, there!" I cried out, loudly. "Ho, there! What are you doing here? Who are you! Get away from there! We do not permit pilfering on these wharves!"

The man trembled with rage. He advanced a step.

"Begone, Thief!" I cried. "Begone!"

"Be silent, you fool!" said the man.

"Thief! Thief!" I cried. "You may not steal here, Fellow! This is Victoria, you know!"

"What is going on there?" called a voice, from along the wharves, behind me.

"A thief!" I cried. "Assistance! Assistance!"

Glancing back I saw a lantern approaching. Two men were there, advancing with slaves.

"Sleen!" said the fellow with the mask, and then he turned and made his way rapidly away.

"Is that you, Jason?" asked one of the men.

"Yes," I said, sheathing my sword.

"What is it?" asked the other man.

"Some fellow prowling about the docks," I said, "doubtless not up to much good."

"He seems to be gone now," said the first man.

"Yes," I said. "Before he was over by the quarry warehouse. He was busying himself about the granite there, that of the defaulted shipment."

"There is nothing of value there," said the second man.

"That is true," I said.

Twenty Eight

Two Captains Come
to the Tavern of Tasdron;
We Prevent Bloodshed

"It is the second Ahn," said Callimachus. "Surely they are not coming."

Peggy knelt with her head to the feet of Tasdron, her master. The heavy chain, with the girl bell and coin box, was still locked on her neck.

I pulled her head up by the hair. I lifted up the chain and Tasdron put his collar again on her neck.

"Did you do as Jason told you?" asked Tasdron.

"Yes, Master," she said, her neck now again locked in Tasdron's collar.

I thrust the key to the chain in the chain lock and opened it, pulling away the apparatus of the Coin Girl from her neck.

"I sought out Aemilianus, Captain of the Guardsmen of Ar's Station," she said. "I put myself naked before him, kneeling, and humbly began to lick and kiss about his feet."

"Yes," said Tasdron.

"I then, in seeming to try to please him, whispered to him of the topaz, and that I had been sent to his feet by those who knew its whereabouts. If he wished information as to its location he was to come to the tavern this night at the twentieth Ahn."

"You yourself," said Tasdron, "did not return until the first Ahn."

"I did not even find Aemilianus," she said, "until near the twentieth Ahn."

"Why?" asked Tasdron, not pleasantly.

"I was detained by men," she said. "I was naked. I wore the bell and coin box."

I moved the coin box, on the chain, which I held. There were now several coins in it. When she had been sent from the tavern it had been empty.

"Aemilianus himself used me," she said. "He tied my hands tightly behind my back and took me to his private compartments. There he subjected me to—to slave rape."

"Appropriate," I said.

"Yes, Master," she said.

She was, after all, a slave, and an extremely attractive one.

"Did he pay his coin?" asked Tasdron.

"Yes, Master," she said, reddening.

"Did you please your customers?" asked Tasdron.

"Yes, Master," she said.

"Did you yield to them," asked Tasdron, "to Aemilianus, and the others?"

"Please do not make me speak, Master," she begged. She was in the presence of Callimachus, whom she loved.

"Speak, Slave," snapped Tasdron.

"Yes, Master," she whispered, head down, "I yielded to them."

"And well?" he asked.

"Yes, Master," she said. "But I could not help myself, Master," she wept. "I am a slave girl. I am only a slave girl!" She seemed to speak to Tasdron, but I knew well for whom her words were intended.

"I do not understand," said Tasdron. "You are under an obligation to yield, and to yield perfectly, fully and totally. You are a slave."

"Even were I not under such an obligation," she whispered, "my Master, I still could not have helped myself. I would still have had to yield to them fully and totally, perfectly."

"Of course," said Tasdron. "You are a slave girl."

"Yes, Master," she whispered. "I am a slave girl."

Then, head down, she trembled, and wept. How shamed she was that her slavery had been so clarified and manifested before Callimachus. I glanced to Callimachus. He did not seem concerned with the girl. What to him were the helpless confessions of a lovely, meaningless slave?

"Aemilianus is not here," I said.

"When he unbound me and sent me from his compartments," she said, "ordering me to return to my master, he did nothing but dismiss me. I do not know if he will come or not."

"At least Aemilianus knows how to handle a woman," said Tasdron.

"Yes, Master," said the girl.

I put the chain, with the girl bell and coin box, on the low table. There was a sound of bells, and Tasdron had again locked slave bells on Peggy's left ankle. He picked up the tiny bit of slave silk which we had, earlier, ordered her to remove, before disguising her as a Coin Girl and sending her into the streets to fetch Aemilianus to our meeting. He tossed her the bit of silk. "You may put on the silk," he said.

"Yes, Master," she said.

It amused me to see how gratefully she slipped the brief bit of scandalous, diaphanous yellow silk about her body, how pleased she was to do so, though it was naught but a laughable mockery of a garment, one fit obviously only for a female slave. Some free women think they would rather go naked than wear such a garment, but then they have not yet been made slaves. If they were slaves then they, too, I believe, would find it very precious.

"Bring us food and drink," said Tasdron to Peggy.

"Yes, Master," she said, and swiftly, with a rustle of bells, left the room.

"Where is Glyco?" asked Tasdron. "He had only to fetch Callisthenes, whom he knows. There should be no difficulty in that. They should have been here more than an Ahn ago."

"I do not know," I said.

"Perhaps they have met with foul play," said Tasdron.

"I do not know," I said.

"Spies are everywhere," said Tasdron, miserably. "Perhaps our projects have already been uncovered."

"The tavern has not yet been burned," I pointed out.

"Oh, excellent," said Tasdron, irritatedly.

I smiled.

"You understand the dangers implicit in these endeavors, do you not?" inquired Tasdron.

"I think so," I said.

"There is someone now at the door, in the back," said Callimachus.

Tasdron hurried through the rear door of the room, and down the corridor, to the alley door. He slid back a narrow panel, and then shut the panel, and opened the door. Two figures were admitted, and the door was closed and locked behind them. I recognized the figure of Glyco, portly and short-legged, breathing heavily, wrapped in a long brown cloak, which concealed the white and gold of the merchants, in advance. The second man, tall and rangy, was he who had interrogated me in the headquarters of the men of Port Cos a few days earlier, when, on the asseverations of Miss Henderson, I had been taken into custody. I had been released after the testimonies afforded by Tasdron, who had made it clear to him that I, well known in Victoria, and having arrived from the east on the river, could not be the courier of Ragnar Voskjard. He had also taken Miss Henderson into custody, as I recalled. He had turned her over to me, bound, when I had been released. I had not, however, slain her nor sold her into slavery. I had returned her to my house, unpunished and in honor. She was, after all, a woman of Earth. Later, of course, she had been captured by Kliomenes, the lieutenant to Policrates, the pirate, and taken to the stronghold of Policrates. There, in full Gorean legality, she had been again enslaved, as, months before, she had been in the House of Andronicus, in Vonda, when first she had been brought to Gor as a helpless Earth girl, to be branded and collared, and sold to Gorean brutes for their pleasure. Indeed, in my visit to the stronghold of Policrates, she had served me, and well, as a slave, though not knowing it was I whom she served. It was in that visit that I had learned that the little Earth beauty belonged in a collar.

The tall man, behind Glyco, entered the room. He wore a brown cloak over his uniform. In his left hand, held against his body, there was a helmet, crested with sleen hair.

I now knew him to be Callisthenes.

His left shoulder was hunched. His right hand, strong, long-fingered, wide, seemed fit for the hilt of the Gorean blade.

"Greetings, Callisthenes," said Callimachus, rising to greet him.

"Greetings, Captain," said Callisthenes. "Glyco told me that you would be in attendance."

"I am no longer a captain," said Callimachus. "It is now you who are the captain."

"There are various captains in Port Cos," grinned Callisthenes.

"How are the men?" asked Callimachus.

"They remember you, as I do," said Callisthenes, "with warmth."

The two men clasped hands. This pleased me, for I had feared there might be friction between them. It had been on the evidences supplied by Callisthenes that Callimachus had been removed from his command. Callimachus, however, bore him no ill will on this account. Callisthenes, in the circumstances, to the thinking of Callimachus, had had no choice in the matter. He had done his duty, as he should have, unpleasant and painful though it might have been for him.

"We used to drink together," said Callimachus to Tasdron.

"It was largely on the recommendation of Callimachus, after he was relieved from his command," said Callisthenes, "that I was promoted to the captaincy."

"A noble act," said Tasdron to Callimachus.

"He was the best qualified man to replace me," said Callimachus. "Otherwise, in spite of my affection for him, I would not have acted as I did."

"I have tried to live up to your trust," said Callisthenes.

"To the trust of a fallen man, a drunkard?" smiled Callimachus.

"We shall always think of you as our captain," said Callisthenes.

"You are a fine officer," said Callimachus, "and it is a splendid command."

"You taught me much," said Callisthenes, "and you trained it well."

Again the two men clasped hands, warmly.

I stood to one side, not speaking.

"Do I not know you?" asked Callisthenes, turning to me. I saw some recollection in his eyes.

"I was one of several suspects brought in for interrogation in the matter of the search for the topaz," I said.

"Yes!" said Callisthenes. "And here is Tasdron, is it not, who testified on your behalf?"

"It is," said Tasdron.

"What is your name?" asked Callisthenes.

"Jason," I reminded him.

"Yes," said Callisthenes. "Jason, from the docks."

"Yes," I said.

"I would have been here earlier," said Glyco to Tasdron, "but I could not readily find Callisthenes."

"I was about my duties," said Callisthenes.

"Your shoulder," said Tasdron. "It seems injured."

"I fell," said Callisthenes.

"Is there anything we can do for you?" inquired Tasdron.

"It is nothing," said Callisthenes. He then looked about, from one of us to the other. "What is afoot here?" he asked Callimachus. "Is it true that you have some news of the topaz?"

"We shall explain all shortly, I trust," said Callimachus.

"What is the delay?" asked Callisthenes.

"We are waiting for one more person," said Callimachus.

"Who?" asked Callisthenes.

"One whom it is important that you meet," said Callimachus.

"Very well," said Callisthenes.

There was a tiny knock on the door leading to the central room of the tavern.

"Enter," said Tasdron.

Peggy, a tray balanced in one hand, opened the door. "Masters," she said, lowering her head.

"Serve," said Tasdron to her.

"Yes, Master," said Peggy.

"Sit," invited Tasdron, and we took places about the low table, sitting about it, cross-legged. Callisthenes put his helmet beside the table, and threw back his cloak. His tunic bore the insignia of Port Cos. Peggy knelt before the table and began to place the cups, the vessels and plates on the table. One plate was of meat, another of breads, another of sliced fruits, the fourth of nuts and cheeses. Each of us, with our fingers, would eat as we wished from the common plates. She had brought, too, paga, Cosian wine and water.

"She is a pretty slave," said Callisthenes.

We looked at her. She wore the bit of yellow silk. There were slave bells on her left ankle. The collar was lovely on her throat. Her long, blond hair was loose about her shoulders.

"She is an Earth girl," said Tasdron.

"Interesting," said Callisthenes.

Peggy set forth the food and drink deferentially, and in silence.

"We will need another cup, for our friend," said Tasdron, "and yet another, for our other guest, who has not yet arrived."

"Yes, Master," said Peggy.

"I trust," said Tasdron, looking at his slave, "that he will arrive."

"I trust so, my Master," she whispered, trembling. She then rose to her feet and, taking the tray, with a rustle of bells, frightened, almost fled from the room.

I smiled. It would certainly be in her best interest for Aemilianus, Captain in Ar's Station, to have accepted her invitation to our meeting. If he did not do so, she would doubtless be whipped, and well.

Callisthenes looked to the door through which Peggy, a moment before, had disappeared.

"A pretty, well-curved slave," he mused.

"But an Earth girl," said Tasdron.

"I have heard they make excellent slaves, and are hot sluts," said Callisthenes.

"That has been my experience," said Tasdron.

Earth girls on Gor came about quickly.

Once they were put in collars, and truly understood what they now were, and that no alternatives were theirs, they not only adapted to, but thrived within, their Gorean bondage. It releases their womanhood, and accepts and prizes it. For the first time they are relished and celebrated, and appreciated, for what they are, physically, psychologically, and emotionally, what they are most deeply, most profoundly— women. The paradox of the collar is that it liberates the woman to be herself, wholly and without inhibitions. At last she can be as wild, and free, and sexual as she pleases. At last the loving, caring, desiring slave in her is freed. Thus, strangely, while least free, she is most free. Her true bondage, she then realizes, had been that of the free woman, and she now realizes her true freedom, that of the slave.

"Is she popular with your customers?" asked Callisthenes.

"Yes," said Tasdron.

"Fortunate must be the men of the world Earth," said Callisthenes, "to have such slaves."

"On Earth," said Tasdron, "such women are free."

"The men of Earth must be fools," said Callisthenes.

"But here," said Glyco, fingering a bit of cheese, "they are not free."

"Here," said Tasdron, "they have their uses—in the collar."

"Excellent," said Callisthenes.

It was true, of course, women had many uses—and were utterly marvelous—in the collar.

What true man would want one in any other way?

Callisthenes then looked about.

"Who is this mysterious guest, whom we are expecting?" he asked.

"One whom it is important that you meet," said Callimachus.

"Very well," smiled Callisthenes.

There was then a knock on the alley door, a firm knock. It was struck three times.

We glanced at one another. Glyco pulled his cloak about him, concealing the white and gold of his robes. Callisthenes, too, seeing this action, drew his cloak about himself, concealing the insignia of Port Cos. Tasdron rose to his feet and went through the door, and down the corridor to the alley door. The rest of us, too, rose to our feet.

In a moment Tasdron had reappeared in the room.

"Enter," said Tasdron.

A tall man, carrying an unmarked helmet, entered. He threw back the hood of a long, brown traveling cloak he wore. I detected the sound of a sheathed blade beneath the cloak. He closed the door behind him, and regarded us. His hair was brown, and cut short at the back of his neck. He was smoothly shaven. His jaw was square, his eyes clear.

"I am Tasdron, proprietor of this tavern, who has invited you here," said Tasdron.

"I am Jason," I said. "I commonly work on the docks in Victoria."

"I am Glyco, of the Merchants," said Glyco.

"I am Callimachus," said Callimachus, adding, "of the Warriors."

"I know of only one Callimachus, of the Warriors," said the man, "one who was once a captain in Port Cos."

"Who is he?" inquired Callisthenes of Tasdron. His voice had not been pleasant. We were all on our feet. I noted the right hand of Callisthenes had slipped within his cloak, to the hilt of the sword which hung there.

The right hand of the newcomer, too, was then on the hilt of his own weapon.

"We are all folk met in the throes of a common plight," said Tasdron.

"Who is he?" asked the newcomer, of Tasdron, nodding toward Callisthenes.

There was a small sound at the door, and the newcomer, instantly, backed against the wall, watching us.

Peggy entered, with the extra cups.

Tasdron sighed audibly.

Peggy, the two cups on a small tray, turned about, seeing the newcomer.

Swiftly she knelt before him, putting her head down. I saw that she remembered well what he had done to her.

"The slave," said the man.

"Yes," said Tasdron.

"I see that I am in the right place," said the man.

"Yes," said Tasdron. Then he said to Peggy, "Serve."

"Yes, Master," she said. She rose to her feet and then went to the low table and, kneeling there, put the cups on the table.

"Was she good?" asked Tasdron.

"Yes," said the man. "She was paga hot."

Peggy put down her head, reddening. The properties of slaves are discussed openly by masters.

"For what have I been invited to this meeting?" asked the man.

"That we may be of mutual assistance in a project of great common interest," said Tasdron.

"Who is he?" asked the man, gesturing with his head toward Callisthenes.

"Who is he?" asked Callisthenes, menacingly, of Tasdron.

I tensed. I saw the hand of Callimachus move subtly toward his sword.

"Who is he?" asked the newcomer, indicating Callisthenes.

"Let us be patient," said Tasdron.

"I am Callisthenes, Captain of Port Cos," said Callisthenes.

"I am Aemilianus, Captain in Ar's Station," said the newcomer.

Two cloaks, as one, were hurled back. Revealed then in the back room of the tavern were the insignias of Port Cos and of Ar's Station. Two swords, as one, leapt from their sheaths. The girl screamed. I stepped back.

"Port Cos!" cried Callisthenes.

"Glorious Ar!" cried Aemilianus.

But no sooner had the blades crossed then both seemed suddenly, inexplicably, in a flash of sparks, to fly upward. Both men stepped back. Callimachus stood between them. It was his blade which had struck both steels upward.

"You are strong," said Aemilianus to Callimachus.

Callimachus sheathed his steel.

"If you would strike someone, Aemilianus, Captain of Ar's Station, strike me," he said. Then he turned to Callisthenes. "Will you strike me, old friend?" he asked.

Callisthenes hesitated.

"Is this not a trap?" asked Aemilianus.

"Our greatest danger," said Callimachus, "is that we should be as foes to one another."

"Captains," begged Glyco, "put up your steel."

"She lured me here," said Aemilianus, gesturing toward Peggy with the Gorean blade. She shrank back, half naked in the bit of silk she wore. She knew that the slightest touch of that wicked Gorean blade could part her flesh.

"She was merely the instrument wherewith we extended our invitation," said Tasdron.

"Of what city are you?" Aemilianus asked Glyco.

"Of Port Cos," he said.

"And you?" asked Aemilianus of Callimachus.

"I am that Callimachus, of the Warriors, of whom I gather you once heard. Yes, I, too, am of Port Cos."

Aemilianus backed up a step.

"Jason and I," said Tasdron, "are of Victoria. Victoria is neutral ground between Ar's Station and Port Cos. You are both, Callisthenes and you, here met on neutral ground."

It interested me that Tasdron had, without even thinking about it, spoken of me as of Victoria. I, myself, had never given the matter much thought. I supposed that I was, though, in a sense, of Victoria. It was here, surely, that I was living and working. Yet to live and work in a place, and to be of a place, are, in Gorean thinking, quite different things. I wondered if I were of Victoria. I thought perhaps it was not impossible.

"I am prepared to sell my life dearly," said Aemilianus.

"You are not in danger," said Tasdron, "or, at least, in no greater danger than the rest of us."

"You played your part well, Slave," sneered Aemilianus to Peggy. "Will you receive a candy, lighter chains, a larger kennel?"

She shrank back, putting her hand before her mouth.

"Or will I survive," he asked, "to teach you punishments thought suitable by a man of Ar for a female slave?"

Visibly, the girl trembled.

"We mean you no harm," I said to Aemilianus. "Peggy," I said, "go to the captain and kneel before him, and bare your breasts to his sword."

She looked wildly to Tasdron, her master, and, interestingly, to Callimachus. She looked to Tasdron, of course, because he was her legal master, her owner. In looking to Callimachus, on the other hand, she had revealed, inadvertently, not even understanding what she had done, that he was in her heart her master, and that she was, in her heart, his slave.

"Do so," said Tasdron.

"Do so," said Callimachus. She was, after all, only a slave.

Peggy rose to her feet and went, head down, to kneel before the startled Aemilianus. Then, at his feet, she lifted her head, and, with her small hands, kneeling straight, parted her yellow silk. She knelt then before him, a helpless slave, as she had been commanded, her breasts bared before his sword.

I saw Tasdron smile. He had not failed to notice that Peggy had glanced, terrified, earlier, to Callimachus. He now realized that one of his girls, Peggy, was, in effect, the helpless love slave of Callimachus. I do not think that this displeased him. Indeed, such information can be of great use in managing a girl.

Aemilianus, puzzled, lowered the point of his sword. He looked at us.

"We mean you no harm," I told him.

"This is not a trap?" asked Aemilianus.

"No," I told him.

"Callisthenes," said Callimachus, turning to the captain of Port Cos, "is it your intention to strike me with your sword."

"No," said Callisthenes. "Of course not."

"Then put up your sword," said Callimachus.

Callisthenes sheathed his sword. A moment later the sword of Aemilianus, too, rested in its sheath.

"Come and sit at the table," said Tasdron. "We have much to discuss."

We all, then, sat about the table.

"Fix your silk," said Tasdron to Peggy, "and go to the side of the room. Kneel there. If we need anything, you will be summoned."

"Yes, Master," she said.

"Do you wish her, instead, to remove her silk, and to lick and kiss you, and serve you, as we eat and talk," inquired Tasdron of Aemilianus.

This sort of thing is sometimes done at Gorean suppers. Each male has a naked slave girl who is in attendance on him during the supper. She licks and kisses him, and fetches for him, and may even put food in his mouth. It is not unpleasant to be served by a naked, collared beauty in this fashion.

"We are not to be all so served, I gather," said Aemilianus.

"I do not think that would be wise," said Tasdron.

"Then I shall myself, of course, forgo the pleasure," said he.

"That is best," admitted Tasdron, "for there are serious things of which to speak."

I smiled to myself. It was true that slave girls were often distractive. It is difficult for a man to keep his mind or his hands off them. They are, of course, embonded, easily the most desirable of women.

"How much does she know?" asked Aemilianus.

"Very little," said Tasdron.

"Keep her ignorant," said Aemilianus.

"Of course," said Tasdron.

I looked to Peggy, at the side of the room, several feet away. She had now closed her silk. She moved slightly, and there was a sound of the bells. Then she knelt very still, that she not attract attention to herself.

"Speak softly," said Tasdron.

"Very well," said Callisthenes.

"Very well," said Aemilianus.

Peggy was very beautiful. She could not overhear our conversations. She would be kept in ignorance. She was a slave.

Twenty Nine

The Sea Gate; I am Again within the Holding of Policrates

"Had we the support of others, in fuller extent, we could carry this project through," said Callimachus. "As it is, I fear we must fail."

The deck of the low river galley shifted beneath our feet, as the ship nosed through the inlet waters toward the secluded stronghold of Policrates. It lies some two pasangs from the river itself.

"Your original plan," said Callimachus, "was an excellent one, but, now, in its alteration, I fear we must fail."

Callimachus and I stood on the foredeck of the galley. I wore the mask which I had worn while pretending to be the courier of Ragnar Voskjard. I knew the signs and countersigns for entry into the stronghold through the sea gate. These had been given to me that I could convey them to Ragnar Voskjard, that he might use them in his entry into the stronghold. It had been my plan to gather sufficient ships, primarily from Port Cos and Ar's Station, to simulate the fleet of Ragnar Voskjard, who would be expected by Policrates. It would have seemed simple enough, then, to have brought enough men into the stronghold, posing as the men of Ragnar Voskjard, to take Policrates by surprise. He himself had never met Ragnar Voskjard, nor had Voskjard met Policrates. The plan, indeed, was bold, but it had seemed to me sound. Callimachus, who was experienced in matters of war, had liked the plan, and had concurred. Glyco and Tasdron, too, neither of whom could be taken as rash fellows, had been taken by the plan. Interestingly enough, it had been the warriors, Callisthenes and Aemilianus, who had tended to regard the plan as dangerous and barren. Callisthenes, in particular, had been outspoken against it.

279

It was now near the twentieth Ahn, the Gorean midnight. The sky was cloudy. The three moons were high over the trees, bordering the shadowy inlet. I could see the high, dark walls of the stronghold of Policrates in the distance, with its lofty sea gate, with its heavy latticework of iron.

"The fleet of Ragnar Voskjard," had said Callisthenes, "can never join with the fleet of Policrates. It will be prevented from doing so by the chain."

"Why, then," had asked Glyco, "are you so concerned that the topaz never reach Policrates."

"The matter was important to the Merchant Council," said Callisthenes. "I merely do my duty. Some of them are uncertain of the effectiveness of the chain."

"And I am one of them," said Glyco.

"That is known to me," said Callisthenes.

"Has the chain now been placed?" asked Glyco.

"Yes," said Callisthenes. "It is now in place."

"This work was done in secrecy, was it not?" I asked. I had not heard of it in Victoria, nor had Callimachus or Tasdron.

"Supposedly," said Callisthenes, "though its existence is now doubtless known to the western towns."

"It was forged in Cos, in a thousand lengths," said Glyco, "and brought overland, around the delta, and on galleys east from Turmus. Its mountings and pylons were mostly done at night. It lies west of Port Cos, that we may be protected from the pirates."

"It would also allow Port Cos to control traffic on the river from the west," pointed out Tasdron, irritably.

"We are under pressure from Cos," said Glyco. "I am not personally in favor of the chain. As a merchant I think a freer trade lies in our best interest. Too the chain will not make Port Cos popular with her sister cities."

"That is certain," said Tasdron. "Victoria, hitherto at least, has been primarily Cosian in her sympathies."

"We of Ar's Station would not have mounted such a chain," said Aemilianus, unnecessarily in my opinion.

"Possibly you do not have the vision or the resources," said Callisthenes.

"Our concerns, Captains," said Callimachus, "must now be with ourselves and our immediate dangers, not with the politics of Cos and Ar."

"Politics?" inquired Callisthenes. "Cos and Ar are at war."

"Neither Ar nor Ar's Station, Captain," said Aemilianus, "are at war with Port Cos."

"That is true," said Tasdron, hurriedly. It was true. The typical colonizing situation among Gorean polities tends to resemble classical colonization, and not the typical colonization of nation states, in which the colony, in effect, is held subject to alien domination. When a Gorean city founds a colony, usually as a result of internal overpopulation or political dissension, the potential colonists, typically, even before leaving the mother city, develop their own charter, constitution and laws. Most importantly, from the Gorean point of view, when the colony is founded, it will have its own Home Stone. The Home Stone of Port Cos, significantly, was not the Home Stone of Cos. Ar's Station, on the other hand, did not have its own Home Stone, but its Home Stone remained that of Ar. This is not to deny, of course, that the colony will not normally have a close tie with the mother city. It usually will. There are too many bonds, cultural and historical, between them, for this not to be the case.

"The chain was inordinately expensive," said Glyco, "and, I am certain, it will prove ultimately ineffective."

"It was forged in Cos," said Callisthenes.

"We shall be expected, in the long run, to bear its expense," said Glyco.

"That is possibly true," said Callisthenes, "but then, too, it is we who will be the direct recipient of its benefits."

"If there are any benefits," said Glyco, glumly.

"Surely Port Cos will find some benefits in being spared the predations of pirates," said Callisthenes.

"The chain will surely be ineffective," said Glyco. "That is why I came to Victoria, to seek out Callimachus, that he might, in these dark times, with the topaz in transit, lend us his council, and his blade."

"The topaz, given the existence of the chain," said Callisthenes, "is now meaningless, though, to be sure, I am charged with the attempt to intercept it, a charge in which I have, thanks to our young friend here, failed." Callisthenes glanced meaningfully at me. "To have actually delivered the topaz to Policrates," he said, "was little short of an act of idiocy."

I shrugged. "You have heard my plan," I said, "that we muster ships and, under the cover of darkness, posing as the fleet of Ragnar Voskjard, enter and take the stronghold of Policrates."

"It is a foolish plan," said Callisthenes. "You would surely be discovered. Spies abound. The pirates are well informed, I am certain."

"Only we in this room know of this possibility," I said.

"Discuss your plan with Aemilianus," suggested Callisthenes. "The pirates of the eastern Vosk are more your concern than mine. The chain will keep the pirates of the western Vosk out of the waters of Port Cos."

"I do not wish to risk several ships and hundreds of men in such an unusual venture," said Aemilianus. "Besides, how do I know this is not a pirate trick to lure the fleet of Ar's Station into an ambush in cramped waters?"

"You have my word on it," said Callimachus, "the word of a warrior."

"Perhaps you, too, have been fooled," said Aemilianus. "I must think of the security of my men and my ships." Aemilianus looked at me. "Are you of Ar?" he asked.

"No," I said.

"Are you of the Warriors?" he asked.

"No," I said.

Aemilianus spread his hands. "How then," he asked the others, "in so great a matter, can I trust him?"

"You must do so," urged Tasdron.

"Do so," urged Glyco.

"Why should you undertake such risks?" Aemilianus asked me.

"There is a girl, a slave, I want in the stronghold of Policrates," I said.

"You would undergo these risks, these dangers," he asked, "for a girl?"

"I desire her," I said. "I want to own her."

"Is that all?" he asked.

I shrugged. "Too," I said, "I have scores to settle with pirates." Twice I had been demeaned by pirates, once in the tavern of Tasdron, and once in the Pirate's Chain, the tavern of Hibron.

"We are not interested," said Aemilianus. "I am sorry."

"His plan is bold," said Callimachus. "It is brilliant."

"I am sorry," said Aemilianus.

"The plan is not only dangerous," said Callisthenes, "and I would not risk men or ships of Port Cos in such a rash scheme, but it is, at least as far as preventing the gathering of the river pirates goes, unnecessary. The chain will keep the pirates of the west to the west of Port Cos."

"The chain will be ineffective," reiterated Glyco, miserably.

"It will be quite effective," said Callisthenes.

"A chain can be forged, a chain can be cut," I said.

"The chain is patrolled, of course," said Callisthenes. "Too, should there be any massing of pirate ships, we can meet them with the fleet of Port Cos."

"What do you think, Callimachus?" asked Glyco. He was not, of course, of the Warriors.

"With all due respect, my friend, Callisthenes," said Callimachus, "I must concur with Glyco, for his judgment in this matter seems sound."

"He is of the Merchants," said Callisthenes.

"He is a man of shrewd and practical judgment," said Callimachus. "And, in my opinion, his fears are well founded."

"With the chain in place," said Callisthenes, "we need fear nothing."

"Placing the chain," said Callimachus, "is unimaginatively defensive. It will be impossible to defend its length against determined attacks. Do not permit it to lull you into a false sense of security."

"If there is to be an attack at the chain," said Aemilianus, "I am willing to lend you ships from Ar's Station, to strengthen your defenses."

"We can handle our own affairs in Port Cos," said Callisthenes. "The ships of Ar's Station are not welcome in the waters of Port Cos."

"There is no drop of water in this river," said Aemilianus, quietly, "which we of Ar's Station may not put beneath the keels of our fleet."

"You will do so at your own risk, my dear captain," said Callisthenes, grimly.

"Our projects are doomed," moaned Tasdron.

"Captain, Callisthenes," said I, "surely the pirates, as you yourself have suggested, are well informed."

"It seems they know anything that occurs on the river," he admitted.

"If that be the case," I said, "surely the forging of the chain, or at least its transport to Turmus, and later to Port Cos, and the time and effort spent in preparing its mountings, joining the lengths, and setting the chain in place, must have been known to the pirates."

"Supposedly this was done in secrecy," said Callisthenes, "but I think there is little doubt they must have understood what was being done. Indeed, I have heard that there are rumors of the work in various of the western towns, in Turmus and Ven, in Tetrapoli and Tafa."

"Indeed," smiled Glyco. "We have even received a protest from Ven in the council."

"On the assumption that the pirates understood what was occurring," I said to Callisthenes, "does it not seem strange to you that they made no effort to interfere with the placing of the chain?"

"It was guarded, of course," said Callisthenes.

"But no effort, even a small one, or one in force or desperation, by steel or by guile, was made to prevent its placing?"

"None, at least to my knowledge," said Callisthenes.

"You yourself are presumably well informed," I said.

"I trust so," said Callisthenes.

"Does this lack of opposition or interference on the part of pirates as powerful and well organized as those of Ragnar Voskjard not seem puzzling to you?"

"Yes," said Callisthenes.

"What would you conclude from this lack of interest or action on their part?" I asked.

"I do not know," said Callisthenes, angrily.

"The conclusion is clear," said Glyco.

"And what do you conclude?" inquired Callisthenes.

"That they do not fear it," said Glyco, "that they do not regard it as a threat to themselves."

Callisthenes scowled at the portly merchant.

"If that is their belief, they are, in my opinion, surely mistaken," said Callisthenes.

"Do you truly think a chain will stop the fleet of Ragnar Voskjard?" asked Callimachus.

"Surely," said Callisthenes, "the chain—and, too, of course, the vessels of Port Cos."

"We know," said Tasdron, "that the topaz was brought to Victoria. It was doubtless brought as a pledge of Ragnar Voskjard to Policrates. It signifies, in effect, the agreement of Ragnar Voskjard to join forces with Policrates. I do not doubt that the fleet of Ragnar Voskjard, in a short time, will follow the topaz."

"Aiii!" whispered Glyco.

"Voskjard may be on the move now," said Callimachus. "At this very moment his forces may be moving east on the river."

"Policrates is expecting their arrival," I said. "That I know. Indeed, it is that which gave plausibility to my plan."

"The chain will stop them," said Callisthenes. "The chain must stop them!"

"I must return immediately to Port Cos," said Glyco. "Voskjard must be met at the chain."

"But what of the stronghold of Policrates?" I asked. "Would you leave such an enemy at your back?"

"It would take ten thousand men to storm that stronghold," said Callisthenes.

"Five hundred, entered, through the sea gate, could take it," I said.

"Your plan is the plan of a fool," said Callisthenes.

"I have been within the stronghold," I said. "I know it. I tell you it could be so taken."

"I will not risk a large number of men in this," said Callisthenes, "but I will tell you what I might do. I will give you twenty men, if so many will volunteer, and if Aemilianus, of Ar's Station, will similarly supply another twenty. Then, if, truly, you can enter the sea gate, and can hold it, set a beacon at the gate. We can then send supporting forces through the narrow waters to the wall. I have some two hundred men in Victoria and Aemilianus, as my intelligence sources indicate, a comparable number."

"There will be presumably some four or five hundred men in the holding," I said. "You would ask some forty men to stand against them, holding the sea gate for perhaps two Ahn?"

"Surely," said Callisthenes.

"It is not just the sea gate," I said, "and the wall near it, and the tower housing the windlass, but the walks about the walled cove within, and the entry to the main stronghold."

"It would be difficult," said Callisthenes.

"Our men would be spread too thinly, Jason," said Callimachus. "You must forget the matter."

"It is sometimes surprising," said Callisthenes, regarding me, smiling, "what a few men, determined and skilled, can accomplish."

"Ragnar Voskjard," I said, "would come with a fleet, not one or two ships, and forty men."

"Empty grain ships, towed, their identity concealed in the darkness, might suggest such a fleet," mused Callisthenes.

"Accept his plan in its plausible form, my friend, Callisthenes, or let us put it entirely from our minds," said Callimachus.

"Yes," said Glyco.

"That is doubtless best," agreed Callisthenes.

"I am willing to try it," I said.

"I thought you would be," said Callisthenes.

"What chances do you think we might have?" I asked Callimachus.

He smiled, wryly. "One or two," he guessed, "perhaps one or two, in a thousand."

"Surprise would be on our side," I pointed out.

"Support would not be immediately at hand," said Callimachus.

"The portals and walks to be defended are sufficiently narrow," I said earnestly.

"And many in number," said Callimachus. 'Too, there may be circuitous passages, secret, of which you are unaware. In this event you might be easily outflanked."

I thought of the slave, she who had once been Miss Beverly Henderson.

"Give me twenty men," I said to Callisthenes.

"I think I can supply you with twenty volunteers," he said.

I looked to Aemilianus.

"If Port Cos can give you twenty men for such a venture," said Aemilianus, "Ar's Station, surely, could supply no smaller a number."

"It is now foolishness, and madness, Jason," said Callimachus. "Do not embark upon so mad a venture."

"You need not come, my friend," I said.

"I shall accompany you, of course," said Callimachus.

* * * *

We were now beneath the high, dark walls of the stronghold of Policrates. I could see them rearing some hundred feet above us.

We nosed toward the sea gate, our oars scarcely entering the water.

I could see a lamp lit on a wall, more than three hundred feet within, inside the sea gate. The sea gate itself was fifty feet in height, large enough, when the barred latticework was lifted, to accommodate a masted cargo galley. It was reinforced on two sides with keeplike towers. The tower on the right, as I faced the gate, housed the windlass which lifted and lowered the gate. It was turned by prisoners and slaves, chained to its bars, but these men, without the assistance of the gigantic counterweights, also within the tower, could not have moved it.

"Who is there?" called a man from the wall.

"Step back," I said to Callimachus. "You might be recognized."

I then stood alone on the foredeck of the galley. I climbed to the foot of the prow and stood there, my left arm about the prow. I wore the mask I had worn when I had pretended to be the courier of Ragnar Voskjard.

"Who is there?" repeated the man.

"I am the courier of Ragnar Voskjard!" I called. "We are sent ahead, the scout ships of his fleet!" We had only four ships with us, and three were, substantially, empty. Tasdron had arranged them in Victoria, on the pretense of fetching a consignment of Sa-Tarna from Siba, to be brought to the Brewery of Lucian, near Fina, east of Victoria, with which brewery he occasionally did business.

"The fleet of Ragnar Voskjard is not due for ten days," called the man.

"We are the scout ships," I called. "It is only two days behind us!"

"The Voskjard is eager," called the man.

"There are towns to be burned," I called, "loots to be gathered, women to tie in our slave sacks!"

"How did you pass the chain?" called the man.

"The battle has been fought," I said. "It has been cut!"

"I do not like it," said Callimachus, behind me. "There are too few men on the walls."

"I surely have no objection to that," I said. "Hopefully most of the ships and men of Policrates are abroad."

"Now," asked Callimachus, "when they are waiting for Ragnar Voskjard?"

"He is not due, in their opinion, for ten days," I said.

"Let us withdraw," advised Callimachus.

"The cups of Cos," I cried to the man on the wall, "are not the cups of Ar!"

"Yet each may be filled with a splendid wine," he called down.

"The ships of Cos," I called to the man on the wall, "are not the ships of Ar!"

"But the holds of each may contain fine treasures," he answered.

"The Robes of Concealment of Cos are not the Robes of Concealment of Ar," I called.

"What do they have in common?" called the man.

"Both conceal the bodies of slaves!" I called to him.

"Raise the gate!" called the man, turning about.

Slowly, creaking, foot by foot, I saw the heavy latticework of the sea gate lifting out of the water, dripping, shiny in its wet blackness, in the light of the three moons.

"It is too easy," said Callimachus. "Let us withdraw while we can."

"Surprise is with us," I told him. "It is the one hope we have. On it all depends."

"Enter, Friends!" called down the man.

I, standing on the prow, motioned with my right arm to the oar master, and he, in turn, not on the stern deck, but among the benches, spoke softly to the men. He was from Port Cos. I looked upward at the high gate, now hung almost above us. We began to move slowly through the opening.

"Now!" cried a voice above us, on the wall.

I suddenly heard a gigantic, rapid, rattling sound.

"Back oars!" cried the oar master, the fellow from Port Cos. "Back oars!"

But there was no time. A few feet behind me, hurtling downward, crashing through the foredeck of the galley, fell the great gate of iron.

I was pitched upward, the prow of the galley, the forward gunnels, seeming to leap upward. There had been a horrendous sound of splintering, as the heavy gate had cut through the strakes of the galley like an ax through twigs. In that moment I had seen, through the closely set latticework of the gate, the chopped galley leaping upward. I saw Callimachus thrown into the water, and the men, suddenly, lifted up with the galley, some clinging to benches, others rolling on the deck. Almost at the same time the walls, on the inside, seemed alive with archers, who must have been hidden behind the parapets. The prow, to which I clung, then fell back towards the water, and I leaped from it. In a moment I rose to the surface, gasping, trying to see. The debris of the forequarters of the galley was floating about me. Outside the gate I saw the rest of the galley subsiding into the water. From the walls arrows were raining down upon its settling timbers. The men were now in the water, swimming from the scattered wood, darting arrows piercing the water about them, then bobbing upward. I swam underwater to the base of the sea gate. I could not push through the closely set latticework. There was no passage under or about the iron. Its iron posts were received by rounded holes, six inches in width, drilled in a flat, horizontal sill. At last, lungs bursting, shaking water from my eyes, I rose to the surface and clutched at the iron latticework. It was dark outside the gate. I could see some shattered wood, floating in the moonlight. Too, there were numerous arrows, like sticks, floating about. Doubtless they would later be collected, and dried. The three galleys we had towed were now adrift, aimlessly, almost lost in the shadows. I heard laughter on the wall. I was aware then of a lantern, and a small boat, behind me. I felt, as I clung to the iron, a rope put on my neck.

Thirty

I am Interrogated in the Hall of Policrates; A Girl is to be Whipped; I am Taken to the Chamber of the Windlass

"Taunt him," said Policrates.

The red-haired beauty, nude, began to press herself against me, in the long, sensuous, full-body caresses of the female slave. I struggled in the chains. My hair was still wet from the dark waters of the lake-like courtyard of the holding of Policrates. There were rope burns on my neck, from the coarse tether, now removed, on which I had been dragged, bound, into his presence. My clothes had been cut from me. I had then been chained, hand and foot, on my back, to four iron rings set in the tiles, before the dais on which reposed his curule chair. Policrates, indolent in the chair, lifted a finger and another girl, one whom I recalled was called Tais, from the feast, dark-haired, nude, knelt beside me and began to kiss and lick at my right foot and leg.

"For whom are you an operative?" inquired Policrates.

"For no one," I said, angrily.

Again Policrates signaled and this time Lita, who had once been a free woman of Victoria, pausing only to discard the bit of silk she wore on the marble steps, hurried to kneel beside me. I noticed how the bit of yellow silk lay on the steps. She had been humiliatingly and pub- licly stripped and knelt on the boards of the wharf at Victoria, before large numbers of her fellow citizens, inactive and frightened. She, nude, kneeling, the blade of the pirate at her throat, had tied the knot of bondage in her own hair. She had been ordered then to the galley, to be bound there as an exposed slave, to be taken to the stronghold of her masters. The bit of yellow silk lay partly on one stair and, descending gracefully, partly on another. It took the edge of the stair beautifully, for such silk is very fine. It reveals even the subtlest lineaments of that to which it clings. It is slave silk. I could see the graining of the marble through the silk. The girl now began to kiss at my left foot and leg. She kissed well. I saw that she belonged in a collar. It was too bad, I thought, that that discovery had first been made by pirates and not by strong free men, before whom pirates might quail. But free men, I knew, were often too simple or ignorant to gather up the unclaimed booty which might lie about them, even though such booty might beg piteously to serve, and to be taken into their homes, to be treasured. It is not easy always, of course, to recognize a slave who wears the robes and veils of concealment; the identification becomes simple, of course, once she has been put in a collar and slave tunic. It is said on Gor that the garments of a free woman are designed to conceal a woman's slavery, whereas the accouterments and garments of a slave, such as the brand and collar, the tunic or Ta-Teera, are made to reveal it.

"You are Jason, of Victoria, are you not?" inquired Policrates.

"Yes," I said. Kliomenes stood beside the curule chair of Policrates. He was smiling. Four or five of Policrates' cutthroats stood about, with their arms folded. About the curule chair of Policrates, nestling about his feet, and on the stairs about the chair, were several of his girls. Most were nude, but some were silked, or clad otherwise revealingly, as befitted the wenches of pirates. Some wore threads of leather, another a bit of rope, another only her chains. Some of these wenches I remembered from the feast. There were dark-haired Relia and blond Tela, who was still kept in white silk, as a joke, though she must have served the pleasure of pirates a thousand times; and the blond sisters from Cos, Mira and Tala; short, dark-haired Bikkie; the girls who had danced at the feast, and had been thrown to the aroused men at the conclusion of their performances; and certain others. Most, however, I did not know, or recognize. Men such as Policrates are rich in women, as well as in gold.

"You are involved in the conspiracy of Tasdron, taverner of Victoria, who is in league with Glyco, of Port Cos," said Policrates.

"No," I said.

"We will deal with those fools soon," said Policrates. "And we will wreak a vengeance on Victoria of which men will dare not speak for a hundred years."

"There is no conspiracy," I said. "It was I alone, with some few men, who thought to take and fire the holding."

"And what of the beacon that was to be set," asked Policrates, "and of the ships waiting fruitlessly now upon the river?"

I was silent. Policrates obviously knew much.

"Relia, Tela, to him," said Policrates. These two girls, Relia discarding her red silk and Tela opening her white silk, and throwing it back, hurried to kneel near me. Relia began to kiss and bite at the palm of my right hand, and at my right arm and shoulder, and Tela addressed herself similarly to my left hand and arm. I struggled in the chains, but could not resist.

"Did you truly think to gain access to our stronghold with so simple a ruse?" asked Policrates.

"Yes," I said. I gasped in the chains. I could not pull away from the taunting caresses of the slave girls.

"It was the plan of a fool," said Policrates.

"It was an excellent plan," I said. "How did you know that we were not the scout ships of Ragnar Voskjard?" We had, after all, known the signs and countersigns, and, presumably, those of the holding of Policrates would not be familiar with all of the men or ships of Ragnar Voskjard.

"Would not it have been clear to anyone?" smiled Policrates.

"We were betrayed," I said.

"It would not have been necessary, of course," smiled Policrates, "but, to be sure, you were betrayed."

"You knew it would be I, and others?" I asked.

"Certainly," said Policrates. What fools he had made of us. How thunderously had the great sea gate descended, destroying our first galley.

"Who was the traitor?" I asked.

"Perhaps Tasdron himself," said Policrates, "perhaps even Glyco, posing as of your party. Perhaps your dear friend, Callimachus, secretly in our pay. Perhaps even a lowly slave, privy to your machinations."

"It could, too, be a soldier, one even with our galleys," I said.

'To be sure," agreed Policrates.

I struggled in the chains.

"Oh, do not struggle so, Master," whispered the red-haired girl at my side, soothingly, chidingly. "You cannot escape, you know. You are helpless. Be content to feel my hands and lips, and my body, against yours." I cried out with rage. I wondered if it had been Peggy, the Earth-girl slave, who had betrayed us. She could have overheard our doings, and well suspected our intentions. It would have been easy for her in the paga tavern to have informed on us. It could have been done with simplicity in the privacy, in the secrecy, of an alcove, her head to a pirate's feet. "Oh, Master," reproved the red-haired girl, kissing me as the slave she was. I tried to pull loose the chains, but they were of Gorean iron. It seemed to me then as if it must have been Peggy who had betrayed us. She might well have known or suspected all. Too, she was a slave and a woman! Who else could it have been? She, indeed, must be the traitress, so lovely in her collar! It could have been, surely, none other than she, the branded Earth girl! I struggled, and cried out with rage. I did not envy the lovely blonde if she were caught. I wondered if she knew the fire with which she played. The vengeances taken by Gorean men on traitorous female slaves are not gentle.

"Was it you, Jason, he of Victoria," inquired Policrates, "whom we previously entertained in our holding as the courier of Ragnar Voskjard?"

"Of course," I said, angrily.

"Liar!" said Kliomenes. It surprised me that he had said this. Surely they must know that it had been I. Their informant must have known this.

"I do not think so, Jason," said Policrates, "though, to be sure, you wore tonight the same mask as he who posed as the courier."

"It was I," I said, boldly, "none other."

"Do you maintain this mockery?" asked Policrates.

"Can you not recognize my frame," I asked, "my voice?"

"There are surely strong similarities," mused Policrates.

"It was I," I said, puzzled.

"You would have been chosen precisely for these similarities," said Policrates.

"Why do you think it was not I?" I asked. "Did your informant not make it clear to you that I it was who brought you the topaz?"

"The topaz," said Policrates, "was delivered to us by the courier of Ragnar Voskjard."

"Oh?" I asked.

"The true courier," said Policrates.

"Oh," I said.

"What have you done with him?" inquired Policrates.

I was silent.

"I trust that you have not slain him," said Policrates, "for doubtless Ragnar Voskjard would not be pleased to hear that."

"I do not understand," I said. I was genuinely puzzled.

"You intercepted the courier, somehow, on his way back to Ragnar Voskjard," said Policrates. "It was from him, or perhaps from papers on his person, that you learned the signs and countersigns for admittance to the holding."

"No," I said, "it was you yourself who gave to me the signs and countersigns, when I posed as the courier of Ragnar Voskjard."

"That is false," said Policrates.

"It is true!" I cried. "True!" I moaned. I tried to move in the chains. Why would he not call off his slaves!

Two of the men of Policrates laughed.

"Bikkie, to him," said Policrates. I saw Kliomenes smile.

"Yes, my Master," said the short, dark-haired girl, and she, smiling, barefoot, descended the marble stairs of the dais and, taking her place on my left, lowered herself gracefully to lie on her side beside me. She began to kiss and lick at me, and caress me. "I am pleasing him," said the red-haired girl on my right. "I can please him more," said the dark-haired girl. I did not cry out to Policrates for mercy. I knew he would grant me none. I suppressed a moan. Bikkie was excellent. I had little doubt but what she was a valuable slave, and would bring a high price. Bikkie wore, like one or two of the other girls still on the dais, only threads of leather, some dozen or so, depending from a leather sheathing encasing the locked, steel collar on her throat. On the front of the leather sheathing, which opened only at the back, to admit the key to the collar lock, there was sewn a red leather patch, small, in the shape of a heart. The heart to Goreans, as to certain of those of Earth, is understood as a symbol of love. The life of a slave girl, of course, is understood, too, as a life of love. She is given no alternative. The leather threads depending from the collar are stout enough to bind the hands of a girl, perhaps at her collar, that she may not interfere with what is done to her body, but they are not stout enough to bind a man. They may be used, of course, in pleasing a master, not only in setting off the girl's ill-concealed beauty, but in touching him, brushing him, stimulating him, twining about him, and so on. The girl knows that the same strands which can bind her helplessly as a slave, are strong enough only to delight and please her master. This helps her to understand that he is a man, and that she is a woman.

I turned my head to the side.

"Do you still insist that it was you who entered my holding, posing as the courier of Ragnar Voskjard?" inquired Policrates.

"Yes," I said. "Yes!"

"We know that that is not true," said Policrates.

"How can you know that?" I asked. Certainly I was prepared to corroborate my claim, if need be, with descriptions of the holding, and accounts of the feast and of our conversations, descriptions and accounts much too detailed to have been likely to have been extracted from a captive.

"There are many reasons," said Policrates. "One is that you are a man of Earth, and no man from that dismal, terrorized world, where men are mean and small, could have dared to enter this holding."

"How do you know I am from Earth?" I asked.

"We know that from Beverly, a slave in this holding," said Policrates.

"Nonetheless," I said, "it was I who entered this holding and deceived you, in the guise of the courier of Ragnar Voskjard."

"Impossible," said Policrates.

"It is true," I averred.

It angered me that Policrates and Kliomenes, and the others, could not even accept this possibility. Surely not every man of Earth was as meaningless, as trivial, as obedient, as unquestioning, as well trained, as emasculated and effete as their various political imprisonments demanded. I had little doubt but that somewhere on Earth, in spite of censorship, media control, manipulated education and outright political suppression, and the almost nonexistent channels for expressing alternative viewpoints, some males remained men. Not every man can forget he is a man, even when he is instructed to do so. Why, he might ask, should I forget it? Indeed, why should I not be a man? It is, after all, what I really am. You may not like it, but that does not make it wrong. Do you truly know better than nature? There seems no guarantee that the perversion of nature is more likely to lead to general human happiness than its recognition and celebration. Only in remaining true to nature can we remain true to ourselves. All else must be falsehood and pathology.

"I crossed swords with the courier of Ragnar Voskjard in the great hall," said Kliomenes. "He was not unskilled. Jason of Victoria, on the other hand, does not know the sword."

"Accordingly, it could not have been I?" I asked.

"Certainly not," said Kliomenes.

"We have information," said Policrates, "that it was the true courier of Ragnar Voskjard who came to the holding, independently of the evidence that it was he who gave us the topaz, which stone presumably could have been only in the possession of the true courier."

"Information?" I asked.

"Which, further," said Policrates, "has assured us that the true courier was captured, and is now being held by those in league with Tasdron and Glyco."

Suddenly I began to understand what must be the case. Whoever had betrayed us must be, or be in contact with, the courier of Ragnar Voskjard, he who had tried to obtain the topaz from me on the wharves of Victoria. And it must have been he, or one in league with him, who had communicated with Policrates. Of course, the true courier would not wish it known that he had lost the topaz, that a false courier had gained access to the holding. The true courier, in this respect, was protecting himself. Doubtless he did not wish to be bound to the shearing blade of one of Ragnar Voskjard's galleys. He could always maintain later that he had managed to escape from Tasdron's confinement.

An idea suddenly sprang into my mind, one of a possible modality of escape for myself.

"No, it was I," I said, but I faltered, or seemed to falter, as I said this.

Policrates smiled. "Do not be afraid, Master," said the red-haired girl at my side. "No, Master," said Bikkie, the dark-haired wench, so lasciviously active on my left, "you are only chained helplessly before your enemies."

"Do you still maintain the pretense of having posed as the courier of Ragnar Voskjard?" inquired Policrates.

"Yes," I said. "I mean—I mean it is not a pretense. It was I!" I made my voice tremble, as though I had been found out.

"Beware," said Policrates, "there are tortures in this holding to which you might be subjected other than the caresses of slave girls— the twisting of chains, of burning irons, of knives."

The girls laughed.

"Make the fool writhe," said Policrates. I gritted my teeth.

"Beverly!" called Policrates, sharply. I tried to control myself.

Then I saw she who had once been Beverly Henderson hurry into the room, commanded by her master.

She ran immediately to the tiles before the dais on which reposed the large, curule chair of Policrates. Swiftly she knelt there, head down, small and beautiful. She wore a tiny bit of yellow silk, a steel collar, and her brand. "Yes, Master," she said.

"Rise, and turn about, Slave, and regard a prisoner," said Policrates.

Gracefully, swiftly, the girl did so. She looked at me, startled. The girls, as she had entered, had desisted in their attentions to my body. They would resume their ministrations upon the indication of Policrates.

My fists clenched in the chains.

"Do you know him?" asked Policrates.

"Yes, my Master," said the pirate's slave. "He is Jason, from Victoria. Once he was of Earth, as I, your slave."

Policrates lifted a finger and the girls about me again began to fondle, and to kiss and caress at my body.

Beverly, as her masters had chosen to call her, regarded me, unmoved.

"How do you regard the men of Earth?" Policrates asked her.

"I hold them in contempt," she said.

"To whom do you belong?" asked Policrates.

"To Gorean men," she said, "who are my natural masters."

I tried to resist the caresses of the slave girls.

"Could you ever yield to one such as he?" asked Policrates.

"Never," she said.

I looked at Beverly, the slave, standing on the tiles, barefoot, in the bit of silk, almost naked. The collar was very beautiful on her throat, and her dark hair, loose and soft, as a slave's hair is commonly worn, was soft and lovely about her shoulders. I almost gasped at the sight of her beauty, the lineaments of her face, and the exquisite curves of her body. I recalled, long ago, how we had met in a restaurant on Earth, and she had desired to speak intimately to me, of fears and dreams, and matters which troubled her. I suspected that there might have been at least one matter of which she had not spoken to me, to which she had perhaps implicitly alluded, but of which she had refused to explicitly speak. I wondered what it might have been. Then I remembered how she had looked, with her hair drawn severely back, and fastened in a bun, but wearing a svelte, feminine, off-the-shoulder, white, satin-sheath gown. Too, she had worn a bit of lipstick and eye shadow, and had worn a tiny bit of perfume. On her feet had been golden pumps, fastened with a lace of golden straps. She had carried a small, silver-beaded purse. The linen had been very white, and the silver soft and lustrous in the flickering candlelight. Had I been able to see her then as I was now enabled, by my Gorean experience, to see her now, I would have been able to see instantly through the trappings of her freedom to the slave beneath. I would have known for certain then as I knew for certain now that she belonged in the collar. Then, as now, though I was not able to recognize it clearly then, Beverly Henderson was the sort of woman who belonged to men, the sort of woman who should be put naked upon the block and sold to the highest bidder. What an exultant pleasure to own such a woman, and to have her at your bidding, your slave, among your treasures.

"This fellow claims to have impersonated the courier of Ragnar Voskjard, and to have deceived us all," said Policrates to the girl.

The girl regarded me in astonishment, in disbelief. "That is absurd, Master," she said.

"You were given to the courier of Ragnar Voskjard for the night, were you not?" asked Policrates.

"Yes, Master," said the girl. "That was your command. You had me sent to his chambers."

"Did he make you yield?" inquired Policrates.

"Yes, Master," she said, head down. "He made me yield, and many times, and he made me yield totally, and abjectly, and as his full slave."

"Did you find the evening instructive?" inquired Policrates.

"Yes, Master," she said. "I learned that I was a woman, and a slave."

"And?" inquired Policrates.

"And, Master," she said, keeping her head down, "that I loved being a woman, and a slave."

"Was this the man who used you," asked Policrates, "this man chained here before you?"

"Of course not, Master!" she said, lifting her head, scandalized.

"Are you certain?" asked Policrates.

"Yes, Master," she said. "He is a man of Earth. No man of Earth could make me yield like that."

"Are you sure?" asked Policrates.

"Yes, Master," she said. "The arms that held me, Master," she said, proudly, "were Gorean."

"I thought so," smiled Policrates.

I now began to writhe, unable to help myself, beneath the caresses of the slaves.

"May I now withdraw, Master," she asked. "The sight of this weakling offends me."

"Remove your silk, Slave," said Policrates.

Instantly she did so, frightened, commanded.

"To him, Slave," said Policrates.

"But he is only a man of Earth, Master!" she cried, protesting.

Policrates regarded her.

"Forgive me, Master!" she cried, and fled to kneel beside me, with the other girls. Then I felt the lips, too, of she who had once been Beverly Henderson upon my body.

I clenched my fists. I gritted my teeth, but how could I resist them?

"Describe to me, if you were truly one who posed as the courier of Ragnar Voskjard, the nature and furnishings of the chambers in which he reposed the night in which we guested him within the holding," said Policrates.

"I cannot. I cannot!" I said. This was in accord with my plan.

Policrates and Kliomenes laughed. Surely now none would believe that it had been I who had brought the topaz to them. Let them, at least for the time, believe that they had received it from the true courier of Ragnar Voskjard.

I shook and shuddered beneath the attentions of the slave girls. I pulled against the chains. I could not free myself. I writhed and twisted in the chains, helpless before my enemy, being aroused for his amusement.

"Please him, Beverly," he said.

"Yes, Master," she said.

I looked at her. I remembered her from the restaurant, long ago, the svelte, off-the-shoulder, white, satin-sheath gown, the candlelight, the beaded purse. I saw her lower her head, the dark hair falling upon my body. I saw the close-fitting steel collar on her throat. Then I felt her lips upon me.

"Oh," I said. "Aiii!" And I cried out with humiliation, and shame, and with rage, and pleasure and joy.

I looked at Beverly. I knew her from Earth. She was to me the most exquisitely beautiful and sexually exciting girl I had ever seen. On Earth I had never kissed her. On Earth I had scarcely dared to touch her hand. Here, on Gor, she was a slave. Here, on Gor, unquestioningly, commanded by her master, she had pleasured me, and well. I had learned on Gor, in the secrecy of a chamber in the holding of Policrates, when posing as the courier of Ragnar Voskjard, that she was a true slave. I wished that I had known that on Earth. It might have made quite a difference in our relationship. She drew back her head, angrily. I regretted only that it was not I who owned her. "I hate you," she whispered. Yes, she was a true slave. I determined that she would one day wear my collar, that one day it would not be Policrates, but I, who would own her. I remembered the wench from the restaurant. Yes, it would be pleasant to have her at my feet, on this barbaric world, collared and branded, as a helpless Gorean slave girl.

"Take him, and chain him to the windlass," said Policrates. "And let us hope, for his sake, that the courier of Ragnar Voskjard is not harmed."

The girls drew back from me, and stood to one side. Two men began to unfasten the manacles at my wrists. "You pleasured him well," said the red-haired girl to Beverly. "Yes," said Bikkie. Actually she had done so too swiftly. I would instruct her in the proper pleasurings of a master, when I owned her. "It is humiliating to be forced to give pleasures to a man of Earth," said Beverly. "He seems strong and handsome," said the red-haired girl. "I do not think I would mind being his slave," said Bikkie. "You do not know him as I do," said Beverly. "I despise him. He is a weakling, and a man of Earth. We are the rightful properties only of men such as those of Gor."

My hands were manacled behind my back. The shackles on my ankles were then removed, and I was dragged to my feet.

Policrates was talking with Kliomenes.

"You received pleasure from what you did, did you not?" asked the red-haired girl.

"The only pleasure I received," said Beverly, "was in being obedient to my master's command."

"You received pleasure beyond that," said Bikkie. "I saw."

"No!" said Beverly.

"You swallowed, did you not?" asked the red-haired girl.

"I had to," said Beverly. "I am a slave girl."

"You are so low," laughed the red-haired girl, "that you could receive pleasure from even a man of Earth!"

"No!" said Beverly.

"We saw!" laughed Bikkie.

"No!" said Beverly.

"Even if he is from Earth," said the red-haired girl, "he is handsome and strong."

"I think," said Bikkie, "too, that there might be a master in him."

"Not in him," sneered Beverly. "If he owned you, the first thing he would do would be to free you."

"Free us?" laughed the red-haired girl.

"Free us?" asked another of the girls, amused, touching her collar.

"What man does not want a beautiful slave?" asked Tais.

"He must indeed be stupid, or a total fool," said another girl.

"Men are the masters, and we are the slaves," said another girl, "does he not know that?"

"He knows nothing," said Beverly, tossing her head.

"I do not believe you," said Bikkie.

"He once freed me," said Beverly.

"If he owned me," said Bikkie, "he would not free me. He might give me away, or sell me, but he would not free me."

"Why?" asked Beverly, angrily.

"I am too desirable to free," said Bikkie.

Beverly, with a cry of anger, drew back her hand to slap at Bikkie, but another girl seized her hand, that she could not do so. "Do not fight, Slave Girls," said one of the men about. "Yes, Master," said several of the girls.

"Master," said Bikkie, approaching me. "If you owned me, would you free me?"

"No," I said.

"May I ask why not, Master," she inquired.

"Surely," I said.

"Why not, Master?" she asked.

I looked at Beverly, but spoke to Bikkie. "Because you are too desirable to free," I told her.

Beverly looked at me in fury, and Bikkie turned to her in triumph. "See?" asked Bikkie. "There are slaves, and slaves, it seems!"

"So it seems," said Beverly. I smiled inwardly. Should she come again into my power let her try to break the chains in which I would put her.

"Have you ever been mastered, Beverly?" asked the red-haired girl.

"Of course. Many men have mastered me," said Beverly. "I am a slave girl."

"To me," said Bikkie, "you seemed a true slave girl, fully, only when you had emerged from the chambers of the courier of Ragnar Voskjard."

Beverly smiled. "It was he who first fully mastered me," she said. "He was fully dominant over me. He was overwhelming, and I nothing, only an amorous, compliant, frightened slave in his arms. I had not known such a man could exist. He made me weep myself his, it seemed a hundred times, in his arms. That night I was devastated, and taught my collar. It was in that night that I first truly learned my womanhood, and my slavery."

"I see that you have never forgotten him," said one of the girls.

"No," she said.

"Do you love him?" asked the red-haired girl.

"Yes," she said. I was pleased that she had said this. To be sure, I had made her yield, as the slave she was.

"Perhaps sometime you will be his," said one of the girls, softly.

"He did not try to buy me, nor did he ask Policrates to give me to him," said Beverly. "To him I am only another female slave, a meaningless slut, doubtless already forgotten, with whom he pleasured himself one night in a strange holding."

"It is sometimes hard to be a slave," said one of the girls.

"We are all slaves," said another girl.

"The masters are all, and we are nothing," said another.

"Yes," said another.

"I will take our fleet east on the river," said Policrates to Kliomenes. "That will discourage interference from towns east on the river."

"Yes, Captain," said Kliomenes.

Policrates then turned about and regarded me. "Do not look for pretty slaves in the chamber of the windlass," he said.

I was silent.

"Oh, Beverly," said Policrates.

"Yes, Master," said the girl, hurrying forward and falling to her knees before him.

"Earlier," said he, "you hesitated, if only briefly, in carrying out a command."

"Forgive me, Master," she begged, turning white.

"Leading position," he said.

Sobbing, she rose to her feet, and put her head down, at what would be the height of a man's waist, her legs flexed. A guard walked over and fastened his hand in her hair. "Have her whipped," said Policrates. "Yes, Captain," said the man. He then left the chamber, pulling the girl, sobbing, at his side. I was pleased to see that Policrates was a strict master. The girl was, of course, guilty. She had clearly hesitated in carrying out a command. How can a girl expect such laxities to go unnoticed, or unpunished?

Policrates then nodded to the men who held me. "Take him away," he said.

I was then dragged from the room.

Thirty One

The Chamber of the Windlass; I Begin to Put My Plan into Effect

"Cease your lying!" cried the pirate. "Put your back into it!"

"Yes, Captain," I said to him, though surely he was not a captain.

The whip cracked across my back.

I, sweating, chained, pressed my bare feet against the flat, wooden slats nailed on the large, raised wooden disk, the treading platform, some five feet above the floor, encircling the windlass. I could hear the chain turning on its winding axle below the level of the platform. The gate is raised by muscle power, abetted by two heavy, drum-like weights which partially balance its weight, transmitted to the windlass by means of metal windlass poles, or bars, these being used to rotate the windlass. The gate, which is heavier than the drumlike weights, has a gravity descent. In lowering the gate the windlass, under the control of its workers, serves primarily as a brake, sufficing to regulate the speed of its descent. The principles and gearing of the windlass, which is an upright windlass, are analogous, of course, to those of the capstan.

I pressed against the heavy metal pole, or bar, almost five inches in diameter, fixed now, like a spoke, in the shaft of the windlass. My neck, in its collar, by a chain, was fastened to this pole. It was thus that I was kept in my place. My wrists and ankles were also chained. I had some eighteen inches of play for my feet. I had some twenty-four inches of play for my hands. These arrangements represent what is theoretically an optimum compromise between prisoner security and the degree of freedom essential to efficiently operate the windlass.

"Push!" cried the pirate.

Again the whip struck across my back. I thrust again against the bar. The whip, then, struck elsewhere, too, and there were cries of pain, and the sounds of men moving in chains. There were five large poles, or bars, set in the windlass. At each, five men, chained as I was, labored. These poles may be inserted into the windlass and, if one wishes, removed from it. When inserted into the windlass they are normally locked within it, as they were now, by a pin-and-lock device. The collars and neck chains keep men fastened to the pole, whether it is inserted within the windlass or not. When moving about, the pin-and-lock device opened, the men will carry the pole with them. When the pole is on the ground, and not lifted, one can rise no higher, of course, than on one's knees, with one's head deferentially lowered.

"Push, push! Move!" called the pirate.

The lash struck amongst us.

As the windlass turned slowly, creaking, we heard, too, overhead and to the side, the movement and swinging of the great drumlike counterweights on their chains. Without these counterweights we could not have moved the sea gate.

I again felt the lash, as did the others, too. The pirate walked about us.

It is dim, and musty, in the chamber of the windlass. It can be hot during the day. My hands slipped on the bar. Then I had it again. Too, at night, it can be extremely cold. There was a smell of wastes in the chamber. Perhaps it would have been less unpleasant if our captors had permitted us clothing.

"Work, work!" called the pirate. "Work!" But he did not strike us again. The weights were now in motion.

There is little to amuse one in the chamber of the windlass, save, I suppose, eating and drinking, and dreams. There is a shallow trough for water, cut in the stone, near one wall, where we would be chained when not working. This is filled twice daily. Too, at the wall, we would be thrown crusts of bread, and scraps of meat and fruit, usually the garbage of the feasts of pirates, our captors. Then, at night, chained, cold, when we would fall asleep, we would have our dreams. These dreams would usually be of slave girls, soft and warm, luscious, licking and kissing in our arms. Then we would awaken, to the straw, to the cold, to the stones, to the damp, cold, heavy iron of our chains. There were no pretty slave girls in the chamber of the windlass, as

Policrates had told me. But we had our dreams. One girl, more than any others, appeared in my own dreams, she who had once been Miss Beverly Henderson, though she now appeared generally in my dreams not as the lovely, free Earth girl, Miss Henderson, but, under a variety of names, as a Gorean slave girl. When, in my dreams I would encounter a slave girl, perhaps suddenly turning to greet me; perhaps in a market, imploring me to buy her; perhaps on a rounded slave block, I with a purse of gold in hand, having ready the means with which to buy her; perhaps an escaped slave, pilfering in my compartments, then turning, then knowing herself caught; perhaps being pulled from a slave sack I had bought on speculation; perhaps drawn by the hair from the tent of an enemy; perhaps chained in the darkness, and then illuminated; it would generally, almost always, suddenly, somehow, seem she. "My Master!" she would say, knowing herself mine, acknowledging herself mine, kneeling before me. One dream I had had several times. We were having dinner in the restaurant, as we had had long ago. She was wearing the white, off-the-shoulder dress. She had the beaded purse. In the candlelight she was very beautiful. We finished the dinner, and our coffee, and I had paid the check. "Now take off your clothes," I told her. "I am going to make you a slave girl." "You cannot do that," she told me. "You are mistaken," I told her. "How can I be mistaken?" she asked. "It is very simple," I said. "You do not know the nature of men." "This is a public place," she said. "That is all right," I told her. She turned to a man at a nearby table. "He intends to make me a slave," she said to him. "That is all right," said the man. "You are a slave." "Strip now, and do not dally longer, Woman," I told her. Then, in my dream, slowly and gracefully, the clothing, put aside, seeming to float from her, Miss Henderson, standing beside the table, on the carpet of the restaurant, stripped herself. I then unbound her hair, so that it fell loosely, almost floating, about her shoulders. No one in the restaurant paid us the least attention. I then removed a black leather cord from my pocket and bound her small wrists behind her back. The ends of the cord were long, and fell to the level of the back of her knees. "Precede me now from the restaurant," I told her. "I wish to see how you move." She made her way between the tables. On the way out we passed the two women whom we had seen long ago in the restaurant. "My Master has tied me," she said to them, "Yes," said the larger of the two women. "Yes," said the smaller of the two women. As we approached the door of the restaurant we passed, on our left, the hat-check counter. "Excellent slave meat," said the blond hat-check girl, Peggy, behind the counter. "You, too," I told her, "are excellent slave meat." "My Master has not yet claimed me," she said. "Be patient," I told her. "Yes, Master," she said. At the door to the restaurant we stopped. "On the other side of this door, at this moment," I told her, "is another world. It is called Gor. It is quite different from your old world. If you cross this threshold now, you will be in that world. Do you understand?" "Yes, Jason," she said. "And in that world," I told her, "you will be, legally and completely a slave." "Yes, Jason," she said. I then opened the door. Beyond that door lay not the bricks, the gutters, the dingy air, the hurrying of traffic, the triviality and misery, which had previously lain outside it, but now, as the door opened, we saw open fields, vast and green, and a sky that was gloriously blue, studded with scudding clouds. The air was gloriously fresh, pure and clean. She stepped across the dark, stained, flat board that marked the threshold of the restaurant, out onto the grass, into the sunlight and wind. "You have crossed the threshold into the world of Gor," I told her. She turned to face me. "Yes, Master," she said. I turned and closed the door, the dark, heavy door, with the rectangular panes of glass set in it, with the curtains behind the glass. As the door closed, it, and the restaurant, and its world vanished. I turned to face the girl. We were alone in the field, in the sunlight. "It is time to begin to accustom you to your slavery," I told her. "Yes, Master," she said. "On your back, Slave," I told her. "Yes, my Master," she said.

"Do not slack, you Sleen," said the pirate, snapping his whip. "Work! Work!"

We had, in the last few days, many times raised and lowered the sea gate. I speculated that these activities were largely connected with the coming and going of scout ships, and supply ships and fitting vessels. Then, yesterday, the gate had been open for some four Ahn. I speculated that the fleet of Policrates was now abroad. In his own hall, when his girls had finished with me, making me yield in his presence, his enemy, for the amusement of himself and his men, I had heard him, as he had spoken to Kliomenes, declare an intention to move his fleet east. Now, I gathered, he had done so. Doubtless this was to discourage the formation of an alliance among the eastern towns, and to prevent ships being sent to stop or delay Ragnar Voskjard at the chain west of Port Cos.

"Keep moving," called the pirate. Again the whip cracked.

As I made my way about the windlass, treading the slatted, circular platform, with my fellow prisoners, thrusting against the metal pole, I saw, chained to the wall, and at one side, behind the water trough cut in the stone, their necks still fastened to their own poles, two other sets of prisoners. There are thus, in reserve, additional chained crews for the work of the windlass. Too, as was clear, no one at the windlass was indispensable. This comprehension doubtless played its role in keeping order amongst us. We knew that any one of us could be cut from his chains at the merest whim of our jailer.

"Hold!" called the pirate. We stopped, the gate lifted. He engaged the holding pawl. The gate would not now slip. The weights, overhead and to one side, swung on their chains. We reversed our position at the poles, stepping under them and then standing, turning the chain swivels, to which the chains on our collars were attached. We were now in position to brake the gate, in its lowering. I, then, like several of the others, the holding pawl now engaged, put my head down on the bar, resting. It is not easy to raise the gate. Outside I supposed that one or more ships, river galleys, might be gracefully entering or leaving the lakelike courtyard of the holding of Policrates. The signal to raise or lower the gate is given by a guard on the wall, at the west gate tower, one of two towers flanking the sea gate. It is a voice signal. Accordingly its authenticity is seldom in doubt. Anyone, of course, might strike on a bar or blow on a trumpet. The windlass apparatus was within the west gate tower.

It felt good to rest.

Yesterday the gate had been open for some four Ahn. I conjectured the fleet had left. Too, it seemed likely to me that Policrates would have accompanied the fleet. Indeed, in his hall, I had gathered, from what I had heard, that the fleet was to set forth under his personal command. The work afoot, thus, was doubtless too serious to be left now to subordinates. Kliomenes, I suspected, would then have been left in charge of the holding. That, at any rate, was my hope.

"The gate is soon to be closed," said the pirate. "Be ready." It takes less time to close the gate than open it, but that, too, because of the weights involved, the windlass stress and the need to control the windlass, requires a considerable effort. To make the gate fall with extreme swiftness, incidentally, as was done when my galley was shattered, it is necessary only to disengage one of the counterweights. The polelike spokes, of course, by which the windlass is normally turned, or managed, should be freed of the windlass before this is done, a disengagement which is effected by loosing the pin-and-lock devices and withdrawing the poles from the windlass. If this were not done the poles would spin wickedly, turning with the rotating windlass. This eventuality would be extremely dangerous, of course, to anyone within the compass of the poles' movement or who might be, as we were, chained to the poles themselves. There are two counterweights, as I have mentioned, which partially balance the weight of the gate. The disengagement of one is quite sufficient to permit the gate to rattle viciously downward. If both were disengaged the gate itself might be severely damaged.

"Be ready!" called the pirate.

I looked upward, the collar slipping on my neck. A golden shaft of light filtered downward, falling gently into the chamber. In it there danced a myriad specks of golden dust. It was very beautiful. I also noted that the window was too narrow to admit the egress of a man.

"I fooled Policrates himself," I mentioned to the fellow next to me, "when I brought the topaz to him. He did not know me for an impostor, any more than the dolt, Kliomenes."

The fellow looked at me, blankly.

"Liar!" screamed the pirate. "I have warned you about your lies!"

The whip fell again and again on me. "Persist in these lies," cried the pirate, "and I will bring the matter to the attention of Kliomenes himself!"

"Forgive me, Captain," I said, as though frightened. But I had also gathered from his remark that my conjecture that Policrates was not now in the holding was correct. Surely if Policrates had been in the holding he would have threatened me with his name and not that of Kliomenes, since I had expressly mentioned Policrates and he stood higher in the holding than Kliomenes. Kliomenes must now, I gathered, be in charge of the holding. This, I felt, was in the best interests of my plan.

"Lower the gate!" we heard a man call. "Lower the gate!" Then, far above us, and to the right of the windlass chamber, angry, entering out onto a small balcony extending into the chamber, a balcony reached through a guardroom, we saw a pirate. "What is going on down there?" he called.

"Nothing!" called the pirate who had been striking me.

"Did you not hear the signal?" called the man on the balcony.

The pirate with us glared at me, in fury. He loosened the holding pawl. Immediately we felt the stress in the windlass poles.

"Pay attention, you fool," called the man on the balcony. "Listen! Get the gate down!"

"Lower the gate!" cried the pirate with us, angrily. "Hurry, you fools!"

We felt the bars pulling against our arms and, slowly, with effort, as the weights ascended, permitted the descent of the gate.

Then the gate was down.

I met the eyes of the pirate. He looked at me, in fury. I looked down, as though frightened.

But I was not displeased with the occurrences of the day.

Thirty Two

My Plan is Successful; I Take My Leave from the Holding of Policrates

"Let them be whipped," said Kliomenes, "both of them."

Kliomenes reclined in the curule chair of Policrates, holding his court.

Mira and Tala, the blond sisters from Cos, kneeling naked before the chair of Kliomenes, their hands bound behind their back, their necks joined by a length of binding fiber, cried out with misery. They had failed to sufficiently please Jandar, one of the minor captains in the holding of Policrates. Each, in the opinion of Jandar, had not tried hard enough to outdo the other in addressing themselves to his pleasure. Perhaps the fact that they were sisters had to some extent inhibited them, each fearing to appear the most lascivious slave before the other. Yet, of course, such inhibitions, under any circumstances, are not permitted to slave girls. They would get over them, or die. Too, I suspected that Jandar had not handled them well. If he would have handled them with adequate skills I had little doubt that each, indeed, would have striven desperately to outdo the other, each trying to be the favorite. Properly handled he could have had them in moments at one another's throats, as competitive love slaves.

"Should this complaint be brought again to my attention," said Kliomenes to the girls, "I shall have you cast naked into the jaws of tharlarion."

"Yes, Master!" said Mira. "Yes, Master!" said Tala.

"Take them away," said Kliomenes. The two girls, by the binding fiber which tied them together by the neck, were pulled, half choking, to their feet, and dragged from his presence.

"Why have I been brought here, Captain?" I asked the pirate at my side, who had conducted me to the tiles of the hall. It was he who was commonly in charge of the workers at the windlass.

"Kliomenes is holding court," he grinned.

"But I have done nothing," I said, as though frightened.

"We shall let Kliomenes be the judge of that," he said.

"Please, no, Captain," I said.

"Be silent," he said, grinning.

"Yes, Captain," I said. The collar and chain which had fastened me to the windlass pole had been removed from my neck, but I wore still, on my wrists and ankles, the other chains from the room of the windlass.

"What is next?" inquired Kliomenes.

"The disposition of loot," said a pirate.

He thrust five, low, flat coffers of coins across the tiles, and put beside them a tangle of jewelry and a bowl of pearls.

"And there is this, too," said the man. He thrust forward a chained girl. Her ankles were joined by some two feet of graceful chain, and her wrists, too, were linked by some two feet of chain. This type of chaining is not so much to confine a girl as it is to have her in chains, and display her. This type of chaining is very beautiful. The primary bond on such a girl, of course, is her slavery itself. On Gor what stronger bond need a girl wear?

She stood before Kliomenes, graceful in the chains.

"Is she pretty?" asked Kliomenes.

Her head was covered with semi-transparent, scarlet cloth, the central portions of such a cloth which had been cast over her, a large cloth, which fell to her calves. It was held on her by being tied under her chin and about her neck with a soft, braided scarlet cord. I could see the lineaments of her body beneath the semi-transparent cloth. She was left-thigh branded, the common Kajira mark, that mark which can grace the thigh of any girl, from the most average of slaves to the prizes in a Ubar's Pleasure Gardens. And, indeed, does that mark not tell us that they are all, in a sense, from the homeliest pot girl to the embonded treasure of a Ubar, only common kajirae?

The pirate behind the girl, who had thrust her forward, unknotted the cord from her throat, that which held the cloth over her head and kept it fixed, too, upon her body. She could probably see somewhat through the cloth, but not well. There seemed something familiar about her. The pirate drew the cloth away from the slave. He dropped it behind her. She knelt. I stepped back. It was she who had once been the Lady Florence of Vonda. I knew her now, of course, as Florence, who was, or had been, the slave of Miles of Vonda. To be sure, she was delicious loot.

"You may do obeisance, my dear," said Kliomenes.

The girl rose to her feet and went to Kliomenes. She knelt before him, on the dais, and put her head down. Gently, softly, she licked and kissed his feet. She then rose again to her feet, backed away, and then, on the tiles, again knelt. She put the palms of her hands on the tiles, and lowered her head to the tiles. Then she straightened up, her back straight, assuming the position of the pleasure slave, though keeping her head bowed, deferentially.

"She is pretty," said Kliomenes.

"Yes," said the pirate.

"Girl," said Kliomenes.

"Yes, Master," she said, lifting her head.

"How were you taken?" asked Kliomenes.

"By force, Master," she said. "My Master, Miles of Vonda, took ship from Victoria, in the *Flower of Siba.*" I knew the ship. Siba is one of the Vosk towns. It lies to the east of Sais. "He was bound for Turmus. He took two slaves with him, myself and a male slave, he named Krondar." Miles of Vonda, in my opinion, had been rash. I had suggested my reservations concerning traveling on the river in these troubled times to Florence, when I had spoken to her in the tavern of Tasdron. She would, doubtless, in turn, have conveyed these reservations to Miles of Vonda. But, it seems, the proud Vondan had ignored them. Doubtless he had ignored the advice of others, too, in this matter. In the river towns the dangers of these times were common knowledge. Little else, these days, it seemed, was spoken of in the taverns, in the markets, and on the wharves. "We were attacked by two ships west of Tafa," she said. "One, as I understand it, was the galley *Telia*, captained by Sirnak, of this holding, he who has just presented me, and other loot, before you. The other was the galley *Tamira*, captained by Reginald, he who is in the fee of Ragnar Voskjard."

"You were to escort the *Tamira* back to the vicinity of the chain," said Kliomenes, regarding the pirate who had presented the loot before him. "How is it that you dallied en route to engage in more prosaic transactions?"

"It was gold lying on the sand, fruit ripe to be plucked," shrugged the pirate.

"The *Tamira* is carrying the signs and countersigns, as you know," said Kliomenes.

"They are safe," the pirate assured him.

"What is the *Tamira*?" I asked the pirate next to me.

"The scout ship of Ragnar Voskjard," said he. I had assumed this must be the case. I myself, in my unsuccessful ruse, betrayed, presumably by the Earth-girl slave, Peggy, had posed as a commander of scout ships, supposedly sent ahead by the fleet of Ragnar Voskjard. Now, it seemed, so soon, the actual ship, or ships, though it now seemed there was only one, had appeared, conducted its business, and was now returning westward on the river, presumably to rendezvous with the Voskjard. That a single ship had been involved suggested a certain complacency on the part of the western pirates. Had they truly so little to fear?

"The chain has not yet been cut?" I asked. I gathered that it had not been cut from the nature of the conversation I had heard. On the other hand, it seemed puzzling to me how the Voskjard's scout ship could have appeared in these waters if the chain had not been cut.

"No," said the pirate next to me.

"How could she have crossed the chain?" I asked.

"A single ship, posing as a merchantman, not inspected, it was not difficult," he said.

"The chain was opened for her?" I asked.

"As it is for honest ships," said the man. He grinned.

"She experienced no difficulties?" I asked.

"We have friends at the chain," said the pirate.

"I see," I said.

"She will return, as she came," he said.

"I see," I said. Inwardly I was furious. How futile, how ineffective, was the expedient of the chain!

Kliomenes regarded the flat coffers of coins on the tiles before his dais, the jewelry, the bowl of pearls, and the girl.

"Is this," he asked, "truly an equal division of the spoils of the *Flower of Siba*?"

"We have something of the better of it, in my opinion," said the pirate before the dais.

"I see," said Kliomenes.

"Not much of great value is currently moving on the river," said the pirate. "Men are frightened. Most of the loot is being kept in the towns."

"Once joined with the Voskjard," said Kliomenes, "we can fetch it forth from the towns, as it pleases us."

"True, Captain," said the pirate.

Kliomenes smiled, addressed as Captain, though within the holding of Policrates.

"Put the coins, the jewelry, the pearls in the general coffers," said Kliomenes.

The pirate before the dais signaled to some men and they removed the coins, the jewelry and pearls from before the dais.

"And what of this?" asked the pirate before the dais, taking the girl by the hair and forcing her head up and back, bending then her body back, so as to reveal the bow of her enslaved beauty.

Kliomenes regarded the girl, musingly. "The values of many things," he said, "seem patent, but not the value of a slave." He gestured that the pirate should release her, and he did so. The girl then knelt, looking at him. "Are you only beautiful, my dear?" he asked.

She put down her head, sobbing.

"Keep her in the holding," said Kliomenes. "I myself shall assess her tonight."

The girl, then, in her chains, was dragged sobbing from his presence.

Kliomenes then looked at me, and I was thrust forward, stumbling, toward the dais. Unbidden, I knelt. There was laughter from the pirates in the room. I was the last item on his agenda for the morning. He had saved me for last.

"I should have slain you long ago, in the tavern of Tasdron, in Victoria," said Kliomenes.

"Forgive me, Captain," I said, head down.

"I understand that you are a braggart, and a liar," said Kliomenes.

"No, no, Captain," I said, hastily.

"He maintains," said the pirate who had conducted me to the room, he normally in charge of the crews of the windlass, "that he deceived both you and Policrates, and us all, by posing as the courier of Ragnar Voskjard."

"Are you so desperate for status among your fellow sleen," asked Kliomenes, "that you will risk such lies in this place?"

I kept my head down. I seemed to tremble.

"You warned him, did you not?" inquired Kliomenes, of my guard.

"Many times, Kliomenes," said the man. "But even this morning he persisted in these assertions, thinking I was not within that distance wherein I might detect his boasts."

"I see," said Kliomenes.

"Too, yesterday," said the man, "he spoke disparagingly of you."

"What did he say?" inquired Kliomenes, amused.

"He spoke of you as a dolt," said the pirate.

There was laughter from among the men present. Now, I noted, lifting my head, that Kliomenes did not seem amused. There was resentment of Kliomenes, and jealousy, and fear, I suspected, in the holding. There were perhaps others present who would not have minded usurping his lieutenancy to Policrates. Kliomenes looked about the room, and the laughter instantly faded. "That is indeed amusing," said Kliomenes, returning his attention to me.

"Forgive me, Captain," I begged.

"The courier, or he who posed as the courier of Ragnar Voskjard, though not my equal, was not unskilled with the sword," said Kliomenes.

"Forgive me, Captain," I begged.

"Do not slay him, Kliomenes," said one of the men near the curule chair, "for he might be of use in bargaining for the freedom of the true courier of Ragnar Voskjard, who must have been captured by our enemies in Victoria."

"They would not exchange so valuable a man for this worthless fellow, a dock worker," said Kliomenes.

"Wait for Policrates," said the man. "Let him make decision on this matter."

"In the absence of Policrates," said Kliomenes, "I am first in the holding."

"I do not contest that," said the man, stepping back, angrily.

Kliomenes again looked at me. "Thus," said he, "if you are truly he who posed as the courier of the Voskjard, you, too, must be not unskilled with the sword."

"Forgive me, Captain," I begged.

"Put a sword in his hand," said Kliomenes.

The fellow near me, who had brought me to the room, withdrew his blade from its sheath. He held it to me, hilt first.

"No," I said, "no!"

"Take it," said Kliomenes, evenly.

I took the blade by the hilt, in one chained wrist. I took care to hold it improperly. I held it as though it might have been a hammer, and too close to its guard, which would, of course, in actual swordplay, impair its mobility considerably.

Two or three of the men laughed. Kliomenes then rested back in his curule chair. He had been watching closely. He was a vain and arrogant man, but he was no fool. He had not won his way to the lieutenancy of Policrates by being stupid.

"Can you not kill me as I am, in my chains?" I asked. "Must you mock me?"

"Take him outside," said Kliomenes, rising, and stretching.

"Please, Captain, one favor," I begged, "one favor."

"What?" asked Kliomenes, puzzled.

"Do not let those of the windlass room know what was done to me," I begged.

"Bring them, in their chains, outside," said Kliomenes, to my guard, "that they may observe what is done to this fellow."

"No, Captain, please!" I begged.

But, already, two men were pulling me by the arms from the room.

* * * *

I blinked against the light of the sun.

I felt the chains on my wrists and ankles being removed. Armed men surrounded me. In one hand I still clutched, with apparent inept-

ness, and as though in fear, the sword which I had been commanded
to take from the pirate.

I looked about. I stood on a board walk, some twenty feet wide,
which borders the lakelike courtyard of the holding. We were within
its high, formidable walls. Wharfed within the courtyard were only
some five vessels, and smaller boats. To my right was the large door,
of dark iron, leading into the recesses of the holding. Across the courtyard, some hundred yards or so of deep water, I could see the walkway at the foot of the outer wall, and the stairs leading to the parapets.
Too, I could see the great sea gate.

"You will soon see what your braggadocio will gain you," said my
guard, whose sword I clutched.

There was laughter about us.

I then heard the sounds of chains, moving in a slow cadence. My
fellows, now in close chains and ankle coffle, from the room of the
windlass, were being brought out to observe what was to be done to
me.

I put my head down, as though shamed, to be exposed as a liar
before them. This way, too, my smile, that they were no longer in the
room of the windlass, and were heavily chained, could be concealed.
It would be several Ehn, surely, before they could be returned to the
room of the windlass and manage to raise the sea gate.

"Back away. Give us room," said Kliomenes, approaching. I shuddered, and stepped back. He handed his sword to a fellow and pulled
his tunic down to the waist. He then took his sword back, and, with
a slash or two in the air, tried its balance. I saw that his blade would
move with great swiftness. I was also reassured that mine could move
even more swiftly.

"Clear more space," said Kliomenes.

The men moved back, around us, clearing a broad circle. Two of
the men with Kliomenes, I noticed, had their own blades drawn. If,
perchance, he found himself in difficulties, I did not doubt but what
they would soon interpose themselves on his behalf. It would do
me no good, of course, even if I could manage it, to wound or slay
Kliomenes within the confines of the present situation. My objective
was not to deal with him, so to speak, but to extricate myself from the
holding. My only chance in this rapid, dark matter, as I saw it, was to

enlist his vanity and, hopefully, a recklessness attendant upon it, in my own cause.

"Are you ready, my stalwart simpleton, my handsome braggart, to now make good your showy boasts?" inquired Kliomenes.

I looked to the fellows from the windlass. They stood there, locked in their chains, grim and sullen. A miserable looking crew, I thought. Their despondency pleased me. In spite of my vainglorious carryings-on in the room of the windlass, which doubtless they must have found tiresome, it did not seem, even so, that they were looking forward eagerly to seeing me butchered before their very eyes. This pleased me. It also encouraged me to believe that they would find it difficult to make their way rapidly back to the room of the windlass. Hurried, they might even be expected to fall, or to become entangled in their chains. Such things can happen.

The blade, suddenly, darted toward me.

I stumbled backward, off balance.

"Lucky parry," said one of the pirates.

"There is no Callimachus to rescue you now, Dolt," said Kliomenes, measuring me, the point of his blade moving subtly, a yard or so from my chest.

Then, again, the blade struck, swift as an ost, toward me.

"The dock worker is fortunate," said one of the pirates.

But then I was afraid, for I realized that Kliomenes had intended, that time, to truly strike me. He had now backed away, and was regarding me, warily. One such parry might be fortunate, but that two such parries should follow one another, apparently so clumsy, and yet, both, similarly effective, would surely appear to defy the probabilities involved in such matters.

"He is skilled," said Kliomenes.

"He is clumsy!" laughed one of the men. There was more laughter. "Are you afraid, Kliomenes?" asked another.

Kliomenes glanced to the two men nearest him, those with their swords drawn. At a word from him, of course, both would rush upon me, and then, perhaps, others.

I dropped my sword.

Kliomenes tensed, but did not rush forward. "You could have killed him then," said a man.

I, clumsily, picked up the sword, breathing heavily. I looked at Kliomenes, as though frightened.

Kliomenes was regarding me, undecided. He knew that I could have retrieved the sword before he could have reached me. He did not know, however, for certain, that I also knew that.

"Have mercy, Captain," I said to him.

"He is afraid," said one of the pirates.

I then realized that I must play a most dangerous game. It was not the others I must convince of my ineptitude with the blade, but Kliomenes himself. The others did not matter.

"Forgive me, Captain," I begged. I then knelt and put the sword on the walkway before me. Then I slid it, hilt first, toward him.

There were snorts of scorn from the pirates about.

"Please, Captain," I begged, "let me be returned to the windlass."

Kliomenes smiled. "Coward," said more than one of the pirates to me.

I knelt at the mercy of Kliomenes, defenseless. He could then have rushed upon me and slaughtered me like a tethered verr.

"Please, Captain," I seemed to beg, "let me be returned to the windlass."

Kliomenes looked about himself, and smiled. Then he kicked the blade back to me. "Take up your sword," he said.

I reached for the blade and, as I did so, he rushed upon me, and I met the blade, striking downwards, with a flash of steel and a shower of sparks. He was off balance and I reared upward, close to him, within his guard, seizing him and half turning him in the crook of my right arm, the blade in that hand. "Back away!" I cried to the pressing others. Kliomenes cried out with misery. My left hand was now in his hair, pulling his head back, and the blade of my sword lay across his throat.

"Back away!" whispered Kliomenes, tensely, held. I turned, holding him, seeing that the others kept their distance.

"Do not come closer," I warned the pirates, "or his throat is cut."

"I slipped," said Kliomenes. "I slipped."

"Drop your sword," I told Kliomenes. He did so.

"Release him," said one of the pirates. "You cannot escape."

"Put down your swords," I told them. "Put them on the walk."

They hesitated and Kliomenes felt the edge of the steel, set to slide on his throat.

"Put down your swords, Fools!" said Kliomenes.

I saw the steel, blade by blade, sheathed and unsheathed, put to the stones of the walk.

My steel was then to the back of Kliomenes. "Precede me to the parapets," I told him. "Do not follow," I warned the pirates.

"Surrender your sword," said Kliomenes.

"Hurry," I told him.

"You have nothing with which to bargain," he said.

"I have your life," I told him. He tensed. "Before you could run two steps," I told him, "I could have you half on my sword or cut your head from your body."

"Perhaps not," said Kliomenes, uneasily.

"It is a risk I am content to take," I informed him. "Is it one which you, too, are content to take?"

He looked at me.

I opened my left hand, at my hip. "If necessary," I said, "I am prepared to conduct you to the parapets, bent over, as a female slave."

"That will not be necessary," he said. He turned, then, and preceded me about the walkway bordering the lakelike courtyard. I looked back and saw the group of pirates. They did not follow. They stood near the iron door, the entry into the inner holding. Their steel lay still about their feet.

"Put aside your bow," I ordered one of the men on the walls, climbing toward the parapets.

"Put away your bow," ordered Kliomenes, angrily, preceding me.

In a few moments, walking along the parapets, we had come to the edge of the west gate tower, that which houses, in its lowest level, the chamber of the windlass.

Two or three of the men, their bows in hand, edged near us.

"Put aside your bows," I told them.

"Do as he says," said Kliomenes, angrily.

The bows were put to their feet. They were short, ship bows, stout and maneuverable, easy to use in crowded quarters, easy to fire across the bulwarks of galleys locked in combat. I had seen only such bows in the holding of Policrates. Their rate of fire, of course, is much superior to that of the crossbow, either of the draw or windlass variety. All things considered the ship bow is an ideal missile weapon for close-range naval combat. It is superior in this respect even to the peasant bow, or long bow, which excels it in impact, range and accuracy.

I glanced over the edge of the wall. We were, as I had intended, in the vicinity of the sea gate. I did not know how deep the water was there. Yet I knew it must be deep enough to accommodate the keel of a captured, heavily laden round ship.

"What do you intend?" asked Kliomenes.

"Tell them to fetch rope," I said, gesturing to the men on the wall.

Kliomenes grinned. "Fetch rope," he said.

They hurried down the stairs.

"It seems you will make good your escape," said Kliomenes. He assumed that I had had the men seriously sent for rope. He assumed that when they returned I would use the rope to descend from the wall. By that time, of course, the men would be again on the wall, doubtless some of them armed, and with bows. Clambering down the rope I would be vulnerable, and the rope, too, could be cut.

"Now, we are alone on the wall," I said to Kliomenes, leveling the sword at his belly. He backed away, a step. "Do not kill me," he said, suddenly, turning white. Behind him was the long drop to the walkway below.

I drew back my arm, as though to ram the steel through his belly. He twisted away, and fled. I laughed, not pursuing him. I did not think he would stop until he was safely again among his men. Then, discarding the sword, I ascended the parapet and leaped feet first to the waters far below. It seemed I was a long time in the air. The rush of it was cold on my body, and tore at my hair. I then struck the water, seeming to plummet through it, and struck with great force the mud and debris of the bottom. I sank into it to my knees. I feared my legs were broken. The water was swirling about me, loud, roaring, in my ears. I tore loose, kicking, of the mud, and pushed upward toward the surface, which, after some seconds, gasping, I broke. I shook the water from my head; I blinked it from my eyes. I looked upward, at the parapets, far above. My legs were numb, but I could control them. No arrows struck into the water about me. I gasped for breath, and then submerged, and swam underwater for the brush and trees, half sunken, which bordered the channel leading to the gate. I emerged among roots and reeds. Only then, looking back, from the cover of the half-submerged growth, did I see men first appear on the walls. I had had them sent from the walls. They would not even know in which direction I had set out. I then swam again underwater for a time until I emerged in the spongy terrain north and west of the holding, shielded from sight by trees from her walls. I assumed they would think I would have emerged north and east of the channel, for that way lies closer to Victoria. I would, at any rate, have a good start on any who might wish to give pursuit. It would take several Ehn, I was sure, to get the great sea gate raised. I had seen to that. I could always cross the channel northeastward, at my convenience, under the cover of darkness, to move toward Victoria, or I might, if I chose, move simply to the southern shore of the Vosk. I was certain I could find means from there to make my way back to Victoria. Small ships abound on the Vosk. I began then to move swiftly. I was cold. But I was in good spirits.

Thirty Three

Battle Horns

"We welcome your sword," said Callimachus. We stood in the bow of the long galley, below the stem castle. The single mast had been lowered and lay secured, tied, lengthwise on the deck, between the benches.

Our ship lay to, east of the great chain. I could see little, because of the fog. It was a chilly morning. The water licked at the strakes. Far off, unseen, I heard the cry of a Vosk gull.

"It was not necessary for you to have joined the fleet," said Callimachus.

"It is here that I belong," I said.

"You have risked much already," said he.

"We were betrayed," I told him.

"Yes," he said.

I was bitter. The great sea gate had crashed down, destroying the galley on which I had sought to enter the holding of Policrates. I had been captured, and had managed to escape. I had made my way to Victoria, and hence westward, learning of the movement of ships toward the chain. Yesterday evening I had boarded the Tina, out of Victoria, captained by Callimachus.

"If the Voskjard attempts to cross the chain in force," said Callimachus, "we will not be able to stop him."

"It was the Earth-girl slave, Peggy, Tasdron's property, who betrayed us," I said.

"Can you be sure?" asked Callimachus.

"I am sure," I said. "Was it Callisthenes?" I asked him.

"It could not be Callisthenes," said Callimachus. "He is known to me. Too, he is a captain of Port Cos, and of my own caste."

I looked over the gunnels. To port and starboard, each some fifty yards away, gray and silent, intermittently visible in the fog, each lying to, as was the *Tina*, were two other galleys, the *Mira*, out of Victoria, and the *Talender*, out of Fina.

"Too," said Callimachus, "he is my friend." It was cold.

"Does it seem likely to you that it was Tasdron or Glyco?" I asked.

"It could not have been Tasdron," said Callimachus. "His interests would be too opposed to such an action. Indeed, he is the leader in Victoria of those who would oppose the power of the men of Policrates."

"Perhaps it was Glyco, then," I said, bitterly.

"He is not of my own caste," admitted Callimachus.

"Nor is Tasdron," I said.

"True," said Callimachus.

"Glyco," I pointed out, "has enlisted your aid against the pirates."

"He is not with the fleet," said Callimachus.

"He is now east on the river, trying to raise support for our cause," I said.

"Perhaps," said Callimachus. "But no ships have been forthcoming."

"I do not think Glyco will be successful," I said. "There is too much distrust among the towns, and they fear the pirates too much. Too, the fleet of Policrates is now east of Victoria, to prevent such ships from reinforcing us. I have told you this."

Callimachus was silent.

"Why is it not obvious to you that the traitor was the slave, Peggy?" I asked.

"She could not have heard," said Callimachus, uncertainly, angrily.

"She was in the room," I said. "She must have heard. She could have understood much of what we planned. Doubtless she revealed our plans to the courier of Ragnar Voskjard, or to a pirate in Tasdron's tavern, perhaps while moaning with pleasure in his arms, perhaps hoping to win her freedom by her treachery."

"She would not be freed," said Callimachus. "She would only be plunged into a deeper and crueler slavery."

"She would not know that," I pointed out. "She is from Earth." It can take years to learn Gorean ways, and how Goreans think. They tend not to be patient with slaves.

"Perhaps you were betrayed by one of the men of Callisthenes or of Aemilianus," said Callimachus.

"By trusted warriors," I asked, "who, too, would have had little opportunity to make contact with the enemy?" I looked at him, angrily. "Why can you not see that it was the slave, Peggy, who betrayed us?" I wondered if he cared for her.

"It could have been no other," agreed Callimachus. His voice was grim, and terrible. I did not understand, fully, his tone of voice. It was almost as though he, personally, in some subtle way, had been betrayed.

I looked out, over the bow, into the fog. One could see almost nothing.

"If we should be so fortunate as to survive this engagement," said Callimachus, "I will see that the treacherous slave is dealt with."

"What will be done to her?" I asked.

"She will be dealt with as a female slave is dealt with, who has not been fully pleasing," he said, quietly.

I shuddered.

"Are you cold?" asked Callimachus.

"Yes," I said. I drew the cloak I wore more closely about myself.

"Perhaps there will be no engagement," said Callimachus. "We have been at the chain for two days."

"The *Tamira* has crossed the chain, has she not?" I asked.

"Yes," said he.

"I anticipate an engagement," I said.

"The *Tamira* is a merchantman," said Callimachus.

"It is a scout ship of Ragnar Voskjard," I said. "It has already paid call on Kliomenes, in the holding of Policrates."

"I find that hard to believe," said Callimachus.

"Was she inspected at the chain?" I asked.

"No," said Callimachus.

"Had she been," I said, "it would have been discovered that she was carrying loot from the *Flower of Siba*. More importantly, she would doubtless be carrying papers linking her with Policrates, such papers as the signs and countersigns whereby the actions of the joint pirate fleets might be integrated and directed."

"You are mistaken," said Callimachus. "Reginald, her captain, is a known man."

"I learned these things in the court of Kliomenes," I said.

"You must be mistaken," he said.

"I anticipate an engagement," I said.

"It should have taken place by now," said Callimachus.

"That seems possible," I admitted.

"Perhaps the Voskjard fears the chain," said Callimachus.

"Perhaps," I admitted.

From where we lay to I could hear, from time to time, the restless creak of the mighty links of the chain, suspended on pylons, stretching across the river. The links of the chain were some eighteen inches in length and a foot in width; the metal of the links themselves was as thick as a man's forearm. The chain, in places, lay submerged a foot or so below the water; in other places, and near the pylons, it would range from a foot to a yard above the water. It was anchored to great rings on the pylons. At five places in the river the chain could be opened, swung open on huge rafts, at which points there were guard stations. Too, there were guard stations at the terminal pylons, on the north and south shore of the river.

"Where is Callisthenes?" I asked.

"He is at the south guard station," said Callimachus.

This was regarded as a point of maximum danger. Gorean ships, on the whole, even the round ships, are shallowly drafted vessels. It is common, where wharfage is not available, to beach them at night. Thus the chain, theoretically, could be circumvented at these points, the shallowly drafted ships being brought to shore and, on rollers, being moved about the terminal pylons. The south guard station was regarded as more vulnerable than the north guard station, because of its comparatively remote location. The supply lines from Port Cos to the north station are shorter and it is easier to move troops to that point. Also, the barracks for the guardsmen of the chain are at that point. I was pleased to hear that Callisthenes had taken up his post at the south guard station. It was at such a point that we particularly needed good men. Yet we would miss him in the fray, should the Voskjard's fleet dare to approach the chain more directly.

"Perhaps it is there where we, too, should be," mused Callimachus.

"The chain does seem fearfully strong," I said. Neither Callimachus nor myself had seen the chain until we had come westward. We had been unprepared for its impressiveness. It represented an engineering feat of no mean proportions. Although we retained our theoretical reservations about its effectiveness, these reservations, in the very presence of the chain, seemed, to my relief, less alarming, and more tenuous and abstract, than they had in the urgent discussions which had taken place in the tavern of Tasdron. It was easy to understand, now, why those who had seen the chain tended to be more confident of its effectiveness than those who had not. I listened to the creaking of the mighty links, and to the water lapping at the sides of our galley, and to the occasional cries of Vosk gulls.

"Perhaps the Voskjard does fear the chain," I said.

"There is surely enough predation west of the chain for him," said Callimachus.

"I would think so," I said.

I looked over the rail, to the great wooden, iron-shod ram, which protruded, in part, from the water. I looked over the starboard rail, and saw the great, curved shearing blade, fixed in the side of the vessel. Its mate, anchored, too, in the strakes, forward of the oars, reposed on the port side. These blades were seven feet in height, like convex moons of iron. It is said that such blades were an invention of Tersites, a shipwright of Port Kar. I returned to stand beside Callimachus.

"You have not fought on the water before, have you?" he asked.

"No," I said.

I could now scarcely see the *Mira* and the *Talender*, so thick was the fog.

"It is cold," said Callimachus.

"Yes," I said.

"Callimachus," I said.

"Yes," he said.

"Do you think the Voskjard will come?" I asked.

"I do not think so, now," said Callimachus.

"Why not?" I asked.

"The chain is strong," said Callimachus. "Too, it seems his fleet should have arrived at the chain by now, did it intend to do so."

"Then you do not think he will come?" I asked.

"I do not think so," said Callimachus.

"An engagement upon the water must be a terrible thing," I said.

"I am of the Warriors," said Callimachus. He licked his lips. I shuddered. I wondered what had been his experiences, and what he knew that I did not. I feared him then, in that moment. For an instant I felt I no longer knew him. I felt, in that instant, that he might be a man of a different sort than I.

"Are you frightened?" asked Callimachus.

"Yes," I said.

"That is natural," he said.

"What are the numbers involved?" I asked.

Callimachus grinned. "That is a warrior's question," he said.

"Surely we have intelligence on this matter," I said.

"It is conjectured," said Callimachus, "that the Voskjard is stronger than Policrates. It is thought he commands some fifty ships and twenty-five hundred men. We have better information on Policrates. He commands forty ships and some two thousand men."

"United, they would become a mighty force," I said.

"To be sure," said Callimachus, "and yet some fifty ships can be brought into the river by Port Cos, and some forty-five by Ar's Station. Accordingly in an engagement of fleets Port Cos and Ar's Station, acting together, would bring to bear the superior forces."

"How many ships of Ar's Station support us at the chain?" I asked.

"Ten," said Callimachus. "They would provide no more."

"How many ships of Port Cos?" I asked.

"Ten at the chain, and twenty in the vicinity of the south guard station," said Callimachus.

"Thirty, in all," I said.

"There are another twenty at Port Cos, of course," said Callimachus. "They are, however, held there to defend the town, if need be."

"How many independent ships?" I asked.

"Seven," said Callimachus. "Two from Victoria, two from Jort's Ferry, two from Point Alfred, and one from Fina." Jort's Ferry and Point Alfred lie west of Ar's Station, and tend to follow the lead of Ar's Station, favoring generally the politics of Ar.

"We have, then, forty-seven ships upon the river," I said.

"Yes," said Callimachus.

"And it is estimated that the Voskjard's fleet numbers some fifty ships?"

"Yes," said Callimachus.

"It would seem, then," I said, "that the odds are approximately even."

"Or, with the chain, perhaps in our favor?" said Callimachus.

"It might seem so," I mused.

"But you are skeptical?" he asked.

"Our ships are scattered," I said. "They patrol the chain."

"And the fleet of the Voskjard can, at will, attack at any given point."

"Cutting the chain," I said, "they could, in one or more successive engagements, outnumber and destroy the defending ships."

"You think like a warrior," said Callimachus.

"Our hope, of course," I said, "is that they can be held behind the chain long enough to permit the massing of our full forces."

"Of course," said Callimachus.

"You said, earlier," I said, "that you did not think we could stop an attack in force upon the chain."

"That is true," he said.

"Why not?" I asked.

"Consider the matter," he said. "Those from Ar's Station are essentially infantrymen of Ar, put at the oars of galleys. They are unfamiliar with naval warfare. And the independent ships, like the *Tina*, are not manned by warriors, but by volunteers, stalwart but untrained fellows, mostly of lower castes. Our defensive force, in effect, is the fleet of Port Cos."

"It is then, you feel," I said, apprehensively, "in effect some thirty ships, those of Port Cos, against the fleet of the Voskjard?"

"Substantially so," agreed Callimachus.

"Why, then, are you here?" I asked.

"I am of the Warriors," said Callimachus.

"I see," I said.

"Why are you here?" he asked.

"I do not know," I said.

"You are here," he said, "because you, too, are of the Warriors."

"I am not of the Warriors," I said.

"Not everyone who is of the Warriors knows that he is of the Warriors," said Callimachus.

"I do not understand," I said.

"I have seen it," said Callimachus, "in your eyes, that you are of the Warriors."

"You are mad," I said.

"Ten thousand years ago," he said, "in the mixings of bloods, and in the rapings of conquered maids, the caste has chosen you."

"You are mad," I told him.

"We shall see, shortly," said he. He drew his sword.

"Why are you drawing your sword?" I asked.

"Surely you can hear?" he asked.

"What?" I said. "What?"

"I was wrong," he said. "I thought there might be no battle."

"I do not understand," I said.

"Yet," said Callimachus, "if the *Tamira* were truly the scout ship of Ragnar Voskjard, and if she crossed the chain westward four days ago, and a rendezvous was made in the river, in the vicinity of the holding of Ragnar Voskjard, the times involved are not inappropriate."

"What are you talking about?" I asked.

"Can you not hear it?" he asked.

"I hear nothing!" I cried. "You are mad!" I heard only the water at the strakes, the creaking of the chain, the sound of oars restless in the thole ports, the far-off cries of occasional Vosk gulls.

"There is nothing," I whispered.

Suddenly the hair on the back of my neck lifted and froze.

"See?" asked Callimachus, lifting his sword, and pointing out, into the fog.

"No," I said. I could not see anything in the fog. But, now, clearly, I could hear it.

Then, suddenly, through a rift in the fog I saw, not more than a hundred yards away, across the chain, what seemed a countless number of ships.

"It is the fleet of Ragnar Voskjard," he said. There was an elation which I found incomprehensible in his voice.

I stood, for the moment unable to move, on the deck, at the bow, below the stem castle of the galley.

"Your sword is in your hand," smiled Callimachus.

I could not remember unsheathing it.

"Sound the battle horns!" called Callimachus to the men on the ship. "Sound the battle horns!"

Lightning Source UK Ltd.
Milton Keynes UK
28 September 2010

160476UK00001B/30/A